Also by Lilian Roberts Finlay

Always in My Mind
A Bona Fide Husband
Stella
Forever in the Past

Lilian Roberts Finlay

CASSA

For Barbara
Best wishes!
Lilian Roberts Finlay

First published in 1998 by
Mount Eagle Publications Ltd
Dingle, Co. Kerry, Ireland

ISBN 1 902011 07 4
(Original paperback)

10 9 8 7 6 5 4 3 2 1

Published with the assistance of the
Arts Council/An Chomhairle Ealaíonn

Typesetting: Koinonia, Bury
Cover illustration:
The Verandah by Edgard Wiethase (1881–1965),
Whitford & Hughes/Bridgeman Art Library
Cover design: Public Communications Centre, Dublin
Printed by ColourBooks Ltd, Dublin

To my grandmother, Bedelia Brabazon,
with all the gratitude and all the love of a lifetime.

I remember I lived April once
and the beloved lived me
when, sowing the four winds,
night wandered wide,
and I sang stars,
sea urchins,
I prayed clouds,
built cities,
sowed answers.
White streamers sang myself
through the olive shades green
when the day was April
and the heart knew

Now, I walk here seawards,
so suffer me, whiteness among birches,
impertinence spent
in the starry dusk,
the little lights singing
slip through my fingers
and the heart knows

I remember it was April once I lived.

Leslie Gilette Jackson

CHAPTER ONE

IN IRELAND, THE years of the Second World War were known as "The Emergency", and in an emergency very little progress can be made. Although England had won the war against Germany, they had lost a generation of men. Thousands of Irishmen had died in the fighting, and many thousands more emigrated to England, filling the gap left by the heroes. The state of emergency was continued into the fifties with food and petrol rationing and no increase in poor wages. Throughout the country the stress of poverty was rife.

Little Cassa Blake had never heard about this poverty. There had been distant murmurs of the war, but nothing had really gone awry. Each evening, she heard her Papa's car coming up the long avenue as she waited on the top step for his hug and kiss. No matter if her big sister Nicole had been a mean bully all day, Papa's hug and kiss blotted out Nicky's tortures. Papa was pure happiness. He never made rules the way Mama did, but Mama could be nice when Cassa took Papa's hand and led him into the front drawing-room where Mama always rested. She, too, lifted her delicate face for Papa's kiss and breathed out his name gently, "Ah, Richard, you are home."

Like the century, Richard Blake was into his fifties, a lawyer of repute in the city of Dublin. The recent availability of petrol made the drive home a time for comfortable reflection, a relaxed time for looking forward to whatever the evening might have in store. Once out of the city, along busy Morehampton and on to the Donnybrook Road, a sense of homecoming took over. That was how it had been since the youthful day he had taken his father's desk in their prosperous law offices on Stephen's Green. No change was ever anticipated in this orderly routine, no change at all, until the evening he observed the rows of new earth-moving machinery lined up outside Donnybrook church.

That night at a family dinner party, he questioned his

cousin Denton. "What the devil is going on at Donnybrook church?"

"More to the point, who got the legal work for the sale of the famous six acres?" Denton was obviously rather irked.

"What six acres are we talking about?" enquired Tim Coloquin, another of Richard's cousins.

"St Andrew's College playing fields," replied Denton, "our summer cricket pitch, since time immemorial . That new lot in Leinster House have commandeered it; heard they paid £18,000 for it. You want to keep your ears to the ground with that lot. They'll enrich themselves before they consider our legal rights."

Everyone listened to Denton Blake although no one ever knew where he got his information.

Richard had not looked for any legal work from the new government. The wags in the Four Courts were telling each other to start learning Irish. Richard's education had been in Downside where Irish was known as Erse, and quite disregarded.

Trevor Gilbey had heard that the fellows in Leinster House were moving the radio station on to the newly acquired six acres. "They used to have it on the first floor of the General Post Office. Proper place for it, in the city."

"And now they need six acres?" Richard Blake was thinking that indeed he had valuable acres he could sell. The money would be useful.

"They'll need more land than that," put in Denton. "Rumour has it that feelers are out for architects and builders. Some time within the next five years we'll see television masts further up the road."

"Television masts!" several of them echoed in disgust. "On our own road?"

"Montrose House changed hands last year," said Denton. "You won't have to worry, Rich, your place is too far out. Those little radio acolytes don't have cars; they'll need to be within half a mile of the tram terminus at Donnybrook church."

"Why didn't they buy Mount Merrion and use the Clonskeagh Road?" asked Tim plaintively. The Coloquin family home was at Cornelscourt.

"Toby Fitzwilliam sold Mount Merrion House and the lands twenty-five years ago, on the day his regiment marched out of Dublin. He still has the house on the canal and the tennis courts, but he doesn't come over much nowadays." Richard's cousin, Denton, had been one of the Fitzwilliam set in the old days, before the First World War.

"Anyway," Trevor told them, "Mount Merrion is further out again. I'm nearer in than that and when I declined to negotiate, some miserable little cockahoop in the Civil Service asked me if I had heard of Compulsory Acquisition! Sheer impertinence!"

"This is a country road," protested Richard. "Many more cars and we would be crowded out."

"Well, Richard," said Denton, "now you know the meaning of all the heavy equipment you saw tonight at the church. The widening of *our* road for an Irish television station.

After an untouched century, everything changed.

* * *

When the little girls asked for a story, Richard Blake liked to give them his own version of the history of Dublin, mainly because he could lead the story around to his own house and land, his beloved Firenze.

"In the 1850s the city of Dublin was stretched out on the south side by the wealthy English colonial speculators. There were the Fitzwilliams, the Baggots, the Humes and the Pembrokes, not forgetting the mighty Lansdownes. The Georges were the Kings of England and the Georgian style was very fashionable and it was taken up by the Lords Northumberland and Morehampton in the advancing suburbs."

Nicole was making a delicate show of covering her mouth for a bored yawn.

"Yes I know, Nicole, you've heard it before, but I'm coming to the Donnybrook bit. Cassa loves this part, don't you, pet? Now, listen.

"When Lord Morehampton's men came to the bridge over the River Dodder, they dared not advance further. Beyond Donnybrook village was the countryside and it was rebellious Irish from the beginning of history. Up in the Wicklow mountains lived the O'Byrnes and the Dwyers who had never recognised English rule, not even when they brought their horses down from the mountains to the Donnybrook Fair.

"Every law was under English charter in those far-away times, and the Donnybrook Fair got its charter from the English King in 1204 which was exactly thirty years after Dublin was captured from the Danes by the Normans under Richard de Clare, known as Strongbow, whose consort was the daughter of the King of Leinster."

Nicole looked up at the word "consort". What was a consort to a man with a bow and arrow? She didn't ask.

"The redoubtable Strongbow was afterwards knighted by Henry the Second of England. He became the first Earl of Pembroke. He was a man who enjoyed high revelry and no doubt had an input into the early Donnybrook Fair of 1204. This notorious fair lasted for six hundred years, each year exceeding the pace of wild abandon."

Their Papa was a little annoyed by Nicole's blatant yawning, but he pressed on, delighting in the tales of the Donnybrook Fair which his grandfather had related to him: tales of tricksters and gamblers and dancers and swordsmen and bare-fisted fighting.

"I should like you to listen, Nicole, it will be good for your history in school. Even if you *are* bored. Be good like Cassa. If you *could*! Now please, Nicole!

"In 1855, the moneyed residents in their big Georgian houses on Morehampton Road persuaded their mighty landlord to buy out the royal charter of 1204, and to open up Lord Merrion's country road beyond the ancient stone

4

bridge over the curdling Dodder. That was the last year of the Donnybrook Fair, 1855."

Papa had told the story many times.

"And the word 'Donnybrook' passed into the English language as a description of any riotous assembly. In the following year, 1856, the Blakes, who had moved their law offices from Swansea to Dublin, bought this land and registered the deeds of this house in which we live since then. A hundred years! Wake up, Nicole! Some day this place will pass to you, you are the elder, and it will be good to know how it all began when you become mistress of Firenze!"

Nicole permitted Papa her pretty pouting smile. She liked the ring of the word "mistress".

Papa explained how the old leafy Donnybrook road curved invitingly to the hamlet of Stillorgan, on out through the ravine of the Scalp, to Lord Powerscourt's great house in Enniskerry, and up into the mountains at Glencree. The books called Wicklow the garden of Ireland. Cassa loved this part of the story; the garden of Ireland sounded like fairyland.

"To the wealthy Dublin merchants, bankers, physicians – and lawyers, of course – this country highway then became desirable as a residential road within carriage distance of the city. Horses in those days, Cassa, no cars then! Sites of ten, or more, acres were acquired for the setting-up of mansions with the necessary stabling for their carriage-horses and their hunters; plenty of space for tennis courts, croquet lawns, walled gardens and glass-houses. There was always a neat lodge for the coachman, a cottage for the gardener, and in the house itself ample attic accommodation for the servants."

"We still have a lot of attics, Papa, but they are empty now," said Cassa, "only for some little mice."

And Cassa would share in his laughter, but Nicole never laughed at what she called "this rigmarole". Nicole would have liked the idea of attics full of servants. A housekeeper and a daily woman was not Nicole's idea of luxury. Papa was probably mean, she supposed.

"Not all that long ago," Papa told them, "the servants' wages topped a hundred pounds a year. I have the account books to prove it – not much use to me now!"

"But we still have Tom for the garden, Papa! And his house!" Little Cassa felt sure that Papa liked reassurance.

Richard nodded, but he wondered for how much longer Tom would last. He was getting on.

Every summer, the extended family group of the Blakes was photographed by Lafayette of Grafton Street, against a trellis of Gloire de Versailles roses. These pictures in their ornate frames were a feature in the drawing-rooms. Holidays in Italy, or fishing in the Highlands of Scotland, gave grand lilting names to the fine houses: Dunlochry, Mount Glenavie or, more romantically: Monte Auraylia, Villa Palmyra.

The great-great-grandfather of Richard Blake had named his imposing residence Firenze in memory, it was said, of his six-month-long wedding excursion in Italy with the exquisite Elvira, whose beauty, it was also said, came down to her female descendants. The Blakes were legal dignataries in Dublin city. Four generations of them had resided most comfortably in Firenze on the Donnybrook Road until that spacious, opulent road was turned into a six-lane carriage-way. Many a Villa Auraylia's flowery acreage had become an avenue of expensive modern dwellings, thousands of them by the end of the slow fifties.

Driving home from his offices on Stephen's Green, Richard Blake never failed to regret the magnificent park-lands of Mount Merrion House, now ravaged into crescents and cul-de-sacs with titles taken from local topography rather than in commemoration of glorious faraway places.

Beyond Mount Merrion, his own Firenze was sheltered by its winding up-hill drive as yet untouched by the new plan-ning authority. Compulsory acquisition was a constant threat of financial ruin. The idea of selling his estate for speculative building was out of the question. His wife, Sadora Gilbey Blake, could not countenance living in a lesser residence. If Sadora had given him a son, the young man could have gone forth to seek a wealthy heiress, as Richard himself had done, honouring the family tradition.

Sadora Gilbey had brought her fortune into Firenze and then proceeded to fulfil her own family tradition by becoming a sofa-invalid in the Victorian style. Her specialists, her nurses, her sojourns abroad in search of health had used up his resources and, he suspected, her own. She still murmured of Gilbey stocks and bonds, but what would be left for his two daughters in a few years from now?

Nicole would survive: she had inherited the Gilbey tenacity. But Cassa, how would she fare in the wicked world should his financial resources continue to be depleted? His comfortable circumstances were costing more each year.

Sadora had insisted on the name Cassandra, a name unknown in the family annals, as if she wished distance from a second daughter who should have been a son.

"Cassandra," insisted Sadora Gilbey Blake from her pillows, "that is the name for this one. Cassandra was the daughter of Priam and Hecuba. She was given the gift of prophecy by Apollo. A gift-bearing name."

"Will Monsignor Flanagan swallow that outlandish name when we present her for baptism? I think I should prefer my mother's name."

"And what is that?" enquired Sadora, to whom the Blakes scarcely figured in Debrett.

"It was Maria Cordelia," and Richard's voice was capable of carrying ice when his wishes were not preferred. He blamed Sadora for his disappointment. A son was what he wanted. In their circles the quota was a son and a daughter, and he had rather banked on it.

"Cordelia!" Sadora was shocked. "That name would, nowadays, be shortened to Delia. People are so careless with names. Delia would be quite common."

Despite her name, little Cassa wound her way into his affections. He tried to be fair but she came first. She was his little House Bird, and she loved her pet name. It never occurred to him that Nicole might have liked a pet name.

Cassa looked for a little pampering; Nicole was impatient with his fuss.

The old country road of Richard Blake's childhood with its sunlit cricketing memories of his father and grandfather had become the changing road of his own life, reducing daily from splendid leisurely traffic into six lanes of stridulating speedways.

As the years moved on into the 1960s, the rush-hour on his road had to be avoided although he longed to get home to Firenze, to walk the dogs, to inspect his roses, to take little House Bird strolling along the curving lavender paths.

He often waited until darkness had fallen so he might avoid the inching traffic jams, the parked bulldozers, the gable-ends of new houses where once there were vistas of the Wicklow mountains, hazily blue in evening light.

The club on Kildare Street was a safe haven from the new road. There a man could enjoy the late-night society of his fellows, and take a stroll around Stephen's Green with other cigar-smokers – a vice forbidden by Sadora Gilbey Blake. A deadly vice, she suspected, which led to other deadly vices, even in some cases into secret scented boudoirs.

He was fairly sure that his sainted wife would never understand the effect of the new road on a man's spirit.

CHAPTER TWO

NICOLE HAD SEEN Dermot Tyson for the first time when she cycled into Donnybrook for the Saturday newspapers, a task she did for her pocket-money when she was fifteen.

From her sofa, Sadora Gilbey Blake liked to apportion tasks in every direction, especially to her husband. On Saturday, however, Richard played golf.

Dermot Tyson played Rugby for Bective, and on that particular Saturday he was chatting to a couple of his pals outside Bective gates when a girl suddenly skidded on to the path, toppling her bicycle. She was a pretty girl, and the three young men rushed to pick her up, then stood admiring her as her long mane of blonde hair tumbled out of a ribbon on to her shoulders.

"Thank you, thank you very much." Her accent told the young men that she was not from the village. "You are so kind, all of you. Thank you again."

Her bright glance embraced the three, but it was at Dermot Tyson she looked, taking in his amused dark hazel eyes beneath arched black brows, his black hair, his broad shoulders, his height.

"I am Nicole Sadora Blake," she told him. "My friends call me Nicky."

Dermot took the offered chance. "Will I walk the bike up as far as the church until you get your breath?" He waved and winked at his pals. "See you later, fellas."

Nicole asked politely, "Did I take you away from your friends? Maybe you were all going somewhere?"

"No, just home for dinner. We had a practice. The three of us are on the team."

"Do you live in Donnybrook?" Nicole's voice trembled, her heart was thumping in delight.

"I do," he answered, glancing down at her. "We have a pub at the corner of Belmont."

He noted the upward flicker of her eyes. "I'm in my last year in TCD," he added.

Now she lifted her face in a brilliant smile. Trinity College! Firenze would approve of Trinity.

"Law," she queried, "or languages?"

"Neither. Business Administration. A Ph.D. – got the Master's last year."

"How clever you must be." Nicole glowed appreciatively at him. "I did my Inter this year."

Being fifteen seemed stupidly young; a fellow with those looks must have had a dozen girlfriends already.

"Does your pub have a name?" she enquired.

"Tyson's," he said shortly.

He was handing over the bicycle and would soon be gone to catch up on his friends.

"I go to Loreto," she said, and avoided taking the bicycle.

"Oh, which one?" he asked.

"In Foxrock." She was thrilled by his interest.

"My sister, Della, is in the Loreto on the Green. She did her Leaving this year. She can't make up her mind about College, which course she'll take."

"Have you several sisters?" Anything to prolong the conversation and stand looking at him.

"No, only Della and two older brothers, Tom and Ben. I'm Dermot. Hadn't you better push on? It is beginning to rain."

She sought frantically for the nerve to invite him up to Firenze – to play tennis? Invitations were strictly vetted by her mother.

"I always come in on Saturdays for the papers, Dermot," she angled.

"Next Saturday we have a match away, Miss... er... Nicky."

Had he forgotten her name so soon?

"Blake," she said proudly, "Nicole Sadora Blake. Nicole because I was born at Christmas."

She cycled off up the road before he could advise her to push off again. Rugby seasons, summer seasons, and slow cycling as far as the Belmont corner. Of course, why not?

Nicole tossed back her blonde hair and smiled.

Actually he had caught the Blake name. The Blakes on the Donnybrook Road were very well established indeed. Since he was ten years old, Dermot had often cycled past the magnificent mansion on the hill set among its entwined pergolas and fringed by great chestnut trees.

In latter years, taking his mother for a Sunday drive down to her sister's place in Arklow, she always said to him, "Look at that house, with the sun shining on it, and the same family living in it for over a hundred years. What's the name of it? Firenze? Funny name."

All of the summer Saturdays in the late sixties, Nicole contrived to meet with Dermot Tyson. Even if he spared only a few minutes, if he was cautious, or casual, or uncommitted, she was determined on having him. The idea of falling in love never came to her mind. Loving or falling were not in her nature, nor the analysing of those concepts. Dominant possession was her creed.

Dermot Tyson had his future planned, and in five years time, a well-bred, good-looking girl of means could be part of it. He was wisely aware of the fatuity of falling for a star-struck teen-ager, letting go of the very natural passions aroused and infused by a willing female.

In close friends, brilliant students, he had witnessed sexual rapture ripped apart by the shot-gun marriage: father and brothers on the doorstep, followed by the priest with bell, book and candle to signify the race between the altar and the font.

Dermot had been lucky to have his sexual initiations without aftermath. Right now he did not need Nicole.

Whatever subtle change Mrs Sadora Gilbey Blake discerned in her daughter, she decided to remove the girl from Loreto, and send her to a Gilbey aunt in Gloucestershire. Great-aunt Hilda would give her a finishing education in Cheltenham Ladies College. Not so good a finish as the old days in Switzerland, but times and finances had changed.

Therefore, on the last Saturday in August, Nicole would

11

introduce Cassa to the purchase of the newspapers in the shop in Donnybrook.

"Nicky will tell Mr Jay that you are her sister, dear. Always remember to bring the list of papers. He keeps *The London Illustrated* aside, so be sure he gives it, dear, with the others. That's very important and you are apt to be so dreamy. And promise to be careful on the new road, especially at Nutley where there is a big crossroads. Yes, dear, I know you would rather go off over to Louise's house. Nicky told me that you don't want to go, but you must earn your pocket-money just as Nicky did. Earning, not taking, is one of the Rules, dear. The Rules are so important. Now, off you go."

Nicole fumed under her breath, but no one had ever disobeyed Sadora.

The girls cycled towards Donnybrook, keeping close to the path where new roads were still under construction for ever more avenues of modern houses.

"You can stay near the new houses, Cass. There's no need for you to come all the way."

"Oh but I want to, Nicky. I want to see the little shops."

"I'm only going to the one shop, the paper shop, that's all."

"Please, Nicky, let me come with you," Cassa pleaded.

"It's too far. You can stay at the new cross-roads and wait there for me to come back. Cassa, do as I say! Don't make me cross with you today!"

This would be Nicole's last chance to see Dermot Tyson before her departure to Cheltenham. He could so easily forget her, he must be surrounded by girls. She would say something very special, something secret, something romantic that would keep her forever in his mind. He was so grown-up, so sophisticated, and she was barely sixteen.

"Please, please, Nicky, don't leave me on this big road all by myself. Please, Nicky," Cassa begged.

"Don't be such a baby – you're twelve, for heaven's sake. You won't blow away. Now, stay there, by the wall. Prop the bike and wait for me. I won't be all day. Don't snivel!"

Nicole raced down the last mile, her blonde hair streaming in the wind. Dermot was actually in the paper shop reading a magazine. Cool as a breeze, he was a vision in black and white: white sweater, white shirt, black hair, dark glowing eyes and white white teeth. He was smiling at her.

Nicole was barely able to get the right papers and pay out the right money. It was not in her nature to fluster, but she came fairly near to it.

"Shall I push your bike up as far as the church, miss?" He was acting the errand-boy in a Dublin accent to make her smile, but now she was seriously wide-eyed.

He knew this would be their last rendezvous. She had told him that her parents and her sister would be spending Christmas with her and Great-aunt Hilda because her mother had heard of another specialist in London who would be able to cure her newest mysterious illness.

"I'm going to be so lonely without Saturdays to look forward to. Oh Dermot, what'll I do!"

Their strange unspoken affair had advanced just that smallest bit.

"Don't get upset, Nicole. Time passes in a flash, you'll see."

It was easy for Dermot. The Rugby season would be starting, and his hopes were high for the trials. His last year of study was over and he had come out on top. There would be awards.

"I might be able to write to you, Dermot. I just might be able to post a letter; they are very strict about that kind of letter, but I will try to find a way."

He had a mental image of mawkish amorous phrases in childish writing to which he would be expected to respond. He said firmly, "Our friendship is special because it is known only to us. Only to us in the whole world – not even a postman must know."

He smiled down at her, but he was imagining his sarcastic sister's curiosity: "Another letter from England, brother dear?"

Dermot still lived at home; he was very fond of his mother, who took great care of him, her youngest son.

Nicole stood still to draw in an ardent sigh: "Oh Dermot, our secret affaire-de-coeur, how heavenly!"

"Just a secret friendship, Nicole. That is it and that is all."

Even that reply failed to dim the flaming colour of her emotions.

"I'll miss you dreadfully, Dermot. I'll think of you every day."

"And especially on Saturdays?" he asked gaily.

They had reached Donnybrook church, the parting place. The bicycle was put leaning against the wall. Excitedly, the girl expected a farewell kiss. Her first kiss from Dermot, but not her one and only kiss. Not by any means! She was quite adept.

She had stolen perfume from her mother's dressing-table, and sprayed it all around her ears and her neck. Dermot would remember the perfect fragrance of this kiss; it was Sadora's most expensive French perfume.

"Who is that kid!" Dermot shouted in alarm. "The one with the bicycle: she'll get killed in the middle of the road. She's waving at us! She's calling *you*!"

Cassa was trying to get her bicycle across the road through the Saturday traffic. She was crying out to her sister, "Nicky! Nicky!" and her sister was shouting back very angrily, "Stay over there! Go back! Cassa, stay where you are! Go back!"

Dermot moved out on to the road.

"She's scared stiff; she'll get hurt. I'll get her across. She's only a kid!"

He dodged into the traffic, and taking hold of the child and her bike, he manoeuvred them to safety.

"Cassa, couldn't you have waited where I left you!" Nicole exclaimed. "What's the matter with you?" Cassa was crying uncontrollably, the tears splashing down her cheeks.

Dermot Tyson dried the little girl's face with his handkerchief, holding her steadily with his sympathetic arms around her shivering little body.

He was murmuring to comfort her, "Are you lost, what happened to you; don't cry, what's your name?"

Nicole pulled Cassa over to the wall. "She's my sister. There is nothing wrong with her. She's all right."

But the little girl, much smaller than Nicole, was distraught. Blubbering through her tears, she sobbed out something about an old man with black teeth trying to take her bicycle and knocking her into the wall and pulling her up far into the new road.

"I'm sorry, Nicky, I'm sorry. I was so frightened. I tried to get up on the bicycle and, I'm sorry Nicky, and then a woman was passing and the old man let me go and I'm sorry, Nicky. Don't be mad at me. Please don't be mad at me. Please, Nicky."

Nicole pretended to fuss over the child, but somehow Dermot was not impressed with her show of concern. The tearful little girl had the loveliest face, and the palpable innocence of her pleading eyes stirred the young man's heart.

Nicole caught Dermot's eyes on Cassa's face. Cassa would pay for this. Nicole knew a dozen ways to make Cassa vow on bended knees never to spy again.

"Oh come on," Nicole said loudly, pushing the bicycle at her sister. "Get up on the bike. We are late already. Get up. Go on. Go on."

CHAPTER THREE

With Nicky's departure for England and Cheltenham Ladies' College, it fell to Cassa to earn her pocket money by cycling to Donnybrook for the Saturday papers. She came always with another girl, older and taller than Cassa and quite as lovely in a different way. The two school-girls were soulmates.

In the paper shop, they chattered excitedly about the new magazines, calling across to each other.

"Oh Cassa, look at this!"

"Louise, quick, your favourite film-star!"

"Cassa, Cassa, Cassa, The Beatles!"

"Here, here, Louise, more pictures of them!"

Reading a paper in the back of the shop, Dermot Tyson listened and observed, and on the many Saturdays when he was occupied elsewhere, he felt a sense of disappointment at not seeing them. Eventually, the two girls came no more. Perhaps Stillorgan had acquired a paper shop at last.

When summer came, Nicole was back to take up the tenuous thread of the shadowy relationship. In the third summer she felt old enough to issue invitations to her home: a garden party, a tennis tournament. Dermot always found an excuse to refuse.

The decade of the sixties in Dublin city, strange changeling years, brought the ambitious thrill of rapid advancement to Dermot Tyson. Almost effortlessly, he rose into the ranks of the young entrepreneurs; he saw the big money waiting for the ones who had the verve to take it. Among his associates, Dermot was a rock of financial wisdom.

He was clever, but not clever enough to reject the focus of lonely wonder at the centre of his being. In his subcon-scious, and seldom acknowledged as an essential part, was the touching face of the beautiful child who had clung to him at the wall outside Donnybrook church.

CHAPTER FOUR

IN JANUARY 1970 Nicole conspired with her mother to set up an interview with her parents for Dermot Tyson's proposal of marriage. It would be his first visit to Firenze. He had, at last, indicated to Nicole that the time was right and he would soon be thinking of setting up his own establishment.

She had her twenty-first birthday at Christmas, and in Sadora's world the age of consent had come. Another year and the girl would be on the shelf. If the young man were not to Sadora's specifications, so be it. If, on the other hand, he was in every way agreeable, then Sadora had something in store for him. Nicole had been most unwilling to be prised away from Marjorie Kemp's nephew Clive, a wealthy young man but disastrously reckless, and perhaps this Tyson proposal would be Nicole's reward. Dear lovely Nicky needed to be anchored very firmly.

The young man was in his early thirties. Sadora approved of the early thirties for men for most purposes, and marriage was one. Richard had been too settled, over forty when they wed, already a bon viveur, a club man, a sportsman, and (Sadora had found out) something of a ladies' man.

"Papa, if you don't want to meet him, Mama will deal with him." To a lawyer's ears, this meant collusion between his wife and his daughter. The airy manner did not deceive him.

"Of course I should like to meet any friend of yours, my dear." Not strictly true but courteous. "Friday night, you say? Is this the young man from last summer, the brilliant tennis player? Oh, that was Clive. And we haven't met this one yet? So many of them in summertime."

Sadora had decided that the impressive front drawing-room was the place for this interview. Since Christmas, the weather had been bitterly cold, and although the house was mainly centrally heated, a big log-fire was burning in the grate, illuminating the beautiful portrait of Elvira above the marble mantel.

Cassa had inherited the beauty of her great-great-grand-mother, she who had travelled to Florence with an earlier Richard Blake for her first six months of married love; she who had become the mother of famous sons; she who could never get enough of her adored husband's ardent passion, and in his absence at war (it was said) welcomed the advances of his fellow officers.

Elvira's rounded, indented chin, her softly parted lips, her great brown eyes fringed in night-black lashes: Cassa had them all, down to the tiny beauty-spot above her eyebrow. Nicole was a very attractive young woman, but she would never be Elvira.

Richard Blake was impressed with the grandeur of Dermot Tyson's car, and the fine figure he cut in his expensive Burberry as he laid his leather briefcase on the side-table with some ceremony.

He bowed to Mrs Blake seated among her cushions on the couch by the bright fire. "I am Dermot Tyson," he said respectfully. "Thank you for receiving me."

Richard and Sadora nodded graciously.

"My husband and I are here to listen if you care to tell us why you wish to speak to us." Nicole had told Dermot not to be put off by Mama's manners. She had primed Mama, and Dermot would have to impress Papa himself.

"I have set out this portfolio of my business affairs so as to assure you, Mr and Mrs Blake, that in the event of your looking favourably on my proposal of marriage, I am well able to take care of Miss Blake. The documents are ready, also a letter of introduction from my solicitors, Dorman and Company."

Tyson's tone was not subservient, nor yet overbearing. He had pride. He bowed again to Mrs Blake. Nicole had told him her mother ruled.

Glancing at the briefcase but not touching the documents, Richard enquired, "Since when have you known my daughter?"

"Distantly, a little more than five years."

"And how is it you never came to the house?" asked Sadora, creasing her eyes.

"She is young and I waited. I am in the position now."

That seemed fair to Richard. "Are you, by any chance, the Dermot Tyson who played Rugby for Ireland?"

"The same," Dermot answered quietly. "My parents have a licensed premises in Donnybrook. Tyson's."

"A fine place," Richard said approvingly. His heart lifted. He would be glad to see Nicole married off. She was restless and contentious. She had too many needs, all requiring money.

Lately, Richard Blake had felt increasingly anxious that by the time his little House Bird finished at the Loreto, there would be no funds for her further education. She was a good musician, and she must get her chance. And her chance of meeting eligible young men. He felt that Nicole blocked Cassa from view in some way he did not understand. At times, he intercepted a look of entreaty in Cassa's brown eyes directed across the table at Nicole's eyes. Nicole had the glittering blue eyes of Sadora long ago, and the thick blonde hair.

"Yes, Mr Tyson," Sadora was declaiming, "that is the portrait of the great-great-grandmother of my girls. That beauty is Elvira, married to General Richard Denton Blake, a soldiering man and a great advocate of the law in India. I forget the artist's name, British I am sure. Yes indeed, a nice picture. Many people admire it."

Richard thought it best to join in. "Ah, er. Dermot, do you play golf?"

Tyson's eyes were still on the portrait. He could never have bargained for the overpowering emotion that closed off his throat when he looked up into the ardently amorous eyes of the lovely Elvira. Would Cassa look into a lover's eyes in just that way? His gaze came back to his host as if from faraway.

"Golf? Yes, I do – in Hermitage. My father took it up in recent years. Amazing how he enjoys his game."

Took it up? Golf was like religion or political party. You were born to it. Still, Tyson was a proven sportsman, that was clear enough.

Mrs Sadora Gilbey Blake was now all set to bring on the trophy. "So you have come to ask for our dear daughter's hand?"

Mama had been well acquainted with her daughter's determination for some time. Being a dear daughter in her parents' domicile was no longer sufficient for Nicky.

Dermot Tyson nodded gravely. He had come to ask for their daughter in marriage. This was an essential part of his plan. He had grown fond of Nicole. She had class, style, good looks, and he was quite moved by her adoration. Like the final piece of jig-saw, she fitted accurately into his ambitions.

Mrs Blake was now standing, swaying and slowly turning towards the door.

In a moment, Nicole would be ushered into the room although her name had not yet been mentioned. Questions flared madly in Dermot's mind while his normal good sense of time and place bade him be silent.

Now Richard interposed in his lawyer's voice: "Sadora, my dear, if I may? Be seated a moment, if you would? We have not discussed this matter of a proposal of marriage either among ourselves, or indeed with our daughter. Should we not hear what she has to say, my dear."

"That is reasonable, Richard. You understand, of course, that I know my daughter's mind?"

"You do?" he asked vaguely with an uncertain glance at Tyson.

"Undoubtedly I do; I always have a perfect understanding of Nicole's mind." She rose again, swaying regally and turning towards the door.

Tyson jumped to his feet. There was a pause. His thoughts plunged downwards in the same instant as a burning log crumbled inwards on the glowing fire sending a sparkling light upwards to the portrait. He almost shut his eyes. He knew he had not come with gifts of love for Nicole but for the girl in the picture. She had lain across his heart, she had clung to him, her tear-filled eyes had appealed to his pity when she was a child of twelve, and now he was looking into the same brown eyes with the same appeal and now he must respond.

He ended the pause by turning to Richard Blake: "But, of course, you have two daughters, haven't you, Mr. Blake?"

Richard was alerted to his wife's perpetual intrigue. "Truly, Mr Tyson, you can scarcely propose for both of them. My Cassa is only a child, in her last year in school."

There was dry amusement in his voice, but in Tyson's ominous pause, Richard had settled his mind on marriage for Nicole. The young man was eligible, a sportsman, money in the bank; enquiries could be made, but an engagement came first. Nicole was too demanding for comfort, too like her mother. She asked for a sports car for her twenty-first birthday; she was always wheedling tenners. And tenners were not as plentiful as in former times.

"Cassa must be over seventeen now," was Dermot Tyson's next comment, although he saw Mrs Blake's narrow gaze fixed on him.

"Why do you refer to Cassa's age?" Richard Blake wanted to know. "Does Cassa know you are here?"

Tyson's shoulders strengthened as if ready to grasp on a rope.

"Do I not act correctly in approaching the parents of two daughters?" That was a stupid question and he knew he was out of his depth. He began to gather his papers. He had come too soon to this tryst; in a couple of years Cassa would be ready for him, equally right in many ways, and infinitely more desirable because she had scored deeply into a sensitive core where no other emotion had taken root.

"I am in a position to take care of Cassa. . . . "

Richard interrupted him abruptly and harshly: "We look after our daughter, Cassa. We look after her very well. We take good care of her."

He knew he would never let his little House Bird go to this fellow. Who was he anyway? Perhaps Nicole would not be safe with him?

Now Dermot Tyson began to gather his papers and replace them in the briefcase.

Sadora had been silent, but Richard's intuition told him that her turn for speech was about to be demonstrated, and her turn was always the decisive one.

She resumed her place among her cushions. "Do not let us be hasty, Mr Tyson. I have a proposition I should like you to hear. Do sit down, Mr Tyson, do sit down."

Richard Blake walked out of range and studied the dark garden through the French doors.

"Yes, indeed, Mr Tyson, we have two daughters, one as fair as the other, and we love them dearly. We love them so dearly we could not imagine the older one being left aside while the younger one would marry and depart."

Sadora rearranged her numerous silken scarves.

"Unheard of in our world, Mr Tyson. The older sister might never marry, so ignominious is the sting. We are moving into another era where such niceties may no longer matter but we happily adhere to our established way. Mr Tyson, you are a man of profound understanding, are you not?"

He was a man bamboozled by an old woman's rhetoric. He glanced at the turning figure of Richard, obviously equally puzzled.

With the dignity of an empress disposing of her last diamond tiara, Sadora Gilbey Blake enlightened the two men: "My daughter Nicole is the marriageable daughter, and with Nicole goes a dowry of sixty thousand pounds."

Richard Blake gasped. Where would Sadora get her hands on sixty thousand pounds? Did she think he had it? The practice would be put up for sale, and if it should sell, the money was needed, every pound of it.

Dermot Tyson concealed his gasp.

Sadora's gimlet eyes were noting his slight hesitation in biting the lure.

"Mr Tyson, I am the owner of a five-bedroom detached house on an acre, beside, but not too close beside, Stillorgan village. It will be my wedding present, our wedding present, to our daughter, Nicole Sandora, when she marries suitably."

Richard Blake took a grip on his temper. Another piece of Gilbey property given away. He had had some hopes of a sale there; these old houses were now more valuable than ten years ago.

Sixty thousand pounds of a dowry (if such existed) would buy half a dozen houses in this year of 1970. Half a dozen, any day in the week. He had heard Tyson's intake of breath and Richard's temper slipped the rein; the man's pause and his lack of protest were an insult to Richard's dear little House Bird, and Richard knew that Cassa was now the young man's preferment whatever his previous intention had been. Tyson's intent study of the portrait of Elvira had not been unmarked by the lawyer. Tyson must know Nicole's younger sister.

"Then I may as well make my position clear." Richard was never afterwards sure if he had defied Sadora or aided her. "I will not permit my daughter, Cassa, to be made a bargaining chip."

He glared at Sadora, in that moment hating her. "Cassa is not on the marriage market. She is my child. And she is still a child, her interests are those of a child. Marriage is out of the question. You are high-handed, Mr Tyson, but I am sure you are honourable. Marriage for my daughter Cassa is not a matter for discussion at this time."

Nicole was listening at the door. She grimaced. Papa's dear darling Cassa! He had no thought of ever making a fight for her, his elder daughter, his first-born, his heiress, if it came to that.

Her father's affection for silly Cassa was to her advantage. This time she did not care. Nicole knew that high finance would be Dermot's first choice. She had secured her prize, undoubtedly with equal rights. The plan had worked as she had known it would and she had not been sold cheaply.

The drawing-room door was opened and her mother tottered out. She called, "Nicole dear," as if her dear daughter were at the top of the staircase.

In due time, they returned to the drawing-room together.

CHAPTER FIVE

O N THAT SAME wintry night, Cassa and her friend, Louise
Condon, lay snuggled in the eiderdown in Cassa's cosy
bedroom. They had seen little of each other since
September when Louise had started in Trinity College, and
this was the year of Cassa's impending Leaving Cert.

Louise had fallen in love with her history professor.

"Oh Cass, he is the most perfect man you ever saw! And
his voice! I adore his voice. I always thought it was silly to say
that a voice could make me quiver, but it does. Oh Cass, I am
delirious, honestly, and I used to despise all that kind of
thing. I only wish I knew if he... you know... I mean, for
me?

Cassa had no idea if falling in love was always mutual,
which Louise was sure it had to be.

"Describe him all over again. Please, Louise. What colour
are his eyes?"

"His eyes? Oh, let me see, oh yes, his eyes are grey, just like
his name, but steely grey. Robert Gray! What a purely perfect
name. And I told you he has a beard, Cass? And a moustache!"

Louise sighed, a delicious heart-felt sigh.

"But a beard, Louise? Do you mean a long beard down to
here, like the picture of Grandfather Blake, the one on the
stairs?"

"Oh no, don't be silly. His beard is very smart, sort of
French, all clipped and curly – gorgeous!"

"But you said you thought he is old? A bit old."

Louise almost whispered her reply.

"He is thirty-four, Cass."

And Cassa whispered back, awe-struck at the thought,
"But thirty-four is fifteen years older than you."

"I don't care." Louise was prepared to overlook his old
age. "He's rich, Cass. One of the fellows in class told me that
Robert Gray has a country house that's mentioned in the

tourist guide, and that his grandfather fought in the War of Independence."

"Was he shot – one of them? In Kilmainham Jail?"

"No, he was in the government; he was a minister. The Minister for Lands."

"And Robert Gray has written three books?" asked Cassa.

"Not *stories*, Cass, *we* won't be reading them. I'm not sure but I think it is an analysis of revising history."

Cassa gazed in wonder. Louise would never have admitted ignorance – she would catch up somehow on analysis.

"Cass, if I tell you something, absolutely in the deepest secrecy, promise you will never tell Nicole or anyone in school. My mother would kill me if she found out. Promise!"

"You know I never tell your secrets." Cassa was indignantly loyal.

Since they were nine and eleven, they had walked home together after school across their adjoining fields and Louise had let Cassa in on all the mysteries of the Irish declensions, given her the answers to the hard sums, supplied ideas for impossible essays, even scribbled out translations for Irish poems. Louise had never taunted her with being a dumbbell the way Nicole had.

Nicky had been taken out of Loreto when Cassa was twelve, and Louise and Cassa had really chummed-up then. Louise was considered the prettiest girl in the school. Nicole didn't think so, but Cassa knew that every other girl envied Louise Condon for her looks and her brains.

"Cassa, solemn promise, you will never breathe a word? Well," she drew out the word slowly, and she lowered her voice, "I went out with him for a drive in his car. Robert Gray, my dearly beloved gorgeous history professor!"

Cassa's brown eyes flew wide open. A drive that no one knew about? With a man as old as that?

"Where did you go?" she inquired softly.

"He drove out to Howth and, Cass, listen, he hired a motorboat at the pier and we went out to Ireland's Eye!"

"Ireland's Eye!" Cassa repeated as if Louise had

announced one of the Seven Wonders of the World. "Ireland's Eye: it's an island, isn't it?"

Louise glowed with remembrance of the stolen day. "There wasn't another person on the little island, not another single person. He pulled the boat up on the beach and we walked along the sand. Cass, the sun was shining, the day was as warm as summer, and listen, we lay on the big flat rocks and, and he... and he... very slowly and very gently he took off my dress and he... and then he..."

Cassa waited, her eyes fixed on Louise.

"I knew I was in love with Robert from the first day in class. I think all the girls are, he is so fabulously good-looking. But when we were on the island I wanted him so much I could have died. Just you wait, Cass, until it happens to you!"

Louise lifted her long hair up on top of her head, twisting the tresses dreamily.

"I can't describe the feeling, not as it really is, the wanting feeling. Robert says it is the primal desire in every human person. Robert told me it comes from somewhere the way a stream must rise at the source, vibrating, pulsing with the desire to become a great river rushing down the mountain and into the ocean."

Cassa asked breathlessly, "Is the feeling still inside you, Louise?"

"Worse than ever! Every day, even days when I have no class with him! Even when I have no hope of seeing him, I am trembly all over!"

Louise snuggled down in the eiderdown."I really will die if it doesn't happen again soon."

She was melodramatically relaxed, confident of Cassa's compliant admiration.

"But what can happen?" Cassa asked. "Only looking forward to seeing him at class? You know how keen you are to get your degree and travel the world: you always said so."

"I want him so badly, my body is aching for him," she purred.

Louise let the long brown hair ripple through her fingers

and on to her shoulders. She rolled over, burrowing and stretching luxuriously like a beautiful cat.

"Just wait, Cass, just wait until you get that wanting feeling for yourself. Special, special, special. Like warm cream, or honey, running into a thousand tiny streams down, down, down low inside you. Oh, Cass, he is so gorgeous! He promised me it gets better and better – the sheer magic of it! And the things he says: secret things, and the things he did – I dare not tell you!"

"Begin all over again," Cassa begged, "and describe everything about him. Go on, Louise, tell me from the very beginning, and you know I would never tell a single soul."

The rapturous telling took more than an hour.

In that same hour, in the drawing-room downstairs, under the beautiful portrait of Elvira, Cassa's sister became affianced to a man named Dermot Tyson, the one who had rescued a twelve-year-old Cassa from being knocked down in the traffic outside Donnybrook church.

Cassa never forgot parts of that day, especially that night when Nicole burned her fingers by holding them in a candle flame. Nicky could never forgive and forget unless her sister was punished. Over the years, Cassa had found it was better to submit and get it over with. If Nicky was placated, things were easier for a while.

But of the young man or what he looked like, Cassa had not the faintest recollection. No one, least of all Nicole, ever told her that her name was mentioned in the marriage negotiations.

CHAPTER SIX

SADORA PROCLAIMED THE Firenze wedding in June 1970 worthy to be written into the annals of weddings the world over. The bride and the bridegroom were resplendently representative of their class and wealth and generation. It was remarked by many that they were radiantly happy and romantically in love.

The weather had been summery since the first of May so the gardens were a photographer's dream, and there were many photographers from newspapers and glossy magazines. There was colour everywhere.

The glory of the ladies' dresses contrasted with the immaculate black and white of the gentlemen's morning suits. It was apparent that Sadora's gown had belonged to an ancestress at the Spanish court, such was the effect it created. Richard Blake, for a man into his sixties, was remarkably handsome.

Some of the cousins said, although not within Nicky's hearing, that dear little Cassa stole the show: what a complexion, what colouring. She herself was not at all sure why she was giddy with delight. Could it possibly be the departure of Nicky to live somewhere else? Or could it be that her closest friend, Louise, was there across the grass with the delectable Robert Gray?

"Papa," Cassa asked, "would you say that Robert Gray is the most handsome man here today? That is, excepting you, of course!"

"Undoubtedly, my pet, the very essence of charm. But tell me, is not your friend Louise a bit too young to be considering marriage. Pity to miss out on College? She is, so you tell me, so brilliantly clever."

"You see, Papa, Robert is going to America for a year – Harvard, Louise told me – and they just could not bear to be parted. Isn't that really, truly romantic?"

"And what does Mrs Condon think? Widowed last year. That big place of theirs is falling to bits."

"It's up for sale, Papa; in fact, Louise thinks they have a buyer. Mrs Condon is going to buy a little bungalow and she is delighted about Louise. Robert is rich, Papa, with property in the country, a big house, although not as big as Condons', Mrs Condon said."

Sadora had arranged a marquee on the lawn and a band to play waltz music. She had laid down a new Rule. There was to be no rushing away of the bridal couple directly after the reception.

"Barbaric!" she declared in her queenly manner. "To stuff themselves with food and drink and then dash to the airport for a four-hour flight. Barbaric! This wedding is not for the guests. It is for my daughter and her husband to meet all our friends and relations. It is for Nicole and Dermot to enjoy. And enjoy they will."

Richard Blake danced in a lovely dated style with his daughter, Cassa. Looking down on her tawny curls, admiring her, his dearly-loved little House Bird, and wondering all the time if bankruptcy were staring him in the face. The Gilbeys were milling around him in droves. He hoped to God that Gilbey money was paying for this extraordinary show. It certainly was not his.

Then Cassa was dancing with Dermot Tyson. She had scarcely had time to make his acquaintance; Nicky demanded all his attention.

As they twirled around, Cassa looked up at him to smile. She was surprised at the intensity of his face, no light in the eyes meeting hers.

"Welcome to the family," Cassa smiled brightly. "I hope you will be very happy always. 'Member me? The bridesmaid?"

He held her very closely but he said not a word. When the music stopped, Cassa was turning away when his hand on her arm detained her. "Again, Cassa?"

Then she was back in his arms, gliding to some old tune from the forties. She was so close she could feel his heart beating. Her body was touching his. His lips were breathing on her hair.

Cassa's eyes began to seek nervously among the dancers for her sister, his bride. To even look at any of Nicky's possessions was, she knew too well, a punishable crime. To be held like this, strongly yet gently, amorously yet lightly, was an unexpected pleasure generously given by so handsome a man.

The music drew out a long last note of the saxophone and Cassa turned quickly away to greet one of the young Gilbey cousins.

"Hi, Charlie, how about a lemonade!"

She saw Dermot later. He was alone, walking away from the sentimental music and through the open French doors into the front drawing-room.

Alone on his wedding day when Sadora expected him to play courtier to his lovely bride? The stuffy old front drawing-room?

Cassa hesitated, unaccountably uncertain. Then she decided to stay with the crowd, safely observing Sadora's Rules.

After the traditional throwing-over-her-shoulder of the bridal bouquet, Nicole stood on the steps blowing kisses at the gathered guests.

If Dermot Tyson seemed unusually quiet and dignified to the Rugby crowd (who may indeed have been getting ready for their own traditional boomps-a-daisy on their big shoulders), no one else noticed. Sadora approved *haute-élégance* in men.

Nicole gave her hand to her groom and they were driven away, and when the last of the slightly inebriated straggling guests had been ushered into their cars, tranquillity settled over Firenze.

Richard's dogs were released at last from the old garden house. The place had stood empty since the gardener had died a few years earlier and his wife had gone to live in Blackrock with her married daughter. Richard missed old Tom. He had been there since both their boyhoods, and he had made the garden what it had become. In the fading twilight, Richard murmured Tom's name. Tom would have

31

been very proud of his roses today; a great man for the roses, Tom.

The dogs chased each other into the far fields. The fields, Richard thought, which might bring money if only Sadora would agree.

A light went on high up in the house: that was his little House Bird's room. Her laughing face came vividly into his thoughts; how beautiful she had been today.

Cassa stood at the long mirror admiring her bridesmaid's dress. It really was lovely. And she would be a bridesmaid again in September for Louise with another big wedding across the fields in Condons'. Louise and Robert!

Twice a bridesmaid in one year, that just had to be lucky. Maybe a great Leaving Cert result in August? Papa had said he would be able to afford the School of Music, although maybe not college. Cassa hugged herself, smiling into the mirror. There was so much to look forward to.

CHAPTER SEVEN

THE ARRANGEMENTS WERE almost complete, and as the day of the wedding approached the two friends talked about it endlessly.

The reception would be held in the Royal Hotel in Bray because the Condons' house, a great house in its day, was almost depleted of furniture. The house itself had been up for sale a long time. The Condons had been advised to wait, the property market being slow to pick up after the stringent fifties. The smart new houses on the dual carriageway were more attractive than a big old house in need of repair, and Condons' was rather further off the road than Firenze.

Louise was in the highest heaven of delight and she shared with Cassa many moments of that summer when her darling Robert was in Harvard preparing for the coming semester. In between times, he was back in Dublin and taking Louise to visit his country house in the midlands.

Louise had become very grown-up and full of responsibility in the year she had known Robert Gray. Gone was the Louise of wild romantic notions. She dressed very demurely now, going to have her hair done in Marcel Prost on the Green, and wearing court shoes with very high heels. She was still as beautiful as ever and still Cassa's closest friend.

"Cassa, you will be our very first guest when we settle in there next summer. Garlow Lodge is the name. Although the grounds are not very extensive, they are close around the house and very well kept. I was telling you about the aunt and uncle of Robert's who are living there, wasn't I?"

"Yes, and you told me about his parents dying in a hotel fire in Barcelona when he was only ten. That is so sad, both of them to die."

"They were on holiday which makes it all the sadder, doesn't it? He was sent to live with his grandfather in Garlow Lodge, and when his grandfather died, this aunt and uncle moved in. He doesn't seem to want to talk very much about his childhood, but I think the grandfather was very stern."

"Will the aunt and uncle be still there when you and Robert come back?"

"I don't think so. They are getting very old and they find the house big and draughty. The aunt's sister has a little house in Wicklow, near Blessington, I think. The aunt talks of her sister a lot. Robert says it will be a relief to them to go."

"I can imagine a thatched cottage overlooking the reservoir."

Louise smiled fondly at Cassa. "You are always imaging something," she said. "Now, don't forget on Thursday you are to go for the second fitting of your bridesmaid's frock, and I give you permission to take a little peek at my wedding dress."

When Cassa went for the final fitting, the dress fitted to perfection.

Sometime in the early hours of the morning on the last day of July, Mrs Sadora Gilbey Blake suffered a massive stroke.

For many years she had had her couch-bed and all the refinements of the invalid set out luxuriously in the morning-room. She loved the many-windowed sunny aspect of this room with its glass door on to a trellised loggia.

Climbing stairs had been forbidden for Sadora several years before. Now that there was no staff beyond a weekly help, Richard brought her a tray of coffee before leaving for his office, so it was he who found her.

At the first moment when he put down the tray, set just as she liked it (even in small matters, Sadora's Rules were household law), Richard noticed her complete immobility, quite contrary to her usual comfortable posture on the pillows, with the hair-net hidden, the lipstick applied, the perfume sprayed around.

"My dear, are you still asleep?"

There was no answer, no stir of the frilly pillows. Then he saw the wildly rolling eyes.

"Oh my God!" He ran to the foot of the stairs. "Cassa! Cassa! Come quickly. Something's wrong."

Cassa had been down earlier to make sure her Papa had some breakfast, after which she had gone about with polish and a duster. Since the wedding in June, Cassa had been what Richard apologetically called "a general factotumess".

"Soon, my little House Bird, soon we will get some new staff for you."

"Yes, Papa, soon."

And Cassa imagined what it would be like to have a cook, and a housemaid, and a gardener.

Now she rushed downstairs, hardly daring to think what had happened.

Phone calls to Sadora's doctors were quickly made. An ambulance was up the drive and a stretcher was carried into the house. Within an hour, Sadora Gilbey Blake was in intensive care in the private wing of a big city hospital, run by nuns as Sadora had always ordained.

Richard Blake was very distressed. He was overcome by remorse. An eminent doctor (and in the private wing the doctors were very eminent) had informed him that Sadora might just as sadly have suffered this stroke twenty years ago, and that undoubtedly there had been minor strokes through the years.

His wife's health, the eminent one said, had been precarious since her girlhood.

"One has to believe these doctors," Richard said many times to Cassa. "After all they would have to believe my legal opinions. They must know. But how did they know, since girlhood? I did not know. I never thought. It always seemed like fashionable convalescence to be indulged... I scarcely believed... I..."

He sat holding his daughter's hands in his, and she heard the muttered words sobbing in his throat: "Forgive me, forgive me."

Richard and Cassa never left the bedside and Nicole looked in occasionally. Cassa discovered within her private thoughts a cold pity for her mother and a rushing flood of love for her father. She could not bear his guilty contrition. She had never seen him do any action for which he must now be sorry.

One day he said to her, "But the wedding, little House Bird, the wedding? You are to be bridesmaid for Louise?"

And she replied, "Papa, the wedding date is past. Nearly a month ago. Louise is now in America."

He wept brokenly, his head hidden in his hands. "I have done nothing for you, little House Bird. The music, everything, I have let you down so badly."

Cassa lifted his head and held him against her breast. "I love you, Papa, don't be so sad."

He turned to look at the inert figure in the tight white bed. "And your mother, too. Oh God, I'm sorry."

Cassa whispered a lot of jumbled words of consolation. She had never seen him be anything to Sadora other than gentle, sweet, compassionate, helpful, sympathetic. She told him all this as she held him.

Richard's tears were bitter. What did little Cassa know who knew only her own loving heart? What could any outsider know of the highly civilised concealment of charged emotion which lay between a husband and a wife in an abyss of estrangement, a husband and a wife who had never known love, and yet who longed for love in every waking hour?

CHAPTER EIGHT

A T THE END of October they were allowed to take Sadora home to her comfortable morning-room. She neither moved nor spoke and her eyes were rigid in her head. The doctors were of the opinion that she could hear and that they should talk to her kindly. This was easier said than done.

For ten interminable years, Richard and Cassa nursed Sadora with docile devotion and around the clock. The ceaseless worry of dwindling money was coupled in winter with the freezing chill of a large house without heat except in the sick room, and in summer with the cutting of grass even within a limited area. To see his gardens becoming a wilderness was a part of Richard's heartache.

During these ten tedious weary years, Mrs Nicole Tyson was busily engaged in bringing up her two beautiful daughters, Orla and Sandra, and in attending to the demands of her social life. When she came to visit, and visits became rarer as time passed, she engaged her father in talk about antique furniture and rare paintings.

"I should like to consult you, Papa, about the furnishings for Dermot's study. With a room to himself, you know, a room to hold not only his books and papers but also his music and TV, well, he stays very late in his offices where he has all these things. As well as at home, of course."

Her father found this somewhat confusing. "Businessmen have TV in their offices now?"

Richard recognised Nicole's long slow curve; she seldom came straight to the point of any demand.

"I was thinking, Papa, of that desk in the back drawing-room? You never use that room now, do you? And, Papa, there is a table in the hall which Dermot would buy if you are selling."

"Has your husband expressed an interest in that walnut table?" asked Richard in his mild voice. "Has he, quite honestly, Nicole?"

"Well, now, not exactly, Papa. I thought of a birthday surprise."

"I understood you to say that he would buy it?"

"Are you selling it?" she asked with a touch of the old Sadora asperity.

"I have not thought of selling any of my furniture. All of it was here exactly as you see it when my father willed it to me, and his father willed it to him. Since 1856, as you may recall? Along with the house, and the thirty acres. One will after another." His quiet voice had sharpened.

Nicole sought to push a step further: "But you will naturally make a will when your time comes, Papa?"

"All done, my dear Nicole. I made my will a few days after my dearest wife secured *your* dowry for *your* marriage. If your mother has not made a will, then I fear she has left it a little late."

"That seems rather cruel, Papa."

"Life can be cruel, my dear. Go talk to your mother for a while. The doctors say it does her good."

"The next time, Papa. I have to hurry now. We have a big dinner tonight. Say night-night to Cassa for me."

Richard and Cassa made a little time for each other when they had padded Sadora in for the night. They took alternate nights to stay with her. In the morning, they had a nurse come to bed-bath her. Cassa did not feel that Papa should have to witness what amounted to incontinence. He was skilful in pressing the spoon into Sadora's mouth, and getting her to drink a little with a special cup. But in fact, her nourishment was minimal.

Cassa was becoming a good cook, and they both enjoyed the little dinner they shared in the kitchen when they came "off duty", as they put it. It was a special time. Richard attended at his office twice a week now in a consultative capacity. Two junior partners had bought in and, for the present, had bailed him out. The money was not great and he was determined on a sale of the practice.

"Nicole asked me to say night-night to you, little House Bird."

Cassa cupped her hand and blew a kiss at the ceiling. "Night-night, Nicky!" she called.

"There is a thing I have been meaning to say to you."

"What is it, Papa?"

"It is this, House Bird: no matter how much the Tysons cajole you in my absence – either because I am in my office, or away for any reason whatsoever – you must not, and you will not, give her or anyone acting for her, any article of the furniture in this house, any article no matter how insignificant. Not while I am alive, and not when I am dead. Sell to other people when it is yours but not to her and not to Tyson."

"Please don't suddenly go and leave me, Papa. I would be lost."

He came around the table and put his arms about her. "My precious House Bird, I have your word on what I have said?"

"I promise, Papa. I never would break my word to you."

Richard Blake looked at his beloved daughter as she took the dishes from the table. These sad years were slowly rolling away with no benefit to her.

Louise provided the one bright month in the year when Cassa was invited to the summer chalet which Robert had bought for Louise, and where they spent their summers.

"Letto Louise" was their dream of delight, situated as it was on the verge of Caragh Lake, half hidden by ancient oak trees. A stranger would never find it, Louise used to say, unless he knew the exact turn-off where the McGillicuddy Reeks come up over the horizon in all their misty glory. In fact, many strangers found Robert's summer retreat when he became famous, but in the beginning, it was the most hidden place on earth.

Louise loved Caragh Lake; she felt at ease there as nowhere else. Every year she began to look forward to July from Christmas onward. It took a lot of arranging to get a month's help for Papa and her stricken mother. Some years there were a couple of nuns who made a holiday for themselves out of it, some years two student nurses, and some years a couple of women from the village.

Cassa adored Louise and she thought Robert the ideal and most lovable of men. His company was exhilarating, and the company he drew around him was excitingly different from any people that Cassa could hope to meet in the other eleven months of the year. Yet, wonderful and fascinating as was the time with Robert and Louise, she also counted the days to be home again. There was always a timorous fear at the edge of her mind that something would go wrong, that Papa would not be at the door of Firenze to greet her at the end of July.

CHAPTER NINE

SADORA DIED TWO days before Cassa's twenty-eight birth-day. The doctors had told Richard that her heart was fail-ing, but her death struck him with a greater force of shock than had the original stroke. He and Cassa had become unquestioningly accustomed to their dreary days almost to the point of resisting change. Without ever spelling it out to each other, they braved each hour as it came. They accepted the stiff, silent, baleful Sadora as similarly they had accepted the righteous ruling Sadora of ten years before.

When the phone call told them of the death, Dermot Tyson drove with his wife to Firenze.

Cassa had not seen him for years. She did not know if he had ever called to see her father in his Dublin office to enquire about Sadora's health.

Nicole, an elegant young matron, went down the lower stairs with her father. She had brought flowers from her gar-den for the morning-room where her mother lay on a bed covered with a white sheet until a doctor would pronounce her to be truly dead.

Cassa was standing wearily at the hall door which Papa had opened. She was staring out across the fields. Dermot was filled with a longing to console and cheer her. He held out his arms when she turned to him. She accepted his com-fort, going into his embrace, resting against the smooth-surface of his jacket.

She felt his breath on her hair. She pressed closer, scarce-ly caring who was easing the misery of her useless grief. She whispered against the smooth solace of the cloth, "It's been so hard, it's been so long, watching and hoping. I want to cry and cry, but the tears won't come."

She looked upwards, unfocused. "Maybe it is all a dream, a bad dream. Maybe no years have passed. Maybe I will wake up and no one will be there... someone will come to wake me..."

Dermot looked down into her wistful face, the face he could never forget, as frightened now as the little face had been in the traffic outside Donnybrook church long ago. He held her and he gazed at her, the huge brown eyes fringed in black lashes, the soft lips, the unbrushed tangly hair, childlike but beautiful like the magic princess-tales he read to his little girls.

Cassa came suddenly to her senses when she heard her sister's voice on the stairs. Her body shrank back against the wall, her face full of fear. To cover her confusion, Dermot drew closed the heavy hall door, making a slow job as if it were stiff on its ancient hinges.

Nicole's voice was full and decisive. "That you, Cass? Oh there you are. I have told Papa that Dermot and I will take care of the funeral. Everything must be done as Mama would wish. The Gilbey grave, of course; it's quite a mausoleum. Dermot's brother, Thomas, as you probably know, Papa, is in the undertaking business. Don't worry about a thing, Thomas will look after all the details. Papa, I know you are not too happy about the Gilbey grave, and it is a bit out of the way, down in Glendalough, but that was Mama's wish, you know that: beside her own mother and father. She said it many times, and the Gilbeys would wish it. Besides, she was devoted to Glendalough, don't you remember, Cass?"

Richard Blake kept his head down. Why did he find his daughter Nicole so loud and insensitive, even coarse? Would Sadora have tolerated this dictatorial manner? But he said nothing.There would be a big turn-out for this funeral and he knew he lacked the financial resources. Long ago, a few thousand pounds was nothing, but if the Gilbeys were going to claim Sadora's poor wasted body, then perhaps he should give them the privilege of paying. Give the Gilbeys their due, their generosity was princely.

He despised himself for not protesting. He was sure Tyson's eyes were measuring him with contempt. Then Cassa took his arm and they moved away from the door.

"Come, Papa, you must rest. You have had no sleep for the

last few nights." She led him to the staircase. "I will bring up a hot whiskey and settle you down. I turned on your electric blanket."

She hugged him lovingly. "Go on now, you will be all right after a little rest. Yes, Papa, I'll be up later. Hang on to the banister, Papa, we're all a bit shaky today."

There was no contempt in Tyson's eyes; if anything, his eyes were full of envy. Nicole followed him out to the car. She was fulminating indignantly.

"Nothing in the freezer. Mama always saw to it that the freezer was packed. Damn little in the fridge. They knew Mama's death was likely this week. The specialist was out on Monday, and he told them. You would think Cassa would stock up: mourners are not like guests; mourners descend like vultures. My sister was always the same, up in the clouds. I saw not even a sign of a dinner for Papa. They eat in the kitchen now. Not even eggs."

"Look, Nicky, why don't we load up the car with freezer stuff and bring it back to them?"

"The shops are shut in Stillorgan – half day," she told him.

"I meant from our freezer." She looked horrified. Her supplies, all home-cooked by their housekeeper? "Certainly not," she said. "Cassa can go to the shops tomorrow. Papa is at home. She can use his car." She glimpsed the grim set of her husband's face. "Besides, I have no time today. There are so many phone calls I must make – all the relations, all the Gilbeys."

"We have to help them," he said; "they have borne enough. Make a list and I'll find a shop and I'll take the stuff back to the house."

"You!" Nicole made a face of astonishment. "You wouldn't be made very welcome. Papa can't abide you, and Cassa can't stand the sight of you. She never could. Don't go with a load of gifts: you know how proud Papa is."

Dermot Tyson glanced sideways at his wife's face and he dismissed a lot of what she was saying. He could feel Cassa's small figure finding shelter and comfort in his arms; he remembered her quick withdrawal when she heard Nicole's voice. Somehow, it did not seem a part of Cassa's nature to bear ill-will.

And for what reason? In the last ten years, their paths had not crossed. Nicole had paid her visits to her sick mother alone, by her own insistent wish. Sadora had never seen her grandchildren. Vaguely, he remembered the little girls had been taken into Blake's offices on Stephen's Green. Dermot was intensely proud of Orla and Sandra. He wondered had Cassa ever seen his girls, her nieces?

When he pulled up at their own house, he did not turn off the ignition.

"What's the matter, dear?" Nicole enquired in her sweetest tone. "Aren't you coming in? The children are expecting you."

"Sorry, old thing. I have some business in Donnybrook. I should be back in about twenty minutes, or even less."

His business might take longer, but he was alert to the possibility of a wife's suspicions. It was not his habit to express concern for her people. He drove back out to the main road and turned to the left, a short cut to Seacoast. He knew a wholesaler who supplied grocery shops.

His friend was helpful and quickly made out an order of goods to fill a freezer and a fridge, and also a quantity of dry goods like sugar, tea, coffee.

"Cover everything you can think of, Ray," Dermot told him. "There is a death in the family, and no one had the time to stock-up in advance. You know, for the people calling to the house. Yes, yes, spirits, wines, all that sort of thing. And Ray, I would regard it as a favour if these things could be sent up tonight? The upper end of Donnybrook Road: one of the old houses. Firenze is the name of the house. Could you do that?"

"No problem, no problem at all."

Dermot wrote out the cheque. "A last favour, Ray. Would you get your van-man to say the stuff was sent in by the Gilbeys? There, you have the name. Gilbey. *Gilbey*. Sorry for the rush, Ray. See you."

CHAPTER TEN

AFTER SADORA'S DEATH, Richard Blake succeeded in selling the practice. This took a burden from his mind, but there was a slow deepening sadness. The Blakes had been important in Stephen's Green and in the Four Courts for over a century. The protracted years of his wife's illness had aged him. Even the rare game of golf was rarer now, and no longer followed by a session in the bar.

"You will miss your work, Papa," Cassa said, "your friends in the city. Your lunches."

"The one thing I will not miss is that damnable road," Richard told her. "Every morning that I stay home, I look out of the window and I thank God I don't have to battle through that traffic. The three mornings I drive into the office, I wake at six o'clock and begin picturing the accident I am about to have that day." He tried to smile instead of sighing.

"Papa, you are too careful a driver to ever have an accident."

Richard shook his head. "On that crazy road, care has no place. Speed is what counts."

"Papa, your week would be long and tedious for you without your days in town." Most nights, Papa watched the TV for a short while, mostly the sports programmes. He was ready to retire for the night at ten o'clock.

A rare time, Papa would coax her to play the piano for him. He loved to listen to Mozart. Cassa would wrap a wool rug about his legs and he would sit listening, the dogs on the couch beside him. There were no Sadora Rules now, and the two dogs had the freedom of the house. "They keep me warm," he always grinned boyishly back at Cassa as he ascended the stairs, Mindo and Fred at his heels.

The piano was in the front drawing-room which could be very chilly in winter. They no longer used the central heating, and a turf fire could not heat the large room. That was another worry for Papa. Without adequate heating, the furniture and paintings in the house would deteriorate.

When Nicole came to call, seldom enough, she belittled Papa's worries: "How did he ever turn into such a morose old man? Ullagoning, moaning, doing the poor mouth! How do you stand it? He must have money stashed away. He's mean, so he is. He always was."

Cassa was intensely loyal but, as with Sadora of old, one did not contradict Nicky; one changed the subject. "He is worried about the traffic on the new road," she said apologetically.

"With good reason. I've seen him. He drives like Lord Muck in his dotage: right on the middle of the white line in any lane and at two miles a fortnight."

"When Papa was a boy," Cassa said, "his grandfather drove a cabriolet and two horses into Donnybrook and his grandma did some shopping – just for fun, Papa says, because there were only little village shops then. The big carriage was driven into Dublin to the offices in Stephen's Green by the coachman every day of the week."

"What has that got to do with anything?" Nicole retorted briskly. "A load of old glory, meaningless. We're talking about now, and Papa getting with it. He's only sixty-four, after all."

"Nicky, he is seventy-two. His birthday was in January."

"Seventy-two? What's the difference. He's in perfect health, isn't he? There's nothing wrong with him only a creeping paralysis where money is concerned. Get wise to him, sister."

Then, at last, the money for the sale of the legal practice came through, complete with interest. Firenze did not suddenly enter its old age of golden luxury, but many aspects of life improved. Between them, Richard and his beloved House Bird reduced their living quarters to four rooms and the kitchen, and in these four rooms the central-heating was restored. The kitchen had a turf-burning range which gave hot water. There was also an electric cooker.

Richard was smiling: "It's not the Waldorf-Astoria, my darling, but it will be easier now for you to cope. Have I told you that you have been wonderful?"

"A thousand times, Papa."

"And you shall have help, my House Bird. Those two women who came up from the village during Sadora's last days: do you have addresses for them? And I have heard of a garden contractor. There will be a couple of months' work for him. Come and I will show you what I have in mind."

Cassa held her father's hand as they strolled along the paths between the over-grown gardens. He was full of gaiety and goodwill like long ago. She asked him, "Are you sure you will be all right when I go down to Kerry next month, and honestly I would not mind a bit skipping Caragh Lodge this July. And anyway, it is so comfortable here with you now, no hard work at all. Really, Papa, I wouldn't mind not going."

"So comfortable with just the two of us," he repeated, and the greyness was gone from his face as if the words were balm on his skin.

"Already, Papa, you are beginning to get the sun. You always used to tan so easily."

She loved the warmth of his hand holding hers. She loved him so much. Without him she would be lost. Her heart trembled when his step was unsteady, or when his vivid memory failed for a moment as he sought for a mislaid word, usually a name.

"Of course you must go to Caragh Lake, my baby. Even when Sadora was laid low, we managed that. Of course, of course. And you must buy something new – something fashionable! Tomorrow, take the car and go into town. Louise would never forgive me if I kept you here – and you love to go, don't you?"

"Oh I do, Papa, I do. It's the most beautiful place on earth: the lake, the trees, the Kerry mountains. And they are so good to me, so nice, so kind. And the chalet itself. Robert had a big deck built out over the lake. We sunbathe, Papa.

Robert is famous now. Louise told me in her last letter that his books are in the curriculum of hundreds of universities: just think, Papa, all over the world." Cassa's brown eyes were gleaming in the bright sunlight.

She mentioned Robert Gray a lot. "How many years is it now, that you are going on this holiday to Caragh Lake?"

Cassa was smiling blissfully. "It was ten years at the time of Mama's death, and this will be my fourth year since then. Every year, Papa, for fourteen years."

"Did you tell me they have no family?"

"No family, Papa. They don't say anything about that."

His House Bird, he reflected, would soon be thirty-two and he remembered Sadora's Book of Rules. Cassa was already an old maid, a spinster.

The idea oppressed him. She had never been told about Tyson's strange proposal, the manner of it. Richard knew that night of Tyson's "second thoughts". Yes, little Cassa was his second thought as if the man could have anything he fancied. But Richard had detected the intrigue between the older daughter and his ever-scheming wife, and he had taken advantage of it to keep Cassa by him.

But should he have given her to Tyson? Now she would be a married woman with a family. Would Tyson have been the right man? Cassa deserved so much more of love and family happiness than her selfish old father would be able to give her.

"My little House Bird, I am a mean old monster, but you are certainly going to Kerry next month and you will be the belle of the ball in your new finery. Come now, and we will go in. I felt a sudden chill when the sun went."

Richard retired a little earlier than usual. Cassa came to kiss him good-night, sitting on the side of his bed and atting his hand.

"I hope you sleep, Papa. Are you tired?"

"Ever so slightly, my pet. The stairs, you know, a bit dizzy on the stairs. Old age, little House Bird, old age."

He had referred to a dizzy spell a couple of times.

"The dizziness will be gone when you have had a good night's sleep, Papa. Are you comfy now?"

Cassa kissed his forehead and his cheeks. "You're getting a tan," she smiled at him. Then she ruffled the furry coats of the two dogs on the end of the big bed: "Spoiled little monkeys! Be good now!"

At the bedroom door, Cassa looked back: "I love you, Papa. Sleep well."

Mindo and Fred never stirred at night. It was Richard's habit to rise at seven-thirty and take them out into the garden. Rain or shine, out they went and he stood in Sadora's now empty morning-room while Mindo and Fred took their early romp. On the trellised loggia, he dried them thoroughly, gave them a quick brush and they, all three, went into the kitchen for breakfast.

That was the drill, the routine, in the four years since Sadora's death; the four happy comfortable years when all the earlier habits of pleasant living had been restored.

In the early hours of daylight, Cassa was awakened by the frantic barking of the dogs, the thudding of their bodies against the closed door of her father's room.

His dogs, used as they were to his intimate presence, had sensed a change in the ice-cold effigy on the bed. As Cassa raced along a corridor to the doom-laden noise, knowing immediately that her cherished world was in danger, her tears were already falling.

"Papa, Papa, I am coming! Wait for me, Papa! Please, Papa, I am coming."

CHAPTER ELEVEN

WITH NO REALISATION of how early in the morning she was phoning, Cassa rang repeatedly before she got an answer.

"Please, please, is my sister there? Please, please, hurry! I must speak to my sister."

Dermot Tyson answered at last: "That's Cassa, isn't it? I am sorry, Cassa, Nicole took the children up to Donegal... I can't hear you... Cassa, are you crying? I said where my sister Della has the new hotel in Port Salon ... took the girls to the sea for a few days... yes. What is it, Cassa? Is it an accident? Is it a fire? Look, I can't understand because you are crying. I am coming over straightaway."

Cassa dropped the phone. She was crying because no one had answered when she had rung all the emergency numbers she had carefully written down beside the phone. When Tyson said "took the girls to the sea", she realised it was the Bank Holiday weekend in June and everyone was sleeping in late, or had gone away. Not even the Gilbeys had answered.

And now there was no Nicky to say the right thing and organise the way things should be done in case Cassa had got it wrong and must be made to suffer without Papa for shelter.

Cassa opened the front door and sat out on the steps to wait for help. The dogs ran around the side of the house to sit with her. That made her start crying again, tears of helpless grief.

When Dermot Tyson jumped out of his car and rushed to her, it seemed to him the most natural thing he had ever done. She had turned to him when the dreaded Sadora had died, and now she had no one else: the only word she could say was "Papa".

Even as he made the necessary phone calls he was thinking of her as the beautiful child at Donnybrook church, a child who had never been allowed to grow up. There was no doubt but that Cassa was loved devotedly by her father whom she idolised and there were no other men to love, but perhaps Cassa would turn to a man the way a flower turns to the light. As Cassa clung to Dermot in a deluge of tears, he experienced drying her tears as an arousal of sensual pleasure of an unaccustomed kind. He saw her struggling in a torrent of bereavement, and each time she broke down, she turned to him and he took her into his arms.

He left the phone call to his wife until the afternoon. Port Salon was a five-hour drive. With the children to think of, she could not start for Dublin before the morning, and no matter how early she started, it would be late afternoon when she'd reach home and leave the children with Mrs Flynn.

Nicole asked a hoard of questions, but he was an experienced handler of her enquiries. He parried any reference to Cassa: "She is totally distraught, and she is keeping to her room."

"That was Nicky on the phone, dear. She sent her love and she longs to be with you. She'll set out as early as possible in the morning."

He led Cassa into the living-room where he had turned on an electric fire. "Stand near the fire, Cassa, here beside me, I need to say a few words to you." Cassa put out her hands and he drew her into his embrace. "As you may have noticed, Cassa, I sent a taxi for the women who help you. They have come and they will stay here tonight. You will not be alone."

Cassa clutched his jacket: "Oh please, don't leave me with strangers. Please don't go, please don't go, please. Let them go, stay with me, please, Dermot." Tears trembled again on her eyelashes.

"I'll stay with you, Cassa, until Nicole gets back from Donegal. Try not to cry, poor darling." He held her closely, curving his arms protectively. "The phone calls I made this morning will bring a lot of people to the house... your father's doctor and my brother, Tom. Do you wish me to deal with them?"

51

When Cassa nodded dumbly, he asked her, "Perhaps you would like to have a little rest in your own room?"

"No, no, no. I could not bear to be alone upstairs. I sat with Papa before I tried to ring your house and tell Nicole because he was my Papa, and I wanted to be first to say good-bye."

She broke down and clung to him pitifully: "Oh Dermot, I loved him so much, I don't want to go on living any more. Don't ask me to go upstairs. I kissed him and I felt his lips were cold and... and... frozen, and... and... hard, and then I knew. I loved my father, I loved him so much..."

Later in the day, after the doctor had come and gone, the women from the village prepared the back dining-room for the reception of the coffin. Cassa was dimly aware that Dermot's brother had arrived and was murmuring words of sympathy. His face was vaguely familiar from the day of Sadora's funeral four years before.

When he had gone away, Dermot brought her out into the garden, holding her steadily because she was quivering as if in fear.

"Cassa, a few words. It may surprise you to hear that after your mother's funeral, your father made an appointment with my brother, Tom, to discuss his own arrangements for when the time would come."

He felt her shudder as she pressed to his side. "Don't be shocked, poor little Cassa; he was concerned for you. He knew you would possibly be all on your own, and he was right, as it happened. If Nicole were here she would see to all."

A tiny flare of resentment caused Cassa's step to falter. He guessed her feeling. "It is Nicole's way to organise – all for the best, of course," he told her.

The sun was warm as they sat in the loggia outside the morning-room.

"Cassa, about the arrangements. Your father was adamant that he did not wish to be brought out of the house over-night, nor did he wish any mourners beyond the immediate family. So we will keep him with us until we bring him to the church, and directly to the local cemetery."

"That could not have been his wish. Nicky will not agree..." Cassa had not the voice for arguing, but she was distressed and could only whisper, "What about my mother's grave in Glendalough, the Gilbey grave? Nicky will be angry, and... and..."

"Leave that to me. Your father's instructions are on record in my brother's office. He wished to be interred after a requiem mass in the local cemetery in Kilmacud. There is a space beside his father's grave, where his mother also is interred. It is, apparently, an old-fashioned grave with many names, and he wished his name added and the date."

"Is that all?" she asked, and her hands sought his for comfort.

"My poor darling, of course you can add your love and devotion when the stone-cutter is cutting the date."

She looked up into his eyes. "You are so good and kind. I never knew you were."

"Come now, Cassa. The women will have lit the fire in the front drawing-room. They are putting together some sort of a meal. Even tea, Cassa. You need to take something. The night will be long."

Cassa murmured words of thanks. She huddled into the corner of the couch, the cushioned corner where Sadora used to sit and rule over the household with all her Rules.

Cassa had no fond memories of her mother, but now the sudden recall tore at her throat. Tears again filled her eyes and she was grateful to feel a strong arm, like Papa's arm, coming around her shoulders and drawing her close.

"Later on, Cassa, we will keep the night-vigil beside your father. I know you would prefer to be alone. I know how you two loved each other, but let me be with you. I would deem it an honour to be at your side and pray with you."

Cassa could only nod her head, gratitude shining in her brown eyes. Somewhere he found a shawl and wrapped it around her as she sat sipping the tea.

And so they passed the night: at times praying silently in the sombre room beside the elaborate coffin; at times in the front drawing-room close together on the couch. From above the marble mantel Elvira watched as she had been watching for a hundred years, her black-lashed brown eyes glistening in the firelight, her delicately rouged lips parted in a smile betokening secrets unknown to all others.

CHAPTER TWELVE

WALKING DOWN THE steps from the solicitors' office, Tyson asked his wife if they should have made some sort of offer to Cassa. He had observed the ominous glitter in Nicole's eyes.

"What, for instance?" she almost hissed.

"Well, lunch perhaps? Here's the Shelbourne where I parked the car."

"Let that solicitor give her lunch. I have no doubt they have something to celebrate. They are in this together, it's obvious. Papa never made that will. Papa was a fair man, upright. She influenced him, connived with that lousy little solicitor. That will is manifestly unjust, dishonest, illegal. I know Cassa and I can see the way she talked my father into making it. She's a rotten little schemer. I should know, yes, and what's more..."

Early in his marriage, Dermot Tyson had learned never to oppose his wife and, equally, never to submit. He found silence a potent weapon and had a subtle way of letting her know when she had pushed the argument far enough.

"So perhaps you and I would like some lunch?" he enquired. "We could try a new place. You look really good today."

"No," she said shortly, "please drive me home."

Her voice left no room for further invitations and they drove home in near silence.

"Please come upstairs with me," she said to him.

As they reached the bedroom, she exploded wrathfully: "My father never made that will. I know Cassa is in collusion with Dick Boyce. Ever since Papa brought him into the firm she has had her eye on him. He has been out to the house, and why else would he go out to the house if she didn't invite him, getting him on her side? So he now knows the house and the furniture and the grounds. A week before Papa's death, I saw him driving away, out through the gate as I was coming up the road. Only the week before Papa's death! He's not married, not even engaged – I found that out when Papa took him on. I'm not mistaken; I know it was him. I saw him in the office when I took Sandra in to see her grandfather on her birthday. Something about him I don't trust. I tell you, they are in this together, he and my sister. I know it and you know it."

She was rushing around the room taking off her suit, getting into a blouse and skirt. She was replacing her jewellery in a drawer.

Dermot watched her, recalling that Cassa's sad face in Dick Boyce's office had left him saddened. So far from colluding in her father's will, she hadn't bothered to listen, hadn't taken anything in.

To Nicole he said nothing. Now she was brushing her hair savagely.

"I know Papa depended on me. I know he always gave me full credit for good sense, for managing. Whenever there was a crisis, I was there. I always knew what to do. Don't leave it to Cassa, Mama used to say, she is such a dreamer. Mama would know perfectly well that Cassa would be lost all by herself in Firenze; the place could fall down and she would go on playing the piano. For heaven's sake, do you remember when Mama died, there wasn't as much as half a dozen eggs in the place? Only the Gilbeys sent in a load of groceries, we would have been disgraced in front of the hoards of relations who came after. The Gilbeys will not accept this will. Great-aunt Hilda Gilbey has always said that she can see me in Firenze: she calls me the future chatelaine of the chateau, that's what she says of me in her will, and that'll be worthwhile. I've always been her favourite. The Gilbeys agree with me that Cassa hasn't an idea in her head about managing money. Papa told us years ago that the place would go to me because I am the elder. Poor Papa, he was probably starved. Oh Dermot, do you think he was starved to death?"

Dermot was remembering Dick Boyce's voice as he had read the will aloud in a quiet legal style. He had shrewdly noticed the date. It was fourteen years ago, the year of his own marriage to Nicole.

"You know, just as well as I do, Dermot, that Firenze is my home, mine, not my sister's. You know that Mama, and Papa too, wanted me, you, us, to get Firenze and have our place, our proper place. It is not suitable for a spinster like Cassa – an old maid that's all she is, rattling around like a marble in a barrel; as it is she has reduced the central heating to four rooms. Four rooms out of fourteen! The place will be destroyed. And anyway, without Papa's income she could never keep up a house that size."

Nicole was sitting on the bed and she patted a place for him to sit beside her, but he remained standing by the window.

"Oh Dermot, I was planning my old bedroom for Orla. The wallpaper is French silk, a Fragonard design. I know Orla would just adore it; she is so artistic. The playroom is nearly as big as a ballroom, and the girls could have dances later on when they are a bit older. Can't you just see the parties, Der!"

Dermot put his arm around her with a great show of tenderness, lifting her from the bed and steering her firmly to the door. "Come, dearest, you are upsetting yourself. The will must go to probate, and all your suspicions and uncertainties will be tested. Meanwhile the Gilbey shares which are now yours, and your mother's jewellery, may be very valuable. Yes, dear, of course I want the house for our family. Be assured I am fully cognisant of your fears, and fully in sympathy. Rest assured."

On the staircase, he took her arm and bestowed on her his special look, thinking as he did so how easily she chose to overlook the Sadora Gilbey mansion in which she and he lived so richly, and the Sadora Gilbey marriage dowry of which Cassa was never told.

Confident of his ability to control events in his own way and in his own time, he enjoyed his lunch.

CHAPTER THIRTEEN

IN A CERTAIN way, Nicole's estimate of her sister's character was reasonable. Until their father's death all practical expenses were privately settled through the Bank of Ireland, by banker's order, or by Papa's cheque book. Within a couple of months these easygoing arrangements gradually ceased. The car must be taxed, an insurance certificate was necessary; oil and petrol must be paid for in ready cash.

Crestfallen by these demands, Cassa was sure the car must be given up. The problem there was the absence of a bus route, and the drive itself was more than a quarter of a mile. The phone bill, when it fell through the letter-box, was startling, and it was followed by a bill for electricity. Undoubtedly, the grocer and the butcher in Stillorgan were only biding their time.

Cassa made an appointment to see Dick Boyce, who seemed anxious to help. He had spoken to the bank manager where Richard had done business.

"You understand, Miss Blake, that the bulk of your inheritance is summed up in the property. Luckily enough, it is totally freehold and not encumbered by debt. There is, as you heard in the will, a secured untouched amount of money which your father feared might be called in for such matters as death duty, inheritance tax, unearned income tax, etcetera. Some of the other value-added tax is under judicial review at present but may redound later. Mr Blake was in full knowledge of tax laws, as you will know, and he wished to guard you against the eventuality of financial loss. However, Miss Blake, all these precautions which he covered for you used up a great deal of money."

Cassa murmured something about day-to-day expenses.

"You have your dividends from the shares left by your grandfather. Mrs Tyson, as I am sure you know, also receives her dividends from the same source. You understand, Miss

Blake, that dividends come in twice a year, and they are returnable for income tax."

He could see that she understood no such thing. He wondered if she had ever considered looking for a job and earning money. She was very good-looking, she had style and class, but she was a little dim. That enormous house and no cash to talk of. It had begun to weigh on her father the last year or so, not that he had moaned. He was as proud as Lucifer, but you could see the way he had slowed down.

"I am always here to advise and counsel, Miss Blake. I had great regard for your father."

"Thank you. Yes, I am sure. Tell me, when are these dividends due?"

He turned over the file on his desk. "In the months of May and November," and he reflected inwardly that when their grandfather had endowed his two grandchildren the annual dividends were worth many times more than they were worth now. That was almost thirty years ago and the shares were barely holding their paltry value today. Still, that type of person never sold.

Dick Boyce had sympathy for Miss Blake, but destitute heiresses, no matter how pretty, were not what he was looking for.

"Will you continue to live in the house, Miss Blake?"

Cassa was surprised. Her eyes opened wide that anyone should ask.

"But of course, of course," her voice rang clear. "I could never leave Firenze. My father knew that I love the house. I think that he left Firenze for me to care for."

The young solicitor took off his glasses, and then he put them on again. She was really attractive now, but he could see her in a few years, decaying slowly in a derelict old mansion. She had no spunk, and she would moulder away. A pity. Her eyes were really something.

Cassa walked through Stephen's Green with her head high, her heels clicking smartly. When Papa had willed Firenze to her, she thought, he had entrusted her with

59

responsibility. Papa had believed in her. She would justify his belief, somehow.

In the ten dreary years of her mother's illness, friends and family had fallen away, and Papa and his little House Bird had had only each other for company. Then during four golden years they had tried to put serenity and comfort back into their lives and into their home. The goal was almost achieved, but four years were not enough. The circle had not widened; there were no new friends and any old friends had found new circles.

The eerily echoing house bore down on her. The real fight was against loneliness, and it was a battle with no foreseeable end. Sometimes her tears were frozen in a valiant effort to fulfil any one of the maxims she repeated to herself.

Failure came in the evenings of recall, in the times on the clock when she used to hear Papa's car driving up, and Papa's hearty voice calling from the hall, "I'm home, House Bird, I'm home!"

CHAPTER FOURTEEN

D ERMOT TYSON GLANCED up at his wife. "Do you ever get time to read the back page of this newspaper?" he asked.

"Of course," she said. "If we are staying in after dinner, I look at the television schedule. Why? Is there something I should see tonight?"

"I meant the death notices," he said.

"Much too morbid!" She stood up from the breakfast table and then she saw his face. "Why? Is it someone we know?"

He handed the paper to her. "I doubt if your sister buys a daily paper. There, under Gray. Perhaps you should tell her?"

"Louise! Louise is dead!" Nicole read the words again. "But Louise is younger than I am! Cassa never mentioned that Louise was sick. If she was in hospital in Dublin, she'd have gone to see her, wouldn't she? My sister has become very secretive lately: mooning around the house, gazing out the window, even when she sees my car coming up the drive, she just stands up at her bedroom window like a statue. If I hadn't got my own hall door key, she'd leave me standing outside. She..."

Dermot interrupted: "Just a minute, it is only a couple of months since your father's death. It will take time. She may not know about Louise, because if you recall yourself saying so, Louise and her husband were not at your father's funeral. You assumed, at the time, that they were abroad, and for that same reason we both assumed that was why your sister was not invited on their summer holiday in Kerry. Anyway, dear, be a bit patient with her."

"She tries my patience, acting the solitary, lonely, forsaken spinster. God! Is she ever trying!"

"Perhaps you should tell her of this death?"

"I suppose so," Nicole agreed. "I'll give her a ring later."

"It would be a kindness to take the paper over to her. The details of the funeral are in the notice."

Ready to make his exit, he said, "As it happens, I am passing that way this morning. I'll take the paper over to Cassa."

"I said I'll ring her later."

"It would be better if you went to the house. It is her friend who has died." He paused.

"Oh, all right! I suppose she'll need a bit of sympathy. Blub all over again. Will it ever stop? Everyone has to die sometime. When I said that to her the other day, she positively howled and the damn dogs howled along with her."

Dermot spoke again: "I know you are always busy, but try not to forget."

"I'm not that busy this morning. I'll fit it in on the way to Marjorie's for coffee."

When Nicole pulled up at the top of the drive, Cassa was kneeling in a patch of garden. She seemed glad enough to put down the trowel.

"You never told me that your friend Louise was at death's door," Nicole called out cheerfully.

The words were whipped away on the wind, and all Cassa heard was the loud cheerfulness.

"Get those filthy animals off me!"

Cassa called off the dogs. She led the way into the kitchen for the inevitable coffee.

Her sister threw the newspaper on the table. "Take a look at the deaths column," she said. "Do you know what, you're like someone in a trance. Do you want me to read it out for you?"

The name had leaped out of the column into Cassa's face: "Louise, dearly beloved wife of Robert Gray..." She read the notice again and again, but her brain could not pin down the words.

"There must be some mistake, Nicky," she spoke very slowly, putting out her hand blindly to find a chair.

Nicole made the coffee, her head turned to talk back at

her sister, asking a dozen questions and getting no answers.

"Would you give me an answer, Cass, please. How long was she sick? Where did she die? There's no mention of a hospital, is there? Was it at home? In the great country house we heard so much of, or in the Kerry cottage? Don't they stay there till the end of the summer?"

"There must be some mistake," Cassa repeated.

"Don't be ridiculous," her sister told her firmly. "She must have got sick and then she died. A wonder you never heard when she was sick. Maybe it was sudden. A heart attack? That can happen at any age. She was a couple of years older than you, about thirty-five now? He must be well into the forties."

"I just know there is a mistake. Some sort of a mistake."

"In that case," Nicole's abrasive wit found an outlet, "you won't need to go to the funeral, you won't need money for petrol all the way to the midlands and back, and money to stay overnight in a bed and breakfast. It's a printer's error, that's what it is, so money saved all round!"

There was no reply.

Nicole turned on the radio, took her coffee cup in hand and went off to make her customary tour of the house, making sure every item of furniture, every picture, every piece of china, every ornament was securely in its place, its position unaltered, its lustre preserved.

The matter of probate for her father's will had not yet been appealed. In Nicole's mind the appeal was a mere matter of form. Firenze, in its entirety, would be hers. As she walked through the house, she was planning a festival of redecoration, and feasting her eyes on certain rooms which must never be touched, so gracefully were they in tune with the age of the house.

Cassa sat staring at the paper. Her beloved father and now her only friend... could life be so cruel? She had missed Louise and Robert at the house when Papa died. But then, she only ever saw them once a year, for the month of July, that cherished month at Caragh Lake.

This July there was no question of a holiday. She did not

dwell on the thought, or on any thought. Mourning for Papa was all that was left in life. Caring for the house and trying to reclaim a piece of the garden were automatic occupations which did not interfere with grief.

But Louise's death? Could that be true?

Somewhere far down that hidden road there would be Caragh Lake again, sunlit water, leafy paths, friends of many years. It was a dream that came with the promise of ending the ache of sorrow. It was a dream in which she confused Papa's dear face with Robert's.

Her sister came back into the kitchen. "Are you still sitting there, moping? You would want to make up your mind, because the funeral is tomorrow. Don't look so pitiful! Make a phone call if you still don't believe the notice in the paper. Actually, in my view, the husband should have phoned you, Louise's friend. Since he did not, in my view..."

Cassa's thought broke in with the sudden realisation that indeed there had been a long silence from Louise, and no word at all from Robert, not even a letter of sympathy for Papa's death. Maybe, maybe this death notice had to be true?

"The way I see it," Nicole continued, "you'd be better off staying at home. It's a Protestant funeral anyway. Not that I'm a bigot and I know we Catholics are not under pain of mortal sin in Protestant churches like we used to be, but who would you know at a funeral like that? Even if there was a lunch after, even in a hotel, who would talk to you? A bunch of strangers? One woman on her own is always a nuisance at these gatherings, especially at funerals, and weddings are just as bad."

Cassa stood up quickly. "I will go to the funeral. Louise was my best friend since the first day in school."

"Friend!" echoed Nicole. "Some friend!"

"And Louise was a Catholic," added Cassa.

"Read the insertion again. That's the Protestant church. A bit fishy, the way it's worded. You should write a note, have a mass said to spite him – he's definitely not a Catholic – and stay here, safe in your own home. Don't go down there making a fool of yourself, which you always did about him. Robert this and Robert that. Buying all his books which I know damn well you could never read."

With quiet determination she repeated that she would go to the funeral. She would go this evening. "Nicky, could I leave Fred and Mindo with you?"

"Certainly not! Dermot can't stand the smell of dogs around the house. You are quite mad to think of going. You'll have to put up overnight in some frowsty B & B, paying God knows what: it's the tourist season, in case you've forgotten. Not to mention the cost of kennelling those animals. Do you never think of expense?"

Nicole glanced at her watch. "I'm on my way to Marjorie's. Clive is flying in from San Francisco. If you'll take my advice, you'll stay where you are."

They walked out to the car and Nicole got in. She rolled down the window as she started the engine.

"Don't make an idiot of yourself. Your friend Louise won't be there to greet you – remember that, sister!"

CHAPTER FIFTEEN

WHEN NICOLE'S CAR had disappeared down the drive, Cassa forced herself to think clearly, not about her sister's advice, but about a plan of action. She rang the kennels. No problem: she could come now, just bring their baskets if she liked. On the way to the kennels, she would fill up with petrol and check the tyres. Then she would pack a few garments and overnight requirements. She would leave the house well locked up, bolting all the shutters.

There was a faint sense of pride in taking the law of departure into her own hands without consulting her sister. When she took a small travel bag from a cupboard, she suddenly realised that she did not believe Louise was dead, and that her thought was of a visit, not a funeral. She read the newspaper again. She wanted to stand and think. The stupidity of having to hurry to a dead Louise! But if she did not hurry, she would be too late. It was hard to have to hurry. And still she stood with the newspaper in her hand.

At last she began to take out a night-dress and a dressing-gown. Robert would surely ask her to stay the night, and if there would be other guests, she might have to share a room. She chose a pretty nightgown and a flimsy negligee, handling them gently because they had been Papa's Christmas present when the money for the practice came through.

A thousand times Louise had told Cassa that in Caragh Lake she came alive. The mysterious lake gave her over to a rapture in life as if it were her home. In Garlow Lodge her heart beat in a different rhythm.

A vivid vision of Louise came to mind: jangling necklaces and earrings and bangles, wearing the skimpiest little bikini, out on the deck over the jetty at Caragh Lake, like a Romany gypsy in scanty coloured silk waiting for Robert after his morning swim, a tape giving forth the sort of hot music they both loved.

And Robert coming up the wooden steps, a towel wrapped about his midriff. Louise slipping the bikini from her shoulders and going fully into his arms to the tinkling of the gypsy jewellery, his towel dropping on the deck and Robert carrying her away as if, Cassa used to think, as if they had not been in bed together the night before. Nothing to do with being married, rather he was a water-god and he had come for his flower-nymph.

A rapturous Louise and a man enraptured... All their words and their actions were so natural to them that Cassa was not embarrassed. She did not stare but she was wistfully aware. She could never imagine a man and a woman more completely in love with each other, and in love with life.

Poor Robert, how he must be suffering.

Since Papa's death, Cassa's sense of grief was new and raw. To give Robert her heart-felt sympathy would mean so much to him; he would remember so many things about their wonderful friendship. Robert and Louise and Caragh Lake. And Cassa, too?

CHAPTER SIXTEEN

ROBERT'S HOUSE WAS recognisable from the many photo-
graphs she had seen of it: a country house set among tall
trees and a green lawn, almost out of sight behind heavy gates.

There were people on the wide step at the door as Cassa
drove up the avenue and that was a relief. She had been
dreading having to knock on the door and explain her business to a prim maid.

Robert was bidding goodbye to callers, mourners no
doubt. He wore his studied air of absent-mindedness. She
remembered this look, which he switched on for unwanted
visitors, those Louise called "intruders". Cassa was confident
she was not an intruder.

"Robert," she said softly. "Robert."

He frowned heavily, and then his face cleared. He smiled
as if a sudden thought had lit the fog of dim recollection.

"Ah, Cassa! But of course, Cassa." He took her hand and
he drew her in. "Come."

He was leading her along a hall, passing rooms on either
side, and down steps to a green baize door.

Was this where Louise lay, in her coffin? Beyond this baize
door? She had tremors of fear that Louise might be changed
by death, as Sadora had been, shrunk and wizened. No, no.
Louise would be as beautiful as she always was, Robert's lovely dead Louise in a casket covered with summer flowers.

But the baize door led into a big kitchen where a woman
was busily occupied in the preparation of food.

"Mrs MacNeill, this is Cassa. She'll help you. Won't you,
Cassa?"

Cassa was taken aback, struck dumb. No one had mentioned death but there were still mourners: she had heard
voices as they passed down the hall.

Cassa turned to Robert. The doorbell was ringing. He disappeared through the baize door, shutting it firmly behind
him.

"I drove a long way," Cassa said defensively as she tied on the indicated apron.

"Is that right, eh?" responded the woman, who seemed to be American, not stopping to chat.

"I should like to wash my hands," Cassa ventured, putting a delicate hint into her voice.

"Oh sure! Down the corridor, right by the back door."

When Cassa returned to the kitchen, she set herself to the buttering of bread. After all, she reflected, this was a house of death and it was traditional to prepare food for mourners. She had come, after all, to be of assistance to Robert through these sad days.

She wondered, however, at the strangeness of this household, and the lack of female help.

Mrs MacNeill shouldered open the door, carrying a big tray of glasses and empty bottles.

"It's a mighty good thing the lady is dead," she laughed huskily. "They tell me she banned smoking, and there's a pall of cigar smoke in there like the smog over Los Angeles."

She poured out a glass of brandy. "Join me?"

Cassa shook her head.

Mrs MacNeill was laughing again that throaty laugh. "Those guys in there have some capacity! We are running out of hard liquor. You got a car? I am sure the pubs are still open. Are they ever shut around here? Would you? I'll make a list."

She fished out money from a bag on the shelf. "You'll have enough and to spare in that; you can keep the change. Go out the back door, and best come in that way with the parcels."

The tradesmen's entrance, thought Cassa as she turned the car in the drive. She upbraided herself for being resentful. After all, this was for Robert. She thought of her first sight of him this evening, standing out on his steps. He was a very handsome man and although his hair was now silver, it was crisply thick. She looked forward to the moment when they would be alone. They would talk softly about Louise.

Perhaps, a little later, he would escort her to the guest bedroom. Robert could be so gracious. As Louise's oldest friend, she would be invited to stand beside him at the grave, and he would reach for her hand in their shared sorrow as, so often, he had taken her hand in their shared holidays amid the romantic beauty of Caragh Lake.

There was that one poignant moment, and it returned now in full summer colours, when Robert had pressed her closely to him under the shadowy trees. He had murmured, "What a pretty little lady you are."

Was that only last year? Or perhaps much further back? The memory had lived.

Perhaps the early years were best. Often he had teased her about being an unclaimed treasure, and many times he had said that she had the loveliest hair he had ever seen. He always paid his compliments when they were sent shopping into Killorglin because Louise had so much typing to do against Robert's deadlines.

Pulling over the car outside the town, where they could admire the massive curve of the Magillicuddy Reeks, Robert would light up cigarettes for both of them, and sometimes he would suggest a drink in a pub by the roadside. Cassa had never learned to drink or smoke, and he knew that, but it amused him to incite her into this little act of rebellion. Maybe those were the early days when she was nineteen, twenty, twenty-one. How long ago that was. She was alone now, as was Robert, with no one to rebel against.

When she re-entered the kitchen Mrs MacNeill was taking a load of glassware out of the dishwasher. "Put the stuff over there, and polish these glasses. Stack them on this tray, and on that one. This lot are for after the funeral. You going to the funeral? Where did you say you came from? There was a room got ready for Robert's aunt, but she cried off – too old. Other relatives arrive in the morning, so you can stay in the old aunt's room if you want. Right now, there's a load of work to be done, and tomorrow morning will be worse. There will be drinks and sandwiches after the service."

She was unloading the packages, "You seem to have been able to get the stuff. No, you keep the change. I'll get it from Robert later. Okay, let's get cracking; no time for talk."

Cassa had been trying to interrupt, both about refusing the leftover change and about her own special niche in this family, or even in this household.

There had been no loving, regretful reference to Louise, yet this woman was quite at home in Louise's kitchen. She had not been hired in an emergency. Puzzled, Cassa felt that by some under-hand trick she had herself been co-opted on to the invisible staff.

Still, she was confident that when Robert was free at last of the calling mourners, he would correct Mrs MacNeill's erroneous impression. She imagined a different expression on her arrogant face. Cassa stole glances at her as she flew around the big kitchen. The woman must be around forty and her long bright hair was all coiled about her head. She would be considered handsome, Cassa thought, in a foreign sort of way.

It was long after midnight when Cassa was told to fetch her case from her car. There was no sign of Robert although the mourners were gone and the house was silent.

Mrs MacNeill led the way upstairs to a spacious corridor, hung with paintings and lined with bookcases. There were many closed doors.

"Is it up here that Mrs Gray is laid out?" Cassa whispered.

"Laid out?" the woman seemed not to know the expression. "Laid out is right – what's left of her, the poor old thing."

Cassa stood still with horror. "Where is Louise?" she questioned fearfully.

Mrs MacNeill gave Cassa a surprised glance. "The coffin is in the front reception room, underneath that room there, where Robert's bedroom is."

"Louise was my friend," Cassa said faintly. "I should like to see her. Please."

"I don't think you would," the woman said abruptly.

71

At the far end of the corridor, she indicated the bedroom for Cassa. "Here you are, and there's a loo and hand-basin next door. I left towels and soap. I'll give you a call in the morning." She shut the door without so much as bidding good-night.

Cassa sat down on the bed, her mind in a stunned state. Disconnected thoughts and emotions began to surface.

Should she have down-faced this Mrs MacNeill? Should she have argued her right to pray over the body of her dead friend? No one had sympathised with her personally on the death of her lifelong friend. Sent running for messages without a word of thanks, and not even a cup of tea offered to her. And Robert had never come back. Should Robert not have rescued her from this formidable woman?

But then, she thought with a rush of sad sympathy, it was probable Robert was keeping his lonely vigil by the coffin of his adored Louise, his handsome head bowed low over her lovely features now coldly chiselled for ever in marble.

The recollection of her own lonely vigil when Papa died was warmed by the memory of Dermot's presence, of how grateful she had felt to him, and how handsome he was when he held her hands in prayer.

She thought of going to pray with Robert and then she remembered Nicole saying he was a Protestant.

Nicole was right when she jeered about Cassa's tender feelings for Robert Gray, otherwise how could she explain all the dreams and hopes which flooded into this dingy room where she had been dumped like a parlourmaid. Nicole had told her often enough that she was only putty in people's hands. But her sister wasn't always right. When there was a death in a house, you had to do your part. Whether that MacNeill woman was here or not, she would have had to spend the night making sandwiches, running errands and getting up in the morning to help again.

It was all for Robert really, to ease the awful pain of these days. He is such a wonderful man, Cassa thought as she drew back the counterpane. He is the ideal man in every way.

Flannel pyjamas would have been the right choice for the icy bed. In her flimsy lacy nightie, Cassa found it hard to keep in mind the promise of a morrow filled with Robert's appreciation.

There was a dim bedside light but not a sign of a book to read to help pass time. All the luxuries of home were missing: the warmth of her own bed and the dreamy snuffling of Papa's dogs in their basket on the landing.

Papa never liked the idea of kennelling. Nicole should have taken the dogs; it was only for one night. Or had she herself thought she might be asked to prolong her visit to Robert's house? It might very well be so. Just let tomorrow come.

For the fiftieth time, she looked at her watch. It was five-thirty and still dark. A cup of tea, she thought. I will creep downstairs very quietly and make a cup of tea.

In the kitchen there was some heat from the banked-down Aga. She made tea and toasted two of the sandwiches. The second cup of tea made a big difference. Her misgivings gave way to a mild elation. This morning all would be as her imagination pictured it should be. She would stand with quiet dignity beside handsome Robert, be introduced to his illustrious friends, offer sherry to their charming sympathetic wives.

From the kitchen window, she saw the slivers of first light colouring the hedges. Perhaps the sun would shine all day. Now she would creep back upstairs, carefully, noiselessly. She would dress with the utmost attention to detail. Today she would look her very, very best.

On the dim staircase she paused and held her breath. From the corridor above came the sound of a woman's husky laugh and the lower tones of a man's voice. Cassa moved up another step and peered through the carved banister. Robert and the woman were standing in a bedroom doorway, the outlines of their bodies etched in the quickening light from a window. Glimpsed for a moment in the silvery light of dawn, they were as perfect and as natural in their naked splendour as the lovers in some fantastical painting remembered from a gallery long ago. And then they were gone, as he drew her into the bedroom and the door was shut.

An instinct of self-saving pride conveyed Cassa and her belongings out of the guest-room and into her car. Then she was speeding along the country road. As usual, she pondered bitterly, Nicole was proved right. If Cassa had stayed at home, her dreams and her illusions would be safe beyond destruction.

She found herself trying to defend Robert. After all, what did she know of the frustration of a man who had lost the love of his life? What, she thought bleakly, did she know of men?

A strange dichotomy was riven into her heart. She did not want to grieve, but she went on grieving for a precious gift which had never for a moment been hers.

Nicole's car was parked at the steps as Cassa drove up her own avenue, and at the same instant Nicole stepped out through the hall door.

It was all too much for Cassa. No chance now to make up a good excuse. Nicole had read the notice, she knew the funeral was this morning, and she had come to check if her sister had obeyed her instructions.

Cassa's control slipped away as much from the weight of sadness as from the lack of sleep. When Nicole put out a hand to steady her, the tears would not hold back.

"Just tired, just tired," she sobbed. "Just tired, too tired, didn't go to the funeral, didn't go."

"And where were you all night? You're bleary-eyed. You look as if you slept in your clothes." Cassa sank down on the steps.

Her suspicions alerted, Nicole led Cassa into the house and made her comfortable on an armchair.

"Take this whiskey, Cass, your hands are numb with the cold. You look all-in. I'll make a bit of breakfast for you, you awful old thing, all puffy-faced."

Somehow, the story was dragged out. Cassa tried to put a slant on it: a grief-stricken man and a strange temptress. Nicole, who could read her sister's face, guessed the scene accurately.

"The swine! His dead wife in the next room – a faithful wife to an immoral lecher! In her coffin! Not so much as prayed over! Sacrilegious! I warned you, Cassa. I always told you. The filthy bastard. I hope you will have the common sense to listen to me in future. An innocent like you shouldn't be let out. But, of course, you knew best."

Nicole eventually ran out of breath, but it took time.

CHAPTER SEVENTEEN

O RLA WAS THIRTEEN years of age and Sandra was eleven. The older girl was blonde and blue-eyed like her mother and grandmother – the looks her mother proudly called the Gilbey looks. Sandra was a replica of her father: slim build, clean-cut features with a tanned skin which her mother said was sallow, and her daddy said was olive, some-how a nicer word for sensitive little ears.

The sisters were the best of friends, happy in each other's company, although they both had plenty of other pals in Sion Hill where they went to school. The Tysons in Stillorgan kept open house for the family friends, and Dermot insisted on this although his wife reminded him constantly that her tradition, the Gilbey tradition, was rather one of exclusivity, keeping up the tone.

He had ignored this from the start, although in most family matters he was diplomatic enough to allow, in the words of his own mother, the woman to rule the roost. He greatly admired the serenity of his parents' household and their steady prosperity. He liked big birthday parties for the children and great festivity at Christmas.

He would have liked to see Cassa and her father on these occasions, but they were never invited, and he dared not interfere in the years when Sadora's illness was the excuse.

"We saw Aunty Cassa in Stillorgan this morning," announced Orla at Sunday lunch, "in the paper shop."

"We often see her in the paper shop on Sunday," added Sandra. Very casually, Dermot enquired, "Were you talking to her?"

"Of course we were," Orla told him. "She was sad though, really sad, not smiling like she usually is."

"What's the latest catastrophe?" asked Nicole coldly.

"We walked back a bit of the way with her," Orla said. "There's something gone wrong with the car so she had to walk across the fields to the village. It's a long walk although Aunty Cass said it really wasn't far and she..."

Sandra interrupted, "That's not the reason she's sad; it's the dogs."

"What about the dogs?" Dermot asked.

"Orla, it's too sad for me: you tell." Sandra had a long-term hope that Mummy would let them have a puppy, or even a kitten.

"Well," Orla began again, "a couple of weeks ago, Aunty Cassa had to put the dogs in a kennel because she had to go to a funeral, and the man in the kennels told her that both of the poor little dogs had a lump in their shoulders."

"She can't even take proper care of Papa's dogs," observed Nicole.

"I expect Aunty Cassa will take the dogs to the vet," said Dermot casually.

"But Daddy, she can't because the car won't go or she would have. The vet she knows is on holiday, she said, and another vet she phoned doesn't make house calls, he told her. She might be able to get a man out from Stillorgan to look at the car, but really she would like the vet she knows better than the one she phoned."

"And that's why she is so sad: it's for Fred and Mindo." Sandra's voice was full of pity. Dermot patted her hand.

Nicole dismissed the matter. "If it wasn't that, it would be something else. Come, help me gather up the dishes. Orla, you make coffee for Daddy. Sandra can stack the dishwasher."

Mrs Flynn was off duty all day Saturday and until seven p.m. on Sunday. On Saturdays Dermot played golf and Nicole allowed the girls entertain their friends. The new swimming pool was a great attraction.

On Sundays Dermot took Orla and Sandra on their weekly visit to their grandparents in Donnybrook. They adored Granny Tyson, and Granda. Of Grandfather Blake they had a memory only.

Nicole was in her element as organiser for many fundraising events. The bishop of the diocese often called on her to lend her name to his functions. But Nicole had become bored in the last year and felt that she needed a greater challenge than the house and the family.

She took her coffee cup to the long settee where Dermot was seated. When she sat down, he zapped off the TV.

"Yes, my dear?" His voice was amiable.

"Have you thought any more about your idea of taking me on, you know, in the contract cleaning ticket?" She leaned against his shoulder, pouting her lips in a kiss.

"Wasn't that your own idea, my sweet? I am not at all sure that dashing out to work every morning and dropping with fatigue every evening is the way a beautiful woman wants to spend her days."

"That would be only in the beginning, Dermot. You always say that organisation is ninety per cent. You don't collapse into your armchair, dead beat and worn out. At the end of the day, you are ready for a night on the town!"

He smiled. "But I have quite a headstart on you, my dear. And I'm a man – no, don't say a word – men are able to carry fatigue in the brainy cranium where it doesn't show. Of course, that may be why many men go bald."

"My darling," she said charmingly, "you have the most fantastic head of hair. I think you are just putting me off. I would make a wonderful businesswoman."

"Maybe you are too much at home these days. Would you be interested in a movie tonight, when Mrs Flynn gets in? We haven't been at the movies for ages."

"I would but I can't. Tonight is the big fashion show followed by the cabaret in the Burlington. You bought tickets, remember? It's the annual fundraiser for Marjorie's orphans."

"I gave the tickets to the girls in the office. Fashion shows give me the..."

"Don't say it, Derm! We'll go to the pictures some night during the week. It'll be all hours when I get home tonight: these things never get started until after nine."

"Will I come down and pick you up?"

"That's sweet of you, but Marjorie's nephew is doing the honours. You know the one I mean? His name is Clive."

"Oh, that nephew!" Dermot's smile was more amiable than ever, although he had no recollection of Clive. "Does he work for the orphans, too? When Mrs Flynn gets in," he added, "I may go down to Belmont, have a couple of jars with Tom and my Da."

She returned his kiss with her usual expertise, and she whispered, "Don't go asleep until I come home, there's a pet."

CHAPTER EIGHTEEN

FIRENZE WAS PLANNED south-by-west to catch all daytime sunshine, to be warmed and waiting for the setting sun. Dermot Tyson observed the effect as he got out of his car. In the valley, the village of Stillorgan showed myriad sunset windows, the distant Wicklow mountains were saffron-edged and Firenze itself was a miracle of light, as the sun still shed its gold on the picturesque house.

Cassa was sitting out on the trellised patio where Sadora Gilbey Blake's room had been long ago, the patio where her father used to brush the dogs every morning. Fred and Mindo were stretched out on the red tiles. Cassa put down the book she had been reading and stood up to greet him. Her gentle face was welcoming. He noticed how the sun caught up amber lights in her hair.

"If I had a wish," she said pleasantly, "I would wish for a visitor. Sunday is always endless – it's true, it's the longest day in the week. How are you, Dermot?"

"Fine, thank you. And you? Not so good, I hear. The girls told us at lunch that you are having car trouble? Nicole would have come, she was very concerned about you, but there is a big function downtown for the usual fundraising – her friend, Marjorie, her orphans-in-need, I think. I am here to offer help and Nicky sends her sympathy."

Dermot Tyson had been kind on several occasions. She had a lot of problems if she could get up the courage to explain them to him. She hardly knew her brother-in-law. The night of her father's death had been buried in her grief. A cool distance was perceived for a man who belonged to her sister.

"The sun is almost gone," she said. "Shall we go into the drawing-room? It stays warm after a sunny day like today. Perhaps we should sit in the window alcove? There's no fire in the grate, and it is depressing to sit looking into an empty firegrate." It seemed a little odd to be entertaining her sister's husband.

The room was as grand as ever, the heavy furniture, the big piano, all polished like glass. Dermot pulled his chair around to face Cassa across the low rope-edge table.

"Judging by the shine on this table, and all around," he said, "you haven't much time to play the piano?"

"No, not since Papa died. Long ago, he had great hopes of my becoming a concert pianist. Did you know that, Dermot."

"Would you have liked that?"

She forced a glimmer of a smile into her eyes. "It is a good thing that I was never put to the test. But I would have liked to teach piano to little children."

"You could still do that, couldn't you?" he asked.

"'Fraid not," Cassa replied, smiling. "I got good honours for music in the Leaving Cert, but then there was my mother to take care of. In those ten years, the piano may have been opened twice. Then it was too late. In the last year, I played a few times for Papa. He loved Mozart. He said it was beautiful, and I am sure Fred and Mindo loved it."

She looked fondly at the two dogs, now asleep on the hearth rug. "But, really and truly, the piano has needed tuning for ages past."

"Will you have it tuned?" Dermot was rejoicing in this very ordinary dialogue.

"I should like to have it tuned," she said, "for its own sake, but there are other priorities. And even if the piano were tuned, I am not qualified to teach: got to have a degree to teach, even to teach little beginners."

Dermot put his hand on the table. Unthinking, she put her hand in his.

"Now," he said, "is the first priority the car, so as you can take the dogs to the vet?"

Her eyes brightened, and her lips showed the beginnings of a real smile. "Ah! Orla and Sandra told you about Mindo and Fred."

"Yes," he smiled back at her, "and all about the bad vet who won't make house calls. The car, the dogs, the vet. Simple. You must have much more complicated priorities than those? How about a piano tuner?"

The great brown eyes lit up. "Not as much a priority as a chimney-sweep before next winter."

"I will add them to the list: a sweep and a piano tuner. Now tell me about the dogs. Sandra was almost in tears. She loves small animals."

"Oh, I know," Cassa said softly, "she is such a soft-natured little girl. They are both sweet. I am sure they are very much loved."

Dermot nodded.

"Well," Cassa began, "the man in the kennels, he told me that Fred has a bad lump under his shoulder. Mindo is even older and he is limping. They must be taken to the vet. I should not have left them in the kennels when they were sick, but I did not know."

She was very close to tears. "I should not have gone to that funeral at all, but, you see, it was Louise's funeral and I... and I..." She snatched her hand away and covered her face.

"Cassa, what is it?"

She was embarrassed. "Do you remember my friend, Louise? She was a guest at your wedding?"

"Yes, I remember her," Dermot said sympathetically, "a very beautiful girl. Nicky told me she died. I am so sorry. Do you want to talk about Louise?"

"No, no, no. I should never have gone to that funeral. I never saw Louise in her coffin; I wanted to, but a strange woman wouldn't let me." Tears glistened on her black eye-lashes. "The woman referred to Louise as a poor old thing. Louise, who was very beautiful and poised and clever. I keep imagining the most awful tragic things, the most terrible sicknesses. I should never have gone."

Her tears fell on her cheeks, and she held out her hand to Dermot again. He took her hand in his, standing up and drawing her into his arms. Whatever she had set out to tell, it had got lost. As he looked down at her small hand, he stroked her fingers thoughtfully and her head rested against him.

In some other city, London or Paris perhaps, he could take

Cassa into his protection, set her up in an apartment, make love to her all day and all night and grant her all her wishes. His own family need not suffer... in Paris, perhaps... Cassa would... he would bring her gifts – perfumes, flowers, jewels...

His racing thoughts came to a sudden end: Forget Paris; you're not French. Do that kind of thing in your native city and your whole life will come unstuck. Your wife and your mother and your children will repudiate you with a blast of publicity. Your pious clients, including Nicole's bishop, will denounce you for a blackguard. All you have worked for will be taken from you.

"Let me run over our priorities, Cassa. I am sure Nicole will drop in this coming week, and if there is any other way we can help, be sure to say, won't you?"

"You are the kindest person," she said. "I don't like to be a trouble. My sister is always saying what a full life you lead, travelling and meetings and all that."

He smiled grimly. "The motor mechanic in my head office, Art McConnell is his name, will call over in the morning. He will bring a mate who will take your car away for a complete overhaul. Art could take you and the dogs to the vet, if you wish? Within the next month, the chimneys will be swept, and the piano will be tuned." He smiled very genially at her. "How does that grab you?"

Cassa looked a little apprehensive, "Will all that cost an awful lot?" she asked.

"I shouldn't think so," he said cheerfully. "We'll talk about it later in the month."

"Thank you, Dermot," Cassa said fervently, "thank you."

"I won't delay now," he said. "I am due over in my dad's place for a couple of jars with him and my brother Tom."

Cassa had thought of offering a drink, but somehow the words had not come. She stood on the front steps as he drove away. Strange how her sister never talked about Dermot's delightful kindness.

Cassa went back into the drawing-room to call the dogs and put out the light.

CHAPTER NINETEEN

ORLA AND SANDRA were already asleep when their daddy looked in to say good-night. Mrs Flynn was in her bedroom, her light on, probably reading a juicy romance. Dermot had insisted on a portable TV for Mrs Flynn's room in spite of Nicole's giving him Sadora's Rule for servants: "Spoiling staff is burning money." Mrs Flynn seldom used it.

"Good-night, Mrs Flynn!" he called out cheerily as he passed her door.

He wanted to stand at the window, stare out at distant lights, and reflect on the hour with Cassa. Desire for one beautiful woman should be identical with desire for another. Why, for him, was it not? Why did one desire flood his senses, and the other desire require concentration.

In the early years of their marriage, his wife's eager urgent nightly conquests had been sexually satisfying. She learned quickly all the tricks of arousal. She bought books on the subject, perusing them like a traveller studying a road map.

Since the night of Richard Blake's death, he had had difficulty in keeping his mind on the job. This love-making had become tedious. The nights of floating away on a cloud were a thing of the past.

"Hello, my darling!"

Sitting on the bed beside him, she slipped off her shoes. He closed the book he had been pretending to read, and returned her kiss as ardently as she would deem totally lover-like.

It was so much easier to follow her lead than to provoke an inquisition of "Are you tired?" and "What's the matter?" *ad infinitum.*

"Had you a great success in the Burlington?" he asked, summoning up enthusiasm. "Many turn up?"

"Fantastic crowd! Everyone said I looked very beautiful. Do you think I do, darling?"

"Too beautiful for words!"

And it was true. Her hair, always blonde, shone like gold, and the glitter of gold continued into her very blue eyes. He unzipped and unclasped, caressing her white arms and her breasts with as much impassioned fervour as he could muster. As she lay under his hands, a shiver of delight showed that he was succeeding.

There was a slight hint of brandy on her breath, very slight because she was careful about drink. Sadora had laid down the rule that drink and cigarettes were ruinous for the complexion.

Nicole specialised in bawdy, lewd whispers in which he had lost interest. He let his trained body perform its function until he was sure she would not have the will to draw back.

Easing away from her, he asked blandly, "How is it that my solicitous wife does not ask me about my night?"

She murmured drowsily, "You went to Belmont..."

He feigned equally drowsy. "Sure, but I went first across to Firenze to help Cassa." He felt the slight tension, the merest ridging under his hands.

"What did you say?" now a touch of sharpness.

"You remember," he murmured, forcing his body to continue the expected work. "What Sandra was telling us today, about Cassa's car, and the sick dogs."

"Why are you telling me this now?" That was asked in her poutiest voice, but she had not drawn back. She had wanted him since she was sixteen. Dermot at rest within her was heaven on earth. She told him so constantly.

"Not important, doesn't matter, not important," his faked muttering, apparently so drugged with the ecstasy of her surrender, seemed to appease her.

In a while, her even breathing told him she had achieved satisfaction and was sleeping, hopefully too tired for an encore.

He moved away carefully up on to the pillows to stare out into the dim room, puzzled and wide awake. Why had he told her about the visit to Cassa? Why had he chosen that moment? Tomorrow, at breakfast, Nicole would bring up the subject of his visit to Cassa, casually, delicately, politely. In that one vulnerable moment Dermot Tyson had dropped a clanger into the family well. Even in her sleep, the disturbed circles were forming one out of the other, and ever widening.

Sleep was eluding him as it had often eluded him since the night he had kept the vigil by Richard Blake's coffin. There could be no doubt but that Cassa would respond to him if he would create a safe circumstance in which her fear of Nicole would no longer surface. Nor need his children suffer. At the hazy edge of sleep, it was hard to be practical, impossible to discipline his yearnings and remind himself of all he stood to lose. Because he had never experienced the reality of knowing love for love alone, Dermot Tyson thought that love would always be given back by the beloved in abundant measure.

CHAPTER TWENTY

Firenze
Wednesday

Dear Dermot,
Please excuse my sending this letter direct to your office, as it is a business letter with a further request. Your man, Art McConnell, was really nice but I am sorry to say the news is heart-breaking. The vet, Mr Roche, told me on the phone today that the x-rays are very bad and that Mindo and Fred must be put to sleep, he said for their own sake. I had to say yes. He agrees that I may take them home for burial as there is, since my grandfather's time, a little pets' burial-place under the high wall at the top of the vegetable garden. Today I tried to dig the ground there to soften the earth. It has not been touched for years and it is rock hard. Some of the little grave stones have fallen and they are heavy to lift.
Do you think you could allow Art McConnell to collect Fred and Mindo, they will be in suitable sacks for interment, and would he dig the earth for them? The car will be ready as from tomorrow, so perhaps one day will do the two collections.
I was going to phone you at home but every time I think of the dogs (Fred was fifteen years) I am afraid of weeping. My sister would be ashamed of me.
With much gratitude for all your help,
Cassa.

Dermot phoned her immediately he received the letter.

"I am so very sorry about the dogs. I know they were company for you apart from all the memories. I am sorry indeed. Yes, McConnell will do exactly as you ask. I will give him your phone number, and he'll ring. Make use of him. No, Cassa, no need to be thanking me, not a word now. I will come over on Friday, early in the afternoon, to make sure everything is all right. Go and have a little rest, and don't be upset."

Nicole had been craftier than he would have suspected.

She did not immediately bring up her displeasure about his visit to Cassa, but waited until the evening. Then she turned on all the charm, snuggling beside him on the long settee, and she tackled him again about her determination to take over one of his latest business ventures. She chose his contract cleaning department because she had heard him saying that it was expanding rapidly.

Dermot Tyson recognised the quid pro quo as she began her carefully prepared speech.

"I am just the very person you need to liaise between Tyson Associates and the nuns: didn't I hear you saying to Thomas that nuns were holy terrors in business? I deal with nuns and social workers all the time in my fund-raising. Not to mention priests! They are crying out for domestic staff in the colleges, and even in their houses of residence. My Bishop Prole is very concerned that they can't get anyone to cook for them over the weekend. Priests and nuns washing up their own dishes is a bit thick, don't you think? I could sell contract cleaning with a wave of my wand.

"And as you know, Dermot darling, I have a great head for figures. You know very well I would be a super saleswoman!"

Essentially, he believed that married women with children were better off chained to their homes with no temptation to become discontented. Of course, poor women, women at their wits' end who had to go out to work, very often raised great families, but there was no necessity for women like Nicole.

He found Nicole's arms were being draped around him. "Darling, I know you are going to tell me that we don't need any more money. But you know, sweetheart, I would be very good and bank my salary. It's not because I want to be extravagant."

"It's not that," he said shortly, "nothing to do with money. There are two things: one, the girls need you here..."

"To do what?" she flared at him. "To wait around all day while they are in school? I don't cook and launder. I don't garden, dressmake, clean out the swimming-pool. I hate

88

reading. I hate endless TV. I never listen to radio. If you are that concerned about Orla and Sandra, you could stay home more often yourself. Should I be here to help Orla and Sandra with their homework? They'd laugh at me. They enjoy helping each other. You are a fuddy duddy old-fashioned man about women."

She calmed down and became meltingly persuasive again. "My dearest darling husband, that day is over. Women go gaga in the house all day! They become simple! When those women get a night out, they are swopping soup recipes!"

He had to laugh at the accent she put on "swopping soup recipes!"

"And what was the second thing?" she demanded.

"My dear Nicole, you are very beautiful: wouldn't chasing the dismal cleaners day after day bring lines of worry on your lovely face, destroy your skin? The life you lead now suits you, my dear."

"Oh is that it? How sweet of you! But I will delegate. I will run teams from my office. What your people call central control. I am the kind of person who must be obeyed. I will rule those women as I rule my home – just multiply by a hundred!"

He lowered his head, maintaining his heavy frown. Nicole entwined her arms in his and kissed his lips.

"Come on, hero, say yes. You know I am getting hemmed-in. I need the freedom to try a whole new way of life; I want a career and you can give it to me. Why are you being so very old-fashioned? "

He pushed her away very gently. "We must be businesslike about this. You have no idea what contract cleaning is really like. I'll consider."

"You said that the last time!" She flashed her brilliant eyes angrily. "Make up your mind once and for all! I could use my talents elsewhere, you know!"

"Are you sure this is what you want?" he asked. "Have you thought of the demands on your free time?"

"Oh, give me credit!" she answered impatiently.

Still frowning very seriously, he asked, "When would this new career begin?"

"Now, this very minute! Now, Dermot, now, right now!"

"You understand, my dear, that because I know the hard graft involved, I am very reluctant. But I suppose I must give in. There is a full-day course set up for supervisors. Ten women applied and were interviewed. Six have been accepted for the course. They are all working-class women."

She pouted prettily. "Couldn't you tell me what I should know. I don't have to mix with those women, do I?"

"That's a bad start, isn't it? How else will you get to know the work they have to do? They instruct the cleaners in the kind of work, times, schedules. I couldn't tell you what you have to know because I don't know. Also, supervisors are often interchanged, and there is a senior supervisor over the others."

"Wouldn't that be me, darling?"

"Hardly on the first day, my pet! There is quite a lot to learn and to remember." He saw she didn't believe him, and he added, "It is up to you, Nicole."

"When is this course?" she asked petulantly.

"It is on Friday, nine a.m. to six p.m. It is held in Saint Adrian's Hospital. There will be a tour of the hospital included. It is considered important to see how big a place a hospital is, apart from the wards and the theatres, a lot of cleaning. Tough places, I am told."

"I'll do it," she said suddenly. "As you said, it will be a starting point." She was flying out of the room. "I have to phone Marjorie about tonight! Got to hurry! It's Clive's birthday, and we are giving him a surprise!"

How long would she last in the roughness of the workplace, he wondered. One thing was sure, or as sure as anything ever could be with Nicole. Friday would be all his.

CHAPTER TWENTY-ONE

DERMOT TYSON GLANCED at the sky as he turned into the avenue. Not a cloud in the blue, and Firenze was all summer greenery.

Cassa's dress was sober and he thought that accentuated her colouring of creamy skin, brown eyes and russet hair. She led him through the hall and into the front drawing-room. The absence of the dogs was at once obvious.

"You have had a sad week," he said, putting his arm around her shoulder in a brotherly way, "and I was sad too, thinking of what you were going through, losing two pets after all the years. But today, we are going to cheer ourselves up by going out to lunch, eh?"

"Oh no, I couldn't," she said quickly. "Oh no, I don't think so, thank you."

"But we are," Dermot said, "we are going out to have lunch. Do you know the Glen of the Downs, the little hotel?"

She had been there with her father not so long ago; it was a lovely place perched on the hillside overlooking the glen itself. But to go there with her sister's husband was unthinkable. She shook her head.

"As it happens," he said, choosing his words, "Nicole is on a course in Dublin today, since nine o'clock this morning until six, otherwise she would be here too. She is very sorry about what has happened to your dogs, but the course is on today."

"An arts appreciation course?" wondered Cassa.

"No," Dermot smiled, "although that is the usual sort of thing she enjoys. No, today it is a business course. Nicole is now keyed-up to the idea of taking a lot of work off my hands and setting up in business."

As Cassa followed him out to the car, her eyes were wide with surprise. She thought of her sister as a fashionable socialite with lots of friends and loads of money, enjoying a lifestyle in keeping with the very wealthy owner of Tyson

91

Associates. Her father used to remark, a little enviously, "That fellow is into everything. Must be making a million."

"What happened?" she turned towards Dermot at the wheel.

He smiled again, a reassuring smile, "Nothing really. It probably won't last long. I suppose it must be the 'in thing' for well-off married ladies to have a career. A high-flown executive business lady is much the same as a distinguished lady surgeon. Would you think so?"

Cassa looked around at him solemnly: "I think she is lucky to have a choice."

"So we are off to lunch in the Glen of the Downs? I think you will like it." Dermot had glanced at the picture of Elvira over the mantel as they went out. It was a good omen, so like Cassa, and the brilliant sunshine was another.

Normally somewhat laconic, leaving other people to make the chat, today Tyson was offering himself as a gift, laying himself out to please. Cassa responded with unconscious coquetry.

He could see that she was unaware of her lovely inviting smile, unaware of the allure in her dark brown eyes, and of the tantalisingly delicate lift of her shoulders when she joined softly in his laughter as he told her funny little incidents about Orla and Sandra which he had surely stored away awaiting this special listener. The most enchanting quality he found in her was her deference to him, her feminine unassertiveness. A man would have exquisite pleasure in moulding her unto himself.

When lunch was finished, Dermot suggested, "If you have never climbed to the top of the Downs, we could try that. The view is superb." When Cassa looked down at her light shoes, he assured her that although the climb was steep, there was a path all the way.

"A family by the name of La Touche built a house right on the top," Dermot told her, "maybe a hunting lodge, a long time ago. Only the ruins are left."

"La Touche!" Cassa repeated dreamily, "What a musical name. La touche is the key-note on the piano."

When the path became steeper, Dermot gave her his hand and she held it all the way to the top.

At the summit, they sat on the broken wall of the ruined house. To the east, the Irish Sea stretched away to Wales where a misty curtain hid Mount Snowdon. To the south and to the west all the mountain peaks of Wicklow piled one beyond the other. Dermot was able to name some of them, but she knew only Lugnaquilla.

"Look," Dermot pointed southward, "the sky is so clear, you can see Mount Leinster. I think it is Carlow, or is it in Kilkenny?

There was a stiff breeze getting up on the summit. Cassa moved near to him and he put his arm firmly around her.

She smiled up at him: "I love being held close like that."

He knew she could have no idea of the fire that ran sweetly through every vein in his body. Someday he would be her teacher. He had plans and he had time.

CHAPTER TWENTY-TWO

THE SUMMER OF loneliness dragged on. Cassa forced herself to walk the fields every morning, but missing the dogs did not get one bit easier. Fred had had an odd way of coming back every so often to look up at her as if with a question, while Mindo used to limp off into the distance as if rabbits were hiding beyond every tree.

She began to think that Fred had stopped in the middle of his run to try to tell her he was in bad pain. Papa would have understood. Poor old Fred's pain would not have been prolonged. Feeling guilty on top of being unutterably lonely was almost more than Cassa could bear.

She came slowly to understand that the one thing which had enlivened her life during all the gloomy years of her mother's illness, and that she had shared in the telling with Papa, was now the one thing she would never have again: the month of July at Caragh Lake. Gradually the broken pieces of her shattered image of Louise and Robert reassembled themselves into a more bearable picture.

Robert was not the man who had betrayed his dead wife: that was a man driven to a desperate deed by some terrible unnameable tragedy and tempted by a faceless woman of evil intent.

Cassa dismissed from her mind the handsome platinum-haired woman who had taken advantage of Robert's sorrow, pressing her thought on to recollections of beautiful Louise, the beloved lost one of his awful misery, the enthralling bejewelled lover of the balcony over the lake. It was she whom Robert was seeking.

Cassa had absolutely agreed with Louise that Robert was ideal in every perfection a man could have. Who was she to judge a man of Robert's calibre? On his pedestal, properly crowned and fêted, that is where Louise would have wished him to be.

Cassa was able to remember how, not frequently but now

and then, he had drawn her to himself with little compliments, light touches on her bare arm as they walked under the trees. She need not let go of her own special memories of heroic Robert Gray and a silvery outline of Cassa Blake.

At other times, Cassa was unable to hide from the dismal sense of disillusion with which she was finding it impossible to live. Survival tactics became all-important.

She got out her mother's gardening books and she made a valiant effort to recultivate a few patches in the garden. Sadora used to say that gardening was therapeutic. In those far-off days, it was therapeutic for Sadora's trained gardeners. Cassa found it wearisome, and worse than that, it left as much time for feeling lonely and forgotten as did all the other monotonous household tasks.

CHAPTER TWENTY-THREE

IN SEPTEMBER CASSA had an unannounced visit from Nicole. "God! Look at you! You're up to your eyes in muck. Have you no gardening gloves? You'll destroy your hands, such as they are. You would need to take a shower before you could make a cup of coffee for me. When I was driving up, you were staring up at the sky.

Cassa began a fruitless protest.

"Come on, I haven't all day. I've something to tell you, could be of great interest. The last time I phoned, you were moaning about the cost of living. Well, this – for God's sake, Cassa, put down that spade and come in and wash your hands."

Cassa was slowly scrubbing her nails.

"Did you hear me? This is to your benefit if you don't want to be poverty-stricken all your life. Or do you think the old writer is heading up this way, looking for a new helpmate? Are you hoping to step into the dead friend's shoes? You got your comeuppance there – and, in my opinion, you were damn lucky – although I daresay a lot of it is in your own imagination..."

Cassa interrupted quite angrily, "Nicole, please don't refer to that matter again. Louise was my friend, and that is all over now. Please, she is dead."

Always impatient, Nicole was making the coffee. Without question, everything in Firenze was for her use and always would be.

Very politely, Cassa said, "You were saying?"

Ladylike behaviour from Cassa always stuck in Nicole's throat, but this time she shut her lips on yet another rebuke. She lightened her tone: "I am really here on Dermot's business, and when my lord and master entrusts me with an errand, I had better come back with the right message!"

Cassa looked at her in wonder. A Nicole who referred to anyone on earth as a lord and master?

"I am up to the eyebrows in Dermot's newest brainchild, contract cleaning. Only three months into the business and I am practically the boss of the show; in another couple of months he will give me an office all to myself in a new building. Are you following me?"

"You came to tell me this? You usually phone"

Experience warned Cassa to watch out for the trip-wire, but when it came she forgot her instinct.

"Dermot has just got the franchise on Dublin's two biggest hospitals, both secular. And, wait for it, on San Salvatore, which is run by nuns. You know Salvatore, the big one in Seacoast? You must know it, overlooking the sea, near the harbour?" Cassa responded happily to this friendliness, rare in Nicky.

"Maisie Foley: she drove me out to Seacoast last week, to see the new shopping centre. We had coffee and looked in all the shops and boutiques. The lifts are like glass balloons and..."

"Yes, it's terrific," Nicole interrupted. "I saw it. What I want to say... Cassa, listen to me for a minute."

"All I was going to say is that people were buying loaded trolleys of groceries, poorer-class people, and I wondered, where do people get the money? That's all."

"Everyone says that: where do people get the money? If you had a job, Cassa Blake, you'd have the money too!"

Very politely Cassa said, "Papa is dead four months. You were the one who told me it was my duty to look after him when Mama died, and that was ten years from the day I left school and you got married, remember?"

"No need to get uppity, miss. Well, if I had known that my mother's stroke would keep her alive for ten years, I wouldn't have got married, and I wouldn't have let you take on the job of nursing her. We could have got a nurse if Papa wasn't so cautious about his money and you could have gone to college, maybe become a music teacher and..."

"Nicky," Cassa's voice was tired and quiet, "you know very well there was no money for college, nor for a nurse."

"Oh, stop being so goody goody about it. I know what I'm talking about. You might have got some sort of a job. It would have got you out of the house, and you could have met people, maybe got yourself a man."

No use in Cassa's protesting. There never was.

"Anyway," Nicole muttered, "I'm glad those bloody dogs are gone, hairs everywhere."

Then she remembered her mission. She tempered her voice and fluttered her hands over the coffee cups. "Dermot wants you to take the supervisor's job in the San Salvatore Hospital. Just supervising, you know. A lady's position. No rough work."

Cassa stared in surprise. A job! "Supervising what?"

"The cleaners, of course. I told you: the new contract cleaning. They come in every day to clean the hospital. The supervisor walks around and checks their work, recording it in her book. Simple. They begin at seven-thirty a.m. and are all out and away, work completed, by midday. Four and a half hours work a day and not on Sunday."

Cassa began to gather the cups. The idea of earning money was attractive. She would be able to repay Dermot Tyson for the vet and the car.

"Cassa, stop fussing over two cups. Sit down for a minute and give me an answer. Dermot wants an answer today. Is the job not an answer to your question, 'Where do people get the money?' You could do with a job. Sooner or later, you will wake up to find yourself having to pay rent. Have you thought of that, miss? Work experience is what you will need and good references. You couldn't even put a CV together!"

"I could learn," Cassa said defensively.

Nicole jeered: "Don't be silly! It's young ones out of school get office jobs, young ones with big blue eyes. You can't even type."

"I was thinking of getting one big dog, a watch-dog," Cassa offered hopefully.

"Could you afford to feed it?" Nicole asked sarcastically. "Is this big dog to be an excuse for not taking the job. You'd only be out of the house for a few hours in the morning."

"A dog doesn't like to be on his own in an empty house."

This was too much for her sister. She jumped up, ready to fly out the door and into her car. "You would try the patience of a saint. I have an appointment. When I get home, I'll phone you. Have your mind made up. It is a good job and Dermot is very good to offer it to you. He is prepared to interview you in his office on Friday at five-thirty. And for heaven's sake, get something done with your hair."

When Nicole had driven off, Cassa sat down in the sunny garden. They used to bring Mama out here on a good day on her long wheel-bed, and Papa used to give a running commentary on progress in the garden.

Cassa wished she could discuss this job idea with an adviser, or with a friend. There had been so little time left over to cultivate friends of her own age. There was Maisie Foley with whom she played bridge occasionally, when Maisie was stuck for a brighter player, but Maisie simply assumed that all her friends were rich.

Anyway, why would the super-efficient Dermot Tyson offer her a job? He had given no indication of a job when he took her out to lunch a couple of weeks ago. The job had to be Nicole's suggestion, and Nicole had even less respect for Cassa's capabilities in any work-place.

It occurred to her that work experience might be a good idea. With work experience, she could move on to a different job, perhaps a nicer job, or at least one not under Nicole's wing. Maybe she could save a little money and start taking in student lodgers, with a deep-freeze full of things to eat, eggs and rashers and sausages. That thought pulled her up short.

When would she be told whether Firenze was really and truly hers?

In the hall, Cassa caught sight of herself in the mirror. Nicole was right about the hair: it was like a furze bush. She made an appointment with Nicole's hairdresser for Friday morning. With a bit of luck she would appear nicely groomed for the interview. When Nicole phoned, the interview was arranged for five-thirty on Friday evening, in the head office of Tyson Associates in Harcourt Street.

"Once inside the office," Nicole instructed her, "just give your name to the receptionist. No sister, or in-law – just plain Miss Blake, and dress ordinarily. It's not top-level management yet, you know."

Cassa thought, someday Nicole will quite accidentally remember that I am over thirty.

When Cassa went up to her bedroom, she took out the good dark suit and the delicate blouse she had planned to wear to Louise's funeral. The taupe colour of the suit seemed to tone in with the colour of her hair, and the creamy blouse only needed a little pressing. "Dress ordinary" probably meant no earrings, no bracelet.

She tried to think only of the interview and the job experience.

CHAPTER TWENTY-FOUR

"**W**HY DID YOU make the appointment with the solicitors for the same time?"

Nicole was perched on the edge of his desk displaying her slim legs. She never knew how this irritated him in the office.

"The solicitors made the appointment," he lied nonchalantly. "Since you have berated them for keeping you waiting, there was no sense in asking for a change of day or time."

"I should be here when my sister comes in for the interview, although I don't really see why I am not the one to interview her. Or couldn't Miss Kenny interview her?"

Tyson walked to the far end of the big office and looked out of the window at the crowded car-park. If she wanted him to talk, she would have to get off his desk and follow him.

"For the obvious reason that she is your sister..." He raised his hand as Nicole tried to interrupt: "All right, all right, you told me it is to be 'no family favouritism'. You are right, and since San Salvatore is your particular charge, you have the say. Nevertheless, it is only courtesy to treat her differently here in my office, and as an introduction to my business..."

"Dermot, that's not fair. It is *my* business. You are not even going to regard it as coming under Tyson Associates until the end of the year."

"My dear, let's not have an argument. In a few months, when you have made a success of San Salvatore (remember, the workload could become a bind, and you could become tired of it) and when you have this hospital up and running, then we shall consider the other hospitals. One step at a time, Nicole."

The very prospect of sixteen hospitals under her control made Nicole's eyes glitter. To be top cat over all the supervisors was the very idea she had in mind, and the first recruit to her army would be the supervisor in San Salvatore, her biddable sister Cassa. Soon there would be half a dozen women running around these hospitals and reporting directly to Mrs Tyson. To rule as one would rule a kingdom, as Sadora Gilbey Blake had ruled Firenze. Nicole shuddered to think of its present deterioration, with no staff and no central heating. This visit to the solicitors would change all that. She would be queen at home and queen in the world of finance.

Close to his shoulder, she said, "I do see your point, darling. Of course poor old Cass is going through a tough time just now. We have to be nice to her."

"I know," he said, "I know."

"Are you not going to kiss me and wish me luck with these ghastly solicitors?"

"Good luck, my dear."

She blew another kiss from the door. He went into his cloakroom to wash the lipstick from his mouth.

Nicole Sadora Blake Tyson's luck was out, and soon she would know it. He had the solicitors' letter in his desk, but he had insisted that Orpington tell her to her face. The Orpingtons and the Gilbeys were connected, old family friends, and Nicole would have to believe them.

In Dermot Tyson's unexpressed opinion, it was right and just that Firenze and all its contents should be willed to Cassa, who had sacrificed her youth for her parents. Nicole had been given her dowry of £60,000, and the house in which they themselves lived and which was now worth, he was sure, well over £100,000.

However, his wife believed, and it was the single sincere belief in her life, that her mother intended for her to own Firenze, and everything in it. Dermot Tyson foresaw that there would be ructions in Orpington's office, such as only Nicole would know how to create .

His role would be to shelter Cassa.

*　　*　　*

Cassa was enormously impressed with the splendour of Tyson Associates, all shining glass and stainless steel behind the modest Georgian exterior in Harcourt Street.

On the dot of the clock, she was ushered into Dermot's office.

"Miss Blake, for her interview," said the secretary.

"Please sit down, Cassa. May I say you are looking very well."

The new hair style surprised him. The tawny curly hair had been trimmed close to her head, showing her small pretty ears. It was a boyish look suitable to her neat slim figure in the well-cut suit.

"Thank you."

Cassa was a little unnerved by his look of admiration. It was a sham interview anyway. She had no references to offer, and her main skill (if she had any at all) was playing the piano.

He had stood up at the massive desk when she entered the office. Now he came around the desk and sat down beside her.

"I was surprised when Nicole told me how much you want-ed to join the firm. Had I known, I would have suggested some other kind of work, but Nicole assures me that you are very much in earnest in joining her team. I suggested you come today so I could, myself, put you in the picture. She would be here but she has another, unavoidable engage-ment."

Cassa had assumed so respectful an air that he wanted to pick her up and hug her like a little girl who must not be afraid of grown-ups.

In fact, she was covering her indignant anger over the lies told by her dear sister. "Dermot is offering you this good job..." But it was not new to be deceived by Nicky. That went back, painfully, into earliest childhood. Oh well, she thought wearily, a job is becoming necessary.

"Yes, you were saying?"

He was talking on, but he had noticed her abstraction, and could guess the cause. She was here because her sister said to be here. But, in fact, the main purpose of the visit was to indicate to her that she had been given the freedom of his office.

"About contract cleaning, I was saying that it is the coming thing. No one can, in big institutions, afford live-in domestic staff. Not nowadays. In this country, the public hospitals were dependent on nuns and brothers, but wages now are high and nuns are becoming fewer. But someone has to clean. Hence contract cleaning, which I think of as team work."

She could not think of an enthusiastic response, but she recognised the tone of his voice as kind and, indeed, gentle. She had guessed at the nature of a cleaner's work in a hospital, and reassured herself that she was going to be a supervisor – just supervising, was what Nicole had said.

Cassa counted to ten. "Dermot, my sister did not exactly say, but perhaps you could tell me what are the duties of a supervisor?"

He repeated more or less what Nicole had said. "Simple! We supply the supervisor with eight to ten cleaning women, all fully trained at base. The supervisor allots the work areas as she sees fit, different from day to day, I understand. There is a map of the working area, a large area I am sure, and a chart to show times allowed per job. All done by rota. The supervisor walks around, keeps on the move. Like a stop-watch, eh?"

This surely called for a smile, but her features were set.

"Cassa, you do want this job, don't you? Nicole says you begged her to get you this very position? You are looking for work, are you?"

"Yes, yes, I am. Very good of you and Nicky to think of me. The work experience is what I need."

He was relieved. "You see, Cassa, this is the first hospital controlled by nuns which we have been asked to contract. I was influenced by Nicole's saying that you had many friends among nuns, and that you had a great understanding of them. She was educated in England, but she told me you continued to Leaving Cert with the Loreto nuns. She said you would be good with nuns. Personally, in business, I find them tedious."

So she was good with nuns? Tyson probably thought she was a nun herself, a dried-up old spinster.

"Cassa, so that you know just what you are facing into, I would like you to work for part of a week in Boley's Hospital. Do you know where it is? Oh good. Not exactly work, rather train under one of our established supervisors, a grand woman named Mrs Slattery. She will be the best one to show you the ropes, as it were. Give it a few days?"

He was smiling hopefully at her again. "Then, if you decide it is for you, you could start in San Salvatore on Monday of the following week."

It took a bit of courage but she asked steadily, "How much do I get a week?"

"I was just coming to that. Nicole is dealing with the wage packets of the other supervisors, but I wish to deal with you directly. I am not sure if all are paid equally. The cleaners are deducted for missing days, and she keeps the book on that also. Would £120 per week pay you, do you think? It means your car expenses to Seacoast six days a week, maybe other expenses?"

This was riches she had never expected. The pleased expression on her face was enough.

"Cassa, we have to work out such things as PRSI, and tax on your dividends, so I will pay you either in here, if you are in town, or I can call out to the house, maybe bring the girls. They often ask about you."

To Cassa, life suddenly looked a lot brighter. "Thank you very much."

He put his hand on her arm, "So, we will meet more often? And, Cassa, there is one more thing: I am here if ever you are in need of a friend."

A sudden vision of her sister's face screwed up in rage wiped the smile off Cassa's lips: "Touch anything of mine and I'll push you into the sea!"

That threat was for trying on a lacy bra long before she had need of a bra herself. She must have been ten on that occasion, but bullying went back much further.

Looking into Tyson's handsome face, she remembered the giddy joy she felt on Nicole's wedding day because she had realised her sister was leaving Firenze for ever. And now she was agreeing to work for Nicky's husband and come to his office every week for her pay. That particular pay arrangement would be swiftly changed when her sister heard about it.

"So you will be at Boley's Hospital as early as possible on Monday morning, Cassa? Mrs Slattery will look after you. She knows to expect you."

He had insisted on Mrs Slattery and Boley's Hospital for Cassa's introduction to the work, although Nicole had advised Sir Patrick Dunn's Hospital and a tough woman there named, aptly, Mrs Fury.

He took her hands to lift her to her feet and he drew her gently towards him. In the manner of a benign foreign uncle, he held her to him while he kissed her cheeks. She quivered from fear that Nicky would come through the door.

The little quiver fired Dermot's own pleasure. "Cassa, always remember we are friends. I am here for you."

He held open the door of his office, but she could not meet his gaze. "Thank you again," she said escaping out on to the stairs down which she fled.

She had come in on the bus and left the car in Stillorgan. Now she hurried all the way to the bus station. She would ring him and tell him to stuff his old job. The humiliation of the interview was scalding. How could her own sister say that she begged for a job? But spinning along in the bus, she knew she would not make the phone call. Her wages at £120 a week would make all the difference between poverty and the ability to pay her way.

CHAPTER TWENTY-FIVE

Late on sunday evening Nicole phoned, full of instructions. "Are you all set for tomorrow? Don't take the car. Boley's Hospital is in a rough area and the parking is only for doctors and nurses. Go in by bus and take another across the city. No, I don't know the numbers of buses. Don't carry a lot of money, just bring your overall. I said your overall. What? I know you have two or three white overalls. The maids wore them in the kitchen. For heaven's sake, Mama never gave them away. Look in the wardrobe in the small return-room. I know you don't expect any dirty work, but a white overall looks efficient, that's why. Now, do you remember the name? Yes, it's Mrs Slattery. Pay no attention to her language. You won't have that problem in the nuns' hospital. Just bring your bus fare and sensible shoes. I know, but I'm reminding you again. There's a lot of walking, it's a big hospital. Don't dress for Grafton Street, for heaven's sake, and go easy on the make-up. I know you don't, but it's better to look your age. Sensible shoes and a raincoat and your umbrella. An umbrella looks the part."

Then Nicole switched to her sweetest tones. "Dermot is so delighted that you are happy to take on the new job. He has great hopes for you. He said how well you are not showing your age!"

Cassa laid the receiver down on the table. She could hear Nicky's voice echoing on and on as she moved out of the hall. Later she would replace the receiver. Nicky always hung up on the last word of her own sentence.

The second bus on Monday morning set Cassa down at Boley's Hospital, and she found the side door of the Out-Patients open to let the cleaners in.

Mrs Slattery was a large friendly woman prepared to give fifty thousand instructions to the newcomer, who fervently hoped she would remember them all.

"You're going out to work in Salvatore? I'd a loved that. It

is a new, modern hospital. Not like this place! This fuckin'
hospital was built in old God's time. Nothin' works. The
shaggin' hot taps go on and off. I wouldn't send me worse
enemy in here for an operation. It's written up over the front
door in stone: 1862. The sluices is the very devil, the bloody
things get clogged up with lumps of gizzard. Well, that's what
it looks like, anyway. Come on, Miss, I'll roll-call the women.
On Mondays they start on the wards, always filthy after their
fuckin' visitors on Sundays."

Mrs Slattery had a large notebook. She called each
woman by name, passing a jocular remark to each one, and
out of an under-the-stairs cubbyhole each took her brush
and duster and a bucket for rubbish. Cassa thought the women,
mainly middle-aged, had a resigned look about them.

"We keep the machines, the vacs and the floor shiners on
the different floors," Mrs Slattery told Cassa, "because the
lifts never work right." To the women she said, "Forty
minutes back here for reassignment."

"It is an enormous hospital," Cassa said to Mrs Slattery.
"Will eight women be able to clean it in four and a half
hours?"

"A lick and a promise, as me Granny used to say. These
wans wouldn't be able to put a shine on it if they had eight
hours. I make them cover all the places that show. I do the
main entrance hall meself because you know what they say
about first impressions."

Mrs Slattery handed a kit of dusters and spray polishes to
Cassa. "I'll vac and do the marble floor and you can look
over the tables and ledges and the sills of the windows. Out
of the ark, that hall, wait'll you see it – fuckin' enormous and
bloody freezin'. Come on."

Despite the fact that people were walking through the
hall, in and out, Mrs Slattery kept up a running commentary
of gossip mixed with instructions, admonitions and an
account of her own absorbing life story. After the forty
minutes, Cassa had assimilated the fact that Mr Slattery was
a lousy bowsy, but she wouldn't swap him for Prince Charles,

that she had eight children, nearly all grown-up and married, and mostly living in the same block of Corpo flats as herself, which was not to say that they couldn't afford to buy houses if they wanted, and they would buy them when these houses were being built in the city.

Neither her married sons nor her married daughters were going to spend good money to go out and live in the Dublin mountains. "Me sister bought a house out in Tallaght – back of beyond – the bus fare 'ud beggar ya."

When the cleaners reassembled around the cubby-hole, rubbish was dumped in plastic bags and clean rags and spray polishes were handed out. This time they went off in pairs to do the corridors and landings.

"Lucky for us," Mrs Slattery told Cassa, "they only do emergency operations (God love the poor buggers!) on a Monday. Tuesday and Wednesday, last thing is the swab-out of the theathres. I supervise that meself and take a hand. Them consultants is that particular they'd sicken ya. Any loose ends and we'd have Mr Tyson's boys in on us like a ton of shit. Have you met him? Tyson I mean. Well, if you do, walk the tightrope."

After two hours of Mrs Slattery, Cassa was exhausted. How that woman kept going was a mystery. She talked non-stop but she worked as well. "The tops of the doors must be done daily," and she rubbed vigorously, "and the rims of the panels. It's the fuckin' age of the bloody place, the dust breeds itself overnight. The feckin' brass handles must be gone over daily. Brass handles in this day and age when we could have plastic and bakelite! Sweaty hands and some-times bloody hands on them handles! I make the women scrub their own hands before they leave to go home. Ye'd never know what disease ye'd pick up in a place like this. Never touch anythin' broken, miss, get a brush and a dust-pan. The filthy diseases that are goin' nowadays are all got from other people's blood. Oh, that's a fact!"

Once in a while, Mrs Slattery paused to draw a wheezy breath.

"On Thursdays I get Mary Mooney to do the Drugs Treatment wards along with meself. She's a very reliable cleaner. Never misses a day and has great devotion to Our Blessed Mother. The drugs patients' wards would frighten the livin' daylights outta ya! The nurses make their beds for them, but it's what's under the beds – spit and vomit. Mary Mooney says they can't help it. Shite too on the floor, although they could walk to the latrines, they don't make it in feckin' time. Mary Mooney says she offers it up for the holy souls in purgatory. I'd bang their heads together for gettin' into that state. Mixin' their blood, that's what it is. And for what? To die in a charity ward. There's only one of them in there ever has a visitor, his poor mother, and he's a creature from the back end of the country. A fuckin' long journey she comes, and half the time he hasn't a clue who she is."

Cassa went into a lavatory and threw up. Despair settled on her heart. She would never be able to face a day full of rubbish and spit and vomit, and worse. Washing her hands and her mouth, she longed for her garden and for her father.

Surely Nicky must know that this job was dirty and degrading and repulsive. She wanted to sit on the steel chair and cry her eyes out, but she was now a working woman and Mrs Slattery was waiting outside. The days of being a beloved daughter in a luxurious home were over. For ever.

Mrs Slattery glanced at Cassa's face. "You'll get used to it," she said sympathetically. "The first few days is the worsest."

She bustled Cassa ahead of her on the stairs. "Never let the women see you weaken. You have to be like an old soldier leadin' the troops into bloody slaughter."

When Cassa looked around in surprise, Mrs Slattery said, "I got that from me Da. He was in three wars. He's ninety-two and not a bother on him. Talks about lookin' for a new mott since me Ma passed on last Christmas."

Two women started at the top of the mile-high staircase full of rope-edge banisters. Two other women were dispatched to the nurses' kitchens, of which there was one on every floor.

"They're all right," Mrs Slattery said. "They'll probably nick a cup of tea. I try to vary that job, different days different women. Gives them a bit of a chance of a break for a fag."

Four women, one to each floor, went to the lavatories and sluice-rooms. "Vary that too, if you can," said Mrs Slattery; "that's a tough one. And, Miss, never make favourites. Some of these women would have your guts for garters if they thought they were ill done by."

With the last two women, Cassa went to the nursery wards while Mrs Slattery stayed near the cubby-hole to write up her daily roster. The cleaners, Cassa noticed, had not been allotted a room to themselves.

While the women scrubbed the floors, Cassa dusted and tidied. The nurses had made the rooms cheerful and bright for the children, but not many of the children were well enough to take much notice.

*　　*　　*

"Let the women all clear off first," said Mrs Slattery to Cassa, "then we'll lock up and let ourselves out."

Cassa was feeling that her leaden feet would scarcely carry her to the bus. Out in the yard, a large polished car was waiting to receive Mrs Slattery. A fine-looking chubby man sporting a thick black moustache pushed open the door. He was grinning good naturedly.

"This is Shay, me husband. This is Miss Blake come to learn her job."

Shay leaned out to shake Cassa's hand. "Hop in," he said, "if you want a lift."

Cassa hesitated. "Perhaps I should walk a bit," she said. "A walk might do me good."

"Get in," said Shay. "Strangers don't walk in this district. Where to?"

"It is very kind of you," Cassa smiled in relief. "I am going to the bus station. I live out Seacoast direction."

"She's got the job out in that hospital where Tysons have the new contract. With the nuns."

"We had them nuns where I went to school," said Shay. "Very fond of the rod, one of them was."

"And of course," put in Lotty, "you didn't deserve the rod!"

There were loud guffaws from the happy couple. Within a few minutes, Cassa was getting into her south-city bus and waving goodbye to the beaming Slatterys.

CHAPTER TWENTY-SIX

T HE GARDEN OF Firenze was like the Garden of Eden to Cassa after the slum area around Boley Square. She walked slowly on the curving paths, drawing in the perfume of old lavender and green grass. She had taken off the shoes she had worn to work and put them up on a ledge to air. The smell of the hospital was hard to shake off, and the ringing of Lotty Slattery's voice took time to fade from her ears.

To sit drinking tea in Sadora's loggia, idly drinking tea, was a greater luxury than she had remembered. She and Papa had always taken their afternoon tea out here. How had she not noticed what a heavenly place it was? This was home, this was happiness.

She tried to count her blessings, "always a salutary thing to do". It was one of Sadora's Rules. She tried to fight off the crestfallen thought that this day just over had sealed off and ended all the pleasant parts of her life. From now on, daily life would be unremittingly grim. The past was finally at a conclusion. But must she submit? Was there no job possible without work experience?

In the hall she paused beside the telephone. Ring Nicole and tell her that you've had a heart attack. Nothing less would let her off Nicole's hook. Tell her you just can't.

But would that backfire on Lotty Slattery? In her own way, Mrs Slattery had been helpful and kind although her voice was like a fire alarm. Praise Mrs Slattery but plead sickness. What sort of sickness?

She lifted the receiver and dialled Nicole's number. Surely her sister would understand?

Cassa put down the phone and climbed the stairs. A long hot bath would be easier than talking to her sister. Her head ached and her feet felt like stones.

Soaking in her hot bath, recollecting the dire elements which had gone into her day, the thought came that she knew very little of the world she lived in. Out beyond the hornbeam hedges of Firenze there was a work-place and a language with which she must learn to cope, to make sure of survival. The longest four days in Cassa's life ended on Thursday.

Mrs Slattery's Shay was always there in his car to take his wife home, and every day they insisted on delivering Cassa to her bus. On Thursday, Lotty Slattery gave Cassa a thousand warnings, instructions, counsels and recommendations. They finally wished her every success and good luck. Putting her head out of the window of the shining red car, Lotty shouted, "You'll need all the fuckin' luck ya can get! Them nuns is holy terrors!"

On Sunday at midday, she had a phone call from Nicole. "I have an hour to spare this afternoon. Dress yourself up to be introduced to the nuns in San Salvatore. I have your cheque for you."

"Oh Nicky, have I got to? I was going to go over to Maisie Foley to make up a fourth."

Cassa was longing for a couple of hours' relaxation. A game of bridge would take her mind off the ordeal awaiting her tomorrow in the unknown San Salvatore and Maisie was always good for a laugh.

"Ring Maisie and put the game off to later on. Dermot wants the Reverend Mother to see you all togged up like the day you had the interview in his office. What were you wearing that day? Did you get your hair done? Wear high heels. Dermot says she is a very tall nun. What did you say? Of course height counts. An insignificant supervisor is not the right image. Put your heels on. Do your hair. And look nice. Be ready at three." Nicole put her phone down on the last word.

That was what Maisie had said: "Come over at three." It was short notice for Maisie to get someone else. With a big sigh, Cassa wondered why life had suddenly become so difficult. She explained to Maisie.

Maisie was a widow and she was a forgiving sort of a woman. "Sure I understand, Cass. Don't be so worried. I must hear all about the job. Of course I understand. I know

Nicole could steamroll a stone mountain.... I'm on one of her committees! Next Sunday, maybe? I'll be in touch. Bye!"

Nicole was glamorous in a pale yellow suit, her hair freshly tinted, her perfume most exotic. She looked Cassa over. "Yes, you'll do. Almost too sober, but you'll pass. I'm not mad on that shade of lipstick, a bit insipid, but for this occasion, I suppose dull is better. Get in. I have to be back by five. We are going down to the Brosnans in Gorey for dinner. Business friends in Dermot's Wexford branch."

The suburb of Seacoast was less than twenty minutes in the car.

"You got on all right with Lotty Slattery," Nicole informed Cassa. "She gave a good account of you to the office. Just one or two comments about your being too pleasant with the cleaners, I think friendly was the word she used, or was it polite? Maybe it was all three! You will have to develop a stiff neck – and keep your distance."

"Nicky, it sounds so depressing. Where do you get all this stiff neck stuff?"

"I am quoting Dermot's words, and it is a good idea if you take them in."

Nicole pulled in to the hospital drive. This place was very different from Boley's; there were white painted garden seats, lawns and flowering trees. Cassa's heart lifted. Things had to be better here.

The Reverend Mother stood up from her desk when Nicole and Cassa were shown in. Evidently she had met Nicole before.

Towering over Cassa at six feet, four inches, she addressed the air above their heads: "Ah, you are Miss Blake. Welcome to San Salvatore. Please be seated, both of you. I have asked for tea to be sent in. My deputy, Sister Calasanctius, will be along shortly. If you..."

"Well, Reverend Mother," Nicole put in her speech quickly. "We will be here as briefly as possible. Miss Blake should be supplied with the chart, the map and the names of the women you have engaged."

A shrivelled elderly woman carried in a tray and placed it

on a side table. Whether they liked it or not, the idea of afternoon tea would not be deflected. The china was delicate, as were the tiny sandwiches in brown and white bread. Reverend Mother Bede had come of titled people and could not be expected to tolerate low standards for herself, and certainly not for her hospital.

"All in due course, Mrs Tyson. There are priorities in all things. Firstly, we will take our tea."

Out of the corner of her eye, Cassa saw the muscles tighten on Nicole's face, but nothing was said. She would be reporting back to Dermot. Her smoothest voice came out of her tensed mouth: "Oh, but of course, Reverend Mother, how charming of you to think of it."

"I take mine black," intoned the nun, "but there is cream and sugar."

Afraid to be caught munching should questions be asked, Cassa did not take a sandwich. Nicole, taking her cue from the nun's manner, disdained the offered plate. The nun had three of the delicious-looking titbits with her black tea.

Reverend Mother Bede made quite a ritual of afternoon tea, finally using a serviette to polish off the corners of her mouth.

Now another nun entered, older, and angular in face and figure. Her nose jutted, her cheekbones jutted, even her elbows under the heavy habit were poking sideways.

"Sister Calasanctius," announced the Reverend Mother, "Mrs Tyson of Tyson Associates, and she has brought for our inspection the prospective supervisor, Miss Blake."

Cassa lowered her eyes for fear a tell-tale grin would escape on to her face. There was a silence during which the two nuns weighed and assessed Miss Blake like a pound of haddock.

"I will take you on a tour of our hospital, Miss," said Sister Calasanctius. Cassa and Nicole stood up.

"Only Miss Blake," said Sister Calasanctius, and her tone indicated who was boss in these quarters.

Out in the corridor, she produced several folders from behind her pelerine. Her fingers were skeletally bony.

"Take this in your hand, Miss; this is the map of our hospital. This other lists the women who aim to be engaged – probationers of course, the same as you are. The chart of jobs, time allowed and days of the week will be supplied to you on Monday morning. It is a confidential document, never to be removed. You will lodge it in the office before you leave the building, collect it each morning. I hope you are listening? The chart must be in my office every night of the week."

"What happens to it overnight, Sister?"

"I study it, Miss. That should be obvious."

Cassa began to feel as if she were being hypnotised. She shook herself and looked around.

"We are now in the convent," said the nun, "not as large an area as it used to be. A strictly private area and forbidden to the cleaners. You saw Annie who brought in the tea? Annie is our personal help. She is responsible for the convent. She has been with the Order of San Salvatore for fifty years. She does all the work, cleaning, cooking, laundering. With the exception of our private chapel, which task will fall to you, the supervisor.

"Sister Chapel-Sacristan is in sole charge of our private chapel and she will direct your work. Do you speak German? A pity you don't. Sister Chapel never learned English. However, I have written out some words and phrases which you would do well to commit to memory. Our private chapel will be your own sacred task: none of the other cleaning women may enter the convent."

Cassa felt a natural repugnance towards this nun, but she kept telling herself that the hospital was hygienically airy with many of the windows looking out to the sea. The contrast with Boley's dingy wards was in itself reassuring. Here the female wards and the male wards were on different floors. The top floor was given over to children's ailments and provision was made for the children's visitors in an enclosed roof garden.

"Do you have drugs-treatment patients here, Sister?" Cassa asked.

"Certainly not," the nun answered sharply. "Alcohol units, yes. Drug units, no."

Well, that's a relief, Cassa thought.

"Now, in this wing," the nun told her, "we have rooms for full-paying patients. These rooms will be cleaned meticulously every day at the same time, eleven-thirty a.m. to twelve midday. Some of these rooms are occupied long term. Some occupants treat their rooms as they may have treated their homes, neglectfully. You will oversee these rooms yourself, and you will not allow the cleaners to forget that these are private hospital rooms, not a bed and breakfast. A hospital, remember!"

A middle-aged nun with a high complexion emerged from one of the private rooms. Cassa noticed that Sister Calasanctius looked critically at this nun before she effected an introduction.

*   *   *

"Sister Gentlemen's Privates," she said, "this is the supervisor of the cleaners. Her name is Blake. She will be here on Monday. If you have any special instructions, you can give them to her then."

She did not touch Cassa, but seemed nonetheless to guide her rapidly along the corridors. The tour was over. Sister Calasanctius maintained a grim silence until Cassa was delivered back to the Reverend Mother's door, then the nun said abruptly, "I expect punctuality. Seven thirty on Monday morning."

On the way home, Nicole was in great form. The first obstacle was out of the way. She felt she had been at her best with the overwhelming nun.

"I certainly have clinched that deal – did you ever see anything like the size of that nun! I knew I could handle them. You were a bit cringey, Cass. Remember what I told you about the stiff neck. Watch me more than you do!"

Nicole knew how expert she was, and Dermot was

learning. One of his partners had used the gilded word "professional" about her work only yesterday.

"You were almost right," she said to Cassa. "Almost. At least you were quiet and ladylike. That's what nuns like. The women are not engaged yet, so you will be able to train them from the start."

"Train them?" Cassa echoed.

"Yes, of course. The way Mrs Slattery trained you. Don't dirty your hands. Let the cleaners do the work. You supervise."

"Did you know I have to clean the convent chapel on my own, with a German-speaking nun to supervise me?"

"Sure, what dirt could there be in a chapel?" asked Nicole cleverly. "There are only a few nuns left now. Fifteen minutes, probably less."

"Maybe it's a big chapel from the days when they had many nuns."

"A bit of a little oratory," said Nicole who had not seen it.

"Incidentally," she added, "one of Dermot's right-hand men will be here in the morning in case of a hitch. The contract is signed up for a year, and at the end of the year it will be permanent. This fellow, I think his name is Garry Something, has been dealing with these nuns. They had their own skivvies up to now and they may be trying to hang on to them. Leave that to him. No, I'm sorry, I can't come in for a cup of tea. I have to rush. Don't look so dismal! Think of the invaluable work experience you are going to get. Oh, I nearly forgot. This is your cheque from Dermot. In the future, I will be the one looking after your cheque."

Unfolding the cheque and reading the amount gave Cassa a lift. A hundred and twenty pounds a week would make it possible to keep the car, and there were a few bills outstanding, including the vet who had put Fred and Mindo to sleep.

She heard the phone as she opened the door. Unexpectedly, it was Lotty Slattery.

"Ya don't mind, do ya - I got your number from Tysons. Shay and me were talkin' about ya. Yer too good fer that job,

Shay can get ya a better job in a bookie's office, bigger pay and easier. Shay doesn't think ya have the hard gall for the nuns. He says it's their vocation to work like galley slaves. The rest of us is only human, Shay says. Think about it, Miss. Here's my number."

Cassa wrote it down. "I am so glad to hear from you, Lotty," she said.

"Shay an' me took a fancy to ya, Miss. Think about it, Miss, an' keep in touch."

If only she could be truthful to Lotty Slattery and admit she was in this unwanted job simply because she was the sister-in-law of Mr Contract Cleaning. She hoped Lotty would never find out.

CHAPTER TWENTY-SEVEN

O N MONDAY MORNING Cassa pulled up her car in the
hospital car-park at the same moment as Dermot
Tyson's deputy.

"Good morning. I am Garry Delaney, and I think you must
be Miss Blake? Mr Tyson hopes I can smooth the path for
you in here. The nuns are not used to the idea of contract
cleaning. It is probable that they feel they are losing control
of the reins of power." He had the accent of a New York TV
cop. Cassa's smile was timid as they walked into the hospital
together.

The night porter was in the hall, and he indicated a straggling queue of women along a side corridor. "Here since six
o'clock," he announced.

Exactly at seven o'clock, Reverend Mother Bede sailed
down the staircase, her robes billowing to each side. She lost
no time in lofty salutations, nodding and waving impartially.

"As I told you last week, Mr Delany, I am literally your only
friend from the convent on the committee, the consensus of
opinion being that we should retain the domestic staff we
had before the hospital was re-sited."

"Yes, yes, Sister, of course," Delaney put in quickly, "and
you were very wise to change. May we..."

The big nun held up her hand to silence him. "And I am
repeating this because I want to make an impression on Miss
Blake. The contract is for one year only, and it will take at
least that number of months to convince the committee, and
indeed to convince the teaching staff here, that contract
cleaning can do a good job, compared to the fact that previously we had cleaners to hand round the clock.

Delaney was ready with his reply. "Sister, that day is gone.
No one can get twenty-four-hours-a-day service, not even paying four times what the hospitals are paying. That's a fact.
Far better a mechanised cleaner fully supervised: in, out and
gone! Hasn't to be housed or fed, or endured underfoot!"

The Reverend Mother seemed to be prepared to argue. "Glancing at those potential mechanised cleaners in that corridor, I find myself very doubtful. I see there the parochial derelicts sometimes employed by San Salvatore in extreme shortage of staff. They could start the mechanics of cleaning on themselves!"

Cassa was taken aback at this lack of charity in a nun, but Garry Delaney had a quick response. "We'll weed them out! Miss Blake is a top-notcher at that game. You understand, Sister, that we are bound to try to attempt hiring all those referred to us by the local Labour Exchange. But not bound to take them, not at all! We have a nucleus in reserve!"

Cassa made a conscious effort to keep the wonder of all this weeding and notchering out of her eyes.

"I am glad to hear about your nucleus in reserve," said the nun. "There was another matter. We had two good women on our staff for many years: Mrs Lacey and Mrs Casey. Excellent workers. Sister Chapel is very particular. If the job is not done absolutely correctly, she insists on redoing it entirely. Now I must save her that, as she is getting old, almost eighty-three, and full of arthritis, poor soul. So, I am suggesting Lacey and Casey be employed for the convent as before."

Cassa gave an inward sigh of relief. That chapel had begun to loom in her mind like a cathedral.

"Certainly, Sister," Delaney replied. "But of course, on the same terms and hours as the other women starting today."

The Reverend Mother gave the impression of being shocked. "Oh dear me! I promised Lacey and Casey that I would get them an extra shilling or two more than the others – per hour, that is. For their long and loyal service. You could joggle the contract a little, I am sure you could."

"Joggle means splitting, Sister, and I could not do that. Contract cleaning is costed to its very lowest, down to the last penny. You are suggesting the impossible, Sister. To give two women more would mean employing fewer women, and making it harder for the rest. Those two women can come along and be part of the full team. If the chapel is their choice, that could be arranged as Miss Blake sees fit."

The Reverend Mother now flounced away rather than sailed, but her skirts billowed out as before.

Now another woman appeared on the scene.

"Miss Blake, meet Doris Kenny from the office. Weeding-out is Doris's speciality!

Miss Kenny and Mr Delaney smiled rather grimly at each other as two people sharing a bad joke. Miss Kenny stepped in front.

"You can stand back now, Miss Blake, and watch this performance. Many of these women will fall by the wayside, and you will be the one to engage new cleaners, or cleaning staff, as we are to call them. So this is how it is done."

Mr Delaney was now ready to leave. "My blessing on the work, Miss Blake," he said. "I am under orders to take you and Doris out to lunch. Would you two honour me?"

Cassa, surprised at being invited out for lunch, hesitated. But why not? By the time this first morning was over, she would really need a lunch. She smiled her acceptance, and he went off.

"Let's get started now," said the formidable Miss Kenny. "We need to have these women dispersed to their jobs well before eight o'clock. Take this ledger, Miss Blake, and get the names down as we go along. Now, first please."

There was a constant shuffle and push as the women edged forward. The first woman gave her name as Jinny Corcoran. She sidled up to Miss Kenny.

"Ye know me, Miss. Jinny Corcoran."

"Oh yes, I remember you, Jinny. Put her name down now, Miss Blake. Cleaning over in the Training College, wasn't it. What happened?"

"We were moved out to the new flats, miss. The bus fare back would ate the profit. Miss, would you take on me daughter along with me. She's a thumpin' fine worker, strong as a bull-elephant." And Jinny pushed forward a stout teenager.

"What's your name?" Miss Kenny asked the girl.

"Annette, that's what her name is. I'll look after her, Miss," said Jinny.

"What age are you, Annette?"

"She's sixteen, Miss. Sixteen with the help of God."

"And dumb, apparently," said Miss Kenny, "or are you her spokesman, Jinny? Now, shut up and let me hear her voice. You want to work here, Annette?"

The girl mumbled and Miss Kenny repeated the question.

"Naw," muttered the girl and her mother gave her a resounding clatter on the back. "Naw," she repeated loudly, "but I suppose I'll have to!"

The mother pushed the girl over to Cassa to get their names down.

A fine busty woman now pushed her way forward. "My name's Jane Duffy. I never worked at cleaning. I was a charge-hand in the Felso Laundry. The Labour Exchange sent me."

"A charge-hand! Nice pickins! What happened?"

"Laundries are closin', aren't they?" said Jane belligerently, "washin' machines on the Kathleen Mavourneen the same as fridges."

Show your reference to Miss Blake, Jane, and get your address in the book. Oh, by the way Jane, what age are you?"

"I would have thought that was my own business, but I'm forty-six for your information!"

"Oh indeed!" said Miss Kenny. "Long life to you! We start punctually at seven-thirty a.m."

"I would rather go on the afternoon shift, miss. I never get up early: bad for the nerves!"

"There is no afternoon shift," said Miss Kenny shortly. "Next."

"I was only askin'!" said Jane Duffy. She gave Cassa a haughty look, and departed through the front door, without leaving her address.

"It takes all sorts!" Miss Kenny glanced at Cassa. "Better without her sort! Next."

Two women stepped forward together. "We'd like to work together. We live next door to each other in the new flats. We worked in the old hospital before it was changed to here."

Miss Kenny looked them over. They were long past middle age, frazzled and shabby.

"What are your names? One at a time please."

"I'm Mrs O'Connor. Everyone calls me Bid."

"I'm Mrs Kinch, Teresa."

"And you worked for the nuns before?"

"Yeh. We worked for Sister Fidelis."

"Ah, that will be the womens' wards. Well, we will see if she will have you back. Put your names down. If Fidelis turns you away this morning, report to Miss Blake. Now, you. What's your name?"

An old lady shuffled into line. She had a sweet wrinkled face, and was painfully slow.

"Loney, Mary. I worked in the old hospital. In the kitchens. I left to nurse me man. Sister Cathaldus will remember me. He's dead now, me husband."

Miss Kenny consulted her record book.

"And sad to relate," she said, "so is Sister Cathaldus. There is no indoor kitchen work. All that side is leased out to a catering company. Why not ask the nuns about their kitchen?"

"I done that, Miss, and they said to come to you. Please, Miss."

Miss Kenny made an aside to Cassa, "Nuns take the biscuit for passing the buck."

The little old woman pleaded gently, "Please, Miss, I'm a good worker. If you could speak for me..." Miss Kenny did not seem able to be as brusque with this woman as she had been with the others. Cassa was pleased to see a softer side to this stiff presence.

"I need the extra money very badly to pay me debts: Maskey's Funeral Parlour has me hounded to pay off the balance by the week for me husband."

"The funeral was expensive, was it?" Miss Kenny asked.

"It was the family, Miss, they wanted to do him proud. He was a good father to them sons."

"And can't they help you?"

"Oh but they would, Miss," and the old woman trembled, "only two of them is after gettin' laid off and the third one went on the boat to Liverpool."

Miss Kenny turned to Cassa and asked in a low voice, "Could you keep her by you, and work out some odds and ends?"

"Of course," Cassa responded warmly as if she had been dealing with such problems for years. Her head was in a whirl. She wished with all her heart that she was Lotty Slattery.

Miss Kenny was glancing at the women left in the queue. A mini-skirted teenager stepped forward. She had bright blonde hair caught up on the top of her head, large inquisitive eyes and long legs in green tights.

"And who are you?" asked Miss Kenny. "Have I seen you before?"

"You saw me in Adolfo's Café this morning. I served yer coffee, Miss."

"So you did! You are the waitress there?"

"Was, Miss. I just gave me notice. Adolfo grabs me tits every time I go up to the counter, and if I go in behind it, he's lookin' up me pants. I just told Adolfo to piss off."

"You have never done cleaning work," stated Miss Kenny, to which the teenager replied loftily, "What's in it! Nothing to it!"

"Take her name," Miss Kenny told Cassa, "there's bound to be dropouts. She looks as if she has a bit of energy, but by the end of this morning, she may prefer Adolfo!" The girl's name was Margaret Riley, and she lived at the back of the flats, she said.

Miss Kenny walked along the queue. "We only need four more. Are you two together? Are you sisters?"

They were young women, both heavily made-up with rouge and lipstick and eyebrow pencil. One spoke for both.

126

"I'm Frolie, and she's Dolly; we're sisters. We worked for the nuns in the Training College. They know us."

"Are you married? Have you children?"

"Yes, we are," said Frolie, "yes we have – one each."

"And your long-suffering mother will crèche them for you?"

Cassa was watching Miss Kenny's eyes, rejecting as she walked. Oh, I'm glad she is not taking that woman, Cassa was thinking, she is like a scarecrow. And that one: what a pong! Oh, she is taking the next one.

"What's the name? Em McLaughlin? Oh, sorry, just M. Fine, I have that."

She looks a steady solid sort of middle-aged woman. Maybe she will be one of the standbys. Cassa failed to notice the flinty eyes of M. McLaughlin behind the spectacles.

"One more, and that's it," announced Miss Kenny. A woman stepped timidly forward, "I'm Mrs Clarke. Sister Fidelis said she would speak for me."

"Fidelis said your husband is here in hospital, is that you? Yes, I see your name here. Rita Clarke?"

"Yes, Miss. He came in sudden."

"What's wrong with your husband? Heart attack?"

Mrs Clarke was very humble. "Miss, they said he would have to take the cure, but he doesn't want to."

"Oh, a one-over-the-eight man?"

"Whiskey, Miss, the sister said."

"Oh indeed! Is it to be near him you are looking for this work?"

"Oh, I shouldn't go near him, Miss. He'd kill me for drawin' attention. It's for the money, Miss. When he's in hospital, there's nothin' comin' in. There's five children, Miss, the eldest is eight."

Doris Kenny looked gloomily at Cassa. "I've said it before and I'll say it again: a pack of lousy bastards! Men in general. Who'll see to the kids if you are working here?"

"Me mother is comin' up from the country, Miss, from Wexford. Can you take me in?"

"Well, normally I wouldn't do it. It never works out if a woman has a husband a patient in the same hospital. You're the one who should be in hospital. You look very poorly to me. But the nun spoke for you. Is she related to you?"

Mrs Clarke hesitated. "Well, a kinda cousin."

"Right then. It is just on eight o'clock. Time for the day to begin, and here come my trusty lieutenants, Rose and Ethel. On time as ever. Girls, meet your new supervisor, Miss Blake – she's nearly ready."

Cassa had finished writing down the names; now she was rewriting them clearly:

> Jinny Corcoran and Annette
> Mrs Bid O'Connor
> Mrs Teresa Kinch
> Mary Loney
> Margaret Riley
> Frolie Molloy
> Dolly Callaghan
> M. McLaughlin
> Rita Clarke.

"Ten names," Cassa said looking up from the ledger. "Is that enough?"

Now Miss Kenny was bright and cheerful. "Two more," she smiled, "Rose and Ethel, for whom, in due course, you will thank God."

CHAPTER TWENTY-EIGHT

GARRY DELANEY TOOK the two ladies to the Seacoast Inn for lunch. The lunch itself was nice and the view over the sea was superb. Cassa's brain was fairly pulsing with a dozen questions, but long habit made her a good guest. Work experience, she reminded herself, that is what you need: work experience and then move on.

"So, the morning went off well," said Garry. "I rang the office, and they sounded pleased."

"Oh, thank you," said Cassa as she returned her gaze to the waves breaking over the white rocks. "A lovely scene is a cure for a disturbed imagination." That was one of Sadora's Rules.

She would guard her tongue. No doubt, every syllable went back to the godalmighty Tyson, to whom she was not related at all. Nicole had informed her that Dermot had said so: "You are plain Miss Blake."

"It was a first day," said Doris Kenny, "and I was there, so the nuns kept their distance, although I saw a dark skirt disappearing behind a door now and then. We had the same problem at the start down in Cork. The good nuns get on with their teaching, the disgruntled ones interfere. It's never the way it was done in their day!"

Garry Delaney's manner was soothing. "Cassa is exactly right for the nuns. No need to worry; you will have them eating out of your hand before long!"

A gruesome prospect, Cassa thought.

"I must not prolong this delightful lunch," she said. "I promised myself a long afternoon in the garden while this weather lasts. You will excuse me?"

"You live on your own?" enquired her host.

"I am never alone," she replied. "My sister and my nieces are in and out all day."

Miss Kenny went on at some length about a dog she used to have. "His name was Walkabout," she said, "but he always landed back on the doorstep at night. I had to have him put down when I bought the apartment. No animals allowed! But he was fifteen years old and going deaf. I never knew how he escaped being knocked down by a lorry which he couldn't hear."

Mr Delaney was not interested in Walkabout. He kept on returning the conversation to Cassa, and her house and her garden. She supposed he was trying to put her at her ease. Afterwards she remembered that she had failed to ask him any questions. His wife? His children? His garden?

She was unused to hearing her name so freely spoken on short acquaintance. Was she being patronised? His over-cordial attitude confused her and prevented her from asking Miss Kenny the questions about the hospital which seemed important to Cassa. For instance, was there a cloakroom and toilet, for the use of the cleaners? A room which the supervisor could lock, to hold their coats, their bags, wet shoes and umbrellas, all the paraphernalia they were carrying this morning in plastic bags. A room was essential for daily women. She had noted the need for it in Lotty Slattery's domain.

She tried to formulate the questions and could not, for lack of what she thought of as the necessary work experience. Inept questions on her first day would betray how little she knew. "Right for the nuns" must be proved to earn Nicky's begrudged praise.

CHAPTER TWENTY-NINE

OVERNIGHT, CASSA'S RESOLUTION hardened. Face the nuns with courtesy, or the battle is lost. She presented herself at the hospital at seven a.m. The night-porter was yawning behind his desk.

Cassa smiled nicely. "Had you a long, hard night?" she asked in a deliberate effort to make a friend of him.

"Not so bad, Miss," he replied, "one street accident for casualty. Prefer to be busy. A couple of heart attacks keeps me on me toes. You're early, aren't you, Miss?"

"I was hoping to have a word with Sister Calasanctius?"

He glanced up at the hospital clock. "She is about due," he said. "They have their mass and then they have their breakfast, but I doubt if that nun bothers to eat! Is that her now?"

"Sister, may I have a few words with you?" Cassa stepped forward.

If the nun was surprised, she did not show it. "I am leaving yesterday's chart in the office for you, but as you are here, here it is. You will find my remarks in red ink." The nun turned away.

"Please, Sister!" Cassa's heart sank as she realised the meaning of "red ink". "Please, Sister, I have a request."

"Yes?" The nun's tone was even colder on the single interrogative note.

Cassa steeled herself. "I would be obliged if you would indicate to me the rooms designed for the cleaners' utensils and their coats."

"There is no 'room designed'."

"There has to be," Cassa said steadily. "The contract says so." Well, it should say so, Cassa thought.

The nun led the way to the side corridor and flung open the door under the stairs. With a bony finger she indicated the cubby-hole.

"That won't do," Cassa said politely. "That won't do at all.

The women need a proper place and their own toilet. They need, and I need, privacy."

"Privacy for cleaners!" The nun was shocked, quite genuinely so shocked she was rooted to the ground.

Cassa, whose knees were shaking, was politely adamant. "Yes, Sister, privacy. There must be available space here, with all the recent cut-backs and closures."

The nun had not climbed down, and her voice was as frigid as ever, when she replied, "Reverend Mother Bede decides these things. If she agrees to the empty room on the end of this corridor, I will let you know."

Which could be weeks, or never. Cassa said firmly, "I need this room within the next few minutes."

The nun marched ahead of Cassa to the far end of the corridor. "Temporarily!" She uttered the word as she opened the door.

"And the toilet?" enquired Cassa.

The nun pointed, then she indicated a key hanging on the door.

"Temporarily!" she said again as she walked away. Cassa took the key, went into the room, and closed the door. She let out a big sigh that was almost a triumphant whoop of confidence. The room must have been used by medical students. There were books on the wall-shelves, a stack of chairs and a table.

As the women straggled in, Cassa indicated the where-abouts of the toilet for their use and encouraged them to select an individual hook for their coats and bags. Then they took all the polishes, buckets and dusters out of the cubby-hole and into the room. The women took the change for grant-ed. Cleaning was cleaning even if the cloakroom was a palace.

Quickly, and in a very friendly way, Cassa indicated the red ink markings on the chart, warning them that some of the nuns were on the lookout for complaints because they were not in favour of the new system. They could see in their tired way that the supervisor was doing her best to be reasonable.

Rose and Ethel were always the last to get in, but they were never late. They arrived in an old Morris Minor, decked in their overalls, carrying their own buckets and polish, all ready to go, like stock characters thrust in to get the show on the road and keep it rolling.

The very sight of them started off Cassa's day with a degree of optimism. Rose and Ethel were born to clean big hospitals. Each was a genius on the job, swift and eager, oblivious of the lowliness of the task, perpetually light-hearted, always at the supervisor's elbow when things went wrong.

They went as a leaven among the other women, got twice as much work out of the sloppy bunch and did four times more work themselves. As the days turned into weeks, Cassa would come to depend totally on Rose and Ethel, bluff-callers and knockers though they were, and to dread the day when their high destiny would move them on to get another contract going in another hospital.

In the first week, Cassa went forward in a state of panic-stations on all floors. It was plain to her that the nuns were well aware they were not getting the promised crack corps of top-efficient cleaners. Whenever she came on the scene, a black veil whisked into an office. The cleaners very quickly re-named Sister Calasanctius, Callous Anxious, and they imitated the way she dragged her bony finger on sills and ledges.

After a month, just as Cassa was beginning to breathe easily, the first pounce came. They were all emerging from the lift on different floors, Cassa with old Mrs Loney and Margaret on the second floor. She had put them together because Margaret from Adolfo's Café was inclined to be skittish. A grim-faced nun was waiting.

"Yes, Sister?" asked Cassa apprehensively. The nun had a rosy-cheeked face, which could have looked pleasant, but didn't.

"I am Sister Gentlemen's Privates. Are you the supervisor, or who?"

"I'm Miss Blake."

"The supervisor. You sent these two women to work on my

floor. I object to that girl; she is too young, also she is stupid. I object to that woman; she is old, slow and foolish."

Cassa was taken aback by the unfeeling hardness of the nun's tone. "Sister, they are good workers. Is something left undone?" And in an aside to Margaret, she said, "Run and fetch Rose from the nursery floor."

"You get that young one off my gentlemen's privates immediately. Whatever about the old woman, I cannot have teenagers hereabouts. Gentlemen's privates are the élite of San Salvatore and I intend them to remain so." The nun wheeled off up the corridor.

Rose and Margaret appeared. "Hark at that!" said Rose. "Gentlemen's privates are élite! Come on, Granny, we'd better shift." She pushed Mrs Loney ahead.

"We will go down in the lift," Cassa said to Margaret, who was grinning.

In the cloakroom, she asked, "What did you do to vex the nun? She was very angry."

Margaret went on grinning. "Vex her? Ya couldn't please her."

"Margaret, the nun was really mad. Speak up, or take your coat and go. What happened?"

"That nun's an old pig. I was only talkin' to a fella in his room. He's a bank manager. His name is James Butler. He said he liked me."

"A sick man? When was this?"

"Oh, several days ago. And look it, are we supposed to dust the tops of the doors, every day? I had to stand on a chair. That's when it started."

Cassa looked at the tiny skirt, and sighed. "Tell me why the nun was angry?"

"I was kissin' the man in the bed when she put her head in around the door."

"A sick man? "

"He wasn't sick. He broke his leg fallin' off a ladder in his garden. Anyway he was old: he must be nearly forty. And he asked me, anyway!"

"Margaret, do I recall that you objected to Adolfo? You gave up your job there for a worse job here, because of Adolfo's attentions?"

"Adolfo is a bleedin' pervert. Work you to the bone and expect you to oblige him in the lav..."

"Margaret, I don't want to hear this. All you did was to give, when asked to give, Mr Butler a kiss?"

"Well, she caught me before when he was payin' me for a bit of a rub. Honest, that was all, Miss, a bit of a rub. Sure, you know what I mean."

"Margaret, I knew you were young, but I took you on because I really thought you were in moral danger from the café man."

"Oh, but I was, I was – moral everything. Adolfo is a moral shit."

"Now I think you are well able to look out for yourself. Give back the money you took from that sick man."

"Took? Me? He shoved it in me pocket and now it's spent – a week ago. I was goin' to be given more when that ole nun walked in."

What should she do in a situation like this? The girl was actually a very quick cleaner. Cassa said, "You go to the nursery floor, and I'll fill in with Mrs Loney."

"I won't do it again, Miss, I promise on me oath." The great big inquisitive eyes filled with innocent tears. "I love bein' here, and I'm stoppin' with Loney in her two rooms."

"We are wasting time," Cassa said, but she had to smile as she shooed the girl out of the cloakroom.

The efficient Rose had whisked through the work leaving only a few dishes for Mrs Loney to wash in the nurses' kitchen.

Although most days were monotonous, some brought calamities, large or small, which gave Callous Anxious the opportunity to fill her notebook with complaints. The supervisor had to be on all floors at all times, and she found that as time went on, she had to cover up for the cleaner who was not a true perfectionist and some who were bone idle. Others were great, and Jinny Corcoran was the hardest worker of all.

Jinny and her daughter Annette were cleaning out the long Common Room which doubled as an examination hall. A nun was peering through the door jamb at them. When she saw Cassa, she moved swiftly into another room, shutting the door behind her. Cassa trusted Jinny to do a thorough job as she herself proceeded to spray and polish the bookcases lining the corridor. It was impossible not to overhear their conversation. Jinny was a tireless talker and worker, but Annette was flagging.

"Gawd, Ma, I'm not goin' to be able to stick this work much longer. Jeez, I'm after breakin' one of me nails!"

"Your nails are like Chinamen's: why don't you cut them? Keep goin' till we get up on the third landin'. I want to see out the winda if Eileen brought the babby to the clinic. I told her to stand in out of the wind where I'll be able to see her. Can you see the time on the church clock out that winda? I told her to give me the beck if the babby is all right."

"What'll y'do," asked Annette, "if Eileen doesn't give ya the beck?"

"I'll go down, of course!" said Jinny, and Cassa could judge by the breathy voice that Jinny was vigorously rubbing away.

"'You-know-who' will love that! Throw over the can."

Annette must have been at the window. Cassa heard her cry out. "Look, Ma. There's Eileen comin' out of the clinic. Ma, she hasn't got the chisler with her! Ma, she's cryin'!"

"Keep beltin' away," shouted Jinny. She ran out and down the stairs. Cassa slipped behind a bookcase as she saw the peeping nun step out of the office and into the Common Room.

"Jeez Mary an' Joseph!" shrieked Annette, "I never heard ye! Ya give me clots in me blood!"

"There is dust between the banisters," accused Callous Anxious, "and where is your mother, or co-worker?"

"I don't know where she is!" Out of Jinny's presence, Annette is less than respectful. "Buzz off!"

136

"How dare you speak to me like that! Brazen impudence. I will report you to the supervisor!"

Cassa stepped into the room. "I will take over with you, Annette. Just go as you were going." With her back to the nun, Cassa began to work.

"The other woman left her post!" said the nun loudly. "Reverend Mother will hear of this!"

CHAPTER THIRTY

LIFE WAS DIVIDED now: the supervisory Cassa was shrugged off on the short journey from the hospital to Firenze; turning the car into the avenue, the gardening Cassa took over. Although she still missed Fred and Mindo, the house did not seem a lonely place now, but rather a sanctuary.

Cassa found the work tiring and the endless bickering of the women very hard to take even though she had sympathy for them. To knuckle under to the nuns who didn't want her there was not easy either.

She stared out at her mother's fading garden and thought of the Sadora Rules: "It will strengthen your character, dear." And that was only about making her bed properly or standing her books upright on the shelves; if she had any character at all to strengthen, she would never have agreed to take this rotten job.

Every day when she closed Firenze's big hall door, she shut it resoundingly. When the echoes died down, the rest of the world was left outside.

Sometimes she met her nieces, Orla and Sandra, on Sunday mornings in the paper shop in Stillorgan. She evaded their questions about her job in San Salvatore, even if she thought an incident funny enough to make them laugh. She was resolved not to let a word of criticism get back to Dermot Tyson, to be reinterpreted en route by Nicky, whose lecturing phone calls almost reduced Cassa to tears.

"Of course, the nuns are all very nice, Sandra."

"But Daddy said that... about all the complaints... I heard Mummy telling him..."

"Oh well, they work so hard and it is a great hospital, and anyway, I'd much rather hear about your nuns in school and how you two are getting on. Come on, the whole story for Aunty Cass!"

An odd time, she rang Lotty Slattery for sensible advice on some of her work problems. She assured Lotty that the nice nuns were really nice; just one was hard to take.

"I never could stand nuns," Lotty told her, "the way they used to pick on us in school. Shay says they must be frustrated for want of a man."

So Cassa said less about the nuns, and more about timing the jobs in cleaning. There, Lotty was brilliant.

Well into the fourth month, she had a phone call from Garry Delaney.

"I should have got back to you much sooner." To her surprise he added, "You have been on my conscience."

"Thank you for ringing. You should not have had to worry. I got a special room for the cleaners."

"I told you the nuns would be eating out of your hands."

Cassa let that go. "And how are you?" she enquired politely.

"Glad to be back in Dublin," he said cheerily. "Cork, Limerick, Tralee. Next week, Waterford and Wexford."

Politely, she asked, "Introducing the great new idea, contract cleaning?"

"That's it," he said, "and it's going very well. I rang to invite you out to dinner." Said as if he assumed she would accept.

"Mr Delaney, is this a business dinner?"

"No way! What a thought!" He laughed. "Did I put it badly? Would you have dinner with me before I go off on another trip?"

How old was this man? Scarcely thirty. "What night had you in mind?" she asked cautiously.

"Friday would be perfect." His voice was very pleased.

"If you please," Cassa asked, "may I get back to you? Perhaps you would give me a phone number?"

Would I like to go out to dinner? Not especially with him, Cassa thought. Delaney was what Lotty called, "one of Tyson's boys". Best to ring Nicky.

"I haven't much time, Cass. Have you something on your

139

mind about San Salvatore? I have my own office now, down two doors from Tysons. Come in there and I'll sort you out. Right?"

"Hold, hold, it's not exactly about the hospital."

"Well, what is it about, and don't take all night."

"Is is all right to accept a dinner invitation with Garry Delaney?"

There was a second's silence before Nicole got the name into context, then she squealed, "Of course you said no? Do you mean lunch, a business lunch?"

"It was an invitation to dine with him on Friday night," Cassa spaced out the words patiently.

"Why would he invite you out to dinner? What have you been saying to him? Has he been up to the house?"

"Nicky, I don't know. Nothing. And no."

"What's the matter with you, Cass? You never used to talk like that - abrupt! Have you got a swelled head because you are out in the big world with the grown-ups? In a job? Enticing the men? What have you said to Delaney?"

Cassa sighed. Some great job to get puffed-up about. "But Nicky, didn't you say that if I got a job, I might get a man?" She made a face at all Tyson's Associates into the mirror over the walnut table.

Her sister was shrieking into the phone: "You certainly cannot go out to dinner, or anywhere else, with one of Dermot's employees! Are you out of your stupid mind! The arrangement is, and you were told, that you are Cassandra Blake, a person in poor circumstances, a plain spinster," and the phone was banged down.

Later in the evening, Nicole was on the phone. "Just when everything was going along fine for me, you have to act the donkey as usual. Dermot is furious with the idea of your testing your strength – that is what he said, testing your strength – after less than six months on the job. Dermot will deal with Garry Delaney. Don't you dare phone this man. Dermot will see you in his office on Friday at five o'clock."

Cassa sat at the piano. She looked across at the fireplace

140

and pictured her Papa in his armchair, a rug across his knees, a book in his hands.

"Mozart or Chopin, House Bird? I think this is a night for Chopin."

Her fingers found their own way across the keys and the melody filled the room.

Brahms was Robert Gray's favourite composer. At Caragh Lake, he used to praise Cassa's playing, although the piano there was not a good one. Louise often said, "Cassa should have gone on with her music".

Cassa closed the piano and she closed her eyes to banish the face of a dead Louise, her beautiful face now made of jig-saw bits of marble, the once-brilliant eyes glaring up at the ceiling beyond which her adored Robert fornicated with a hoarse-voiced woman of low morals. Had it been Robert, sil-ver-haired and silver-tongued, or had it been the green and gold of Caragh Lake which created the deluded enchant-ment for twenty years?

Cassa made an immense effort, and, for the thousandth time, she forced her mind to think of something, anything, to draw down the misty curtain over the lake.

CHAPTER THIRTY-ONE

O N FRIDAY CASSA dressed carefully for the interview with
Dermot Tyson in Harcourt Street. She had things to say
about her job if she got the chance and if she were smart
enough with the words. At least she could look smart.

So she took the car all the way into the city and parked in
Tyson Associates' car-park. The staff were pouring out, free
for the weekend, all chatting and relaxed. Without even a
secretary in sight, she was ushered into his office.

"Ah there you are, come in, come in."

He had a decanter of sherry and two glasses on his desk.
"Your late father's favourite sherry, I am told, Croft Original.
I thought a little snifter would be nice after your long drive."

He poured the sherry and extended a glass to her. "Sit
down there, Cassa, where I can admire you. How is it you
never change a day?"

Cassa kept her eyes on the sherry. He must be drunk, she
thought. "Thank you," she said in an uncertain whisper.

"You are doing a great job out in Seacoast. I have reports
on my desk from Mother Bede, and also a daily sheet of complaints from Sister Calasanctius."

She raised her eyes in resentful amazement, and then she
lowered them back to the sherry. "A great job full of complaints?" she questioned fearfully.

"Cheer up, Cassa, not complaints about you personally,
although they made a big fuss about taking a room for the
cleaners." He was smiling.

She took heart. "That room was really needed."

"Oh, I'm sure, and once established, it will remain so.
Cassa, this is a personal matter, nothing to do with the nuns.
About Delaney."

Tyson came around the big desk and stood by her chair.
He took the glass from her hand and placed it on the desk. She
tried to stand up but her nerve was weak. Always with this man,
she saw over his shoulder her sister's face, and she was afraid.

She gathered her wits and her voice came out fairly strong: "I have seen Mr Delaney once on the day I started at San Salvatore, only on that day, and Miss Kenny was present all the time."

Tyson's voice was friendly, "You must have talked a lot during the lunch, all of you."

"Mostly about Miss Kenny's dog," that was all Cassa could remember.

"More than that, I think. He came away primed with information about your garden and your comfortable home left to you by your late father."

Cassa showed her surprise in her candid face. "I don't remember talking about Papa. About the garden, yes. He seemed interested in the garden."

"Having got your phone number, he now knows your address. It would not take an Agatha Christie to find out that my wife and you lived there, two sisters."

Cassa hoped it was anger rising in her throat, and not frustrated tears: "I did not ask for this job, and I am prepared to give it up this very minute." She stood up. "Right now," but her voice broke. She sought blindly for her handbag and a handkerchief.

To her horror, Tyson put his arm around her. Her head was against his chest and he was stroking the hair curling around her ears. In a moment he would be pressing against her. She recoiled in fear, knocking against the chair blindly.

"I'm all right! I'm all right! Look, I had no intention of going out to dinner with him or with anyone else. And I never told anyone that my sister is married to you. I don't know what Nicky has been saying about that."

Tyson pulled her towards him. She felt the force of his strong arms. "But I am," he said, "married to your sister, and I have your best interests at heart, as has Nicole and the girls. You need us to guide you, Cassa my dear."

He lowered his tone to one of tender concern. "Delaney is married and divorced. In America. He is paying alimony. The thought of your very comfortable home was very attractive to him, I am sure, your house and, no doubt, your extensive grounds."

Tyson's strong hand enclosed Cassa's shoulder. "In no time at all, he would have wormed his way into your confidence, started making up to you, staying late, maybe overnight on some excuse, the weather or some damn thing . I know his type. It is not a question of our close relationship, my dear Cassa, it is a question of your good name."

Tyson's breath was hot as fire against her cheek, his good looks like some tempting fruit so close to her face.

"Nicole knows I am speaking to you for your own good. I have spoken to Delaney. Employees at his level in Tyson Associates do not mix outside office hours. You will not be troubled by him again."

Cassa was afraid now that if he let her go, she would waver down to the floor like a small cloud.

His voice took on a confiding note: "I remember how you looked at eighteen, and you haven't changed a bit. Of course, you won't give up the job. And the job will improve. We will just remember we don't mix business and pleasure." Cassa could scarcely breathe. Tyson was not done. "Now we will kiss and make up," he said.

He released her very slowly as if he too were aware she might slide to the floor. He steadied her against the desk. "Never changed a bit, just as sweet as when you were a kid." His kiss was warm and firm. The barest tip of his tongue lightly licking her lips, pausing as if to taste the softness and then licking again. "Poor little Cassa," he murmured, "you need someone to take care of you."

She extended her hand to ward him off and then, when his hand also extended, she turned her back on him as she groped for the door.

"No, indeed you haven't changed," he laughed gently at her. "Come, this is the back stair. I'll lock up after you." His deep voice followed her as she raced across the car-park: "Drive safely, Cassa!"

Once out on the road, she had to pull in and strive to be calm. She sat staring at the Friday evening traffic for a few minutes. She was puzzled, and very afraid.

CHAPTER THIRTY-TWO

O**N SATURDAY MORNING** Cassa drove to San Salvatore with a firm decision in her mind. Firenze belonged to her and to her alone. She must take her life into her own hands. This was the last morning she would be going this road.

She would investigate the idea of taking in lodgers, students from the university near by. No matter if they burned the furniture, no matter if they played pop music half the night, she would have no one giving her orders, no nuns snooping, and no Dermot Tyson with his blazing eyes. Maybe even no Nicole, but she hoped she could still meet Orla and Sandra.

Nicole couldn't interfere. Firenze belonged to Cassa and to her alone. It was a century old now, and needed work done on it. If she hadn't to go out to work every day she would have time to paint all the doors and windows. Paint cost money, of course, but, as she turned into San Salvatore's car-park, Cassa was thinking that if her house fell to bits, this was her last morning here. Definitely.

On Saturdays, all the women turned up. This was the day they got their pay envelopes. M. McLaughlin always questioned hers, pretending to forget that she had taken a half-hour off here and there. She was an odd bod, not popular with the others.

As Jinny said every Saturday, "Yer woman is on the monopods! It affects the memory – it's the hot flushes: sends the blood to the brain!"

However, on Saturdays they worked well. There was no theatre to scrub out, and this left one woman with extra time to help the others.

Cassa remembered Jinny's conversation of the day before. She put Jinny and Annette on the nursery floor, and gave Margaret sole charge of the floor polisher on the corridors.

Margaret liked rolling the machine, and corridor work let

her see all that was going on. Confidently, she thought the young house doctors fancied her.

To keep Sister Theresa happy, Cassa took Mrs Loney to gentle-men's privates. They combined well and worked rapidly through the twelve private rooms. Cassa never glanced at the men in their beds. Apparently Sister made them stay in their beds until the cleaning was done.

"Supervisor," rapped out Sister Theresa, "Reverend Mother wishes to see you in her room. Is this old woman capable of finishing on her own?"

"We are almost finished, Sister. Mrs Loney will be able to do the nurses' kitchen on her own. I'll do this corridor, and that will be all."

"Reverend Mother said now," said the nun.

"Yes," said Cassa politely, "well, my now is ten minutes."

"Reverend Mother will be told you said so!" said the nun spitefully.

Quite suddenly, Cassa didn't care. She polished away and when she was quite finished she went rapidly through the hospital. Supervising is what I am supposed to be doing, she thought, as she glanced at her watch and hoped she would see no gaping undone places.

"Yes, Reverend Mother, you sent for me?"

The nun rose majestically from her large chair behind the large desk. Today Cassa wasn't cowed by this towering monster of a woman.

"A complaint, Reverent Mother?" she enquired.

"This time a request, Miss. Sister Chapel has been laid low with her arthritis rather worse than usual. Our chapel is always our priority."

Along with a dozen other priorities, Cassa thought, but she said, "The chapel was done yesterday." And Sister Chapel was teutonically efficient yesterday.

"Perhaps so," said the big nun in her West British accent as if addressing the troops, "but tomorrow is the feast day of St Werburga, Sister Chapel's patron saint. Sister Chapel works every day. Give one of the cleaners overtime."

"Is Sister Chapel in the infirmary?"

"No, oh no! She is not one for the lazy bed! She is seated in the chapel waiting."

"Our day ends at twelve-thirty," Cassa said, "and it is nearly that now."

"A request?" the Reverend Mother insisted in the voice that brooked no denial.

For the very last time, thought Cassa.

When the women had all gone, Cassa went into the convent. She gathered up the special equipment used only in the chapel. The German nun was seated in front of the altar, a blanket wrapped around her knees and her two gnarled hands gripped a heavy walking stick.

"I am sorry to hear you are in pain, Sister," Cassa said.

The nun grimaced and muttered some kind of acknowledgment before letting flow a stream of instructions in her own language, pointing with the walking stick. Every time the walking stick was thumped to make Cassa repeat a task, Cassa's decision became firmer. This was the last time she would ever have to take orders from this or any other nun.

The mahogany altar rails were polished three times, and the brass urns and lecterns were gone over and over until Cassa's fingers were stiff. The tiled floor had to be washed twice and mopped dry, and drier. Finally, the flowers were brought in from the sacristy and the nun arranged the vases for Cassa to place and replace on the altar. The heavy walking stick was thumped and pointed a hundred times.

A distant bell clanged in the convent. With what may have been thanks, the nun hobbled painfully away on her stick, the blanket trailing the ground.

Cassa's knees were giving way with fatigue and her head was throbbing. She sat down at the back of the chapel and stared up at the altar.

"Oh Lord," she murmured half aloud, "how did I ever let myself in for this! I hate this chapel. I am beginning to hate nuns. If this goes on, I am going to hate my religion. Oh Lord, I am tired and hungry and depressed."

She put her head in her hands, her eyes closed in fatigue.

"May I help in any way?" A male voice was speaking, and a hand rested lightly on her shoulder.

When Cassa looked up, she looked into the kindly face of a priest. He was a well-set-up man of a little above average height in his mid-forties. His face was vaguely familiar.

"Oh I am sorry. I apologise," Cassa was almost sobbing, her confused emotion close to tears. "I was just tired, that's all. I must go. Excuse me."

"I know you are Miss Blake," the priest said. "You were dusting in my room this morning. I asked Sister Theresa your name."

"Oh," Cassa said, "you are a private patient on Sister Teresa's floor. I thought for a moment we had met somewhere."

The priest smiled, "Let's meet now," he said, "I am Frank Gowan, a missionary priest, and this is my fourth day of recovery from an appendix operation. I came down here to give thanks."

"I will leave you to your prayers so, Father." The priest's bright smile had lightened Cassa's downcast spirit. "I am finished for today."

And for tomorrow and for ever. She glanced back at the chapel. Never again.

"Allow me to walk you to your car," offered the priest. "I am told to take mild exercise."

"If you like, Father," Cassa said politely. "I must collect my mac and my bag first."

As they walked across the car-park, the priest asked, "Do you come in on Sunday, Miss Blake?"

"No, Father," she replied. "Sunday is cleaners' day off."

"Ah," said he, "that is a disappointment. I was going to have the temerity to ask you to have lunch with me, after your hard morning's work."

Cassa was so surprised that she stood without opening the car door. Two invitations from men within a few days!

"You look surprised," Father Gowan said. "Is that because I am a priest?"

"No, because you are a man!"

He took this as a little joke. "I imagine you are probably inundated with invitations to lunch."

"I would like to have lunch with you." Cassa was surprised at her own response "That is, if you are really sure you meant it."

"And why wouldn't I mean it?" asked the priest. "My brother is bringing over a hired car this evening before he goes back to Monaghan. I shall be here for another few days, but I need to get out and about."

"Are you sure you are well enough to drive?"

His smile was very pleasant. "Apparently, the way doctors operate nowadays, the patient could climb off the table and go swimming."

"My home is about twenty minutes' drive from here. Easy to find, not far off the main road." Cassa took her late father's card from her handbag. "This is the address."

"I am saying mass for the students at the Training College at eleven-thirty. May I call for you at one o'clock? Should I book some place you would like?"

"Let me think about that," answered Cassa, who had never booked a table in her life, "and yes, call for me at one o'clock."

She felt no misgiving about his being a priest. The important thing was that he was neither employed by nor related to Dermot Tyson.

The weekend was not going to turn out quite as Cassa had been vaguely planning: some leisurely shopping on Saturday, followed by some quick housework, followed by the writing of a letter of resignation to Tyson Associates, and a quick trip into town to drop the letter into Tyson's letter-box for Monday morning.

Suddenly the idea came that shopping could be very brief, that the housework was not necessary, and that before the letter was written, she must go first of all to that hairdresser.

No, it was not for Father Gowan; it was for lunch in a nice place. It was a gesture of freedom. She was lucky to be fitted in for five-thirty.

The letter of resignation was more difficult. Half a dozen attempts and the letter would not come together in a businesslike way. And after all, Dermot Tyson had tried to be kind, if she could trust him.

There was a call from her friend, Maisie Foley. "Are you coming over on Sunday for a game, I need a fourth and I want to hear all about San Salvatore?"

"Unfortunately I can't, Maisie. I have to take an old cousin out to lunch." Telling her that she was lunching with a priest would only send Maisie's blood pressure up.

"Sunday lunch is always dicey, Cassa. Families! Kids all over the place like demented midgets. I suppose you have to treat the old cousin?" When Maisie got going on a discussion of restaurants, Cassa finally had to mention the date with the hairdresser to get Maisie off the phone.

The letter of resignation to Dermot Tyson would not get written today. But thinking of Tyson, Cassa smiled. Why not? She rang the Glen of the Downs and booked for Sunday lunch. Maybe she would take the pleasant-faced priest up the path to the La Touche ruins and knowledgeably point out Mount Leinster and Lugnaquilla.

Suddenly Cassa was bustling around, thinking of what she would wear, watching the clock for the hair appointment. She was her own woman, beholden to no one. It felt good.

CHAPTER THIRTY-THREE

FATHER FRANK GOWAN arrived, very priestly in his clerical collar and well-cut black suit. "I didn't realise you were here on your own, Miss Blake. I should have asked."

"My father died recently," she told him sadly, "and my mother died four years ago. I miss my father very much."

"You were devoted to your father?"

"I adored him," Cassa said. She had never said that before, even to herself.

"I should like to have known my father," Father Gowan said, "but he died when I was six. I was the eldest, then John, and after him Deirdre. There was a little boy who died in infancy of meningitis."

As they walked across the garden to the car, Cassa took his arm. "That is so sad. Your poor mother. Please accept my sympathy."

The priest did not say anything, but he touched the fingers on his arm.

In the car, Cassa allowed him to concentrate on the unfamiliar road. It was quickly obvious that he was an expert driver.

"I thought," she said, "that on the missions, Father Gowan, you would be out of practice with a car?"

His eyes on the road, he smiled. "In Peru you wouldn't get far without a car. I had a Subaru truck for years, very reliable. Last year, I got a four-wheel drive. My mission is high up where the Andes border on Bolivia, a village called Sonaquera. Tremendous mountains. These dual carriageways are new in Ireland, are they? I wonder have they replaced the old country roads in Monaghan?"

"I don't know," Cassa replied. "It is years since I have been up north. Haven't you been home to see your mother yet?"

The priest did not reply.

The beauty and the comfort of the Glen Hotel gave Cassa and Father Gowan a talking point to ease them into friendship. They drew each other's attention to the oil paintings in the dining-room, portraits of notables of earlier times, and water-colours of Wicklow beauty spots .

"I have seen old houses like this in Monaghan," Father Gowan said, "but they were shabby. Maybe they are hotels now. It is nine years since I have been home. In Ireland much has been changed in that time."

"My father was not very keen on the six-lane highways where once he knew an old twisty country road," Cassa smiled, "but we are bound to have changed. I am not the best person to analyse the situation, Father."

"May I plead for first names?" he asked. "I have been practising the sound of 'Cassa', and I like it."

"If you wish," she smiled at him. "I always liked the name Frank."

"Thank you." He had a good way of smiling with his eyes which she noticed were a nice colour, dark blue. "Your manner is very respectful. I saw that with the nuns."

"We are not going to mention the nuns, or I shall have indigestion! Tell me about Peru. Tell me about your work. Are they black people? Are they primitive?"

"Peru is an enormous mountainous country," he said. "Telling you about Peru would be like settling down for a thousand days: the Arabian Nights, but not nearly so exotic!"

By the time they ordered lunch, Cassa had become accustomed to this newfound friend, with whom she felt extraordinarily comfortable.

"Please tell me about Peru and your work, Frank."

Cassa's smile encouraged him to go on talking. "Thirty years ago, there were reckoned to be eleven million people in Peru. Not black but South American Indian. Many look Spanish, from centuries of inter-breeding."

She noticed how slowly he was eating, and she remembered he was still a hospital patient. "Is the lunch all right for you?"

"It is delicious," he smiled at her, "but it is rich. I have lived on beans and roots for so many years that I have forgotten how food can taste. Look at this china! I keep wondering who has taken my tin plate!"

"Eight years without a break?" asked Cassa. "Was there a holiday at all in that time?"

She waited while he chewed thoughtfully. She remembered how her father used to tell her to masticate properly. The warmth of this priest's manner also reminded her of her father.

"In a way there was a holiday every year," Father Frank said; "the annual retreat in the Domo of Saint Martin in Lima. That is the General House in South America."

Cassa smiled with him. "But isn't an annual retreat fasting and praying?"

"Not too much fasting for those of us out on the mission. They know we men are often hungry, sometimes too tired or lazy to cook a meal, and meditating in a comfortable stall can be a rest!"

"Is Lima far from the mission?"

"Probably a couple of thousand miles. There is a railway – when it functions, and if there are no landslides. When possible, I get to Lima by an old steamer from Antofagasta to Tquique, then usually a better ship from there to Lima. Lima is a big port. It is a very impressive city, created by the early Spaniards when cathedrals were two a penny, but there are horrendous slums."

"Is the weather always sunny?"

He smiled broadly. "Not always. In fact, more temperamental than Ireland! Always extremes. From Antofagasta to Lima can take up to three weeks, sometimes taking shelter under the cliffs, perhaps in a *pueblo pequeño*."

"It sounds fascinating!"

"This is fascinating," the priest said, "an excellent lunch with a pretty woman, who is also a wonderful listener. No more about me now. Tell me about Cassa Blake."

If she were to start now on Cassa Blake, the problems would come pouring out: Tyson Associates, the odd bods of inefficient cleaning women, the snooping nuns, her bossy sister, her financial fears. In fact, with a patient out for the day from San Salvatore, should one even mention contract cleaning apart from the plain fact, which he knew, that she worked at it?

"There is very little to say about me." Her voice was gentle. "I told you both of my parents died, my father this year. I took the job in San Salvatore to... well... more or less to fill the time."

Frank Gowan put his hand over hers. "A beautifully told great big fib."

Then they both laughed and the moment passed.

Back at Cassa's house, it seemed only hospitable to invite him in, and she was very pleased when he accepted. They sat looking out at the neglected garden where the old sycamore trees were beginning to show their greenery. Frank recited slowly:

"You will have the road gate open, the front door ajar
The kettle boiling and a table set
By the window looking out at the sycamores –
And your loving heart lying in wait..."

"That is sad and beautiful, " Cassa said. "Who wrote it? "

"Patrick Kavanagh," Frank told her, "a Monaghan poet. The Kavanaghs lived not far from us. I remember him when I was a small boy, and he writes the way I lived then. His verses have kept me company many a time on a mountain top in Sonaquera."

Frank's eyes rested on Cassa's quiet face and he wondered if he had come, peradventure, across two oceans to find her loving heart lying in wait for him. He remembered another line from Kavanagh, but he did not say it aloud: "We must record love's mystery without claptrap, snatch out of time the passionate transitory." Aloud Father Frank said, "Sister Theresa expects us to be tucked up in our beds by seven-thirty. We may have visitors until nine o'clock, and then Sister Theresa walks up and down the corridor giving out the rosary, good and loud!" Frank smiled, and Cassa noticed again the sapphire blue of his eyes.

"Are you expected to answer the rosary?" Cassa asked.

"Yes, indeed! " Frank smiled. "She leaves each door open!

155

So far I have fallen asleep!"

Cassa laughed at him. "Ah, but you were a sick man!"

"No excuse was what Sister said. Cassa, I see a nicely polished piano. Do you play?"

"An odd time!" Cassa smiled at his expectant face. "Depends on what you hope to hear."

"Anything at all," he said, "but I am not into modern music. We had only classical records in the seminary, and in Sonaquero there is only local folk music."

"My father loved Chopin and Mozart the best."

"Your father's choice then, if it will not make you sad."

Frank is so easy, she thought. I like him.

Chopin's music filled the room as the daylight faded into twilight.

They had tea in the kitchen when it was time for Frank to think of departing.

"May I come back another day for a piece of that cake?" he asked, smiling.

"Of course you may," Cassa replied. "I agree it was a very hearty lunch. Will you find your way to the hospital all right? Are you familiar with the lights in the car?"

"My brother, John, took me out for a run when he brought the car. He might have come with us today but he had to return home."

"To Monaghan?"

"No, the family home is still in Monaghan, the land and some business, but he is into other things in Carrick-on-Shannon. He will be coming down to take me home on Saturday. I should like for him to meet you."

"I would like that."

"I think you would like my brother John," Frank said in a serious way. "I do."

Cassa stood on the steps as he got into the car.

"I look forward to seeing you tomorrow!" he called through the window, as he drove off waving cheerily.

Tomorrow? The resignation! The letter of resignation had not been written, and the rebellious mood had evaporated.

Cassa's mind was happily at ease as it had not been since her father's death.

There was nothing she could do but face into San Salvatore at seven-thirty a.m. on Monday. Mondays were always tough.

CHAPTER THIRTY-FOUR

THERE WAS NO sign of Jinny Corcoran, a stalwart in any emergency.

"Where is Jinny?" she asked Annette.

"She's here but she's not here now, Miss."

Cassa asked patiently, "Will she be in, and when?"

Annette looked around cautiously. "She's in the clinic with Eileen. Eileen's babby has to be put under the knife for something behind his little eye, Miss. Me Ma said could she run in and out. She said you would give permission when you knew."

Rose and Ethel now arrived and Cassa gave them a brief hint of the situation. Jinny must be covered for or she would lose a day's pay.

"Leave it to me," Rose said. "I'll cover. I'll take the full nursery wing with Annette. Send Ethel to the clinic to tell Jinny to stay put until whenever!"'

M. McLaughlin did not like this secrecy. "The nuns ought to be told about favouritism!" she said in a voice pitched at any nearby nun.

Cassa consulted her chart. "M. McLaughlin for theatres and sluices swab-out – and the chrome taps must be polished, not only a dry rub. Forty minutes for re-assignment!" Small hope that M. McLaughlin could keep her mouth shut.

Frolie and Dolly liked their work on the women's floor. Always heavily made-up and watchful while they sneaked a smoke, they were reasonably good workers, and cheerful.

"Margaret, the nurses' kitchens on second and third. Thorough, now!"

Mrs Clarke, who looked frailer each week, was dispatched to x-ray. Callous Anxious had laid it down that if Mrs Clarke was put to work on the men's public wards, she would be sent home immediately. It was a threat that Cassa took seriously.

"Mrs Loney, you go ahead to Sister Theresa and leave the

men's rooms until the visiting doctors have seen their patients. I'll help you then."

Ethel would have started on the women's public wards, so Cassa went to help her. The first three hours of every morning flew by. A cup of tea at eleven would have been very welcome but, officially, that was not on. The nuns had vetoed that, and smoking, in the contract, although most of the women managed to get tea and a smoke through the charity of the nurses.

The hour and a half of the second shift was harder and more rushed. This morning it was chaotic. A phone call brought Cassa to the entrance hall. Jinny, her daughter Eileen and Annette, who should have been in the upper reaches of the hospital, were in tears, screaming loudly. The porter wanted them shifted. Somehow Cassa managed to get them out of the hall into the cleaners' cloakroom.

The baby had died under the anaesthetic. The three women were in so much shock they were uncontrollable. Annette was loudest: "The chisler died under the knife!" she repeated over and over. Jinny's screams were incoherently vowing vengeance on the doctors.

Eileen was wailing, "Send for Joe! Send for Joe! He'll get them! I want my babby! I want my babby! They never let me hold my babby! Mammy, get Joe, he'll make them give me back my babby!"

Cassa rushed out into the hall.

"Get a taxi as fast as you can," she said to the porter. "I'll pay. Quick! Quick!"

The taxi was there within minutes. With the porter's help, Cassa got the three screaming women into the taxi, bundling in Jinny's and Annette's coats and bags. She gave the taxi-man a five pound note which she borrowed from the porter.

"Make sure you get them home," she told the taxi man, "and leave them there. Don't bring them back!"

In the hall, Sister Calasanctius was waiting. "You exercise no control over your staff! This is what comes of casual women! A disgraceful scene! Reverend Mother will hear about this. There is work left undone on every floor! A report..."

Cassa had walked into the cloakroom and closed the door on the nun, who must have heard in the hall that a baby had died.

Cassa remembered Jinny boasting to the other women that Eileen was breast-feeding the baby: "Eileen is as full of milk as a dairy-float! Dribbling out of her it is!"

The women had heard. They assembled in the cloakroom in a tired, dreary silence. They gathered their duds together and shuffled out.

"The work is not all finished," Ethel said. "Rose and me will come in early and give it another go. Callous Anxious was readin' the riot act at the head of the stairs. Go home and have a rest, Miss."

Going through the entrance, she gave the porter his money, and an extra pound for his help. She had never gone up to the private ward, and she was home before she remembered Father Frank Gowan.

The phone was ringing as she opened the hall door. Almost too tired to speak, she picked up the receiver. It was Dermot Tyson. This time it was the godalmighty Tyson of the freezing voice.

"Nicole is here beside me, very upset and angry. A phone call from San Salvatore informs us that there was a riotous exhibition of women in the front hall, led by you, the Reverend Mother says."

"Yes," Cassa responded wearily, "you could say that."

His cold voice scarcely concealed his anger. Cassa could easily imagine Nicky's flashing eyes at his shoulder.

"We will have a report from you on my desk, first thing in the morning. Do you understand?"

Cassa hung up the receiver. As Lotty Slattery would have said to him: frig the lot of you.

The phone rang again and for a while she counted the rings. If Tyson were back on the line, the rings would be limited. After twelve, she answered. It was the warmly concerned voice of Frank Gowan.

"Cassa, are you all right?"

"I meant to go up and have a word with you, Frank. Things went wrong."

"I know," he said. "I heard the whole sad story. Sister Theresa informed the men, when afternoon tea came round, that we would see no more of the supervisor. From her voice," and now he was highly amused, "I gathered the hospital is well rid of you."

"I wish it were that easy!"

Cassa tried to give the impression of a light heart, but she was thinking of Nicole. There would be a visitation from her sister, probably about seven-thirty.

"I took the car out to make this phone call," he said. "I have the feeling that the less the nuns know, the better it is for you?"

"Yes," Cassa said, "but you are not to worry about it. You just have to get well, and get out of San Salvatore."

"May I come over and take the two of us out to dinner?"

Cassa hesitated. Write a report, Tyson said. And he would send Nicky over this evening, nothing surer. Contract cleaning was his big money-spinner. Cassa, silly stupid woman, must be brought to heel.

"Frank, it is very nice of you." Again she hesitated, then she said, "Just give me until six-thirty and I'll be ready."

Nicky had a key to the hall door. Cassa wrote a note, and propped it up on the hall table: "Sorry Nicky! Gone to dinner and the theatre with friends."

I tell lies quite easily lately, Cassa thought as she went up the stairs.

Will I be able to call him friend when he is out of the hospital? I think I love him like a dear friend, and he is so safe to be with. He reminds me of Papa. I don't remember being so at ease with any other person ever before.

CHAPTER THIRTY-FIVE

"THIS IS TWICE you have taken me out to a meal, Frank," Cassa said. "I should like to invite you to Firenze for dinner."

They were going to a little restaurant in Seacoast, an Indian restaurant that another patient in the hospital had told Father Frank about.

"Thank you," Frank said, "I would appreciate that, but today is a day for you to be taken out. This morning was tough. Coming up from their chapel, I heard one of the nuns tearing strips off two of the cleaners!"

"Why don't the nuns consider how much harder that makes the job for me? I am supposed to be in charge."

"I gather the whole idea of women coming in by the hour is new to the nuns," the priest suggested. "They seem to resent it."

"Yes," Cassa told him, "they would prefer to have servants on call, as they themselves say, 'around the clock'."

Frank said, "I cannot help wondering if a different job would suit your nature better, Cassa?"

"You see, Frank, I never worked in any job before, and I am really aiming to get work experience. Right now with so much unemployment, jobs are not plentiful. Now, let's get down to eating. This smells beautifully spicy!"

But Frank Gowan was not satisfied to ignore Cassa's job. From the upper landing, he had witnessed the scene in the entrance hall of San Salvatore. He had seen the distress on her face.

He had great admiration for nuns. He knew very well theirs was a life of sacrifice and loneliness, but like the rest of people, they were only human.

He asked her, "Did you expect that all nuns would be gentle and full of Christ-like compassion?"

She looked surprised. "Well, yes, I suppose I did. I got on well with the nuns at school."

He smiled, Cassa was probably an exemplary pupil. The nuns, no doubt, liked her in return.

"But you never thought of entering the convent?" he asked.

"My father would have had a fit!" Cassa laughed. "My one ambition in school was to become a music teacher — he approved of that."

She saw Frank's thoughtful eyes on her.

She put down her fork. "Yes, I am aware that I mention my father very often. You see, Frank, it is only this year that he died. Only this year that his health failed. He and I had been the best of friends for all my years, especially since I left school. He was a most lovable man. We had so many interests in common."

"Interests? Like what? Tell me." His eyes lingered on her face, softly rounded in the candlelight from the table.

"Everything!" Cassa said, "music, gardening. The dogs: I loved the dogs as much as he did. We loved to walk through the far fields with them. Films. Books. I shared his love of sport – golf, tennis. In the good years he took me to the links with him. I had 'promise' he said. We loved board games, chess, draughts, Scrabble. In the winter, we used have friends in for cards; he was a great bridge player."

"And were there never any young men coming calling?" the priest asked gently.

She was suddenly remembering the sunsets across Caragh Lake. "Unclaimed treasure" Robert Gray used to say of her to Louise.

"No," she said, and she smiled at the priest, "not really. No young men lining the drive to have their credentials checked out by my father."

"And your mother?" Frank asked. "Is she part of the tranquil family picture?"

"When I was eighteen, that summer, my mother suffered a massive stroke. Nearly five years ago she died, after ten years of total paralysis. You don't want to be listening to this sad and sorrowful tale," she said softly to his kind face across

163

the table. "And that is enough, altogether enough, about me. Now, let me ask the questions."

"Let us finish the meal," he said, " I see some people are taking their coffee out to the veranda where they can watch the moon shining on the waves."

It was in Cassa's mind that he mentioned his brother as much as she mentioned her father. Were his parents dead?

"This is good coffee," Father Frank said, "don't you think so?"

He is stalling, Cassa thought. So she said nothing and contented herself with gazing at the sea.

He touched her hand where it rested on the table. His dark blue eyes were pensive. "You are allowed four questions," he said.

"Oh, I am glad!" Cassa said, "I was beginning to feel put back into my box! I recall you told me your father died when you were six. You do not mention your mother. Is she at home with your brother, or maybe he is married? With your sister then?"

"My mother?" The priest had asked a question of himself, not of Cassa, and he paused. "No, she is not in Monaghan with John. He lives in Carrick-on-Shannon and a house-keeper looks after him and the house. Deirdre is married to a decent man from Donegal town. They live there. They have three teenagers. I believe they are a happy family. I have not seen them for eight years. But they all write great letters."

There was a long pause. Cassa was about to withdraw the question. She was not a person who would intrude on grief. At last the priest spoke. "I was six when my father died. He drowned in a boating accident out on Lough Erne – a day's fishing with the Anglers' Club. He was thirty-three. My mother was thirty-one."

"Oh my God," she whispered.

"My mother's grief was appalling. She could not stay in the house. She walked the roads day and night. She must have looked like a saint of olden times: ragged clothes, hair blown in the winds, the rosary beads in her hands, her voice crying out her prayers to heaven. When I was a grown man that picture was still in my mind."

They left the restaurant and got into the car.

"Would you like me to drive you home now, Cassa?" he asked.

"May we stay out a little bit longer?" she replied.

At this moment, Nicky could be sitting in the front drawing-room, among Sadora's cushions, seething with rage because the stupid sister dared to be out.

"Might we drive out along the coast road?" she asked, "and talk a little more. Unless you are tired, Frank?"

"As it happens (cuteness is a Monaghan trait, Cassa), I said to sister Theresa that I might miss her prayers tonight. Direct me to the coast road."

He drove beyond Dalkey and Cassa pointed the way to the Vico Road. The moon was still high in the sky, and the sea shone into infinity. They sat in the car and let the seascape sink into their vision.

Then she asked him very gently to go on with the story. "Please," she said, "I want to know about your childhood."

Frank Gowan drew a long deep breath. In the Andes as a functioning missioner, he listened rather than talked.

"Cassa, it is not so easy to tell, and I have tried to forget." He paused as if wondering should he go on. "Our house was set so far back from the road that we had no neighbours. The land was in the family for generations, and our grand-parents were all dead. My distraught mother accepted no help from anyone. 'Frank would see to it.' While she prayed all day."

For a while, the priest gazed into the distance of the night, remembering. "Frank was my father's name too. The Frank who had to see to it was six years old, then seven, then eight. My brother John grasped the situation early on. He is a bare year younger than I, and very quickly he grew taller and stronger. We bonded, there is no other word. Between us we managed the place. We managed Deirdre, we got ourselves fed. Eventually we got to school with a teacher's help – he passed on the road a mile below us every day in his old Ford Prefect."

There was a long pause, perhaps a reluctant pause.

"The worst time was when the baby got sick. When at last the woman let us get the doctor, the baby was dying. He died in the hospital. They diagnosed meningitis. Maybe he could not have lived, but she blamed us. That was a bad time. His name was Eugene. I have never forgotten his little flushed face, his little whimper of pain."

There was silence again for a long time. Cassa was very close to tears. If the man had not been a priest, it would have been possible to put an arm around his shoulder, even hold his hand in hers. Without touching him, any words were inadequate.

"When I was twelve," Frank Gowan said heavily, "things began to improve. She cooked a bit for us. She washed our clothes. Her uncle died and left her a farm of good land over the border near Lisnaskea. This was sold and money became a little easier, but not much; her grief had made her miserly. I was clever in school, and in fact the three of us were, but Deirdre was kept home a lot to help, and John had so much farm work to do that keeping up with the lessons was almost impossible. We helped each other and we helped Deirdre, but the woman watched her doves like a hawk. I was the scholar, she said, John was the farmer, Deirdre was the maid. When I was in the last year in the secondary school, still being taken to the school bus by that teacher, she decided that I was destined for the priesthood. Frank would be offered up to Almighty God for all she had suffered. Frank would be sacrificed."

Cassa waited while the priest drew a long shivering sigh from the depths of him. The minutes went by. "There you have it," he said. "Amen!"

"Had you expressed the wish to become a priest?" Cassa asked. "If I am not pressing you too hard."

Now he turned to her and his face was drawn. "No," he said. "Never for a single moment did I express any such wish.

166

Nor did I want to become a priest. Often I stood out in the fields and I cursed God, the God who took a good father and left us a vixen for a mother."

"So did you refuse?" Cassa's voice was scarcely above a breath. "Did you think of running off?"

The priest's voice too was low, and taut. "For almost twelve years, we had struggled upwards, swimming always against the tide of her eccentricity and her wrath. To refuse her vocation would be to open the gates and let loose the demon we remembered and, at times, still experienced. For me to run away would be to leave John and Deirdre to sink in the abyss. When I was seventeen and a half, I entered the seminary. Her votive offering."

"Did that set the others free?"

"In my first four years as a seminarian, I was attending university and having a lot of study and thereby a bit distracted from the thought of what might be going on at home. The rule was strict on detachment from family. Then came time for the year of enclosed novitiate in the south of England. I was packing my few clothes and books ready for departure when a note came from the prior to say there were visitors in the reception for me."

He turned to Cassa, there was a gleam of tears in his eyes. "Cassa, I had never had visitors in four long years. For a wild moment I thought it might be John and Deirdre, finding the money somehow to come down for a farewell. I raced down the stairs, I was ready for a big family hug after the lonely years."

Cassa held her breath. His voice when it came was dry.

"In the priests' parlour were my mother and a stranger, a stout bald man."

"'Meet my husband, Frank!' she said at once. 'Mr Will MacLaren!'

"I think I stumbled backwards.

"'Shake hands, Frank!' she said loudly. I fled out of the room, back up the stairs. I have never seen her since. She lives in Belfast. MacLaren is a very very rich man."

"But you went on to become a priest."

"It was a long time ago," he said a little more cheerfully, "more than twenty-five years. In those days, a 'spoiled' priest was an outcast. I did not even think of walking out. I knew there was nowhere to go. I was not qualified to earn a living and I had no home to go to. Although I had shown my ability to deal with life since the death of my father, I was still too young at twenty-two to realise that I had done so."

Neither spoke, each waiting for the other.

Cassa, near to tears, spoke first: "Frank, please believe that I feel an overflowing sympathy for all you have gone through. Thank you for telling me. It was not easy for you to talk about yourself."

"No," he said. "I am not given to confidences. But, Cassa, there was a purpose in my opening up to you. The first morning I saw you, furbishing around my room in the hospital, I saw a person who was doing something I did for years: swimming against the tide. A stubborn resentment expressed in the set of your shoulders.

"Cassa, you are working in a job that is utterly unsuited to you. You could walk away from it at a moment's notice, yet you stay. I have been very open with you, after the shortest acquaintance in history. I want to help you. We should let our nice friendship develop, but there is not time. In a day or two, I shall be gone away. Please, then, Cassa Blake, tell me what is at the back of your persistence."

So she told him. She really needed a job to hang on to the house and keep it in good order. Her sister had told her that she, Cassa, was the ideal person to deal with nuns.

"But I am not, you know, Frank. I am not the right person at all. I am as weak as water when they raise their voices. I had a few days' training in a city hospital and the supervisor there told me that I would need 'hard gall' for the job."

They laughed together when she told him all about Lotty Slattery and Shay's magnificent car.

"Are you going in tomorrow morning?" Frank asked.

"Well, I have to," Cassa said, "because while I have been

dining with you, I have left no time in which to write a report on what happened today. So I guess I have to face the music."

On the hall table, Nicole had scribbled under Cassa's note: "I waited long enough for you to be home, and for the report. Ring me when you get to the hospital. D. is furious."

CHAPTER THIRTY-SIX

As CASSA WENT through the hospital reception at seven a.m., the porter handed her an envelope. My notice to quit, she thought.

It was a one-line note from Father Frank: "Look unconcerned: let it blow over."

Cassa was smiling as the women straggled in. Rose and Ethel had been in since six, and there was no problem in distributing the work. Two of the women who always worked together, Bid O'Connor and Resa Kinch, stayed back and asked Cassa if they could make a complaint about M. McLaughlin.

"Is it about her work?" Cassa asked cautiously.

"No, Miss, it's about her dirty tongue."

"But you all use the same..." Cassa began.

"It's not that, Miss," Resa Kinch interrupted. "She says we are a pair of lesbians. She says Callous Anxious has us spotted, and we are bein' reported to the Reverend Mother."

"M. McLaughlin is talking the usual rubbish," Cassa said robustly. "I have absolute faith in you two women, top marks in the bunch! And all reports come to me. The Reverend Mother has nothing to do with it any more."

"We're respectable married women," said Bid O'Connor as they prepared to leave. "Which is more than M. McLaughlin is," added Resa Kinch. "We know about her ."

While Cassa hurried up and down stairs, along the endless corridors, in and out of wards, outwardly looking the picture of white-clad efficiency, she was inwardly expecting a summons to the Reverend Mother's office, or to the telephone to hear the voice of Dermot Tyson's secretary, or an encounter with Callous Anxious.

Mercifully the morning passed without incident, and the women assembled in the cloakroom to get their things together.

"Me and Annette won't be comin' tomorrow, Miss," said Jinny Corcoran dolefully.

"It's the babby's funeral." Annette's eyes were swollen from crying.

"I am sorry, Jinny. May I come over to your house to sympathise with Eileen?"

"We're goin' down to the Coroner's Office at six o'clock in a procession from the flats. The morgue is behind the office. They'll have to give the babby. We have a white coffin." Poor Jinny's face was wrinkled in grief.

"We're havin' a wake," Annette told all the cleaners, "a proper wake. Everyone in the flats is comin'. They're makin' the food."

"Would eight o'clock be a suitable time?" Cassa asked.

"Make it after nine," Jinny said mournfully. "Most of the childher will be gone home for bed by nine."

The women stood back to let her pass out first. Jinny would be a woman well supported in her neighbourhood. All the women around her, and all her relatives, would share in her grief.

Driving home to Firenze, Cassa realised that her world was expanding.

Within her home, with her beloved father, she had been contented. The highlight of every year had been the summer month in Kerry, in the lodge at Caragh Lake. Those had been her limits. She had not stepped intimately into the lives of any other people. Now, she had formed a friendship with a man, a safe man not unlike her father and doubly safe because he was a priest. Overnight, she had been drawn into the heartbreak of a family unknown a few months ago. She felt Jinny's woe as closely as a family sorrow.

In the late afternoon, Father Frank was on the telephone. "I had a feeling I would not see you this morning. You were playing safe?"

"I followed your law for survival," Cassa told him. "So far it has worked!"

"It will always work," he assured her. "All things, right or wrong, blow over. How are you, apart from that?"

"Sure, I'm fine! And you?"

"I too am fine, completely back on my feet. And that is the good news." His voice invited comment.

"Don't tell me you have bad news?" Cassa queried.

"Well," he said, "this is my second last day here, and tomorrow is my very last."

She laughed gently at his voice. "That is all good news," she told him: "quite cured – free from pain – off on a holiday."

"I had just become used to going out to dinner with a pretty lady who listens to me as if I were the star of a radio show. Only two nights left, and tomorrow night I shall have a rival at the table – my brother John."

Cassa thought, I will miss him when he is gone.

"Father Frank, I cannot come out with you tonight, much as I would like to. The baby who died – you remember yesterday – is being brought home tonight. I must go and show my sympathy."

"Of course. Of course. And that will stand to you among the women, while you are here in this hospital. As you know, I hope you won't be in this position too long."

Cassa had the same hope, but dimly.

"Then my last day," he said. "John comes down from Carrick on Friday. A celebration dinner? Please, Cassa?"

"Celebrating your homecoming, and your return to health?" He had told her that the appendix had been rumbling for a year.

"A celebration to friendship," he said, "and would you like to ask a friend, and make it a foursome?"

Apart from the bridge club, she had not many friends. "Will I do, all on my own?" she asked.

"Actually, I like that best," he assured her. "I would like to go to the same place, the Glen of the Downs."

"I wonder now would we be expected to dress up for dinner there? Shall I phone and enquire?"

Father Frank was amused at this idea. "We'll dress up anyway, to celebrate. I'll phone John to bring a dinner jacket. I have a new black suit and the collar. I look forward to seeing you in evening dress, gloriously attired."

And I look forward to seeing your brother in a dinner jacket, she was thinking. She had a vague picture in mind of a swarthy big farmer driving the cattle, his Wellington boots covered in dung, a stubble all over his jutting chin. A brother accustomed to a tuxedo was a different image altogether.

When it was time to go to Jinny Corcoran's, she filled a carry-bag from her father's drinks cupboard with two bottles of Irish whiskey and a bottle of port. She had never been to a wake, but she was sure that lots of drink was traditional.

CHAPTER THIRTY-SEVEN

CASSA HAD NO difficulty in finding the flats, high up the hill out of Seacoast. The big crowd of people gathered at a crossing, evidently mourners and sympathisers, indicated the left turn. Many of the crowd held bottles. There were kids with lemonade and elderly women with mugs of tea. There were girls passing plates of sandwiches. It wasn't exactly a party but neither was there a funereal sadness.

On the tiers of the flats were many more people. Could this be all family? She pulled up the car, uncertain whether she should intrude. A woman came from the iron staircase outside the flats.

"Jinny told us to look out for a white car, Missus. Are you the lady?"

"I'm the supervisor from San Salvatore."

"Jinny said you'd be comin. Billy, keep an eye on this lady's car."

"Disastrous about the babby," another woman said. "Poor Eileen's desolated. Her first! But I coulda told her. The little eye twisted, it's a sign. I seen it before."

They were now on the crowded top storey and the word had mysteriously preceded them that a stranger had arrived.

Annette was at the door of their flat. "Come in, Miss."

Although the room was packed with Jinny's sons and daughters and in-laws, the immediate impression was of cleanliness and order. There was no sign of the near-poverty that Cassa might have expected in the home of a humble cleaner. Jinny was seated in the midst of them. She rose to greet the new arrival with a gracious dignity suitable to the sad occasion.

"Good of you to come, Miss. This is Miss Blake. Me husband Mick; Eileen and Joe; Francie and Tim; Lena and Pat; Danny and Gertie; Violet and Anthony; me daughter-in-law Jane and me son Eamonn – they just got in from Manchester; Rory and Dodo – the poor lamb, as ya can see,

174

she's expectin' her fifth. Do we know what's before us? And me unmarried son, Michael – he came over on the mail-boat. He works in Wales. And you know Annette, Miss. We had the ten grandchilder, but they're all still only small, so we got them off to bed."

"Will I offer the lady a drink, Ma?" asked Rory. Violet was offering a cup of tea, a nice china cup on a nice china saucer.

"Oh thank you very much," Cassa said. "Tea is just right."

Annette was offering a plate of sandwiches, and Cassa took one gratefully.

She handed the carry-bag to the husband Mick, and he opened it to show the contents to Jinny. They all looked into the bag, but solemnly and without comment. "Now," said Jinny when Cassa had handed back the cup. "I'll bring you in to see our Joseph Anthony laid out in his little crib that Eileen decorated with her own hands. We've given over our bedroom for our poor babby."

Mrs Jinny's manner was queen-motherly.

Again Cassa could not but observe the freshness of the paint and the wallpaper in the bedroom, the crispness of the white curtains. There were two young women sitting quietly, their rosary beads in their hands.

The crib, embellished with satin and silver frills, had been placed in the centre of the big double bed. The baby, still fresh and chubby, was dressed in a little ski outfit in blue and pink.

Eileen had followed them into the bedroom. She was weeping helplessly and hoarsely.

"Oh Mammy, look at him! Can I pick him up, can I?"

Jinny pressed Eileen against her shoulder, "Better not, pet, better not."

Jinny motioned to the two young women: "Dodo has a bit of supper for you two girls, now. Mrs Murphy and Bella are comin' in to keep the next hour for Joseph Anthony."

Cassa had knelt down to say prayers, since that was expect-ed, although her heart told her that prayers for his happy repose were scarcely necessary.

Through her fingers she watched as Jinny Corcoran lifted the dead baby and placed the rigid unyielding little form in Eileen's arms. Then Jinny replaced the tiny corpse, adjusting the many frills, and held Eileen against her until she was reasonably calm.

Two women came in and took up their places with their rosary beads. Jinny indicated to Cassa, "Come on, Miss."

Driving home again, she pondered on the strange world she had never considered. I am halfway through my life, she thought, and I have not really lived.

CHAPTER THIRTY-EIGHT

THE DINNER WAS a great success. Father Frank paid compliments, and his brother John had a charming way of echoing them, adding, as Frank remarked, his own grace-note.

John was not unlike Frank, taller and broader but with the same sapphire blue eyes. He looked very fit and tanned, as, she thought, a farmer ought to look, but his voice was quiet, and his manner pleasant and restrained.

"Do you have this great tan from being out in the fields all day?" Cassa asked.

He smiled easily. "I rent out the fields in conacre. I still keep the house, although it is far too big. I have an old lady who looks after it. I have a farm machinery business in the town, left to me by an old uncle of my mother's. That's all in Monaghan, but I live in Carrick-on-Shannon, mostly on the water."

Cassa looked mystified, and Frank laughed at her expression.

"Begin at the beginning, John. Eight years ago, you talked nothing but Tourism, in capital letters. You got my signature, and Deirdre's, to get money out of the bank. So you bought a houseboat. Now proceed, son."

John grinned, "Not a houseboat, Frank, as you well know: two cabin cruisers, and now I have over fifty, and the loan has been redeemed. A lot has happened in the last eight years. Our old home and farm and land belong to the three of us now. I bought out our mother's share of the place two years ago. Only for having to rush you into hospital when you arrived at Dublin airport, you would have heard all this. I am sure Cassa doesn't want to hear the family saga."

"She does, you know. I told her little bits about us already, and she is a great listener."

Courteously, Father Frank went on encouraging the talk.

John told Cassa, "Men told me, years after my father died,

that he was an expert sailor. I think I inherited the love he had for the water. I discovered that when I was twenty years of age, a couple of years after you went away, Frank. The lakes and the rivers began to plague my mind, especially the mighty Shannon. Deirdre says that river is my one passion, and she might be right."

"Oh," Cassa broke in, " I remember when I was in school, one of the girls used to have holidays cruising down the Shannon with her family, but that must be nearly twenty years ago."

"Yes," John said, "well-off people had cruisers twenty years ago. Now it is for everyone, big tourist stuff."

John took up the story again. "There were always cruisers around Carrick, even when I was a boy, and Uncle Eugene used bring me with him to buy tractors in Sligo. Yachts also, but the weather around Cuilcagh and the flow of the tide favour the flat-bottomed cruiser. The canal system will be restarted eventually, if only for tourism."

Frank remembered the lock cottages. "Long ago the lock cottages were picturesque: flowers and hens scattered about, nasturtiums growing down the walls. Which sounds impossible, but don't mind me, go on with the bank loan and two cruisers becoming fifty cruisers, not to mention that car you are driving. Are cars that size necessary?"

John laughed in his quiet way: "A Bentley impresses the bank manager in a lean year. Deirdre calls it my ego trip but she finds it comfortable."

"So do I," Cassa said. "Tonight is the first time I sat in so gorgeous a car. Please go on with your story."

"His meteoric rise to fame!" added Frank.

"I have been helped in the last five years by the increase in the interest of Continental tourists in the boat business."

"Have you lost your own interest in farming?" Frank wanted to know. "Will you be selling the ancestral land next?"

"Deirdre and James may be considering it for their eldest, Peter. He is down in Grange Agricultural in County Meath –

his mother says he's top of his class What do you think, Frank, about the land and the house for Peter?"

"It's up to you, John. And it would be grand to keep it in the family."

"I would like to hear more about the cabin cruisers," Cassa said.

"So would I," said Frank.

John smiled. "You'll see everything! In the high season, I have thirty cruisers afloat on the lakes, and many more of different capacities on the rivers and canals. Local day-trips are very popular and profitable. Excursions, outings."

"Is the cabin cruiser hard to operate?" enquired Frank.

"Of course not! It's easier than driving a car! It is actually a do-it-yourself holiday. There are a number of us in this particular tourist area now."

"You mentioned in a letter that you live aboard a lot; do you go back to the house at all?" Frank asked, again the hint of envious nostalgia.

"I have a house in Carrick now, and Melia Tracey looks after me. She's over seventy and nimble as a goat. I like to stay afloat when it is off-season time. I cruise far up the Shannon and I fish. Wait till you see my flagship, Frank. Very snazzy."

"Like the Bentley?"

When the meal was ending, John Gowan issued an invitation to Cassa.

"Easter is not far off," he said. "If you have no other plans, you are welcome to come up to Carrick-on-Shannon. *La Vie En Rose* is an eight-berth cruiser, very comfortable. Bring a friend if you like. Our sister Deirdre and her husband James O'Donnell are making a holiday of it to welcome home the long-lost brother. The three of us will be together for the first time in eight years, and it was eight years before that, but I did not have the big cruiser then."

When they arrived back at Firenze, the two men got out of the Bentley to see Cassa to her hall door.

"You know," she said a little bit sadly, "nights like this night hardly ever come again, and we may never meet."

"We will meet, and you will spend Easter with us on this famous old wreck of a boat. Right, John?"

"Dead on," and John was smiling at Cassa. "Tonight was only an introduction."

Frank embraced her warmly. "As John said, only an introduction, Cassa."

"Thank you," she said, "both of you, for the loveliest evening I ever had."

She sat at her dressing-table, looking into the mirror and wondering why this evening had been the loveliest evening she ever had. That wasn't just politeness, it was true. Because Father Frank was at the table, because she watched the thoughtful way he ate the meal, the way he placed his fork at an angle to the knife on his plate. No one else did that. He is a priest of God, she thought... better to remember the old loyalty to the image of Robert Gray, now restored to innocence and still at the edge of her mind.

She thought of Frank Gowan while the woman in the mirror gazed back.

Suddenly she became aware that the phone was ringing. She glanced at her watch: after midnight. It had to be Nicole, and she didn't want to hear that hectoring voice at the end of her beautiful evening. She let it ring, but it went on so long that she ran down the stairs to answer it.

"Yes, hello?"

"Cassa, I was worried about you. I have been ringing since eight o'clock. You are always at home. I began to think of a car accident."

It was the slightly aggrieved voice of Dermot Tyson. "Are you all right, my dear?"

Puzzled, Cassa answered, "No accident, Dermot. I was out."

"Out? Out with friends?"

She did not stop to think, the instinctive lie came out. "You know," she said, "there was a very sad death. A child of one of the cleaners. In the flats in Seacoast. A wake."

"Ah," he said, relieved and confidential. "That is the very

thing about which I wanted to talk to you tonight. I was about to come over, but when I phoned, you had not come home. Are you just in now?"

"Yes, just now, and on my way to bed."

"I promised Nicole I would look into this matter of your becoming personally involved with the cleaners. You are too trusting, too soft-natured, Cassa. It doesn't do in business."

"I'll remember to be more discreet," she said.

"Perhaps a little talk in my office, tomorrow? Call me. Or perhaps I shall come over during the week?"

She replaced the phone, almost reluctantly. He could be so kind. But surely he must know that the most meagre friendship with her, even a kind word, would bring Nicky flying at Cassa's throat.

She fled up the stairs, as terrified of her sister as when she was six and Nicky was ten.

CHAPTER THIRTY-NINE

KNOWING THAT FATHER Frank had departed from the hospital made San Salvatore even more uninviting, which was silly when she had hardly seen him there. Saturday was usually the easiest day to get through and since he was not in Sister Theresa's care any more, she went with Mrs Loney to help out.

Ignoring restrictions, she took Mrs Loney with her to the chapel. The German nun, seated there with her heavy walking stick, thumped and garumphed every five minutes. Mrs Loney, who was sweet and forgiving, looked on anxiously, but Cassa knew there was little enough crabby Sister Chapel could do. No doubt new bad reports would be issued, but Cassa was finding it hard to care.

Almost finished, she was called to reception. The hall porter told her there was a woman to see her in the waiting-room.

"I'm Margaret's mother," the woman said at once. "I was sent to bring her home – immediate, if not sooner!"

"I thought Margaret's mother was dead," Cassa said hesitantly, "and you look too young to be her mother."

"Thanks a mill," the cheeky-faced woman said. "Wouldya believe stepmother then? Her oul fella wants her outa here pronto."

Cassa would not be too sorry to see Margaret gone as she was always up to mischief, but she was a rapid worker. How quickly could a replacement be found?

"Perhaps you could allow her to work this coming week?"

"Her oul fella said now, this minute. Me babby is due and overdue, and Magser has to look out for her Da while I'm laid up."

"All right, you stay here, and I'll get Margaret."

"Wait here, is it? In my condition?" The woman lowered her eyes modestly.

"Would you wait over across the road in Adolfo's Café?"

"Adolfo's? Adolfo charges a pound to rest yer bum, never mind a cuppa instant."

Cassa got a pound from the porter and ushered the woman out. There was still a half-hour's work and Cassa let it run.

In the cloakroom, she spoke to Margaret. "Your stepmother has come to take you home."

She handed the pay envelope to the girl.

"She's not me stepmother and I'm not goin' home. She can fuck off, so she can."

Margaret hid the pay envelope deep down in the yellow plastic hold-all hitched on her shoulder.

"But what about your father, Margaret? She says you will be needed at home while she is laid-up."

"Fuck her anyway. Please, Miss, please don't let them take me back. I share a room with Bessie Loney. I haven't bin home for three weeks. Miss, don't let them. They're bloody dirty and all they want is the money. Couldn't you help me, Miss? Please, would you have a little spare corner. I saw the big house you live in, Miss. Me fella had a loan of a motorbike an' he showed me yer big house. We sheltered outa the rain under them big trees that go down to the ground."

"Margaret, it was your father's woman who was looking for you, so he knows where you are. He is your father, Margaret. He could get the Guards to bring you home. You are only sixteen."

"Nearly sixteen, Miss. Me Da wouldn't call the Guards, Miss. He's only after bein' let out after servin' time for manslaughter."

"Are you saying your father accidentally killed someone?"

"Accidental me arse!"

Margaret gathered up her anorak and the yellow plastic shoulder-bag she always slung on her shoulder. "He won't go to the Guards, but if he finds out where I am in Bessie Loney's, he'd come after me himself and use his fuckin' belt on me bum – he likes that. Don't breathe a word, Miss, about me kippin' in Bessie's. Please help me, Miss."

"Are you telling the truth, Margaret? Who did your father kill?"

"Me Ma, Miss. In a bleedin' row. He got offa murder because he was plastered up to the eyeballs. Accidental? After he tied us to the end of the bed and split her open with a hatchet. I was eight years old and me sister was ten. It was what he was doin' to me sister started the bleedin' row. Me mother's sister took me in while he was in the clink. He took me back from her. It was all right there, but she is strict-like, about boys and smokin'."

"When did he marry your stepmother?"

"They're not married, Miss. She's the local bicycle. All the cleaners knowed her if they saw her here today. Tessie Tuite is her name."

"She is obviously about to have a baby."

"An while she's havin' it, he'll fuck me as usual..."

"Margaret, don't talk like that, it's wrong."

"I'm goin' now, Miss. If I meet Tuite, I'll belt her with me bag, and I'll put a big stone in it. Will ya think over about helpin' me, Miss, I'm sick to death of me Da. I know where you live, Miss. It's a very big house, I'd be real good for you, Miss. I'd do a great job of cleanin', honest I would."

"If I don't see you in the morning, Margaret..."

"I'll be here, Miss. Me an' Bessie comes with Jinny and Annette. Riley wouldn't cross Jinny Corcoran, Miss. She was the one had him put behind bars."

CHAPTER FORTY

WHEN CASSA LEFT the hospital, she drove home in a state of rebellious shock. She hated this job. Words were spinning around in her head: resign, give it up, say you don't need a job, say you are sick, advised by the doctor, say anything, anything at all!

BUT GET OUT OF IT!

As she went in through the kitchen, the phone was ringing.

"Where were you? I was over to the house, but I could not open the front door. You were supposed to be home an hour ago. What have you done to the door? Well, you are in now, so stay there." Nicky banged down the phone.

Rapidly Cassa changed into slacks and a sweater and took a couple of tools out to the small enclosed garden beside the loggia.

She practised saying, "Been neglecting the garden, much too busy to talk. Perhaps another time, Nicky."

Look unconcerned; it will blow over. She knew very well that Nicky's bossy dominance was a relic of childhood that she should have grown out of long ago. But if she parted with her only sister, who was her tenuous link with their dead parents, and indeed with the Gilbey cousins far and wide, and especially Orla and Sandra, who would she have?

"What are you doing out in the garden? I told you, didn't I, that I was on my way over? Why aren't you ready to drink coffee with me, or even offer me a drink? What's the matter with you? You're filthy, why don't you wear gardening gloves? Go on, go ahead and wash your hands. I suppose I'll have to make the coffee."

Nicole was a fashion plate in cream linen and the sheerest of silk stockings. She had been in to see Dick Boyce earlier. She had sworn to him she would never give up her beloved Firenze. Never. Despite Dermot's advice, she was determined to make a legal stand. Or illegal if it came to that.

Boyce was equally adamant. "Mrs Tyson, we have been

over this ground several times. The will is unassailable. Your late father was of sane mind when he made the will. He was thus assessed by various medical men at his own request. He may have foreseen that the will would be contested. He was sane, no question."

"But my sister may not be sane. Has that occurred to you? Cassa is light-minded, untrustworthy, foolish. I am prepared to swear to that fact."

Dick Boyce shrugged his shoulders. This was the third such encounter with Mrs Tyson, and each time she shifted to new ground.

"Think seriously, Mr Boyce, if you are acting in the best interests of your client in trying to incarcerate her in a huge gloomy mansion for which she has no means for upkeep. She becomes morose and she is lonelier with every week. Standing at the window staring out at nothing, the lawns unkempt, the hedges uncut, she herself shabby and sad, unable to invite a friend. Indeed she cannot afford a dog whatever about a friend. Weighed down with the awful responsibility of a decaying mansion."

"I am not my client's detective, but, as her sister, you will be glad to know that I have seen Miss Blake on a recent occasion, dining with a couple of men in the Glen of the Downs Hotel, happily chatting with her friends and quite at her ease. She had not the appearance of a shabby person; quite the contrary."

Nicole Tyson had shot out of Boyce's office with all doors crashing.

Now she was banging a spoon against a coffee cup.

"Cassa, I am talking to you. I presume you have not gone deaf along with everything else!"

Here it comes, Cassa thought. Time to look very unconcerned.

"Under the circumstances," Nicole could sound imperially magnanimous, "I am prepared to go easy on the bad reports from San Salvatore, this being your first job." Cassa had not eaten since seven o'clock that morning. She stood up to open the fridge. Look unconcerned.

"Did you hear what I said?"

"What was that, Nicky? I am feeling hungry. Would you like a sandwich or something?"

"Oh forget it! What I want to know now is this: who are these men who took you out to dinner in the Glen?"

Cassa drew a deep breath. Papa used to say that everyone knew everyone in Dublin.

Nicole began again to tap the spoon on the cup.

"I'm waiting, sister."

"Friends of mine," Cassa said, "Father Frank Gowan and his brother John from Monaghan, County Monaghan. Father Frank was a patient in San Salvatore."

Her sister was aghast. "Friends of yours!" she said scornfully, "a sick priest and a farmer from Monaghan! What were you thinking of? You know my views on that subject. It is a scandal of our day the way women are encouraging our priests to take liberties. Bishop Prole blames the women for making free, and now I think he must be right. How could you? Did you bring those men back to this house?"

Cassa longed to say, Yes, and we cavorted till dawn. She said nothing.

"You couldn't snare that old writer and now you are tossing your hat over the windmill for an old priest. Or is it the brother? I presume he is a farmer, being from the country?"

Deliberately, Cassa said, "He sails a boat on the Shannon."

"One of those!" Nicole was horrified. "A tugboat with turf?"

"Or maybe with slurry," offered Cassa, "or pig meal."

"It gets more disgusting. How can people like that afford the Glen? Or did you pay? Answer that."

"I forget," Cassa drawled out, and in her mind she quoted Jinny Corcoran: 'Frig off!'

"So I presume you did pay – more madness. I know the prices out there, and priests never have much money. Are you absolutely certain that you did not bring those men into this house?"

The thought of strangers eying the beauty of her Firenze was choking Nicole. Cassa would pay for this.

"Answer me, I said. Were they here, in Firenze? "

Making wide innocent eyes, Cassa asked, "Don't you believe me?"

"You are like a stupid child, foolish and ignorant. Dermot was furious when I told him about the Glen of the Downs."

And did he tell you he took me there? Cassa thought not.

"The Glen of the Downs, indeed. What would Papa say? You have gone peculiar lately. Dermot says you are head-hunting – the last try of the old maid. I have advised you but you never listen. First it was the lecherous writer. Then Garry Delaney, the notorious womaniser. Now a revolting tugboat man or worse still, a sick priest.

Nicole fled out of the house like a sudden squall, all doors swinging behind her.

Cassa sat quite still, letting the echoes fade.

Time was, she murmured, when I would burst into tears at this point.

All I am now is hungry.

CHAPTER FORTY-ONE

EVERY MORNING IN the hospital, Cassa observed that Mrs Loney and Margaret came in hotfoot behind Jinny and Annette, Mrs Loney rather puffed because Jinny walked too fast for her comfort. Bid and Resa were always next. They were permanently assigned to the intensive care units because they were silent and thorough.

Jinny and Annette worked well together. Sister Calasanctius complained of their endless "confabulation", and they complained of her sudden trap-door appearances which, Jinny said, "gave Annette clots in the blood".

M. McLaughlin's spiteful remarks about "the lesbians" came to an end when she was put in charge of cleaning the entire x-ray department, where she seldom encountered the other cleaners.

Rose and Ethel were still the stars of the circus, everywhere at once and indispensable.

Frolie and Dolly had found favour with the nun who controlled the female floor, both public and private. It was a tough morning's work, but they got along very well together and that made it possible. They actually liked their work. Cassa observed that they were a pair who managed the odd cup of tea and cigarette. No one had ever seen them without mascara and false eyelashes. They always put in a few rollers to redress the morning's ravages, so to speak, and with their heads tied in scarves, they swanned off from San Salvatore arm in arm.

That left Rita Clarke, and Cassa worried about her as she became paler and thinner as time passed. She had been put on the nursery wing where the nun in charge was young and amiable. Cassa went constantly to the nursery wing to help.

It was tacitly accepted that the nun in her kindness gave Rita a cup of soup if it was available. On the odd occasion, this nun said that Rita was missing: "She goes off for a few minutes, not every day".

On these occasions, Cassa took the lift to the male floor, often to see Rita Clarke hurrying back up the stairs. Rose and Ethel and Jinny were asked, in confidence, to head Rita away from the ward where her husband Richie was a patient, especially if Callous Anxious were prowling.

Rita claimed that Richie was "taking the cure", but as the weeks passed, Cassa began to wonder if the man was, perhaps, past the cure. At last, she cornered Rita on the stairs. She queried her gently, noting the trembling of the woman's frame.

"You do remember that the cleaners are not supposed to visit relatives during cleaners' working hours?"

"Oh Miss, I wouldn't dream of visiting him!"

"Why are you here, Rita, off your floor?"

The woman's eyes were full of tearful weariness, "Just to get a glimpse of him, Miss. It's been weeks. I wouldn't go into the ward, Miss."

"But you could visit him at visiting hours, couldn't you? At night between seven and eight."

"That'd be worse, Miss. He'd lep out of the bed at me. Ye see, Miss, it was me got him put in here. Well, it was me mother done it really. And me mother is going home to Wexford. She is fed up with me." The woman's face was a plea for understanding.

"I think you would like to talk about it, Rita, but we dare not talk here. Would you like me to come to your house?"

"It wouldn't be much comfort for you, Miss, and there's all the kids. But me mother would be honoured. I tell her all about you, the way you stick up for us."

"You live down by the harbour, don't you – the cottages? I'll come over tonight about seven o'clock. Stay on your own floor, Rita."

Sister Calasanctius was on the bend of the stairs. "Have you been told that that cleaner, Clarke, smuggled a bottle of porter into the ward for her husband? Reverend Mother was told by one of your cleaners."

"Who?" asked Cassa, knowing what the answer would be.

"The one who goes by the name of M. McLaughlin."

Cassa showed some anger. "That cleaner couldn't know of such a thing, Sister. She is permanently on the ground floor in x-ray."

"She saw it in Clarke's bag." And the small red-faced nun stepped erectly up the stairs as if in triumph.

Strange indeed, Cassa thought, the pleasure it gives that nun to put poor Rita Clarke further down than she already is.

At home, when the phone rang, she did not recognise the voice.

"It seems you have forgotten me," the voice said. "It's John, John Gowan."

"Of course, I haven't forgotten you, John. I was abstracted and worrying about things in the hospital. Do forgive me. It is nice to hear from you."

"We have not been in touch for several reasons, nothing to do with forgetting about you."

"How is Father Frank?" asked Cassa, a little at a loss.

"He is the reason we are out of touch. He wanted to be the one to make the phone calls, but he went up to Donegal to see our sister Deirdre and her husband, James. They brought him out with them from Killybegs for a few days fishing and they ended up in Aranmore and appear to be stuck on the island until another day or so."

"And how are you, John?" she asked politely.

"I am here in Dublin for the Boat Show, early this year. There is the AGM this afternoon, finishing about six. Would you, by any chance, be free to meet me for dinner?"

"John, I love that 'by any chance'. My hectic social whirl! But as it happens, I offered to call to one of the cleaners tonight, a poor woman in trouble and needing help."

"What time would that be?"

"I said I'd call at seven, so I should be back here at eight or thereabouts."

"So may I call for you at eight-thirty? I could phone and book for us at that same place. I picked up their card when we were there."

Cassa put hesitation aside. Why not? She had only seen him once and scarcely thought of him since, but why not?

"That would be just gorgeous," she said.

"And you can share all your worries about the job with me. I am a guy who knows all about job worries." He sounded happily relaxed.

Mrs Clarke's cottage was miserably poor. The children were gathered around a table, and a big stout woman was trying to kindle a fire with a few sticks.

"I'm Rita's mother, Mrs Yourell," she said. "You're welcome, to be sure."

The accent was country but the diction was clear and correct. "Excuse the cut of the place. It's clean but it's crowded."

Cassa had brought packets of potato crisps, biscuits and a couple of bottles of lemonade.

"Oh Miss, you shouldn't have! There's enough here for a week. Look at what the lady is after bringin'."

Rita Clarke's wan face was lit up in gratitude. How pretty she must have been, Cassa thought. She has aged even since my first day.

"There's a box of mixed sweets and some apples in this bag," Cassa smiled at the small expectant faces around the table. "Perhaps Mammy will take care of those?"

"Granny will," said the grandmother, seated by the fire. "My daughter Rita never learned to say no to those children – nor to anyone else either."

Rita pulled a chair nearer to the fire. "Sit down, Miss, and warm yourself." Rita herself sat on an upturned box, as did the children.

"You've noticed, I see!" said the grandmother. "The good chairs are all in the pawn, and the china cabinet, or down in that auction room. Everything that furnished this house is sold. Beds. Presses. Cups and saucers. All the best! Two big vanloads of stuff Rita's father sent up from Enniscorthy!"

"Mammy, don't! Miss Blake doesn't want to hear all that!"

"But I do," Cassa said quickly, "because I see you are very distressed every day. I want to help."

The frail woman clasped her hands together.

"If my Rita doesn't change her tune and listen to me, she'll leave those children in an orphanage. And what's more, Miss Blake," the grandmother became vehement, "he'll never lift them out of it. He's a drunk."

"He's only an alcoholic, Mammy."

There was a hush around the table as the noise of crackling crisp packets was stilled. It was evident the children were aware that a flood-tide of argument was rising. Mammy crying again. Even a nice lady bringing lemonade would not be able to stem the tide of the tears these children had come to dread.

Cassa stretched out her hands to Rita's clasped hands. "I don't think you are able for the hospital work," she said, "certainly not the scrubbing you have had to do on the nursery floor."

"Scrubbing!" the grandmother echoed the word in horror. "Scrubbing! You never told me that, child?"

"I like the hospital work," Rita Clarke said faintly, casting a look at the children.

"You like it because you are trying to get a look at your husband in his sick bed. He is not 'taking a cure' girl; he has liver failure. You know it and I know it."

"He'll get better this time, Mammy." In a low broken voice she said, "He's my husband, he's the children's father, and we love him. Don't we?"

This was an appeal to the kids. They did not seem to be sure of their response, nodding and shaking their heads. The little one slipped off her box and nestled into the grandmother's lap.

Cassa was touched by this scene. "I'll change your work, Rita. I'll get help for you as well."

"You can't save her from that snotty nun," the grandmother said. "We are not Catholic, Miss, and that nun has Rita hounded. It is not only about Richie Clarke who is out and out rotten, Miss, but because it was a mixed marriage and the children are going to the Protestant school."

"Religion has nothing to do with cleaning," Cassa said indignantly.

"In a Catholic hospital, Miss? Run by nuns?"

The grandmother had a point there, Cassa thought.

"I don't go along with the nuns in a lot of things," Cassa said, "and certainly not in this matter, I do assure you. And Rita, you should have told me of this persecution. Is it Sister Calasanctius?"

"It was M. McLaughlin who told the nun," Rita's voice was barely above a whisper, "I thought she was my friend. I told M. and she swore to secrecy."

The grandmother tried to control her anger. Quite obviously she was fond of her daughter, no matter how feckless, and fond of the grandchildren too.

"It makes no difference where you put her to work because this unfortunate creature's one object in life is to get into her husband's favour. In his health and strength, he treated her badly. I won't say in front of the children, Miss Blake, but badly is badly. And no one on this earth should have to hide their religious beliefs when sincerely held."

"Mammy, there's nothing anyone can do." Rita Clarke looked the picture of guilty despair. "I can't go and leave him. I can't."

"Of course you can," her mother said. "Miss Blake, could you talk sense into her? We have the place below outside Enniscorthy, room for all. Her father would receive her and the children with open arms. She knows that. And our people hold no ill-feeling for a misconceived marriage. She thought it was love, Miss Blake; she was young, she would not be talked out of it. You tell her. She will listen to you. That hospital will kill her. She was never reared for that. Talk to her, Miss!"

Cassa stood up to go. Talking another woman out of love would be the kind of talking more suited to Nicole.

"I am full of sympathy for you, Rita, and I will help you all I can."

She turned to the older woman. "You are a great mother,

and I think you will see progress soon. I give you my word, I'll look after Rita."

She walked around the table, asking each of the children their names.

"I'll come again soon," she smiled at them.

Cassa was glad she was going out that night. If she were to sit and brood on the scene she had witnessed, she would become very depressed.

John Gowan arrived just before half past eight.

When they were sitting down in the Glen Hotel, Cassa told him a little about her visit to the Clarkes' cottage, keeping the sad tale very brief.

"On my own tonight," she said, "I would have been very down. I felt so helpless! So thank you for the invitation, John."

"And thank you, too, Cassa," he said, "I too would have been on my own – or worse still, holed-up in a pub with a few hard drinkers who would be looking for a bit of diversion, or davarshun as we say in Monaghan."

He enjoyed Cassa's laughter; it had a gentle echo.

"All sound married men, too," he added.

"I never got around to hearing the whole story," she said, "but I presume that you, too, are a sound married man?"

"A bachelor," John answered, "and you?"

"What used to be called a spinster!" and she laughed again. "My sister thinks that I am on the warpath for a husband, so beware all good bachelors!"

She realised that she had not been hurt by Tyson's remarks, relayed to her by Nicky. Her voice was open and amused.

"I must admit that I am surprised you are not married." John was candid.

Cassa surprised herself by saying, "What a friend of mine used to call 'unclaimed treasure'."

John talked about the Boat Show until at last he fell silent.

To keep the talk flowing, as she thought a good guest should, she told him about the walk up to the top of the

Downs. That day with Dermot Tyson was a pleasant day to remember, and although she did not say with whom she had made the climb, she recounted the little adventure graphically, her eyes shining.

"Perhaps you and I could make that trip to the top," John said, "if we come some future time in daylight?"

They ate placidly at ease for a little while, then John asked, "Putting my feet in it again, you must have had strings of admirers, Cassa?"

"You specialise in compliments, John, but I must disappoint you. Quite honestly, there were never any admirers – never even any prospectors for the treasure!" She laughed again in candid friendship. It was good to talk, even if to disclaim his jovial flattery.

He raised his eyebrows in a way which said he didn't believe her.

Cassa said, "I could say: how come so fine a fellow has not been pursued by hordes of lovely ladies? But you know what I think? Aren't you very happy the way you are?"

It was an unintentional leading question and he did not choose to answer it.

"How is the dinner, Cassa?"

"It is very good, thank you. "

"I was admiring the dessert trolley as we came in. Cooking aboard my cruiser, I seldom think of dessert. I think I have a sweet tooth." His grin was that of a schoolboy.

They called over the waitress with the trolley. To please him she chose some chocolate gâteau.

"Have a piece of several," Cassa suggested to John.

"Frank would never approve of this!" John smiled down at the laden plate. "And speaking of Frank, he talked a lot about you, Cassa."

"Oh?" she questioned pleasantly, "in what way?"

All evening, she had been waiting to hear of Frank.

"He knows you don't like your job, and he wonders, for instance, if the work will be any easier for you at the end of the year when the contract is worked out and the nuns are no longer up on the battlements with their binoculars!"

Cassa was delighted. "Did he say that? Oh that's lovely! But, all I want is to get work experience, for a different job. I told Father Frank that."

"But the work experience will be for that kind of work, and you do not really like it. Won't it be another hospital, another set of nuns?"

"I have been sticking it, being patient with it, so I can say I have experience of going out to work," Cassa told him, "experience of work."

"What work would you like to do, Cassa?"

Innocently, and smiling, she said, "What I have always done since I left school. Look after the house and the garden, keep a few dogs, join the odd game of bridge, play the piano when I feel like it, listen to radio, look at television, and read a lot."

"Is there a reason you cannot have that life?" he asked.

Cassa was amused. "Of course I can't," she said. "Everyone has to work nowadays. My Dad left some shares and stuff, but it doesn't go far now. He couldn't foresee the way things would turn out."

"Of course," he said carefully, "you might get married? To someone who had enough to keep things going."

Now Cassa laughed in the gentle echoing way that he found so attractive.

"What a hope!" she said as she took up on the fork the last piece of chocolate gâteau, eyed it carefully and put it back regretfully. "Just too much!"

John insisted on an answer. "Why do you say 'what a hope'?"

"At my age!" Cassa's eyes opened wide with the wonder of it. "At my age, women do not get married. There is a time for all things. The time for getting married is in the twenties. You know, what you read nowadays about the biological clock?"

"I don't know," he said. "Is it about having a family?"

"It is the present wisdom," she smiled at him. "I read it

everywhere in magazines and newspapers. You know, about women who go out to work, pursue careers for which they have studied and trained, and which they are loath to give up. At the same time, they do not want to go childless into old age. So, they consider the biological clock."

"So you do believe in this clock thing?"

"I have no worry, it's too late. My sell-by date has passed. On my next birthday, I shall be thirty-four."

She was highly amused by this unlikely conversation.

"On my next birthday," he told her, "I'll be forty."

"If I knew the date, I would send you a birthday card. Forty is a nice round comfortable figure!" she was teasing.

"You have the nicest face I ever saw," he said, "and as it happens, this year my birthday falls on Easter Sunday, which is the middle of April, the latest Easter date for years or so Melia Tracey tells me. So you have to keep your promise to spend Easter aboard *La Vie En Rose* – she's a beauty, and you will love her!"

"There is nothing I should like more." Cassa's brown eyes told him she was happy.

John had made a tentative step into his future life. Cassa's light-hearted remarks had assured him there were no rivals and certainly no commitments.

As they were leaving the dining-room, Cassa caught a reflection of the tables in a large mirror. There, undoubtedly, was the back of Nicole's head, and the companion at her table was Clive Kemp. Cassa took a second glance. The couple, toasting each other with up-held glasses, gave the impression of intimacy.

Cassa held closely to John's arm as they walked to the Bentley. Clive Kemp, of all the boys Nicky had brought home for tennis, was the young man most sternly forbidden by Sadora's Rules .

None of my business anyway, Cassa assured herself. I've escaped for once.

CHAPTER FORTY-TWO

A S THE WEEKS passed, Cassa had a premonition that there was a catastrophe waiting around every corner. She woke up with it, she went to bed with it. As each day ended without the hospital roof caving in on her, the premonition grew. If only she had the nerve to walk out, or simply not to show up.

Perhaps, she thought, it is the silence of the Tysons: not even a phone call. Maybe it is the threatening atmosphere in the hospital or the constant fear that the women are doing something wrong; all the talk nowadays about drugs. Oh, rubbish! All those cupboards in the pharmacy are securely locked.

It was almost a relief when the blows finally fell, one after the other.

On a Saturday morning, the small red-faced nun was waiting in the entrance hall. She began a tirade which continued as the women straggled in, slowing down to listen, even as Cassa tried to wave them onward to the cloakroom.

"I have here my reports for the past six weeks – no, the time is past for interruptions. You will listen, Miss. Now we have a complaint against you from the highest quarter, Mr Ronan Loughnan-Marr, the neurological consultant who has patients on male, female and private floors. He comes through on Tuesdays and Fridays at nine fifty-five. You have been told this repeatedly. Mr Ronan Loughnan-Marr, who has high expectations of hygiene, has complained to the Hospital Committee! Yes, Miss, the Hospital Committee, that on more than one occasion he has observed tissues and fluff under beds. No, there is more. The sluices inadequately cleaned on three occasions, caused offence to visitors, who had never, they said, smelled anything like that in this hospital before. You, Miss, sent a request for a plumber to repair the destruction left by your cleaners! When we employed our own staff, there was never any necessity for a plumber. Our plumbing never went out of order."

"Have you finished, Sister?" asked Cassa, trying to hold on to her temper.

"I have this to say: Reverend Mother will see you in her office at twelve-thirty."

The nun had turned on her heel and was gone before Cassa could say that she went home at twelve-thirty.

Out of the corner of her eye, when the nun started her rampage, Cassa had noticed that Margaret was not one of the bunch.

She flew all over the hospital to see if Margaret had come in and was at work. Jinny and Margaret had been asked to keep an eye on Rita Clarke, and between them to help her, but Jinny had not seen Margaret. She supposed she was helping Rita Clarke. But Rita was slogging away slowly and dispiritedly in the nursery.

"Annette, have you seen Margaret today?" Annette, being the same age as Margaret, might know.

"She's not in, Miss. It's her fuckin' father. He took her outa the chipper last night. Bessie was knockin' on our door lookin' for Magser, at midnight . She musta never came in to Bessie's."

"Who said her father took her home?"

"Our Rory said he saw them. Ma sent him down to Tomko's for a basin of chips for our supper. I cooked the sausages and..."

"All right, all right, we are being watched. I'll talk to you later."

Annette had spotted the nun. "Shaggin' snitcher!" she sang out as she leaped into the elevator.

Cassa let the matter drop for now. Mrs Loney was apt to get upset when questioned. Cassa thought, not for the first time, that if only the nuns were more approachable, she could use advice. It was a pity that the nuns felt they had been let down in front of their nurses by the Hospital Committee and took out their frustration on the contracted cleaners, who really were, and Cassa knew it, an ill-assorted and inefficient bunch.

I'll have to find out about Margaret or replace her. She wished it wouldn't nag at her mind that Margaret had pleaded for help.

"Jinny, could we meet somewhere in Seacoast tonight? I need your advice or help about Margaret Riley."

"I'll give you any help I can, Miss, but those Rileys are fuckin' losers. Be better you'd steer clear of them lot."

"Yes, I know, Jinny – Annette told me when I asked her. I am worried."

"Look, Miss, you know where I live. Come over after eight. I'll be on my own. They are all on the darts team and will be off down the pub. I'll find out what I can before you come. Don't be frettin' yerself about the Rileys, Miss: sure, they were never out of trouble, seed breed and generation, as me mother used to say."

Cassa took off the white coat, tidied her hair and washed her hands. It was a little after twelve-thirty. With a bit of luck, the Reverend Mother would have gone to her prayers or her lunch and a note left on her door would suffice.

No such luck.

As usual, the enormous Reverend Mother rose from her desk. She motioned Cassa to a chair opposite, and then she slowly subsided, indicated a pile of papers on the desk. Her head went up and down as if in great distress, a sad distress caused by the person about to be reprimanded. Disappointment was evident on her broad face.

"Oh dear oh dear oh dear! Miss Blake, you are a trial to me. A sheaf of bad reports from all directions, from the highest to the lowest. From Sister Intensive Care (very serious, that one), Sister Gentlemen's Privates, Sister Chapel, etcetera. Sister Calasanctius has annotated your daily charts and the omissions are all there in red ink. Now, it appears, you have now taken on the habit of visiting the cleaners in their own homes. I require a few explanations. Speak up."

Cassa kept her eyes bent down on her hands. She felt like Alice in Wonderland shrunk to twelve inches. She dared not raise her eyes in case she would not be able to see up over the desk. Speak up, she said to herself, if you can think of anything to say.

"Speak up," the big nun ordered, sounding like a general addressing the Bengal Lancers.

Cassa stood up. It had been a hectic morning, she was tired. The only thing she wanted to say was: Here is my resignation.

"I have photocopied all the detailed reports Sister Calasanctius has prepared for the Hospital Committee, and I am sending them personally to Mr Tyson of Tyson Associates."

He'll be thrilled, Cassa thought irreverently.

"Your time is almost up," said the nun. "What have you to say, Miss Blake?"

"Only about Easter, Reverend Mother. I intend to take a week's holiday."

The words flew out like birds winging to a safe place, although they were words previously unconsidered.

In majesty, the Reverend Mother arose and extended a large hand to the door. Her voice was the condemning voice of a Supreme Court judge.

"By Easter, you will be gone out of San Salvatore!"

All this news would percolate to the Tysons tomorrow, so Cassa had one more free day.

She wished with all her heart that her conscience would let her off worrying about Margaret Riley.

*   *   *

When Jinny's door was opened, the gleam and glitter of the living-room was revealed as if all lights had suddenly flooded on. Jinny had been ironing.

"Come in, come in. Sit down, Miss. I'll get us a cuppa tea in a minute. I'm just finished the ironin'. You can't be particular enough about ironin' – and airin'! Ye know, Miss, I wouldn't let them use a handkerchief that wasn't ironed and aired, and as for an undergarment, the vest or the knickers or the men's drawers! Fatal! Fatal!"

Jinny folded every garment with scientific precision.

"That was what worried me sick about Eileen's babby, Miss. I cross-questioned her did she put a vest on Joseph Anthony that wasn't right dried and ironed and aired. Eileen is the best in the world, but she has a lot to learn."

Cassa was nodding sympathetically, and waiting for the right moment to interrupt.

"That nun that day, Miss, it upset Eileen. It nearly killed her. The lack of feelin', Miss. Them nuns is buggers. And the doctors! Half the time you could be dead before you knew the reason and maybe nothin' much wrong with you at all."

The ironing board was closed up and the neatly folded clothes taken away. Cassa took the opportunity to change the subject, hopefully to a less long-winded one.

"I must say, Jinny, I admire your sitting-room. The colours are warm and comfortable."

Now Jinny smiled with the pleasure of receiving admiration. "Ah now, go on! Do you like it really? I'm mad about decoratin'. They give out to me here. Killin' yerself, they say. As soon as I have a room the way I want it, that's the very minute I change it! Can't resist wallpaper and the new drip-dry paint. I mix the colours meself. Annette has no interest."

"But she is a great little worker, Jinny, better than expected."

"Providin' I'm there lookin' at her. But she's not a slut, I'll say that for her: she respects herself."

Jinny was now putting the kettle on.

"I don't spend all the money on decoration, Miss. I buy smashin' gear for the lads, too. and I put down a big nosh-up for them every night. They're good fellas, and I have a good husban'. Gets work when he can! The money is not bad these days."

"Will you soon be able to retire?"

"Never!" said Jinny vehemently. "I'll die with me boots on! I don't go out to work in the afternoons the way I used to when the lads were childer, but besides the hospital (and that suits me with Annette), I do usherette two nights and Sundays down in the cinema in Palace Street. I do a house in Foxrock on Saturday afternoons, the same I'm doin' for the last twenty years. There's only her and him now, a retired lawyer – gettin' on they are. The clothes that woman has given me! Good enough to sell! Like yourself, Miss, she's a real law-de-daw," and now Jinny drew breath to heave a sigh. "She hasn't been well lately. I'll lose a good friend when she goes."

Jinny drew breath to set out the teacups.

"Lovely to hear all about you," Cassa said gently. "It's so hard to get to know each other in the hospital. Some of the nuns resent the younger ones, I think, especially Margaret."

Jinny was judicious in her own way. "When we've had our tea," she said, "I'll take you round the backa the flats and we'll knock on Riley's door. He's rough and the bleedin' place he's livin' in is bloody awful rough. I told you, Miss, a fuckin' animal, and please excuse the language. He's barred from the pubs this end of Seacoast, but if he has money he'll have found a pub up the top of the hill."

The squalor of the Riley dwelling was appalling. The door opened directly into a room with a large bed. In the dishevelled bed lay the woman Cassa recognised as Tessie Tuite, now even more largely pregnant.

Margaret had opened the door, standing behind it. Now she saw Miss Blake.

"Jaysus, Miss, what are you doin' here! Howya, Jinny? Tuite, you know Jinny and Miss Blake."

Tessie struggled to sit up. "The woman from the hospital – she gave me a pound. I hope she hasn't come to collect it!"

Squeals of laughter at her own joke convulsed Tessie.

Jinny Corcoran was looking around. "Margaret, why don't you go back to Bessie Loney? Where are you sleepin'?"

"In the bed, where else?" answered Margaret, politely enough.

"In alonga me," chortled Tessie, "until I go in to have me child, any day now."

"How many little Tuites will that be?" enquired Jinny.

"I'm after losin' track." Tessie laughed again.

"And whose kid is this?" Jinny asked, pointing at the bed, "or does it matter?"

"It could be Riley's."

"What does Riley say?" asked Jinny.

"Sure he's de-lired. He loves kids." Miss Tuite rolled over the better to squeal loudly and enjoy the fun.

Cassa made her voice kind and quiet. "Have you left the hospital so, Margaret?"

Margaret's eyes were bright, but she only nodded her head.

"I'll go, then. I wanted to make sure you were all right. You are, aren't you?"

Please, Margaret, trust me. Don't put yourself in danger. The words would not come out against the squeaks and squawky convulsive laughter of the woman in the bed.

As Cassa turned towards the door, Margaret gripped her by the hand, but nothing more was said.

"We failed to see Riley," Cassa said as they walked across gritty ground.

"An hour later and he'd a been in the bed alongside his women," Jinny retorted.

"I don't understand," Cassa said, "surely Margaret..."

"Oh, she's been through it all before. No use goin' for the Guards. She's tough as hob-nails."

CHAPTER FORTY-THREE

THERE WAS A car pulled up outside the house. Cassa slowed down and put on the full beam. A man stepped out of the car and Cassa saw at once that it was Father Frank.

"I am so glad to see you, Father Frank. Come around the side of the house; the front door is bolted inside. Oh, I am so glad you are here. Come in, come in."

In the kitchen, Frank gave her a swift hug.

"What have I done to deserve this lovely enthusiasm? I was a little apprehensive that when you saw a car at your door so late you would reverse and go for the Gardaí? I was here earlier, and chanced coming back. Did I scare you?"

"Just for a moment."

"Good," he said, "but I get the impression that I am like the relief of a besieged citadel. Let's have tea and a big long talk."

"I could do with a bit of counselling."

"So what's the trouble? Let me help."

"Wait," Cassa said; "tell me about yourself first, and how your holiday is going, and why you are down in Dublin. You look just great," she added.

"All right then," he smiled at her, "we will dispose of me first. The holiday is so enjoyable that I wish every day you were there instead of in that hospital. I am in Dublin to interview three young priests who have applied for mission work in Peru. Well, to fill them in really. I did not know the exact date this was coming up or I should have phoned you. I only got their bishop's letter yesterday back in Carrick. We have been moving about."

"Did you catch many fish?"

"My brother-in-law James is the fisherman. I dossed on the half-deck. We were lucky with the weather and the scenery from the water is postcard picturesque – you will love it, Cassa. You are coming for Easter, now, aren't you?"

"This very day, Frank, I announced that I was taking a week's holiday at Easter! This very day!"

And then the whole story spilled out: the anger of her sister because of the anger of her sister's husband because of the angry dissatisfaction of the nuns. The constant battle to get the women to take the work seriously, to be respectful to the nuns, to avoid the "language" in the nuns' hearing. The vigilance of the nuns in looking for sins of omission, but never noticing work well done.

"I get so upset that I get angry, and being angry is so upsetting."

"Tonight, Frank, this girl Margaret. She's hardly sixteen and I was worried in case she had done something drastic, like an overdose. She told me her father abused her and she was never going back to his house – not even a house, his room in a horrible shack, and Margaret had begged me to help her, and, and..."

"And tonight you found her back with her father?" Frank guessed.

"And the father's woman is about to have a baby and no one knows whose child it is. Oh Frank, I wanted to be sympathetic and helpful, and all I felt was degraded and frightened."

He could never have guessed how much he would want to cradle her in his arms and comfort her with soft words and caresses when she raised her eyes to his in a plea for understanding.

But in her eyes he was not a man, he was a priest of God, to whom she could pour out her heart in full assurance of his friendly sympathy. He sat still and quiet across the table as the story went on, until Cassa could emerge into calmness.

"Thank you for listening so patiently," she said at last. "You never touched the tea! It has gone cold."

"You can make coffee in a moment, Cassa. You and I both know that the mistake in all this was made on the very first day. You are giving of your utmost in a place where you are not wanted. And you are going on from day to day for fear of hurting your sister, whom you believe is trying to help you to be independent. But, for you, Cassa, she made the wrong choice."

Frank took Cassa's hand and rubbed it gently as one would warm a child's hand. "I wanted to walk out so many times but it would mean a break with the only family I've got."

"Of course you would miss your sister and her husband out of your life."

"I miss you most," she surprised herself by saying, "I know it was only an acquaintanceship for a few days, but I really felt how far away you had gone."

"You had John down to keep in touch. How did that go?"

Now Cassa smiled. "We had a great evening. He is a lovely man. We chatted away like old friends."

Well, Frank thought with just a hint of resentment, isn't that something? If I can't have everything in this woman's life, I can have a percentage, maybe. A small percentage.

"Cassa, my dear girl, I knew you were unhappy, and unsuited to the work, even before I saw you crying in the nuns' chapel. You were cleaning my room when Sister Theresa gave you a dressing-down. I was half asleep, half awake, but I was waiting for you to pick up a brush and give the nun a good brush-off."

Her tremulous smile was almost too much for him, and then they laughed together. Frank watched the light reviving on her face, the easy way she was made happy again, the brown eyes lit from within.

"In the years you passed in this house with your parents, were you always contented?"

She was considering his question.

"You know, Frank," she lifted her eyes to his, "it is difficult to answer a question which one has never been asked before. It comes to my mind that my father and I were boon companions. I could not have left him anyway, even had I a career or a position in the world. There was my mother, you see. Before her stroke, in June when I was eighteen, my sister's wedding to Dermot Tyson had to be arranged. I remember my mother was determined that Nicky would get a good send-off. She was twenty-two. She looked so beautiful on her wedding day."

"Were you a bridesmaid?"

Now Cassa's smile lit up her face. She too is beautiful, he thought.

"Yes, I was the bridesmaid," Cassa said. "There were several hundred guests: all the Gilbey relations, all Nicky's friends and Dermot's family and Rugby friends and business friends and all the legal people that my father knew all his life. There was music and the garden was lovely, not like it is now."

"It must have been a wonderful day."

"It was absolutely perfect. I can never forget how beautiful Nicky was that day. She is like Mama, who was the most admired debutante of her day, it was said."

Frank kept his hands firmly clasped, his feet firmly on the ground. He had never suspected this depth of emotion within. He had always been sure that his own mother had disillusioned his heart of frail human love.

Father Frank gathered in his straying images, looked at his watch and pretended alarm at being locked out of his hotel.

"Ah Frank, you don't have to go, do you?" Cassa was disappointed. "I didn't realise it was so late. I could make up a bed for you. Do let me, it would only take a minute and there are five bedrooms to choose from. Do say you will stay."

He was fully in command. "Cassa, you are a real Irish darlin' lady, but thank you just the same. My effects are in the hotel. And, you forget, we have tomorrow."

"Will you let me make dinner for us tomorrow night? Please say yes. I really am a good cook. Please, Frank."

The invitation to come again tomorrow was too tempting to refuse. "Won't you be expecting a visit from your sister tomorrow?"

"And if she comes, wouldn't you like to be here to pick up the pieces? My friend?"

She stood back demurely as he passed through the hall door. She was hoping for a hug, but he had not dared. The soft warmth of her could very well overwhelm his strength of purpose. In the car, he drew a deep breath as if he had been running for miles. He smiled ruefully as he steered in a circle to the avenue, and he saw her close the hall door.

Sometimes she called him Frank, and sometimes she said Father Frank. There was an unconscious warning there. He was her friend, and she had quickly grown to love him, but much, much more than that, she respected him. That was an icy cold thought carving through hot emotion. He consoled himself with the thought that she needed him. The desire of needing her must be locked away.

Prayer was more necessary than usual tonight.

CHAPTER FORTY-FOUR

WHEN HIS TWO beloved daughters were settled into secondary school, Dermot Tyson converted an upstairs bedroom into a comfortable study for them. Each had her own desk and bookshelves, each had a cushioned armchair and chairs for their friends. A special big chair was known as Daddy's chair, and he seldom missed his own half hour there on weeknights.

Nicole would have preferred boarding school for them, but Dermot could not bear the thought of such separation. He was proud of them, and rightly so, for they were beautiful and very bright. From their infancy, he had built up a warm and confident relationship with his daughters, who adored their Daddy.

This slowed down the headlong pace his heart was willing him to take. The girls must not be hurt.

Tonight, Orla was trying to concentrate on her schoolwork while her inquisitive sister was ear-wigging.

"Sandra, please don't open the door. You are so nosy. I am trying to concentrate on this essay, and it takes me ages to begin. If you shut the door now, I'll help you with your algebra. Pleeease, Sandra, the door."

Sandra almost shut the door but, still listening, she hunkered down inside it. Usually she had to strain to hear, but tonight the tone of the voices sounded as if Mummy was getting worked up.

"They are talking about Aunty Cass," she whispered.

"It's rude to listen to other people's conversations," Orla said, but she moved over to the door and knelt down beside Sandra. "What are they saying about her?"

They always looked out for Aunty Cass in the paper shop in Stillorgan because they liked her so much. They agreed that she was the nicest person they knew, with the nicest hair and the most beautiful eyes. They wished she would come to visit in their house, or ask them to go to her house.

Sandra put her finger on her lips and breathed the word "Listen".

"How many times do I have to tell you, Dermot? It's not just the hospital complaining about Cassa. She's gone very careless what people might say. When I questioned her about what that lousy little solicitor said about her, she admitted that she had gone out to dinner with two men, one of them a sick priest out of San Salvatore, and brought them back to the house. A sick priest!"

"Maybe they were old friends. Why get worked up about it? The complaints from the hospital are more important. The nuns are against signing the contract, but Cassa will bring them round."

"You don't know my sister like I do. She is as airy-fairy about the hospital as she is about everything else. She's as lazy as hell, always was."

"Oh, come on now! She looked after Sadora for years, and then after your father. Richard can't have been easy. Cassa never asked us for help in all those years."

"She had her reasons, remember. She was working on my father all the time about the will and the house. She's mighty sneaky, his little House Bird. No need to raise your eyebrows. You know and I know that Mama intended Firenze for me. When we called over to Firenze after the honeymoon, you remember what Mama said when you admired the portrait of great-great-grandmother Elvira in the drawing-room?

"She said, 'It will all be yours some day: the pictures, the silver, the piano for your children.' I saw your face, Dermot, you were pleased. My sister has no right to anything in the house, nor to the house."

"Nicole, don't get wrought up. We've been over all this before. As it turned out, Firenze was not your mother's house to give. It has been a Blake house for over a hundred years."

"On the contrary," Nicole's voice almost shrieked at him, "it was my mother's Gilbey money which secured it for Papa. The Blakes were spendthrifts. My Mama was an heiress, a Gilbey."

"And you, also, were an heiress, weren't you?" His voice was dry and tired.

Behind the jamb of the door, Sandra whispered to Orla, "Did you know that? About Mummy being an heiress?"

Their Mummy's voice returned to normal. Very firmly she said, "I'll let Cassa go. She is a very great disappointment to me. I interviewed a woman yesterday who would be more suitable."

"Wait a minute, Nicole. Do you mean you are going to sack her? You can't do that."

"Why not? She's useless. Every day, complaint after complaint. She must be let go – this week."

"The nuns will go on complaining no matter who is the supervisor. It's a question of convincing them that they have no alternative to contract cleaning in this time of cutbacks. The trustees have not complained. Cassa is probably doing as good a job as possible under the circumstances."

"We did agree, Dermot, that the policy decisions are mine." Her voice sounded, to the listening girls, very hoity-toity.

Now Daddy's voice hardened, and the girls glanced at each other. "If you insist on letting Cassa go from the hospital, I shall find a position for her elsewhere – lighter type of work."

Orla and Sandra heard the ice cracking in their mother's voice, a sound not unknown to them.

"You said that before, but she is my sister. I am responsible for her and I will decide where and when she will take up a position." Nicole switched to cloying sweetness: "It must not be any concern of yours, my love. Leave Cassa to me. Come, darling, come over and let me kiss you. Let me..."

Orla closed the door very quietly. "That's enough for today, Sandra."

"Poor Aunty Cass," Sandra said.

They both jumped when they heard the bedroom door slammed shut and Daddy's footsteps running downstairs. Then the hall door was opened and closed.

"That's Daddy's car driving off somewhere," Sandra said. "I thought they were going to bed."

CHAPTER FORTY-FIVE

CASSA INTENDED TO do quite a lot of preparation for Father Frank's dinner. First, shopping. She dressed neatly, used a little make-up and brushed her hair until it shone.

She sat down to make a list, having checked her almost empty fridge. Lately she had lost interest in food.

She was all set to go into Stillorgan with her list when Nicole walked into the kitchen through the open door.

"Strange not to see you in your gardening rig-out," was the greeting. "Oughtn't you to cut the grass circle; it looks very neglected."

Cassa ignored this remark. Uppermost now was the urgency to get Nicole out of the house.

"Come into the sitting-room," she said, leading the way out of the kitchen and away from the tell-tale list on the table.

"I hate this room," Nicole said, taking a sheaf of papers and note books out of a briefcase. "It could do with decoration."

"Easier to heat," Cassa said as she switched on the electric fire.

"You must have money to throw away," said Nicole severely. "Don't you realise that an electric fire eats electricity?" Now she eyed her sister critically. "A much brighter lipstick would be a help to your lack of colour. Your idea of make-up is disastrous. Sit down, I have something to say to you."

Cassa sat down and gripped a cushion. Look unconcerned, she told herself. "So? Fire ahead."

"Don't try being cocky with me, Miss. I am your employer and I'll get straight to the point. Dermot has come to the conclusion, and I must say I have to agree with him, that you have no interest in the fine position he gave you in San Salvatore. The letters from the nuns, not only the Reverend Mother, not only Sister Calasanctius, but all the nuns and other staff, continue to pour in. Personally, I am not only disappointed, I am shocked. I should have thought you would have given us your best because of family loyalty."

Nicole's straight blonde hair was swept attractively into a stylised roll at the back of her head. Her suit was pale grey, as were her shoes. Her earrings and her delicate neck chain were of fine gold. Her appearance was rich, elegant, studied.

Cassa waited to be bowled over. Unperturbed is my only hope, Cassa thought. "Yes, go on," she said quietly. "Is there more?"

"Certainly there's more: trotting around the car-park in contract time, exercising your lazy muscles. Ignoring the exact method in which you were asked to polish the nuns' chapel. In fact, always doing the work in a way that suited yourself, contrary to the established, customary way of doing things. Sending, at great expense, for a plumbing firm to unblock drains, the damage caused by your inept instructions. Calling taxis to the entrance hall for women who didn't feel like finishing their day's work. Borrowing money from the hall porter. Indulging the cleaners in unspeakable, vulgar coarse talk within the nuns' hearing. Never making the slightest attempt to apologise for them. Worse still, hobnobbing with these women in their homes after working hours, and drinking with them in some cases."

Ah, Cassa surmised, that would be M. McLaughlin.

Nicole riffled the pages in her hands, impatient to find an accusation to which she could demand a reply.

"A lot of the reports would be much the same," offered Cassa blandly.

Nicole almost snorted. "Have you seen any more of those people? That sick priest?"

Cassa contrived to look slightly puzzled. "Oh yes," she racked her brains, "you mean the wonderful dinner in the Glen of the Downs? That was most enjoyable, a great night out!"

Nicole jumped to her feet, blazingly angry. "Whatever you are at, you are up to no good. As regards your own behaviour, remember that men are only out for what they can get.

In your case, a valuable property and the money Papa left you. Since Papa's will was published in *The Irish Times* last week, these fortune-hunters know now that you have something saleable. As regards San Salvatore, you are on a month's notice as from Monday. After that, you are out of work and you will get no more from us."

Nicole stormed out the door and into her car.

A pity to be fired now, Cassa thought, because she had just at that very second worked up the momentum to tell her sister she could stuff her old job up her jumper!

She switched off the fire. If she hurried, there would still be time to get the good things she had planned for Father Frank. Her heart lifted at the thought of her best friend coming to dinner.

Seldom had preparing a meal given Cassa so much pleasure. She made a pretty arrangement of daffodils from the garden and raided her father's drinks cupboard. She had bought mixers.

She debated should she dress up in a low-cut afternoon frock bought before her father's death and never worn, but decided on a blouse and skirt with a cardigan. At the last moment she clipped on earrings which Nicole had disdained as too grandmotherly. The earrings complemented her short hairstyle.

Hearing the car, Cassa greeted her guest at the open front door. He was wearing the good black suit and his clerical collar. He looked rather formal, but his dark blue eyes twinkled merrily and his smile was youthful.

Cassa said, "Every time I see you, you look younger, Father Frank. You must give me the secret!"

And you look even prettier, he thought, and you are so glad to see me that I must be very, very careful.

"I read up my etiquette book today," he told her as they went into the front drawing-room where she had lit a fire of turf and logs. "My book decrees that a gentleman visiting a lady should bring flowers and wine but nothing too personal. I brought two books, but they are parcelled in

216

flowery paper, very ladylike, done by a nice girl in the shop in Nassau Street." Having got this opening speech off his chest, Frank felt able to breathe.

Cassa was thrilled and excited. "Surely books are far more personal than wine!"

"*Perdóneme – lo siento*! I mean, why is that?"

"Because," Cassa said solemnly, "it is revealing to know what kind of book one's friend thinks one likes to read." She was carefully removing the wrapping paper, not letting it tear. "Oh! Books about Peru!" Cassa wanted to fling her arms around him and give him a big thank-you kiss, but the clerical collar was a gentle warning.

"You could not have given me anything I would value more. Lately there has been so little time for reading, but the summer is coming and I will be able to take my books out to the garden and read until the sun goes down."

She read aloud the titles of the books: "*A History of Peru*, and *The Mountains of South America in Pictures* – and oh look, such splendid pictures! Thank you, Frank, thank you. I wish I had a gift for you!"

You have given me your gift, he thought as he watched her turning the pages. Cassa Blake, you have watered the desert in a heart that had lost hope. Prayer will flower again in the depths.

"You will never know, Cassa, how much you have given me in allowing me to share your life for a little while."

"A little while? But, Father Frank, we are surely going to be friends for ever and ever?"

"But of course!" He hoped his smile looked sincere and persuasive. "From Ireland to Peru is only a postage stamp!"

"But you have months yet, haven't you, Frank? Aren't we going to sail up the Shannon together? I woke up this morning thinking immediately about you and John and the locks and that little place John talked about: Rooskey."

Settling down to the delicious dinner, Frank tried not to watch the play of light in her eager eyes. He concentrated on describing his recent expedition in John's cruiser, but it was hard not to treasure each feature of her face: the laughter lines, the tiny frown, the cleft in her rounded chin.

"Just wait, Cassa, until we sail across Lough Key, and maybe land on the island and climb the castle."

"Will there be time for reading as we sail along?" she asked.

"Hours of time, but you will take your turn up front steering the cruiser!"

"I just can't wait!" Cassa's face was alive with the thought of a holiday such as she had never dreamed of. "But if there's a wet day, will we read?"

"And play cards, or chess, or even Scrabble! My sister Deirdre's husband, James, fancies his genius as a Scrabble player. He brings along dictionaries and special-words books. He likes to play for money, a gambling system he invented himself."

Frank watched every movement as Cassa cleared and replaced dishes. Watch it, Frank, he warned himself. It is easier to slip over backwards than to climb upwards.

"I just looked at the calendar in the kitchen," she said. "It is only a little while to Easter! I meant to ask you: how did your interview with the three priests go off today?"

"Very well, indeed. They are keen, and strong and healthy. Medical examinations have to be thorough: parts of the Andes are very, very primitive."

"Were you ever very sick, close to death, Father Frank?" Her voice was caring, concerned.

"No, Cassa, I have been one of the lucky ones. My upbringing as a child and as a schoolboy must have toughened me."

She so admired this man. She longed to hold his hands in tender sympathy to show him that in her heart was love and sympathy for all that childhood sorrow. One glance across the table told her that Father Frank would not countenance impropriety, no matter how heartfelt. His priesthood had begun as a sacrifice to his mother, but it had become his enclosed sacred place, devoted totally to the mission field. Cassa understood.

Watching her face, he was reading her thoughts. It might very well be easy to let go. Cassa did not know it, but he was halfway there. Almost thirty years of his life would have been used up just to be thrown away. But would it be thrown away?

"Forget about me for a moment," he said deliberately and he noticed the slight movement of a muscle in her throat. "The main agenda for tonight is: 'Cassa Blake: The Rescue'."

She brought a tray of coffee into the drawing-room, setting it on a fireside table. Frank sat at ease in Richard's chair.

"When we have settled your future, Cassa," he smiled at her, "perhaps there will be a little of your music?"

"Frank, my future is in the past! After my sister's visit today, I am a hopeless case."

"I want you to tell me exactly what transpired, but before we get to that, there is something I want to tell you, Cassa."

His dark blue eyes were warm and happy, the firelight sending out their sapphire twinkle. Cassa's eyes rested on him with love, a love full of peace and hope.

"What do you want to tell me, Frank?"

He etched this scene into his memory: the family setting, the fireside, the coffee cups. This moment might never come again, and it was best that it should not, but memory could hold it in all innocence for ever.

"Cassa dear, I want to tell you that in my entire life I never tasted food so beautifully cooked and served. I enjoyed every particle. It will be for all time the most enjoyable dinner I ever had, along with the most delightful person who made it, and who shared it."

Perhaps the danger was passing. Frank held her eyes steadily.

Cassa was ecstatic. "That is the most fabulous, fantastic, splendiferous and nicest compliment I ever had. I did want it to be special. I am so glad you liked it!"

In the amber glow of the table lamp, her face rejoiced. Frank had said the right thing.

Frank remembered John's impressions of Cassa: "She does not play hard to get, she is quite simply uninvolved.

And yet she is definitely not unbending."

Frank wondered how much experience John had of women? And how much did he himself know beyond what he had learned in confessionals?

"Nicole has put me on a month's notice. She departed at the exact moment I was about to tell her I was finishing."

"You are not going in any more?"

Cassa considered for a moment. "While I was preparing the cooking, I was thinking. I don't want to go on working there a minute longer, but I would like a reference when I finish to say that I had worked as a supervisor in a large hospital for so many months. Surely that would not be too much to ask? It doesn't have to be a glowing reference, just a reference. And I have got used to the extra money. I need to earn that little extra."

"What about a week's notice? Or make it a condition of working a month, say until Easter, that they then give a good reference?"

He saw the perplexity on her face. Obviously bargaining with the Tysons would present insuperable difficulty.

"What do you think, Frank?"

"I would like to phone your sister this very minute and tell her that I think you need a holiday far worse than you need a job. I wish I could tell her what I think."

Cassa's brown eyes were shining. "I always dreamed of having a champion to stand up for me against Nicole, but my sister would be impossible to impress. Thank you all the same. You are the very nicest person I ever met, Frank. "

"I could be very tough on a person who is putting you through the torture in that hospital. I could give those Tysons a scarifying for ever letting you in for that."

"Lately, I got the queer thought that Nicole is punishing me for my father's will. Is that a very disloyal thing to say?"

"Did your father's will displease her?"

"I guess she thinks I did very well out of the will, Frank. When Nicole married, she got a dowry of £60,000 and a large house in Stillorgan."

"Surely that was a great dowry, a huge dowry fifteen years ago?"

"I did not know about the dowry then. The solicitor who was dealing with Papa's will told me all that recently."

Cassa knelt down to put turf on the fire. Frank would have wished to touch her hair, tawny in the firelight.

"The solicitor said that my father thought Nicole got a very generous dowry indeed and the solicitor said he was of the opinion my father made his own will accordingly."

Still kneeling on the hearth-rug, Cassa looked up at Frank. "I have never had a friend to talk to, about all this, I mean."

"Go on, Cassa."

"Now, Nicole says that I should have got the money and she should have been given the house. She says that Dermot Tyson is of the opinion that I should hand over the house due, he says, to the depreciation of what she got, and the appreciation of land around here. The solicitor told me all that. Nicole feels defrauded. They tried to overturn the will but they could not. I feel miserable about the whole thing."

Frank's eyes opened wide with amazement.

"You do realise, I am sure, that your father was fully aware of the provisions he was making for you in his will?"

"How can I be sure, Frank? You see, forty odd years ago, my mother's fortune came with her marriage. She was a Gilbey. Nicole was always saying, when we were growing up, that the Gilbey money was propping up the house, that the house really belonged to Mama." Sadly she added, "Nicole always came first with Mama."

"Or so your sister would have said," Frank's tone was cryptic. "Are you trying to tell me, Cassa, that your clever father was not aware of the undoubted fact that in this house he was sitting on the fortune some day coming to you? That they could give Nicole her Gilbey dowry because he had secured yours for the day you would need it?"

"Did he have that kind of foresight?"

"For you he did," said Frank decidedly, "and he knew you

221

loved him. Forgive me for saying it, but you gave up your life for him."

"Well, there was also my mother to look after."

"That too you did for him. He knew very well exactly what he was doing the day he wrote the will, and he never changed it."

"What shall I do about the hospital?"

"You are an adult and your own advice is best for you. I could suggest you give a week's notice. Or work out the month making it clear that's your sister's instruction. Demand your reference from that gigantic head nun – she would not court publicity, or indeed altercation." He smiled at her, and winked mischievously.

"I am thinking of the earnings which I put in the bank each time I get Tyson's cheque, and you are making fun of me." But she knew he was not. "With no earnings, what will I do then?"

"Then, Cassa dear, you put a few warm clothes in a suit-case, jerseys and jeans, and you drive up to Carrick-on-Shannon for Easter. Maybe for the summer, Cassa, if you fancy the place. Loads of jobs up there for the season."

"I was very lucky to meet up with a friend like you, Father Frank. I am so grateful to you."

Frank gazed into the glowing fire. Friendship and grati-tude. A man should be content and safe with friendship and gratitude. In the smouldering turf he could see castles in Spain.

CHAPTER FORTY-SIX

IN SOME MYSTERIOUS way, known only to the almighty Tysons, there was no mention from the nuns of dismissal notices.

Monday morning began in the same way as any other Monday morning: the women slothfully adjusting to work as if it never would come naturally, and the red-faced nun beetling in and out of every door, her notebook at the ready.

There was no sign of Margaret Riley, which meant Cassa had to fly up and down faster than ever to give a helping hand.

At eleven-thirty, she was called to the entrance hall.

"There's a woman in reception," the hall porter told her. "She says her name is Mrs Jane Duffy, and I seen her in Seacoast, she's local."

The woman was glancing through a magazine. She did not stand up. "You Missus Blake?" she asked lazily.

"Yes, I am. Weren't you here on the first day? Are you looking for work?"

The woman, busty and dyed blonde, threw the magazine back on the rack. "Now that depends, doesn't it? The Labour Exchange said 'Supervisor'. The one here now is leavin'. That's you?"

"Are you applying for the job as supervisor, then?" asked Cassa politely. "It requires training, or perhaps you have been training? Where?"

"Training?" The busty woman sounded incredulous. "Whatcha mean?"

"If you come with me around the hospital, you will get the idea. If a cleaner is off work, the supervisor fills in."

"Fill in? That's a bit Irish. D'ya mean, down on me hands and knees? I'd want danger money for that."

"We'd better get on," Cassa said, "the morning is nearly over. We'll get an overall for you in the women's cloakroom. You can leave your coat and bag."

"Ya must be jokin'. A cleaner's overall? If I wear anything, it'll be a white coat like yours. Even that's a bit demeanin'. Go on, I'll folly ya and see what I think."

"We'll start on the male public wards. There are two excellent cleaning women there, Dolly and Frolie."

Cassa's thoughts began to spin merrily. A new supervisor: the end in sight! Someone was praying for her.

On the male floor, bedlam had broken out. Rock music was blaring out of a transistor and a couple of nurses at the ward door were clapping and laughing When Cassa looked around the door, she was astonished to see Frolie and Dolly jiving   madly in the middle of the ward. Men in their beds were applauding the two wildly gyrating figures, arms and legs flying to the music.

Cassa switched off the radio. The two women collapsed in a swinging halt to the vociferous disappointment of the audience in the beds.

The nurses quickly disappeared.

Frolie and Dolly flew around gathering up their overalls and buckets and landed out on the corridor almost knocking down Mrs Jane Duffy.

Before Cassa could draw breath to speak, Dolly fell down in a dead faint, and Frolie began to bawl loudly as she tried to lift Dolly up off the floor.

"Jaysus, she's after killin' herself! I told her not to do it! I told her! Josie Horgan died after takin' them. Fuckin' poison! I told her she'd kill herself. Dolly! Dolly! Jaysus, Miss, do somethin', she's nearly gone! Looka her! Conked out!"

An alert was sounded. Two nurses lifted Dolly into a wheelchair, one held water to her lips, the other rubbed her hands.

Frolie bawled even louder when a young doctor appeared.

"What happened this woman?"

"She is one of the cleaners," Cassa said. "She was dancing a minute ago. It looks like a faint."

Frolie now yelled in earnest. "It's not a faint! She's dyin'. She took twelve of them pills. Dolly! Dolly!"

"Pills?" the young doctor asked, "what pills?"

Frolie was sobbing and hiccuping. "The ones Josie Horgan took and died from!"

"Get the woman down into observation," the doctor told the nurses.

He turned to Frolie, "Are you related to her?"

She nodded vigorously, the mascara running down her face.

He asked again, "What pills?"

Frolie was not sure should she tell the truth and maybe get Dolly into trouble.

"Say whatever it was, Frolie, just in case Dolly is in danger. There'll be no harm, I promise. Depend on me. Just tell the doctor the name of the pills."

"The name on the bottle was Penny Royal. She won't die, Doctor, will she?"

The young doctor hurried after the wheelchair.

Cassa took Frolie down in the elevator. "You go on home now, Frolie. I am sure you will know how Dolly is in a couple of hours. You could ring up, couldn't you? Fix yourself up at the mirror."

Poor Frolie's face was a sight. Runny mascara had settled on her chin and the vivid lipstick had spread up under her nose, but she still had her senses.

"That oul dyed-in-the-wool blonde up there when Dolly passed out – if she's workin' here, I'm goin'. Savin' yer presence, a bloody oul rip, that one! We were nearly leavin' so we were, then she went. We knew her in another job. She's vermin, that's what she is."

"You're tired and upset, Dolly. Hurry on home."

When Cassa turned back into the entrance hall, she was confronted by Sister Calasanctius and Mrs Jane Duffy who was gripping Rita Clarke by the arm.

"While you were condoning riotous behaviour, this wretched woman was breaking the most important rule of San Salvatore: she went without any permission into Saint Aloysius Ward and was about to give a very sick man this bottle of whiskey. This woman here saw what was happening, and only in the nick of time."

Cassa took Jane Duffy's hand off Mrs Clarke's arm, and drew the trembling figure over beside her.

"Is that all, Sister?" she asked politely.

"You take serious matters very lightly, Miss. The man is in the last stages of alcoholic poisoning. It is plain murder to give him drink of any sort."

Mrs Clarke shrank in against Cassa's side.

"Thank you," Cassa said. "Now, if you will excuse me, my women are coming to their cloakroom."

As she turned to unlock the door, Sister Calasanctius spoke loudly to Mrs Jane Duffy. "You would do well to contact the person in Tyson Associates who recommended you to the Labour Exchange for the job of supervisor. Be sure you give a full account of what you have witnessed here today."

The cleaners were all pushing into their cloakroom.

Jinny had wheedled the news out of a nurse: "They didn't use a stomach pump on Dolly in case she might be pregnant."

Bid Kinch had even more information. "I coulda told them she isn't."

"And how would you know – up to the minnit, like?" asked Annette.

"Because Dolly's husban' works on the mailboat. He's able to get trunkfuls of French letters. Been doin' it for years. Supplies loads of us – for a price, of course. Dolly isn't up the pole with a babby. Them pills she was takin' is for slimmin' ya down."

Resa always backed up Bid: "Them pills, I told her about Josie Horgan, we all did. Each of them pills has a tapeworm inside in it that eats up the food in yer stomach so ya never put on weight. Looka Dolly, she's as narra as a pencil."

Annette chimed in: "Maybe she is havin' a babby and she thought the worm would eat it as well."

Jinny gave her daughter a big thump on the back. "Watch yer tongue, young wan."

"Jaysus!" said Bid Kinch, "I never thoughta that: nothin's safe nowadays."

Cassa detained poor Rita Clarke until the others had gone. "I'll run you home," she said. "We'll get some crisps for the kids."

In the car, Rita told Miss Blake that all the kids had the measles. "Only for that, Mammy would have gone on down home. We will all go now. That's what I was tryin' to tell you. That's why I got the bottle of Powers for Richie. Powers is his favourite. Me Daddy is coming up tonight with the van and Mammy has our things packed in boxes."

Rita's voice was a thread.

"Miss, did you hear what that nun said about murder. I wouldn't harm a hair on Richie's head. I saw the bad news in the face of the nurse who let me into Richie's ward: he's not gettin' any better."

The cottage looked poorer than before. Rita's mother had lost her fresh country look, but her greeting was warm and friendly.

"Sit down, sit down, Miss. I hope you had the measles when you were a child. It's very catching. The school had to close. I have a blind up over the window to protect their eyes. Children can get red eyes out of the measles."

Cassa had stopped at the shop to get tea, sugar, milk and currant buns, as well as the crisps. Money must be at a very low ebb; she saw the relief in the old woman's face when the milk was put out on the table.

Where, Cassa wondered, did the whiskey come from? Some last object pawned to show her undying love for the ginger-haired man in Saint Aloysius Ward. Poor Rita.

"You must build up your health now when you are back in your own place, Rita," Cassa said.

"Health is it?" Mrs Yourell spat out the words. "Look at her! Skin and bone! And she was the Summer Rose of our townland, admired by all. Working in that place for slave's wages. Neglecting the children to go up every day to look on the face of a man who was never a proper husband to her. I'll say no more about him. I've said it all before. For work-house wages to look at him propped up in a bed."

Frail Rita broke into sobs. "But supposin' he got better, Mammy. Supposin' he got let out and came home. What would he do? He hasn't got anyone else but me and the children. We love him no matter what. When we're not here, where will he go?"

Her tears were pitiful and Cassa held her hands to comfort her.

"I know where he'd go," her mother said bitterly. "Miss Blake, this is new to you but her and me have been through all this before. I've done all I can. My own man is middlin' old now, and there's the land. We'll not give it up, nor let it run down. The lads will come home from America with their savings, they're good men, and the farm will be there. Only a neighbour and his wife comes in to help, I wouldn't be here. But it's over, Rita, it's over. Your Daddy will be here at three o'clock and we're going."

"One more week, Mammy, one more week. Miss here would get me another week, wouldn't you, Miss?"

Before Cassa could speak, Mrs Yourell stood up. "I made soup for the children. Bring it to them."

She ladled the soup into cups ready on a tin tray. She added the packets of crisps and opened the door into the bedroom for her daughter to go through.

Cassa heard the children's voices. Poor kids, she thought.

"You'll share the cup of tea with us, Miss – yourself provided it, and thank you. I'll bandage all their eyes for the journey, though it's a pity they won't see the scenery. Another time with the help of God. Life isn't finished, but I hope this awful dwelling is done for ever."

She indicated the cardboard cartons inside the door: "That's all they have worth taking home. Richie Clarke sold and pawned everything we gave them, even the good china cabinet that belonged to my grandmother, and my mother after her. Rita always fancied that cabinet, and she a young child, she'd polish and shine every little twist of it. To please me, she'd do it."

"This money is due to her from the hospital." Cassa

handed over her own small purse. "I would like if you would mind it for her. Today she might mislay it."

Mrs Yourell looked at the purse, and at Cassa. Then she tucked the purse into the pocket of her coat. "I'll give it to her in due course," she said. "I don't know what she told you, but the landlord got an eviction notice on Richie Clarke and if we are not out of here today, we'll be on the street before night."

"I am sorry to have to say goodbye, Mrs Yourell. I am sure there are better times ahead."

"Well, Miss, they couldn't be worse. I hope to hear that Richie Clarke is gone to his merciful Maker. Then she'll begin to mend. The children are great, and they'll soon forget. We have horses, and the river and the fishing. When Richie Clarke is dead and gone, I hope she'll forget him. But, you know, Miss, she is a faithful trusting sort of a girl."

On the way home, Cassa gave some thought to her own situation. She wished Father Frank were still near by. She wondered what he was doing at this moment: maybe sailing on the River Shannon into the sunset. It seemed like ages before they would meet again.

Then she thought of tomorrow. Another woman gone. Dolly and Frolie jiving in the ward: that would be reported within the hour. What evil fate had sent this nemesis of a hospital to ruin her life?

Roll on, Easter. Start counting the days.

CHAPTER FORTY-SEVEN

A S SHE EXPECTED, the phone was ringing when she went into the house. It was Nicole in full vituperative voice, hitting the high notes.

"Where the hell were you? You are supposed to knock off at twelve-thirty and be at home eating your lunch, not out gallivanting. You have become most unreliable."

Cassa barely felt the sting of the words. So many things had crowded into her life where once the empty spaces were waiting to be filled by Nicole's strange type of concern.

"We have had yet another blinder from the Reverend Mother in San Salvatore. What the devil do you think you are doing? You seem bent on destroying Dermot's business – all we have is a year for them to sign the contract. What's the matter with you, Cassa? Every day another disaster! And I was the one who told Dermot that you were the ideal person for that job. He is livid, absolutely livid. He wants you in his office on Friday. Say something, can't you!"

"Friday? Does that mean I don't have to work out the notice you put me on?"

"There's no need to mention the notice to Dermot. Of course you have to work out your time. Five o'clock in his office. You have to train in the new woman, Mrs Whatsername."

"Mrs Jane Duffy?" said Cassa brightly.

"No need to be so damned cocky, a new habit you have. You think none of this is your fault because you have no family feeling, but it is all your fault. The fact is you never knew how to handle anything. Even the old boyfriend, the writer who exposed himself on the landing..."

Cassa replaced the receiver. Family feeling, she thought. At that moment she didn't give a feckin' damn. That was Jinny Corcoran's phrase when she was being polite. But Cassa was not really smiling. It was becoming difficult to get to sleep at night with her head full of foreboding for each next day. She wished with all her heart that she had never heard of San Salvatore.

A morning came when the hall porter, usually yawning loudly at seven-thirty a.m. when Cassa arrived, was wide awake. There were bags, briefcases and coats littered in the hall as if thrown from a rapidly departing taxi.

"What's been going on?" Cassa enquired.

"I'll tell you what's been goin' on," the man positively snarled. "I haven't had a minute to myself since two o'clock this mornin'. Jeez, such a night!"

"What happened, are you all right?"

"I suppose I'll survive, unlike some of them that were hauled in here tonight. An oil tanker and a private car with four men in it. Some crash! Jeez, an oil tanker!"

"Sounds like a very bad accident. Where did it happen?"

"On the new main road," he said, relishing the details. "On the one bad bend in the whole eight miles of it. The one bad bend! The Super of the Guards said to me that it was an accident waitin' to happen, just waitin' to happen, he said!"

"I hope no one was killed?" Cassa asked as she pictured the very bend around which she took her car twice a day.

"They were mangled!" There was a small note of triumph in his voice.

"At least three men must have got their cards, goin' by what I saw, and I'd say I'm a good judge. Jeez, they were in bits!"

Cassa hurried away. Although she preferred the porter who came on the day shift, a silent obliging man, she wouldn't miss either of them when this month was over.

As the women came in, it was obvious they had heard of the terrible accident and each had her own version: the four men were young, out on a skite; the middle-aged men were driven by a young lad with drink on him; the truck driver was a demon for speed and probably plastered; no, he was a local man, a divil for the young wans! Go way outta that! That fella was drinkin' in Tolans last night, off duty. That truck driver is a married man with five childer, very respectable, as sober as a judge, a mean oul shite wouldn't give ya a drain of oil outa his tanker!

Not for the first time, Cassa wondered at the inextinguishable life in these women. To hear their ribald laughter, you would think they had everything to live for in a world of comedy. She always noticed that their miserable wages were budgeted-out in advance: fags and porter for him, a toy for the grandchild, a few shillings for the never-never and the burial society. They put me to shame, Cassa thought: my beautiful home, my sufficient money, and, yet, my twinges of self-pity.

Her mind was occupied by the usual strenuous efforts to get the women started on the cleaning, to redistribute the work to cover the gaps. Then the race began to be in all places at once, supervising of course, but actually doing a lot of the visible tasks herself.

Coming to the end of a very long corridor, she was surprised to see M. McLaughlin on the stairs.

"Shouldn't you be in x-ray?" Cassa asked.

"I'm lookin' for you," the woman said; "you can come down here and sort out that bleedin' doctor. The name on his office is Mellaker and he says he has a clinic behind x-ray. It must be done today, he says. It's up to you, Miss."

"I meant to remind you, M. It's a job that Margaret Riley did twice a week. She's out sick, I think. It's only a small room with filing cabinets. It wouldn't take you long."

"I'm not Margaret Riley. I refuse to go into that room. You can come down and do it yourself if it's all that easy. I'll go on with x-ray, which is what I was doin'."

"A moment, please. Is Dr Mellaker still there?"

"He's in there. I told him you'd do it."

Dr Mellaker saw patients with venereal disease three mornings a week. He was much respected in the hospital, a mild man with courteous manners.

Cassa was followed by the curious cleaner as far as the door of the clinic. When the doctor turned at Cassa's footstep, McLaughlin hid by the wall.

"I am the supervisor, Doctor. Is there a problem?"

"None that I know of. The room has been neglected for a

few days. Forgotten, perhaps? I asked the cleaner in x-ray if she could fit in a little dusting, and perhaps mop the floor. She bid me wait until she fetched the supervisor."

"Certainly that will be done. The cleaner to whom you spoke seems to have fears. Is that not so, M.?

M. McLaughlin moved into the doorway, glaring in her usual manner.

"Oh dear!" said the doctor, smiling. " You are quite safe. I would not bite your hand off."

"I am not going to put my hand to anything in this room," spoke up McLaughlin. "It's all contaminated. I might pick up a dirty disease. I'm very particular, so I am."

Dr Mellaker gathered his papers and prepared to depart. "As you please," he said. "You would be the first person in medical history to contract VD from the handle of a brush."

"They're all feckin' liars," McLaughlin hissed. "They all have it themselves. You can report me to Callous Anxious, let her do it!" She flounced into the elevator.

In less than a quarter of an hour the room was spotless. Another chore that would fall to her lot, she supposed. Another cleaner over whom she had no control.

Roll on Easter. Roll on Freedom.

On other floors of San Salvatore, Mrs Jane Duffy was creating botheration for the women. Resa Kinch had threatened to throw a bucket of dirty water over her if she didn't shut up. At twelve-thirty they were all fomenting with anger. Mrs Duffy had departed by a side door where she had hung her coat.

"Is it true what she said, that she's the new supervisor?" asked Jinny glumly.

Cassa nodded. "She'll settle down in a week or so, I'm sure."

"She does bugger-all work," said Annette, "all the time in cahoots with Callous Anxious, law-de-daw here and law-de-daw there as if she was a manager."

"Talkin' about the way she's goin' to change the way we do things, the nuns' way was what she said to that fuckin' snitcher of a nun." Bid sounded really angry and usually she was the one who led the laughs.

"Will Dolly be coming back?" Cassa asked Frolie, but she evaded the question. "How about Margaret Riley?" and again there was a silence. With Dolly, Margaret and Rita all gone, she would have to ask for more women.

The Friday interview in Tyson's office was lurking at the edge of Cassa's mind. She wished with all her strength that Nicole had never landed her into this ghastly job.

Every second day there was a picture postcard from Father Frank, always of the river and the cabin cruisers. The cards were treasures because they meant that someone somewhere was membering her, feeling sympathy for her, almost looking after her.

This gave her the small surge of courage she needed to pick up the phone and ask to speak to Mr Tyson.

"Who shall I say is speaking?" enquired the secretary.

"The name is Cassa Blake." She cleared her throat and took a firm grip on the phone. It's got to be done, she decided with a new grimness.

"Mr Tyson is expecting to interview you on Friday evening."

With immense dignity, Cassa said, "I cannot keep the appointment on Friday. It is urgent I speak to Mr Tyson now."

"If you would kindly give me the message, I will convey it to Mr Tyson."

"Very well then," she said. "Please tell Mr Tyson that unless Rose and Ethel (I have no surnames) are restored to the cleaning staff in San Salvatore by tomorrow morning, the work cannot go on. Three are out sick. I am finishing at Easter. And please tell him that the cleaning staff are not impressed by the new woman appointed by Mrs Tyson to take my place."

She put the phone down quickly. Giving ultimatums was not easy.

She wished she had Father Frank to talk to now. It was sad

to have no one at the end of the day when this big house filled with twilight.

She took herself for a long lonely walk to the top of the far fields.

CHAPTER FORTY-EIGHT

A T SEVEN-THIRTY THE next morning, the loudly yawning hall porter handed her an envelope; winking his eye, he said, "Sister Gentlemen's Privates is out for yer blood!"

Cassa read the note: "In view of the emergency in gentlemen's privates, two cleaners are necessary. Sister Theresa."

"Is there another emergency since yesterday?" she asked the porter.

"From what she said when she left the note, three of the four men are out of intensive care and into private rooms, and she was already overcrowded."

To Cassa's great relief, Rose and Ethel turned up in triumphant style.

"Just to tide you over the hump," Ethel said. "We are in the middle of the latest venture, in the new Training College, and due for the nurses home in Saint Fidelma's: they are nuns too and they are trying out contract cleaning on the nurses' home first."

Rose added, "You are getting three new ones on Saturday."

Rose and Ethel gave the other cleaners a kick-start, and the morning ahead was full of promise. Even Jane Duffy knew better than to cross Rose and Ethel.

Cassa hurried up to Sister Theresa's floor, where Mrs Loney was already started in her slow but diligent way.

The nun was waiting, her fingers tapping her pocket watch. "You take these three end rooms. These men are out of intensive care, but they are far from out of all danger. The cleaning must be done noiselessly and fast. The other post-op rooms can be begun by the other woman, although she is so slow that no doubt you will catch up on her."

Mrs Loney was cleaning the nurses' kitchen area. Cassa went in to warn her to keep clear of the three end rooms. The old woman caught her sleeve to whisper to her: "The babby was born in Riley's last night. They were all langered with the drink. The Guards were called in."

"Get on with your work!" Sister Theresa barked.

Cassa had developed a thorough and very quick way of cleaning the private rooms, never glancing at the occupant of the bed. Earlier in this job, she had found that the sick person was often lonely and bored, and eager to tell someone, anyone, the full details of his ghastly operation if you caught his eye.

In record time, she completed the first two rooms and went on to the third. She was working away, fully occupied with the task, when a man spoke from the bed.

"It could be the effect of whatever they gave me!"

Cassa stood up. "Shall I call the nun?" she asked softly, glancing towards the door rather than at the patient.

"For a moment," the man said sleepily, "I thought I was at Caragh Lake. It is Cassa, isn't it?"

"Robert! Robert Gray!"

"The same!" he said huskily. "Somewhat battered. I thought I was dreaming, and seeing in a dream a head of curly hair I remembered. You cut it."

"Were you very badly hurt in the accident?" she asked, forgetting to continue her cleaning. "You have been in the intensive care unit since yesterday. Oh, Robert, are you in pain?"

His leg was propped up in a covered cage.

"I'm in god-damned agony," he moaned. "Come over closer. It is Cassa. What are you doing here?"

He fumbled for his spectacles. "Now I can see you. When I saw your head bent down, I thought you had come to visit me and that you were crying. Do you work here?" His voice held all the notes of incredulity.

This recalled Cassa to the danger of being discovered by Sister Theresa.

"Yes, yes," she muttered, "and I must finish quickly."

"But why?"

Cassa did not answer. She was quickly polishing the window ledge and the wainscoting, up down, down up.

"Cassa, stop. Talk to me."

"I dare not," she muttered, knowing that Sister Gentlemen's Privates listened at doors. "I must get finished quickly."

"You can't go and leave me here! I nearly died in the accident. A lovely friendly face... Cassa, don't go. Cassa! Cassa, come back here!"

But Cassa was out in the corridor, his door firmly shut.

CHAPTER FORTY-NINE

O N THE WAY home, Cassa bought a newspaper. If the other injured men in Robert's company were as eminent as Robert, there would be an ongoing account of the accident. There was.

She sat in the car and read it over several times. The driver of the tanker was dead, his death from a heart attack apparently the cause of the accident. The car in which the four men were travelling was a complete write-off.

There was a picture of the wrecked car. It's roof had been shafted upwards, throwing two men, presumably those in the back seat, out on to the road. Their injuries were grievous. The other two men had to be cut out of the car. One was in a stable condition; the other was not. Although medical help was quickly on the scene, the fourth man had lost much blood. Cassa's heart was wrenched with pity, and then she suddenly realised that both Nicole and Dermot Tyson would have read this account. The names of the four men were given, each one a very well known name. Apparently they had been involved in a celebratory function in Trinity College and were returning to the home of one of them in Seacoast.

Her sister would know at once that Robert Gray was in San Salvatore. There would be a phone call to shatter whatever of idealistic love may have risen like a distant melody in Cassa's heart, but what Cassa was hearing now was very different: the note of need in Robert's voice when he cried out to her, "You can't go and leave me here. Cassa, stop. Talk to me."

And the American woman? Maybe he is married to her by now? But wouldn't she have been there, in San Salvatore, by his bedside in his private room?

Cassa hurried through her lunch. She raced around the house for a quick tidy-up. She wanted to be out of the house before Nicole called, or worse, staged a screaming visitation.

239

To be unperturbed, that was the thing if she were caught. As she flew through the tasks, she coached herself to be ready.

In the back of her mind was the dismal vision of the Riley room, the newborn baby, and Margaret (to use Margaret's own phrase) pissed as a newt. Margaret had begged for help. Cassa recognised that her own concern sprang from guilt rather than affection.

When the phone rang, she jumped. So sure was she that the caller was Nicole, she brought out a very sharp, "Yes, what is it?" instead of the usual soft "Hello".

"Oh, I am sorry. Is this a bad moment? I could ring later." This time, she knew the voice.

"John!" she sang out loudly, "is it you? It's a great moment! Lovely to hear from you!"

"There's nothing wrong, is there, Cassa? You didn't sound like yourself."

"I've been in the wars, John, and the call I was ready to take was going to be tough. Don't mind that. It is you and I'm delighted. Where are you?"

"Up in town again, this time for a Tourist Board meeting. It was over early. I was going to turn around and head for home, and then I thought I could ring you. Am I pushing my luck?"

Cassa realised he was very unsure of her reaction, but she was delighted. She laughed softly into the phone. "I am flattered to get your call, John. Why not come out and have tea with me? You will cheer me up. Everything has been at sixes and sevens lately. Where are you?"

"Not far away, the RDS in Ballsbridge... I guess about halfway between town and your place."

"I was just about to take myself for a walk. Shall I wait for you?"

"Please do. I should be with you in about fifteen minutes, I think."

Now, for the next half hour, she could dread Nicole's call. She went upstairs and changed into a prettier blouse, a nicer skirt. She brushed her hair. Tried on earrings, took them off, and finally left them on. She took out a warm jacket for the walk.

Still the phone did not ring. Which could mean that Nicole could descend on her later in the evening, maybe when John was drinking tea with her in the kitchen.

My sister was right, she thought. I dither. I am full of doubts. I cannot make a decision. Remember one thing, she warned herself, don't unburden all your problems into the first ready ear.

When she heard the doorbell ring, she glanced out of the window and saw John's Bentley in the drive. She ran down the stairs and gave him a big hug.

"I am so happy to see you," and she smiled up at his nice face. She pulled the door shut and linked her arm into his.

"I want to hear all about you, the Tourist Board, Father Frank, the cruiser, the river. I am counting the days to Easter."

"And we are counting the days also. Have you been getting the postcards from Frank? He has the shops in Carrick driven mad because of the lack of variety in the cards. I told him to add my name. I hope he did?"

"Is he enjoying his holiday?" Only Frank's name was ever on the cards.

"Absolutely! He is the real sailor now: no cleric's collar, decked out in an Aran sweater. He hasn't a clue what goes on inside the engine but he's a super steersman – no collisions, so far. And he is sleeping well now, although that took time. It's a different rhythm, he says, the heart or the lungs take time to adjust. It must be the case because tourists often tell me that their second cruise is much better than the first. We must remember that when you come aboard."

At the top of the road, the houses ended in open heathland, still unclaimed by the planning authorities or the local speculating builders. There were a few bench seats, placed for a view of the bay.

The same view, Cassa thought, that Robert can see from his hospital window. "I am hoping to meet your sister

Deirdre," Cassa said. "Will she be with us at Easter?"

"She certainly will," John said, "and probably her husband – he is a very busy man when the fishing is good. Deirdre is the gentlest person I know. She is already stocking up on food. She is a great self-taught cook. Her favourite reading is the cook book. Rows of cookery books on her shelves!"

"I like cooking too," Cassa said, "and reading cook books. It will be fun to have that in common. Tell me more about the places we will see."

So John talked away. He knew every mile of the river, the lakes, the canals. His enthusiasm was infectious. Cassa liked very much the northern expressions he used, the deep burr of his northern accent. He had built up a great business and he was proud of it, although he regarded it as in its beginning.

"Here am I blathering away," John said, "and when I go home, Frank will expect a full account of your doings. He is very concerned that you are overworked, and unhappy in that hospital."

"I'll tell you all about it later. You will have tea with me?"

"Link my arm like you did coming up the hill, and we can walk in step."

Trotting along happily beside this tall man, Cassa's heart suddenly missed a beat.

A car was coming out of the pier gates of Firenze. The driver glanced left and right, and then the car paused as the driver looked again to the left, a long look, before driving away to the right, on down the Donnybrook Road. Dermot Tyson, Cassa thought.

"Let's take this side gate," Cassa said to John. "There's a short cut across the fields." John, unfamiliar with the road, had not noticed the car.

No Nicole? Tyson by himself? He had seen her and John Gowan, but surely she had a life of her own as well as being their employee? It occurred to Cassa that Dermot Tyson would have seen the Bentley in the drive, right outside the hall door. That will give him something to think about.

"Shall we eat in the kitchen?" Cassa invited. "I am going to cook rashers and eggs. You just sit there and talk to me."

"Rashers and eggs are great," said John loyally, although she guessed he had probably had rashers and eggs for his breakfast that morning.

"I used to have lots of things in the freezer," she said, "but, apart from money, one person eating alone requires some sort of genius I don't have. I never make a cake nowadays because, by the end of the week, I would have eaten a whole cake!"

"You've never eaten a whole cake in your life," John smiled at her. "You look to me as if you live on fresh air."

"I like that! I think in the last six months I have used up more energy than in the rest of my life on the endless corridors and mile-high staircases in San Salvatore!"

"So what am I to tell Frank? When does it all come to a full stop before you fade away altogether?"

"You are a dab hand at the back-handed compliment," and Cassa smiled most beautifully, her brown eyes glinting with the sheer fun of their easy exchange. "I should be doleful: from Easter I shall be unemployed, on the rocks! I intend to finish in the hospital on the Thursday and set off on the Friday, Good Friday, for Carrick-on-Shannon."

Now the words were out, she would have to go. "You know, John, for the first time in my life, and on a Good Friday of all days, I shall have broken loose."

"Would you like me to come for you," he asked, "or would you like Frank to come?"

"Thank you, John. That is very nice of you. But," and she paused for emphasis, "I see my driving up to the north as a time for a sort of contemplation. I was thinking that yesterday. A time to think about the second half, of making a change, a beginning of an end. I am not the same person I was a year ago. I hope that doesn't sound self-important to you?"

He held his breath. To him who had not known a different Cassa, she was perfect.

She said softly, "For months I have been watching the clock, trying to please people I don't even know. I am like a person in a faded negative. Maybe I never had an appetite for life. I resist nothing."

John was speaking but she was hearing a different voice, the deep cultured voice of Robert Gray with its new note of pleading: "Cassa, don't go!"

"Think about it, Cassa," John was urging. "It's nothing in the Bentley, but your car is, well, it's getting on. No offence, Cassa."

It was after seven when he left to drive back to Carrick. Twice Cassa said, "Be careful, won't you. Be very careful, John. Accidents are horrible."

He laughed at her: "I'll try to stay on the road."

CHAPTER FIFTY

CASSA TOOK HER time washing up, drying the dishes and putting them by. Slowly the buoyant mood drained away. Any moment now Nicole (and maybe her big-boss husband) would drive up to the door and demand half a dozen explanations.

How explain away John Gowan, whose Bentley had undoubtedly been seen parked outside the door?

How excuse the shortage of staff in San Salvatore, and Mrs Jane Duffy's account of two cleaners jiving in a hospital ward?

Most important of all, what answer to give when they questioned her about Robert Gray? They would forbid her to go near him. If only she had never told Nicole about the lovers in the doorway in Garlow Lodge. Why, oh, why hadn't she kept silent?

To hell with them! I've tried and I won't try any more. Let her come now, and let her darling Dermot come! I won't be here to receive them.

All afternoon, far back in her mind, was Mrs Loney's whispered message. She would go over to Riley's place and make sure Margaret was all right so she wouldn't have to worry about any of them ever again. In case she had to go into the Corcorans' flat, she put a bottle of Jameson in her bag.

She left her car in the hotel car-park and walked up the hill to the flats. Two police cars and a crowd of people blocked the area.

"What's up?" she asked a woman at the edge of the circle.

"They're interrogatin'! Jaysus, Missus, they're at it all day! Them Guards must have no homes to go to. Before I went home to give the kids their dinner, I saw them walkin' Riley up and down and up and down, to sober him up. The drink was runnin' out of his eyeballs. He brung a new young wan in there and Tessie Tuite in the labours. And then they locked the door! Such a carry-on! The screams of Tessie was awful!"

"Was Margaret in there?" whispered Cassa fearfully.

Now another bystanding woman cut in, but she only added to the confusion. Maybe she was there or maybe she wasn't. No one knows! Willya look at the cut of Riley's new young wan! Bleedin' twat! That's all she is!

Two of the Gardaí were hustling a half-clad girl into a police car. Cassa saw Jinny Corcoran coming towards her.

"You best come up to my kitchen, Miss. No place for you here. Tim saw ya leavin' yer car down at the hotel, and he gave me a tinkle. We guessed you'd have heard the commotion. It beats all, so it does."

They went up the iron steps to the top tier.

"Come in, come in," Jinny said, "only the girls are in tonight. The lads are gone to the hotel bar for the semi-final of the darts. Put the kettle on, Francie, there's a love."

Cassa was seated into the best chair near the fire. She handed over the bag with the bottle she had brought.

"You keep it," she told Jinny. "I didn't know what else to bring."

"I'm glad you come," Jinny said, "because Magser gave me a message for ya." Jinny paused significantly, her eyes going around her family circle. "I didn't know it was a message... not at the time she said it, if ya follow me." Then Jinny continued most solemnly. "'You ought to be back at yer work in the mornin',' I said to her, 'and get out of that stinkin' dump.' That's when she gave me the message, only now I know it was a message. 'Tell Miss Blake,' she said, 'that she's the nicest decent skin I ever met. And tell her,' she said, 'if it hadda been a boy, it woulda been different. But,' and this is what she said, Miss, 'but another female girl in this kip would go through it all again.' Now, do yeh get the meanin' of it?"

Cassa was completely mystified. Jinny was assuming she knew of some event to justify the police, the crowds, the message. She looked around at Jinny's girls, whose names were hard to remember. Their eyelids were discreetly lowered.

"I had a friend to tea," Cassa said, "and we went out for a

walk. I wasn't listening to the news on the radio and I didn't buy an evening paper. Please tell me what happened, Jinny, please."

The girls now inclined their heads. This family had its own sense of theatre: the drama would be given to the queen. When Jinny began to speak, all the eyes were opened again and fixed unblinkingly on Jinny.

"The birth of Tessie Tuite's latest infant began at ten o'clock last night. Riley had come home with a young woman – he said she was a midwife. Around here, Miss, unless we're run into hospital, Mrs Loney acts midwife, but Riley's door was bolted and barred against Mrs Loney. Bolted and barred!"

Cassa heard her own low question: "And Margaret?"

"Magser had brought her fella in earlier. Petsey Farl is his name. He works in Adolfo's Grill." There was another weighty pause. "Petsey had won on a horse and was celebratin' and he brings in a truckload of drink.

"So there's Tessie Tuite bawlin' in the bed (and maybe others in it too, for all we know), Magser and Petsey, Riley and the new midwife, all barred and bolted in with loads of drink.

"Then Tessie Tuite's babby began to be comin', and she started screechin' for Loney. Screechin', Miss! You'd hear her in Holyhead. A crowd gathered outside the place, but would Riley open the door? Nor could the crowd push it in. It was like – a what do you call it, Violet?"

"A siege, Mammy."

"The very word. Well, of course, the Guards were sent for. We didn't know what was keepin' them, but there was that bad accident on the main road. So, the Guards were all investigatin' the accident. Women who were peepin' through the slats in the broken blinds said that Riley was in murderous form, his monkey up... if ya get me... leppin' on the three women! Riley and the mott he brang in was supposed to be assistin' the birth, God bless the mark!

"Before the Guards had time to arrive, the babby was

born. A beautiful baby girl, Miss. Well, the bolts was drawn back, the neighbours poured in, and the drink was poured out. When the Guards got there, the whole population was admirin' the new babby. Drinkin' its health – much good that was to its health, the misfortunate creature."

Jinny drew a long deep wheeze. "And we'll do the same," she said. "Get the little mugs out, Francie, and fill a jorum out of Miss Blake's bottle for each of us. For a bit of respect, and for luck."

Jinny began again on the last drain out of her little mug.

"As we all know, and can attest to in a court of law, we all went about our own business this mornin'. Those of us who work are signed in and said for," she looked around with pride, "and that's all of us. Petsey Farl was all present and correct in Adolfo's Grill. Riley and the new midwife and Tessie Tuite were sleepin' it off in Riley's bed. Yes, Miss, all three of them. The fella from Tolan's pub collectin' the empties heaped up on the window ledge, he looked in and saw them. The new babby's basket was neatly laid on the end of the bed, and the new babby was supposed to be in it.

"At ten o'clock a.m. Magser Riley took the beautiful babby in that plastic yellow shoulder bag, yiz'll all have seen it, she never moved out without it, and she walked down to the pier, beyond the cottages, near as far as the lighthouse.

"The tide was full in at the harbour. She walked into the sea off the rocks, the yellow bag on her back." Jinny's eyes searched Cassa's face in another dramatic pause.

"Two young lads mitchin' off school, on the lag, they saw Magser Riley walkin' into the sea off the rocks. Yiz all know the very spot below the lighthouse. They belted all the way home and told their mothers. They called the Guards."

Tears were running down Cassa's cheeks. She could scarcely whisper, "Were they saved, Jinny?"

"Swept out to sea!" Jinny gave the words immense tragic dignity. "Recovered late this evenin'. Dead! Both dead! Now, Miss, ya know the meanin' of the message poor Magser meant for you. If the babby had only been a boy...?"

"Have you told the message to the Guards?" Cassa was stunned, scarcely able to speak.

"No, nor need you. Eileen's Joe advised me. Tell them nothin'." Jinny looked around her circle, eyeball to eyeball. "Yiz all hear that. Tell them nothin'. We have our own lives to lead. Joe says, it's down to them – they're paid for it."

On her slow way home, Cassa thought sorrowfully of Margaret's pitifully short life, the bright inquisitive eyes and the poignant message.

CHAPTER FIFTY-ONE

F ACING INTO WORK next day was the hardest thing Cassa had ever done. She dreaded the loose talk of the women. She dreaded even more the assault on her already frail emotions when she must go into Robert Gray's room in the humble capacity of a hospital cleaner.

Driving reluctantly through the misty morning, the previous afternoon spent in the warm presence of a tall strong man seemed like a year ago. The hospital porter handed her yet another envelope. When he saw her apprehensive face, he grinned.

"Keep yer heart up! It's not the nun this time, Miss. I got a feckin' big tip to make sure you got this!"

Cassa slipped the plain envelope into her bag. Undoubtedly it would be from Nicole. She would have to read it, but she put off the moment until she had some privacy from the gossiping women.

Rose and Ethel were pillars of strength and practicality. They had no interest in the terrible story of Margaret's throwing herself into the sea with a newborn infant strapped to her back. Ethel and Rose never listened to gossip.

The nursery ward fell to Cassa to clean.

She always locked their cloakroom when the cleaners had finally been urged out to their separate places. She took the letter with her, knowing she must read it, but dreading to know its contents. A break with her sister and with her nieces seemed inevitable.

At last a moment came when Cassa could go into a wash-up, lock the door, and open the letter.

Cassa, what happened? I was sure you would come in the visiting time. They are taking me into a city hospital for tests... gone all day today. Be here for the visit tomorrow. I must see you. As always, Robert"

Cassa had the joyous feeling of her heart flipping over.

Be here, he had written. Be here! Wasn't that assured power one of the qualities she had always found so fascinating in him? She wanted to read the little note over and over, to analyse each word, to study the handwriting, but she had to fold it away safely, knowing it was there waiting for her to savour in her own time.

Cassa flew through the cleaning on gentlemen's privates. The other two men from the accident were still there, but they were both sleeping or perhaps sedated. The head nurse on this floor was reasonably friendly and Cassa approached her when Sister Theresa had gone to her prayers.

"I cleaned the last room," Cassa said. "It is empty."

"Oh yes," the nurse said, "but that man will be back tomorrow, so it will be ready for him."

"I thought maybe he...?" Cassa chanced.

"Oh no, he'll survive. He's just gone for tests. His left leg was very badly lacerated, especially the foot. He may be diabetic, which could be dangerous under the circs. He demanded to see a specialist he knows. We could do the tests here of course. Sister and he nearly came to blows. Apparently he insisted on sending for the paper man again."

Cassa had been wondering how Robert got the note down to the hall porter. The newspaperman, of course.

"They are havin' a post-mortem on Margaret and the babby," Jinny told Cassa later in the cloakroom. "The babby was still in the yellow plastic bag, zipped in, and the bag was still buckled on to Margaret's back. They got them on the turn of the tide."

"And a funeral?" asked Cassa sadly.

"Riley hasn't a tosser. Around the flats we are puttin' our hands in our pockets. We'll be able to get a coffin, one for the two, I think. Riley used to be in constant work and he may have his first wife's grave papers, but some sell the grave papers cheap when they're hard up. I don't know, but Joe is enquirin'. There's a plot in the Noggin graveyard for paupers. Joe is lookin' into it. In any event, we'll all be goin' to the church for the takin' in. All night in the side isle, mass

251

in the mornin', and then the burial. Joe will be able to get the details and I'll keep ya informed."

"Please count me in for the subscription," Cassa said. "Tell me tomorrow, Jinny."

The garden of Firenze looked peaceful and lovely as she drove up the avenue, a world apart from the world of the hospital. There were daffodils everywhere. She would have to look for help in the garden if she got another job with no half-days for outdoors work.

Her mother had loved the garden, always reminding them that her money maintained the roses. Cassa remembered when she was little in her first school, when the yardman drove her home in the pony and trap, her mother would be in the garden, her arms full of flowers.

There was a card in the hall from Father Frank: a picture of cabin cruisers on the river and in the background among the trees, a village with a church spire.

Cassa's heart lifted. There were good things in life as well as the bad things. Easter was coming. Robert Gray would be getting better in San Salvatore for weeks and weeks ahead, and she would be a free agent, able to visit him whenever she chose. And after Easter? Well, after Easter, who knows?

CHAPTER FIFTY-TWO

SHE WORKED IN the garden for a while, which eased her mind as it always did. She got most of the side lawn cut and some of the climbing roses tied back. She smiled to see Ena Harkness already in bud, a family favourite in deep red. A cup of tea and a cosy sit-down with today's newspaper, that would finish a nice afternoon, free from worry.

The phone rang. It was Nicole, and Cassa's heart sank.

"Glad to find you in, Cass." A very subdued Nicole? "I am coming over to Firenze now, if that is all right?"

So polite, so friendly and polite, that Cassa knew there was something amiss.

"Cassa, are you there?" the slightest shade of her more natural impatience.

"Yes, I am here. I am not going out."

"Right, see you then," and Nicole rang off.

Cassa could not imagine anything in the whole world that would unseat Nicole. Maybe the godalmighty Tyson had run off with that glamorous secretary in his magnificent office? She could not see that happening. Nicole was his right hand, and his daughters were his treasured jewels.

No, Tyson was too complacent. As Great-aunt Hilda Gilbey used to say of her famous nephew, Peregrine, "The world is his oyster, complete with the pearl of prosperity."

Nicole in low key? This was an occasion to be honoured: the sherry decanter, the crystal glasses, the fire lit in the front drawing-room.

Cassa's hopes soared: maybe the bad reports were all at an end? Maybe a reconciliation? Friends at last, no more harsh words. Maybe all good things come to those who wait. She had found Robert Gray, Robert Gray waiting even now for Cassa's visit.

Let it be so, O Lord: family harmony, a soft-spoken sister, a kind brother-in-law and two beautiful nieces who could come every day to Firenze. Together they would restore the tennis lawn, only needing a little care. She might be allowed to teach Sandra the piano. The little one had expressed just such a wish to Aunty Cass on an occasional meeting in the paper shop in Stillorgan.

"Good news, I hope?" Cassa enquired as she poured out the sherry and handed the glass to her sister.

Nicole was wearing the slimmest of slacks and a blouse the colour of her blue eyes. She seemed, to her sister, the most beautiful woman ever, and her face was not frowning but pleasantly focused on Cassa.

"About the hospital, Cass," Nicole said; "the woman we sent you, Jane Duffy, could she take over as supervisor straightaway?"

Cassa thought instantly of Robert Gray in his private room in San Salvatore. Quickly she said, "I'm prepared to stay until Easter."

"Yes, well," Nicole never liked to be diverted but she kept her voice even, "The thing is... there is something we want you to do."

"I am going on holiday."

"Dermot will see you get it, and indeed he will finance it. But not over Easter. Maybe a few weeks after Easter."

Cassa forced the words out: "I have to have my holiday at Easter, and at Easter I finish in San Salvatore. I have made up my mind and nothing will change it."

Nicole's face hardened, and her voice became the familiar commanding voice. "You'll change your mind when I tell you what I want you to do, and, make no mistake, what you will do." Nicole drank the sherry and clinched her eyes into her sister's eyes, as if the sherry had acted on her eyeballs.

Cassa knew the signs. Silly to think that Nicole could ever alter her ways. Even to glance at her struck flint in flying sparks.

"And what is it you want me to do?" Sooner or later the blow must fall.

"We want you to accompany me to a clinic in London for an abortion."

The crystal wine glass fell out of Cassa's hand into the fender, shattering in fragments. In blank amazement, she stared at the fashionable young woman in the slim close-fitting slacks.

"And on our return," the toneless voice continued, "I will remain here overnight. In my own room, of course. Be sure to have it heated."

An abortion? But Dermot Tyson was a devout Catholic. Cassa had seen him at mass with his daughters, and sometimes Nicole was there too.

"But abortion is a mortal sin."

"That has nothing to do with the present case. Your main concern in this matter, Cassa, is to make sure that woman, Jane Duffy, is in full control in San Salvatore while you are absent."

"Nicky, you cannot be serious. You could never go through with a thing like that and you..."

"What the hell would you know about it! And," Nicole added rapidly, "Dermot would never allow me to put my life at risk. A baby at my age!"

Nicole was not yet forty. There was no fear of her dying. She was superbly healthy.

"Nicky, please put this idea out of your mind. An abortion is murder. Please don't brush me off, please Nicky, give me a chance to tell you what I have read. You could never do this, to kill...?"

Nicole almost laughed in her sneering way. "Don't be a silly donkey, Cass. A woman has a choice nowadays. An abortion is like any other small operation, over in half an hour. Unfortunately, getting to England is necessary and I don't want to be on my own. Come on, Cass, cheer up, it won't cost you anything."

But Cassa was counting the cost to her own life. If she could persuade her sister to drop this terrifying plan, and if there should be a baby born, would she be given in return a nursemaid's job?

All hope for a future of her own would have to be relinquished: that little dream of Garlow Lodge, a woman in her own right at last. Robert in his book-lined study writing his famous books.

Or even, come to think of it, that idyllic vision of a cabin cruiser on the Shannon, Father Frank at the helm, John pointing out his favourite landmarks, and all of them sailing into a many-coloured sunset. The image of the sunset had become woven into the sequence of Father Frank's post-cards. Goodbye to all that. The foolish useless tears were beginning to burn her eyes.

Cassa's sister was expatiating, explaining, excusing, deny-ing, but Cassa could not pick out the words from the misery of her own inner lamentations.

Suddenly there was a crashing knock on the front door.

"Good Lord!" Cassa breathed, "Who's that at this hour?"

"Go and answer it," Nicole said in her normal dismissive tone; "probably some of those men you entertain – sick priests and the like."

Cassa went into the hall. "Who is it?" she called out.

"Dermot Tyson. Open the door."

When she opened the door, he brushed past her with a bare apology.

"What's going on?" he demanded of Nicole. "It was under-stood that you were not to keep on at Cassa, that she is doing her best at the hospital. I can see by her face that you have been following up on the nuns' endless complaints. Come, we'll go."

"I suppose I can visit my sister?" Nicole yawned delicately.

Cassa cried out to him, "Please don't let this happen! Please!"

Tyson turned stiffly. "There is nothing for you to get upset about. Come, Nicole."

This damned house was at the root of all his wife's jealous resentment of her sister. He had offered to buy it and move the family into it. Cassa could have the money and he would persuade her to travel, perhaps to study music abroad. Nicole stamped that plan into the ground.

"Give Cassa money for the house which is legally mine? You are mad. I'll get the house if it takes years. I am taking

256

an action to declare that will cannot pass probate. Cassa is incompetent, feckless, juvenile, puerile. Look at the mess she is making of our contract with the nuns." Last week there had been endless abuse.

Now Dermot Tyson turned to look at Cassa and he realised she was crying and trying to speak to him, repeating what she had said when he came in.

"Dermot, if we never meet again, please believe me when I beg you not to let this happen. Please, please use your influence with my sister." Tears splashed down her face as helplessly as if she were twelve again.

Nicole jumped between them, "Cassa, don't say another word. Dermot understands why I have to say these things to you. All in the interests of our mutual business deals."

Nicole took a grip on Cassa's arm, a familiar vicious grip, and Cassa quailed. Suddenly she wrenched her arm away as an unexpected spirit of rebellion surged into her.

"Business deals?" she shouted painfully. "An abortion in the interest of business deals!"

Tyson swung away from the door. "What abortion?" he thundered.

"That's enough, Cassa." Nicole moved swiftly to stand beside her husband, her attitude fiercely protective of his hurt that her stupid sister should dare to shout at him.

She put out her hand to open the door, but Tyson touched her arm. "I will hear her out!" he barked.

Cassa felt blindly for a handkerchief; she tried to dry her face. Her sister must not do this awful thing. She remembered a poem which had touched her deeply, and maybe it would also touch the heart of her adamant sister.

The pleading words came trembling out in the urgent necessity to persuade Dermot Tyson to listen.

"I was the price you paid for a candlelight dinner

That starry winter's night

By crocus time you knew of me and of my father's betrayal

Why did I cause you such bitter tears of anguish, fear, rejection?

Little mother, I could have loved you so..."

Tyson gripped the door handle. "That is enough!" he shouted at her. "You are an ungrateful woman who rejects everything that is done to help you. Everything."

"No, no, Dermot. That is not the way it was. I haven't got the words, but just listen, please, please, just hear the rest and you will understand..."

He interrupted harshly, "I understand nothing. I don't want to hear this." His broad shoulders were rigid but he did not open the door. Nicole tried to divert his attention, but Cassa's voice had grown clearer.

"Near Eastertide I was to die

I struggled in that awful moment when they crushed my tiny body..."

This was too much for Tyson. He pulled at the door with words so angry they choked his throat and made no sense. Cassa ran towards him trying to hold his arm, but Nicole, her eyes blazing, pushed her aside. They were gone, both of them; the door slammed violently.

Cassa knelt down and buried her face in Sadora's cushioned couch. Cassa saw plainly that Dermot did not know. How quick he was to assume that Cassa was the pregnant woman. So kind, Cassa thought, when she needed help for Mindo and Fred who were, after all, only dogs. His harsh judgment had been instant, contemptuous.

Now she took in, very slowly, the actual meaning of the scene. The lines of the poem came back to her. These words must be her shield against the danger of submission to her sister. If only Nicky had heard all of the pleading in the little poem, but would Nicky ever listen to a poem chosen by her sister, her stupid little sister?

Why would the Tysons not welcome a baby, a symbol of their love in their successful married life? Or was it only Nicky? An abortion might be the last desperate resort of a helpless impoverished woman, but surely not her sister Nicky?

CHAPTER FIFTY-THREE

D ERMOT TYSON STOOD on the steps of his house until his wife's car was beside his on the drive. He used a phrase he had never used before: "We have to talk."

In the lounge Nicole lit a cigarette, to give him something to object to, but he said nothing.

His wife could be discursive with the truth, so he usually found his own way around events. Tonight, he was at a loss.

"What's going on?" he demanded.

Nicole shrugged delicately as if the subject might be distasteful.

"You tell me," she quipped, flicking the cigarette into the ashtray. "How about bed, darling?"

She draped herself on the settee, slipping off her high heels. "Sweetheart, I need a hug."

He stood inside the door and he repeated, "What's going on? Answer me, Nicole."

"What do you want me to say, my pet?" She pouted in her appealing way and blew a kiss to him.

"What was that about an abortion? What was she saying about the price she had to pay for her candlelight dinner?"

Nicole had noted, with a certain amount of surprise, her husband's violent rage at Cassa. Very revealing, taken in conjunction with his early insistence on sending Cassa's weekly pay out of his own accounts, and with the many battles he put up to rescue Cassa from contract cleaning?

Sympathy for her sister, poor orphan, was allowed. But he would do well not to get notions.

She took another cigarette. Waving it in the air, she drawled casually, "Just Cass being a silly donkey! The usual rubbish! Something about one of the cleaners."

"I told her not to get involved in a personal way with the women," he said. "A tender heart in business never pays off. But if she was talking about herself, you would tell me, naturally?"

Through half-closed eyes, Nicole watched his face. "Perhaps she was?"

Now his anger exploded. "I would not allow her to have an abortion. That is utterly against the Law of God. No, Cassa is too much of a prude to have anything to do with any man. Perhaps she is taking sides with a daughter of one of the cleaners against the mother? Do you think?"

Nicole laughed up into his face. "What an imagination! Scriptwriting! Cass is acting the nitwit. It's the same way she carries on with the nuns."

"A few days ago you mentioned men in Cassa's company. How do you know what she does, or whom she sees?"

"For godsake, Dermot, if you sneeze in Stillorgan, someone reports it. Let's forget it, like a darling man, and come on down here."

He had pictured Cassa in the arms of a man, some unknown man to whom she had surrendered the virginal purity which belonged to him, and only to him. Dermot Tyson had persuaded himself into the belief that Cassa remained untouched because she was destined to be his.

His plan was in place. He would not heed this abortion scare. He was convinced that such a thing could never touch Cassa. His voice hit a light note to convince himself that the scare had vanished.

"So, this is all to do with some unfortunate woman in Salvatore? You should have stopped me from losing my temper, Nicole."

As he stretched out on the long settee, he determined to see Cassa tomorrow night for an apology. She was due an apology, and he would tell Nicole so in the morning. No secrets at this stage.

"I thought you had forgotten me," Nicole whispered, "and I want you so badly."

She lay very closely. Her tongue caressed his closed eyelids. Tonight would be one of her gentle nights of slow allurement, nothing too fast because she sensed his divided mind, but of an enchantment to bring him back to dependence on his wife alone.

Her husband's physical flawlessness had never lost its charm for her and, while she felt free to live her own life by her own rules, she would not permit as much as a single thought in his head to go in the direction of any other woman, especially her sister.

CHAPTER FIFTY-FOUR

CASSA GAVE JINNY thirty pounds to help with buying the coffin. "I intend to be at the chapel when the poor things are brought in, but if I cannot come, it will be for some urgent reason, and I know you will all understand."

Her usual small routines had been given a jolt. "I see Dolly is back but, of course, Rita Clarke is not with us any more. Maybe Mrs Duffy has got confirmation that she will be the next supervisor."

"Look at her," jeered Rose. "She's dressed up like me Granny's turkey cock in a red kilt and a yalla blouse."

And Ethel added, "But Callous Anxious is in full confab with her, and the bleedin' nun is writin' names in her book. She says there are more absentees than workers. She keeps appearing outa every door, like a feckin' miracle!"

Cassa said, "We are supposed to be getting three new recruits on Saturday – if the nun doesn't frighten them away."

Rose, always a comfort, told Cassa that she would look after the new three. "Callous Anxious'd frighten the crows. Wait till Jane Duffy gets the measure of her. There'll be skin and hair flyin'."

"What do the women think of Mrs Duffy? They will agree with her, won't they?"

"They wouldn't agree with her if she was the angel Gabriel," Rose grinned, "but what option have they? They'll hound her as much as she'll hound them, and they'll be delira at the chance. You maybe don't know it, Miss, but they're as good as gold for you. No? I didn't think ya did."

As soon as the women had cleared off home and the cloakroom was locked up, Cassa drove over to the hotel. After three attempts, she got an operator on the line. She dared not wait to phone from home in case her sister was there already with her suitcase. The documents Nicole had put on the hall table were airline tickets, addresses in London, and a heap of credit cards.

"The name is Gowan and it is a cabin cruiser office number. Yes, it is Carrick-on-Shannon. Thank you. Yes, I'll hold on, but it is very urgent."

At last, the operator came back. "There are three firms of cabin cruisers in Carrick-on-Shannon, but I think this is the Gowan one. Will I dial the number for you?"

By a miracle, it was John who answered. She recognised his voice when he said, "Miss Brady is at lunch, but perhaps I can help you?"

"John, it is Cassa. I am ringing from Seacoast, not from home. I need help and advice. Could Father Frank ring me at home this afternoon?"

"Are you, yourself, all right?" he asked anxiously.

"Yes, yes I am, and thank you for asking. But I have a problem and I would like to talk to Father Frank, if possible."

"He just now went ahead and I was about to follow him. We invited some people to the inn for a business lunch. I am glad I was here when you rang."

"But he will ring me, won't he, John? About three o'clock this afternoon?"

"Yes, he will. Of course he will. Cassa, Easter is still on, isn't it?"

"Bye for now, John."

A saying of her mother's came to mind: "It is in the lap of the Gods." Funny thing, whenever she thought of Sadora, it was to recall some phrase of hers. When she thought of her father, it was like clutching a treasure to her breast for fear it would be lost. Long ago, all of life was a dream which would, some day, become reality. She wished reality had never come.

When Father Frank's call came, Cassa explained, stumbling over the words, that the travel arrangements and expenses were all in place for an abortion. She could not keep the shocked hurt out of her voice.

"Nicole will force me to go with her – she always gets her own way. And, Frank, apart from the awfulness of it, I cannot bear the thought of losing you and John and Easter and the river. It's mean of me when my sister is in trouble, but the hospital has been a heartbreak in the past few weeks, and I was thinking of Easter with such longing."

And so was I, he thought. Longing for your presence, Cassa, longing, longing for the echo in your laughter.

"Stay calm, Cassa, you are upset now."

"Oh Frank, all this is so repugnant to me. Perhaps Nicole is strange, different."

"It is hard to understand. Cassa, whatever happens, we are your friends. Tell me, so that I can note it down: the exact details of departure for London."

"She left a sheaf of papers here on the hall table: a dawn flight on Easter Saturday. She intends to stay overnight here, Friday. The time at the clinic is twelve, midday. Return flight on Tuesday late evening."

"I will phone you on Holy Thursday about four. Take care of yourself, try not to be so upset, and we will talk on the Thursday."

She wanted to keep him talking, the deep timbre of his voice with its slightly foreign intonation was attractive, reassuring, comforting. She fancied she could see the flash of his strong teeth in the movements of his lips. She thought of telling him about Margaret Riley's funeral in Seacoast tonight. Or maybe prolong the conversation by recounting the terrible motor accident on the high road, and Robert Gray's injuries. No, what had been of moment had been said.

"Bye for now, Frank."

CHAPTER FIFTY-FIVE

W HEN CASSA PULLED over near the church, there was a crowd outside. They were mostly women, but Riley was in the midst of them wearing a bowler hat like a man about to walk in an Orange parade. Jinny, her back very deliberately turned on him, was pointedly conversing with some of the cleaners. Two of Jinny's sons were standing by a handcart on which rested a coffin.

The daughters whom Cassa had seen in Jinny's house were all holding little posies of flowers, presumably ready to lay them on the coffin when the men brought it into the church. The women, conspiratorially whispering, were shuffling to and fro, anxious to move into the church out of the chill breeze.

"Why the delay?" Cassa asked Dolly, who was beside her.

"The clerk of the chapel is gone to find out, Miss." Dolly took out her compact to freshen her nose. "The bloody gale comin' offa that harbour makes yer face go purple – always the same, even in summer."

"Will the P.P. himself come out to tell us?" asked Bid Kinch.

"Some allow it and some don't, Miss," put in her friend Resa.

Cassa moved over to stand beside Jinny Corcoran. "Is there something wrong, Jinny?"

Jinny was so angry that she found it hard to speak quietly. "Who was it shouldered all the burden of gettin' the bodies outa the morgue? Who bargained for the friggin' deal coffin – no cheap coffins in Massy's Parlour? I felt like cuttin' the joojoos off the fuggin' upstart; I worked with his oul wan in the old hospice. They're nothin', an' they were always nothin', them Massys! I stood over him until he handed out that coffin and charged fifteen pound for it. Rory and Tim brought it home on the handcart: that's them over there, Miss. Who was it bedded Magser down in the coffin, dressed lovely in a lace dance dress given me by my lady in Foxrock – old but pure white as the driven snow."

"And she put the poor oul babby folded into Magser's arms, God have mercy on them." This was from Eileen who had so recently lost her own baby. "And Mammy made the wreaths, and posies for the babby."

"Two babbies," countered Jinny, "the other one in Magser's belly. Sure, she was only a child herself, never outa trouble. I gave money outa what we collected to the friars over in Church Street for a novena of masses, and now the feckin' P.P. won't let us in to leave the coffin for the night. Eileen's Joe is after goin' in to sort out His Worship."

Jinny's husband now took up the story: "The clerk of the chapel said His Reverence was only follyin' the rule. Suicide is a mortal sin, the priest told the clerk, a deadly sin and for that you go to Hell. So suicides are not given Christian burial."

Now Dodo took up the story, helped out by Violet, "Suicide and murder!"

"Murder of the babby, too!"

"And the clerk of the chapel said that even the pauper's grave is not allowed to suicides to be buried in because it is consecrated ground. Joe is gone in to find out if there is a bit of ground that is not consecrated."

"We're waitin' for Joe to come out," Eileen said, to which Dodo added, "If we're not let into the chapel, Mammy doesn't know what we're goin' to do with the coffin with the remains in it."

Jinny turned round, "Will ya look at Riley in the hat! He's feckin' useless and the feckin' cause of all the trouble. He gave a load of oul guff outa him to the clerk of the chapel, when the unfortunate creature suggested that Riley keep the coffin in his own house. He went to batter the clerk!"

"There's no room for the coffin there, anyway! Tessie Tuite is inside in the bed in the room," added Dolly, "and you could hear her bellowing in Holyhead. And, y'know, Miss, she's the mother of at least six other chislers, and who knows where they are!"

"They could be all at the bottom of the ocean for all she knows, or cares." This was Annette's opinion, for which Jinny gave her a thump.

"Jeeze, Miss, do y'know what: it's a bleedin' pity we didn't let the fuckin' sea keep Magser and the poor oul babby," Jem added.

Eileen nudged her mother: "Here's Joe. Holy Mother of God, he's carryin' shovels and spades!"

Joe addressed the crowd as if it were a political meeting, hoisting himself up on an old tombstone.

"Men and women of this parish, I am deputed to give youse a message from the parish priest, the Reverend Father P. Starkey. Under the special set of circumstances, His Reverence says, of the misfortunate manner in which the deceased met their ends, by their own hands as it were, one a day-old infant, the coffin may not rest, nor be deposited in the sacred precincts (that's what he said, I have it written down) of his church tonight, nor tomorrow, nor in the paupers' plot. There is, however, a small patch of earth, he said, unconsecrated for the purpose, under the high end-wall of the graveyard. If we dig the grave ourselves before it gets dark, we can inter the coffin. Which, His Reverence says, will solve the dilemma."

He handed out the shovels.

To Cassa, all this was unbearably sad. She was remembering the cheeky girl in the mini-skirt and her message.

Jinny's son-in-law, Joe, certainly had the gift of oratory. There was a small sarcastic note here and there as he flickered his eyes over the crowd, but his hearers were convinced. They might not have obeyed the P.P. with the same alacrity as they obeyed Joe, when he added another few words.

"That's me brother-in-law comin' up now with a couple a dozen stout! Share them out now, men, an' don't forget the wimmen."

It did not take four men more than twenty minutes to dig out a big hole under the high wall. Tim and Rory trundled the handcart up the path between the graves. They lifted the coffin down and the clay was rapidly shovelled in.

Jinny handed a wreath to Mrs Loney and another to Riley. Her daughters and daughters-in-law arranged their little flower-offerings in a circle on the rough grave.

Then she stood up very straight and turning to the crowd, she said sharply, "I heard what some of yiz said: if poor Magser couldn't be let into the chapel, yiz didn't think there'd be any use in prayin' for her soul. Well, the soul is immortal, so it is. Yiz are all very smart and yiz know feck all. Magser was only a child, and she never got a chance. If youse want to go home, youse can go. Me and my family is goin' to say a decade of the rosary. The First Sorrowful Mystery..."

When the prayers were finished, Cassa stole away. She had failed to help Margaret, through ignorance and inexperience, and she knew that failure would be for ever a sad memory of poor little Margaret.

Driving home, she passed again by San Salvatore with its every window brightly lit. Late evening visiting time. She pulled into the car-park.

Then she hesitated. Tonight she doubted if she could show the happy cheerful face a sick man would expect.

Tomorrow, Robert, tomorrow.

Reluctantly, she switched on the ignition and regretfully moved back out on to the road. She would love to have gone into the hospital, to be with him, to hear his melodious voice, to wish him a happy recovery

But not tonight. Tomorrow she would look better. It was essential to look her very best. Robert Gray was a very special man. Any distant misgiving to the contrary had been banished.

CHAPTER FIFTY-SIX

CONTRARY TO CASSA'S expectations, the three new cleaners turned up early. They were reasonably young and they had worked before. The small red-faced nun asked their names and wrote them into her notebook. She was about to give them a lecture, no doubt on the great honour of being allowed work with nuns in a prestigious hospital, but Cassa shooed Callous Anxious out of the women's cloakroom with scant courtesy.

Rose and Ethel took charge of the three new cleaners. Jane Duffy was all set to be officious, but no one noticed her.

"Rose, could one of them fill in with Mrs Loney on gentlemen's privates? I will have to do the nursery, and this is the day for the nuns' chapel."

Incredibly the morning passed without incident. Perhaps contract cleaning could work, most days anyway.

Cassa decided she would go home after work to change her clothes for visiting hour in San Salvatore. She had ascertained that Robert was back in his private room. She was a little apprehensive at the thought of visiting Robert. She still harboured a vague fantasy of a real liaison with Robert Gray. Just a friendship of course, but a close friendship. But maybe the American woman was still in his life, or maybe some other woman?

He was a very attractive man; there had always been feminine admirers for Louise to keep at bay. Louise had enjoyed a teasing amusement at "Robert's fan club" and there had been times when he did not seem too pleased. Cassa wondered if perhaps Louise could be a little bit jealous? She was left in the background rather more than so lovely a woman might expect.

Ah no, in Cassa's memory they were madly, feverishly in love, and Louise had enjoyed her life to the full. Cassa had always felt the smallest tinge of envy when she witnessed Louise's adoration for Robert. A man in a million.

The day porter smiled nicely at Cassa as she passed through the entrance hall. She went up in the elevator to the male private rooms.

There was no sound of Sister Theresa's voice. Cassa knocked politely on the last door, and peeped into the room. All was well. Robert was propped up in his bed, surrounded by newspapers.

"Cassa! Cassa! I thought you had deserted me. Bring over a chair. Sit down and talk to me, and let me talk to you."

He talked about his tests, his treatment, his pains and aches, his resentments, the hospital food.

The thing is, she was thinking, I could listen to his voice all day. It does not really matter what he is saying. It is the music of his voice, not like any other voice I know.

He went on complaining most musically: "I can't stand this bed-bath thing, and this blasted bed-pan thing is even worse. They won't let me put my foot to the ground. I have demanded a wheelchair – it is supposed to be available first thing tomorrow. Three months, that doctor said, three months before I can walk. Bed rest for three months!"

"Here? In San Salvatore?"

Cassa gazed at his face, grey eyes under jet-black brows although his hair was silver, a mane of hair that fell over his forehead. "Here? In hospital?"

"I do not believe so, and I hope not." He gave her that famous smile, the smile always on the covers of his books. "I could be home in Garlow Lodge in a few weeks. At least it is home, nowhere else ever is."

"You have good help there to look after you?" Cassa ventured to ask, but very quietly, so as to keep the burning curiosity out of her voice.

"I don't have anyone," he said.

Cassa was surprised. "I thought there was staff?"

"We had had help, Bridget and a man who did the garden and odd jobs, but Louise had let them go."

"Expensive, keeping staff," Cassa murmured.

"It was not the expense," he said. "After Louise's tragic

death, I took six months writer-in-residence at Yale. I had some Americans staying at the time – Enda MacNeill and his wife. He had to go back to California, but she stayed on to give me a hand with the funeral. Maybe you remember her? I know you came for the funeral, Cassa, but there were so many people coming to the house, I hardly saw you. Are you working here, or did I dream it?"

"I have been working here," Cassa said, "but this is my last week: I finish on Thursday."

"How are your mother and father?"

"My parents are both dead. My father died suddenly last year. I am quite alone – same house, of course."

"I never knew of this!" He was sincerely moved. "Did Louise know? Did she write to you?"

"There was a whole year in which I never heard from Louise. No Caragh Lake that year." Cassa's voice was sad.

"You know the circumstances, of course?" His voice was puzzled. "You came to the funeral."

"I came because I read of the death in the deaths column of *The Irish Times*."

She wanted to ask why he had not let her know. After all, she was Louise's lifelong friend.

"Did Mrs MacNeill not tell you?" he asked.

"We did not talk," Cassa said. "I left quickly."

And vividly into her mind came the dawn-lit scene of the naked lovers. Lovers of a single night? Were such things possible? A man seeking oblivion in lust? Not two impetuous youngsters trying to give each other a lasting memento of passion, but a man with a dead wife and a woman with an absent husband? The impression in Cassa's memory, on that misty morning, was of two mature people fully accomplished in the art of mutual seduction.

"Louise had barred all our friends. We went to Caragh Lake, but we went alone. In that year I began to realise that she had grown to hate me." His voice trailed away to a whisper, an almost theatrical whisper.

"I am sure that is not true," Cassa said gently. "Louise

adored you."

"Louise changed, Cassa. I blame myself. I was away a lot – lecture tours. But you know, you must have heard?"

"Robert, I only saw the newspaper notice."

Almost inaudibly he said, "Louise took her own life. In Caragh Lake. While I was in New York to receive some damned honour, she drove down to Caragh Lake alone. She left a letter with the Reverend Slater, of our local church."

Cassa was stunned and shocked; tears burst from her eyes. She buried her face in her hands, murmuring her sorrow and her sympathy.

Robert Gray was very moved by her distress. "Poor Cassa! Poor Cassa! You and Louise were such close friends. Don't, my dear, don't."

He leaned from the bed to take her hand. "Tender-hearted Cassa!"

She had to get away. She would have to sort out her tangled thoughts. Once again they were dominated by the dawn-lit nightmare of the lovers.

She stood up, gathering her scarf and her handbag. "I am sorry, Robert. I didn't know."

"Cassa, my dear. Please come tomorrow," he urged her. "I will expect you. Please be here tomorrow."

At the door, she looked back at him. Before Cassa Blake entered Robert's life as a cleaning woman and returned to his room as a visitor, he had probably rarely given her a thought. Cassa Blake had had almost twenty years to think of Robert Gray as the ideal man, and in spite of that scene at Garlow Lodge, she could not quite let go of the dream.

The man in the hospital bed was awarding her his handsome, intellectual smile, his long fingers pushing back his heavy silver hair. "You will be back tomorrow, won't you, Cassa?"

Cassa shut the door.

In the car, she sat very still and tried to take hold of her thoughts.

Margaret Riley's suicide was understandable and very forgivable. What had the poor kid to live for? But Louise? The beautiful and regal, the brilliantly clever Louise. Why? Loneliness? Louise had known how to fill the gaps when her husband was away earning ever bigger money. Louise had said so to Cassa many times.

There had to be a better reason for Louise to commit suicide. A suicide often aimed to punish someone, to make someone wretched and repentant. The one left behind was the victim.

Robert Gray a victim? He had taken up his life, he had re-assumed the mantle of fame. Would even this present awful accident change his sense of his place in the centre of his world?

"Be here," he had said.

Cassa supposed she would obey.

CHAPTER FIFTY-SEVEN

T HE LAST WEEK started well. The new women were indoc-
trinated and all the others set-to with their nearest
approach to good will. Cassa got an opportunity to say a
word of appreciation to Jinny as they worked together in the
nurses' examination rooms.

"You and your family were wonderful, Jinny, the way you
handled Margaret's funeral. I shall never forget it."

Jinny was slightly surprised. "You were very good yerself,
Miss. But sure, poor oul Magser was only an outcast, but she
was our outcast. That's the way it is, Miss."

"Do you think the new women will fit in?" Cassa asked.

"They're as good as ye'll get nowadays, and they need the
jobs, their men unemployed this ages, and they've worked
before – two of them anyway. Always providin' Jane Duffy
doesn't tongue-lash them to death. Some people is more
thin-skinned to the mean remarks than to the flamin'
drudgery of the work, if ya follow me?"

"What about Annette, Jinny?" Cassa had seen the growing
resentment in Annette's eyes.

"What Joe was sayin' to me husband is that Annette'll go
off the rails if we don't let up naggin'. She has brains to
burn, Miss – the stuff she does be readin'! Joe is enrollin' her
in the Vocational School for September. She won't be sixteen until October. Joe says she'll be a credit to us yet. Jaysus,
I hope so!"

"I hope Eileen is a little better now?"

"Ah, Miss, as true as God, ye never get over the death of
yer new babby. The gap is there for ever, in yer heart, where
it counts, Miss."

"I am sure Joe is a comfort to Eileen."

"Joe," repeated Jinny. "God sent Joe to the Corcorans. As
my husband Mick says, Joe is our Book of Wisdom."

Cassa tried to nod wisely. She was glad for Annette.

Disaster struck on Wednesday almost in the same moment

as Cassa was saying to herself that there was only one more day to go. The antiseptic smell of the hospital had become like inhaling poison, and her good humour had stretched to breaking-point.

"Miss, Miss, come quickly. There's somethin' goin' on in x-ray."

Cassa rushed down the back stairs to the ground level.

Members of the public, who had been waiting in the queue for x-rays, were gathered in a tight circle, and M. McLaughlin's unmistakable Northern accent was addressing this little crowd.

"Ye all saw the bitch! Came up behind me, she did. Never laid eyes on her. Snatched the cigarette out of me jaw and jammed it into me face, so she did. An' then, the hoor knocked me to the stone floor with swingin' the machine at me. Ye all saw it! Ye'll bear witness! Me fist is all I used on her, the bitch!"

To Cassa's horror, Jane Duffy lay stretched out on the tiled floor, blood leaking from her mouth and one arm twisted behind her. A stretcher was rushed out and nurses were hurrying to help.

The local Gardaí had been sent for. The public were ushered out into a corridor and a doctor took M. McLaughlin to an inner room to attend to the burn on her face.

Cassa was shaking with fright. She was convinced Mrs Jane Duffy was dead. And who would be blamed? The supervisor, who else?

Nicole would say that it was expected of a supervisor to have telepathic warning of disaster and that she should be on all floors at the same time. After his angry condemnation in the drawing-room in Firenze, she could not throw herself on Dermot Tyson's mercy.

She gazed with loathing at Jane Duffy's blood on the tiled floor.

So much for Easter: the next days were going to be a straight-jacket of investigation by Tyson Associates and the Guards.

She went up to the cleaners' cloakroom and waited for the police.

The thought of Robert, which had gone completely out of her head, now returned, and with it came a host of loves and hates, yearnings and revulsions. The promise to visit Robert Gray must be honoured. There was a time, she thought... Now there was room for nothing else but the murder of Jane Duffy.

CHAPTER FIFTY-EIGHT

SISTER CALASANCTIUS HAD never known a more exalted moment. No door was locked against her authority now. She was fully into this cloakroom with all these cleaners assembled, together with their supervisor.

She was Reverend Mother's deputy, empowered to ask each of these women where she was at the exact moment of Mrs Duffy's deadly fall at the hand of M. McLaughlin. Despite the fact that every woman's name and place were recorded on the supervisor's daily work chart, it was necessary that Sister's notebook would bear the record and each statement be signed by each individual cleaner.

The joy of justification was often denied to this red-faced nun, but not now, not now O Lord.

"I will take your names in alphabetical order," she intoned, "Step forward as I name you. State your name, your place of work at the exact moment of eleven-fifty. I will call the supervisor last."

Cassa sat well back in the corner and watched the proceedings. The women, for the sheer gas of it (as Cassa knew) contradicted each other, and barracked the nun, demanding to know if she knew how to spell their names and querying the necessity for their signatures.

"Are ya actin' for the Guards?" Rose asked very politely, and Ethel said piously, "She means the Garda Chickawna, Sister.'

The women found this hilarious and had to mop the tears of laughter from their eyes. Cassa noticed how relieved they all were to be in the clear. Jane Duffy was nobody's favourite, but then neither was M. McLaughlin. These two were well cast in the roles of the villains of the piece, and the rest of the cast would go free.

All except me, thought Cassa. They have no way of knowing that I am the one going to be deprived of freedom.

"My notebook is for Reverend Mother's inspection," said

the nun with a high degree of pride in her voice. "You women may now await the interrogation of the Garda investigators."

As if she had stage-managed it, she flung open the door and the two Guards walked in. The procedure began all over again. When the women had all given their rather more subdued answers, the Guards checked the details against the supervisor's work chart. They took no notice of the nun's presence although she stood her ground like a small sentinel at the door.

The two guards consulted together for a moment. "There is no reason why you all can't go now," one of them said, and the other agreed, asking, "You'll all be in here tomorrow morning?"

The women, already late and anxious, hurried away.

Sister Calasanctius watched as Cassa put on her coat and tied a scarf on her head. "You will hand over the key of this door, Miss!" the nun's voice was peremptory, "and your work chart."

Cassa looked at her. "Excuse me, Sister," said Cassa, locking the door; "tomorrow, perhaps."

Concentrating on the road and concentrating on a plan of action gave Cassa an agitated half-hour driving home.

Isn't it strange, she was thinking: a little while ago I had never heard of the Gowans, and now I seem to know no one else. I seem to be bothering them on the phone every time I can't cope. I have to tell them that it looks as if Easter is out of the question. And what about Nicole? She can't go anywhere now with a murder on her hands.

Cassa found it hard to convince herself that her sister would be baulked by anything, even a murder. On the other hand, who would supervise if Mrs Jane Duffy were lying in the morgue and Nicole made Cassa go with her to the abortion clinic? A faint hope began to grow that Nicole must stay and face this new contingency. The thought of facing a murder enquiry on her own was terrifying.

Cassa had forgotten to put the bolts on the front door.

Nicole let herself in with her own key. She marched into

the living-room where Cassa had just turned on the television, turned it off and swung angrily around on her sister.

"Looking at television without a thought in your head for
the destruction you have caused! You stupid dunderhead!
Why do we have to hear what goes on in the hospital from
the Reverend Mother? Have you ever thought of picking up
the telephone to let Dermot know immediately about a
catastrophe? Isn't that what you were put there for, to
monitor the situation? The local Guards all over the hospital
and not a word from you to us – us who pay you. For Christ's
sake, Cassa Blake, what makes you so bloody awful stupid.
You have landed Tyson Associates in right trouble this time.
The contract will be scrapped. All the expensive equipment
a dead loss. A murder! Legal fees! Compensation! What the
hell were you doing?"

Cassa felt a heap of stones had been thrown in her face.

"No doubt Cassa Blake will be in the District Court by
Friday," she rounded on Cassa again. "You were always the
same. You could have made a success of something, anything, but no! You never learned, did you! I will not have
Dermot burdened with the legal fees in this case: there is
this house, and these grounds; we will see who is responsible
when it comes to a court case."

Cassa found her voice although it was very shaky. "You
probably know you are being unreasonable, Nicky. You
shout at me because you always did. You wouldn't dare to use
that tone of abuse if I was another supervisor – someone like
Lotty Slattery."

Her sister picked up a book from the table; Cassa thought
Nicole was going to hit her.

"I shout at you because you are stupid. That outburst in
front of Dermot the other night. Always the self-righteous
goody-good! You could have kept your mouth shut! And
talking of Lotty Slattery: her deputy will take your place in
San Salvatore as from Saturday morning."

Nicole stood over Cassa the better to pronounce into her
face. "We will travel on Saturday morning as arranged, but I

279

will collect you here at six-thirty in the morning rather than stay overnight on Friday. Have you taken that in?"

"Are you going ahead with this thing?" Now Cassa's voice was steady.

"Yes, and you are coming with me. I want to hear no more of your holier-than-God ideas. When this is over, you can have a holiday at my expense and I will arrange another job where you won't have to work the brain so hard."

"Have you forgotten that we may all be up in court this weekend?"

Nicole, calm now and quite at her ease, walked into the hall and opened the heavy door. "Cassa," she drawled, "try not to be so stupid, and I know about Robert Gray. Watch your step. Old lechers never change. "

Without seeming to hurry, she was at the wheel of her car and driving down the avenue.

CHAPTER FIFTY-NINE

IT WAS IMPOSSIBLE to sleep, but morning came at last and Cassa Blake hurried through the entrance hall. Sister Calasanctius was standing beside the porter's desk.

Cassa was passing without even a nod when the porter said, "Mornin', Miss. There's a message here for you."

Cassa recognised Robert's choice script on the envelope. "Thank you," she said, slipping the letter into her bag.

"What was that, Miss?" the nun asked loudly.

"A letter," Cassa said, continuing on her way to the cloakroom.

"Reverend Mother must be informed of all these peculiarly secretive messages that you receive and..." But Cassa cut her off by closing the door.

Quickly she glanced at the note: "Cassa, my dear, I heard of some catastrophe here which could account for your enforced absence. Come today. I have an idea which you will like. As ever, Robert."

The cleaners trailed into the cloakroom. They all had different versions of the state of events.

"Is she dead, Miss?" Rose asked. "I mean killed dead."

Some said she was, and some said she wasn't.

"I told yiz," said Bid Kinch, "that McLaughlin was on the change, didn't I?"

Resa, as always, agreed with Bid. "We saw her moppin' her face and it was as red as a purple beetroot."

"And that was before Mrs Jane Duffy burned the jaw offa her," said Jinny. "But the flushes can be pandemonium. I read in the *News of the World* about a woman in Liverpool who sliced up her husband with a sharp knife, an' she never done time in jail on account of she was afflicted with the flushes on the change."

"The judge musta had sympathy with the monopods," said Bid.

The women found this a guffaw. "Pity men don't go through the change!" Resa added.

"The trouble with them two oul wans," offered Mrs Loney, who seldom spoke, "was they were both on the monopods. It made both of them act peculiar!"

"Ye mean," said Ethel, "they got the hot flushes of blood to the brain simultaneous like." Ethel liked to tease.

"No," said Jinny, who must have the last word, "not simultaneous, continuous – all the time, if ya follow me."

"Callous Anxious is bangin' the door down." Ethel said. "Get movin', the lot of ye!"

Cassa decided to go straight to the Reverend Mother and ignored the protocol of asking for an appointment. She knocked on the superior's door, having skillfully avoided Callous Anxious on the stairs.

"The door is open," came the imperious voice. Cassa stepped in and stood with her back to the door.

The nun rose to her full height, then resumed her chair, her ample garments billowing out around her.

"Ah, Miss Blake! Have you made an appointment to see me?"

As often before, Cassa was reminded of some old movie of historic heroism. Today she had the voice of His Majesty's Commander-in-Chief.

"If you please, Reverend Mother, the woman who was injured yesterday, Jane Duffy: was she fatally injured?"

"Are you not in direct charge of the cleaning staff? Should you not have this information to hand?"

Cassa swallowed and took a deep breath. "Yes, Reverend Mother. Yes, on all counts. But I don't sleep here. Did the woman die during the night? If you do not wish to give this information, Reverend Mother, I must approach the medical officer."

Again the Reverend Mother rose; an inch more and her head-band would touch the ceiling. Her lifted arms gave the impression of a big bird about to take off. She consulted a book on her desk, taking her time.

"No death has occurred in San Salvatore within the last thirty-six hours." She closed the book ceremoniously.

Cassa stood outside the door in a second, her heart fluttering with relief. She made her way rapidly to the female public floor. There she found Mrs Jane Duffy comfortably ensconced in a corner bed, a white bandage about her head and another on her hand.

Cassa approached the sister-in-charge. "I had marked Jane as absent today. Is she completely unfit for work, Sister?"

The sister gave a small bit of a smile. "I'd say she could be up like a flash if they were paying out in gold coin! She will be let go home after the doctors' rounds. Do you wish to speak with her? Beware: she is talking massive compensation!"

Cassa took a long speculative look at the stout figure in the bed. "Will you be reporting for work tomorrow, Mrs Duffy?" she enquired very civilly.

Jane moaned and turned a mournful face: "No, nor for six weeks to come. You have me address and you can send me wages. I am near death, as you can see."

"Unless you manage to show up on Saturday, I doubt if you will get any wages."

Again the sepulchral voice: "I'll take Tysons' management to the High Court of Justice. I near met me end – there are witnesses. This is a stingy bloody place. I've had nothing to eat. That McLaughlin is a wicked murderin' bitch."

"And I hear her face is very badly injured," Cassa informed her; "in fact, disfigured. She also intends to sue: not the hospital, of course, but your good self, Mrs Duffy."

Duffy would show up on Saturday; Easter without money would be unthinkable. And she still believed she was going to be the new supervisor.

Cassa hurried away. She got on with the usual duties and stopped to talk to no one. Two women short left Cassa with many tasks which the others would deliberately leave undone: what Annette called "the fuckin' fiddly bits!"

Half of the worries were over. No one had been killed and Cassa would be free to leave this place for ever. If I were dying, she thought, I would never enter this hospital again.

The other half of the worry remained, and that was the worse half because it was family.

There had been no call, no visit, from the Tysons to the hospital, which meant that they knew now the storm of yesterday in the hospital was over. No one would be waiting on her doorstep.

As she was leaving the hospital, she gave Robert's envelope back to the hall porter together with a few coins.

"If you can?" she said to him. She had crossed out her name, and put Robert's name. Underneath the name she had written: "If at all possible, Thursday some time."

CHAPTER SIXTY

"AND WHAT DO you think you are doing here?" It was the dreaded voice of Sister Gentlemen's Privates. "Your hours are over. You are not even attired suitably."

Short of knocking the nun down, Cassa was unable to proceed down the corridor.

"Sister Theresa, please, not now." Cassa's attitude challenged the nun's right to stop her. "May I pass?"

"My information from on high is that you are persona non grata, certainly on this floor."

Cassa turned to one side and the nun moved also. Quickly Cassa slipped past and reached the end room, the nun rushing after her.

Cassa got the door open. "Am I persona non grata here?" she said clearly.

"Certainly not!" answered Robert's voice. "Come all the way in!"

She could hear the angry nun erupting verbally outside the door. To have outwitted this hard-faced nun on her last day restored her normal good humour as she took the chair by Robert's bed.

"How are you getting along, Robert? Are they treating you well?"

He looked a lot better.

"I feel ghastly," he moaned. "I am bored out of my mind. The food is horrible: some sort of diabetic diet. I am sleeping badly. I sent out for some Scotch and that hideous nun confiscated it before I got my hands on it. She strip-searches that unfortunate newspaper guy. She made me a present of rosary beads. I'm not even a Catholic – a lapsed atheist, as someone said. She then said I could use this rosary for worry-beads, like a pagan. She walks up and down from nine o'clock chanting prayers which we are supposed to answer. I demanded my door to be shut but she chanted louder. This isn't a hospital, it's a mental asylum."

"You'll be going home soon, Robert."

"Another month, maybe more." Again he groaned. "The only good thing is that I met you again. Why are you working here, Cassa?"

It seemed like the hundredth time she had said it. "To build up work experience, Robert, to get a job, a different job, to supplement my income."

"Louise always said your people were wealthy. She regarded you as an heiress. She was always wondering why some fortune-hunter hadn't tracked you down."

"I suppose we were well-off one time. It didn't last."

Looking at Cassa, he assessed upper middle class. She had always been well groomed and very presentable. She always spoke very correctly.

He continued, "I have just realised I have known you for about twenty years, and do you know what, you really haven't changed much at all."

"Well, thank you, Robert." Cassa's heart lifted.

"Louise hadn't changed much either, only in the last year, although I never suspected she was ill. Not that kind of ill. No one suspected. Did you know, Cassa?"

"No, Robert, I didn't know."

And please, she pleaded silently, I don't want to know. I prefer to know nothing.

"This is my last couple of days here," she said.

"But of course you will come and see me every day. Have you found another job?"

"Not exactly," Cassa said, "but I am going away."

"Oh, why is that?" he asked.

"Well, it is like this," Cassa had not had time to figure out a good story, "I think a change would do me good. Somewhere by the sea, or the river, sailing boats, you know the sort of holiday I mean?"

"Just when I have found you again? I am so disappointed."

She laughed light-headedly. "I'm not going away for ever, Robert."

"Cassa, you do feel for me, don't you? Don't you?" His voice was wonderfully mellow.

"You know I do, Robert."

I did, I did, and I could again. Despite his obvious pain, he was leaning towards her.

"Then forget all this going-away nonsense, my dear Cassa. Listen to my idea, and tell me if you like it. Pull your chair nearer."

Robert had long experience in using his voice. Cassa had heard these fluting notes many times before to Louise and to others: a rise and fall at once intensely compelling and gently pleading,

"Come back to Garlow Lodge with me, my dear. It is a dear lovely house in which you could be at home and secure. You need never worry again about this job experience idea. That kind of thing is not for you, my dear. Garlow Lodge would welcome you and receive you in."

"Would it, Robert?" Cassa murmured.

"Tell me, Cassa, would it break your heart to leave your own home? Is it yours to leave, to rent, to sell? Are you devoted to your own home as I am to Garlow Lodge?"

Cassa was smiling at him. "Yes, I love my home, I love it very much, but lately I have been thinking it is too big for just one person alone. And the garden takes a lot of keeping. Yes, it is mine to sell and the fields at the back of the house, about thirty acres. I could not think of letting it to strangers; it is full of furniture prized highly by both my parents."

"But your sister?" Robert Gray queried. "Is half the property hers?"

"My father left the property and the investments to me. My sister was given a dowry."

"That sounds like a very good father," Robert said. "And yet you think you cannot live without going out to work, Cassa dear?"

"No, I find money has changed. Everything has become expensive. The electricity, the car, everything. Don't you find it so at Garlow Lodge?"

Cassa had felt warmed and comforted by his talk of Garlow Lodge.

"Money has never worried me. I have always been a big earner. Louise looked after everything. She was systematic. Are you a good manager?"

"Reasonably," Cassa said, noticing the assessing tone of his voice.

She was anything but systematic. Since her father's death she had fumbled along, just about surviving. Where was this conversation going?

His voice retuned into delightful persuasion: "Cassa, Garlow Lodge is waiting for you. Waiting among the copper beeches, waiting in the sunshine. You will just take control. Employ help as you wish. Always providing that you assure me that you will not miss your own home. Oh Cassa, we must talk about your plans, mustn't we? You would fit so beautifully into Garlow Lodge!"

Robert was leaning towards her; his ageing classical features were alive as if with a new-found provocative stimulus.

Cassa smiled serenely, but her instincts had shifted into top gear. "Take control?" Those words had shot out as coldly as icicles. I have to know, she was thinking, I have to know. I don't want to know. I can't go out of this room unless I know. Ask him.

Cassa pushed her chair a little back away from the bed and picked up her handbag from the floor. With all the sweetness she could muster, she got out the question. "It sounds really pleasant, Robert. Just what a hard-up woman would be needing. And Robert, tell me, what would my title be in Garlow Lodge? Here I am a supervisor." She managed another smile for Robert.

"Your title, my dear Cassa? Whatever you choose? House-keeper seems so ordinary for someone so nice as you. Manageress? No, manageress is a little hard. Something in French, perhaps. Chatelaine sounds nice. Queen of the teapot?" And he actually laughed... that wonderful manly laugh.

"Leave it with me, but I promise you will be in total charge. Among the Lares and Penates – the household gods, my dear – your word will be law!" He lay back smiling a satisfied smile.

In one graceful movement, Cassa had stood up, well back from the bed.

"Must you go so soon, Cassa?" His voice held amazed surprise.

At the door, Cassa turned proudly. "How kind of you to consider me for the position. Perhaps I should give it my best consideration."

As the door clicked shut, she heard his voice calling her back. Maybe he realised he had put his foot in his elegant mouth. Lares and Penates! And he had translated it for her!

She ran all the way down the stairs, muttering furiously.

In the car, she simply had to smile to relieve the pain. It was a better way than crying – not easy but better.

Nicole had been right again. She had called Robert a bastard and she had said Cassa had had a lucky escape.

When Cassa was eighteen she had idealised this man, and twenty years later it was what it had always been, a fantasy.

Cassa Blake, she addressed herself in the car's rear mirror, you are one of the foolish virgins, but you are learning. Strike out for yourself. Have a bit of courage. Now start the car.

Tonight she would phone Father Frank, whose call she had missed today. She had an idea that Father Frank would think of all possible eventualities in the same way that Cassa was thinking of them to banish the thought of Robert Gray, to stop hearing his marvellous voice informing her that she would be the Queen of the teapot, and rule over his Lares and Penates.

As soon as she arrived home, she rang the number John had given her. Father Frank answered. She knew his voice at once.

"Your voice cheers me up, Frank, isn't that a nice thing to say? I am so glad you answered. John is a darling, but you are my first friend."

"Cassa, thank you. I tried several times. Were you with your sister?"

"No, I went over to San Salvatore to pay a final visit to a person who was in an accident. But I have decided: I am definitely not going to London with her."

"I am greatly relieved to hear you say that. John is ready to go scorching down for you and I am to arrange times. I could come, of course, but he insists on the Bentley and he doesn't trust me to drive it – the nerve! He said you thought of coming in your own car?"

"Frank, he and I talked about that and I want to make the trip alone. It will be an epic journey for me. I need the long drive all on my own.

"I want to go in to the hospital tomorrow to say goodbye to the women. Despite all, they are a great bunch, and I have learned a lot from them. Then I'll pack and start up on Saturday morning. You do understand, Frank?"

"Of course I understand, Cassa. But be careful and take it easy. Start as early as you can. We will be watching out for you. You have a map? You will be careful? The roads are very bad in parts, never repaired since winter."

The tender concern in his voice was most endearing. "I will be careful, Frank, I promise. Just let me get tomorrow over! I am counting the minutes to be free of San Salvatore for ever."

"Won't you miss Callous Anxious?"

"Won't I have you to make fun of me?"

And he was thinking how very, very intently he listened to her every word, every inflection of her voice.

"I wish you were here to share our dinner," he said; "John and James have just tapped on the window. You will be careful driving up?"

"Sure! Bye for now, Frank. Give my love to the others."

Cassa went singing up the stairs. She felt honoured and elated to be the subject of Frank's concern.

The soft warmth of his voice brought her back to the days when her father was in his heyday. His business was booming, he was playing great golf, and he was surrounded by friends. It seemed as if his sick wife would get better. The medical opinions became ever more expensive but the money was there. Cassa was in her early twenties then, and his first thought every evening was for her. As he came through the hall door, he always called out to her, "Cassa, I'm home! Where are you?"

His deep affectionate voice brought her running to him. He always folded his arms around her, and his kisses on her hair told her how much he loved her.

He was the nicest and best father in the world, and Father Frank was the nicest and best friend she had ever had, not that she had so many friends.

Cassa checked her thoughts. The practical thing was to get out a few suitcases. It could be a long visit. Would warm pyjamas be the thing for a cruiser?

This reminded her forcibly of Robert, of when she had packed her best nightdress for Louise's funeral.

She had always packed her prettiest things for the annual month at Caragh Lake. On sunny mornings they had sat out on the balcony for breakfast, all three of them in night attire. Louise and Robert were carelessly intimate on those mornings. Louise came fully to life in bright sunshine, and when Louise was in that mood she was entrancing to behold.

Would warm pyjamas be the thing for a cruiser?

Robert and Caragh Lake lingered still at the edge of her thoughts, but she had only to repeat the horrible epithet "Queen of the teapot" and instead of the balcony over the lake, she saw the pompous groaning professor in his bed at San Salvatore, where he would be for weeks to come while Cassa would be far away, cruising down the Shannon.

Cassa was a little shocked to feel a satisfied kind of glee in this reaction. After all, Robert was not to blame for a young girl's romantic fancies, even if the fancies persisted for twenty years. No one could say he had actually encouraged her.

Cassa tucked two pairs of winceyette pyjamas into the case; the silk negligee was altogether too reminiscent of the past. I am packing, she mused solemnly, like a person going somewhere. But why do I have an empty feeling of belonging nowhere?

CHAPTER SIXTY-ONE

GOOD FRIDAY MORNING was cold and sleety. The women arrived wet to the bone, in no humour for rigorous cleaning.

"If that oul nun opens her beak to me, I'll let her have a bucket of water up her snitch," was Annette's remark as she brushed past Callous Anxious at the cloakroom door. "If they're all that holy, they should do the work themselves on Good Friday for a bit of crucifixion."

"You'll never get to heaven, Netty," said Jinny piously. "Them nuns has to pray a double dose of prayers today."

"Look who's here!" called out Rose as the door was opened again: "Lady Godiva!"

Mrs Jane Duffy lumbered in, heavily bandaged around the head and one hand. She was hunched into a big winter coat and she did not take it off.

"Are you working today, Jane?" Cassa enquired.

"Just supervisin'!" the woman answered, "and not even fit for that."

Cassa wrote the name into the ledger. No point in arguing. "Stay on the top floor, then," she said.

As the women streeled out of the room, Rose held back.

"Miss, is this yer last day?"

When Cassa nodded, Rose continued: "A few of us had a whip-around and we want to make you a little present. It's only a small thing," she said quickly when she saw Cassa's eyes brim with tears. "We were goin' to take you over to Adolfo's, but that eejit is closin' for the stations of the cross from twelve to three. Of course we know where he'll be doin' the stations, under the counter with the new assistant. Anyway, Adolfo's is shut so, if you don't mind, we'll gather here at twelve-thirty!"

"Oh, Rose." Cassa could find no words.

Cassa went across the yard to the nuns' chapel. She sat for a moment, remembering the first day Father Frank had befriended her here. She offered a small prayer of thanksgiving before she set to work.

There was no sign of the German nun, although Cassa felt sure that someone was watching her. It was the same in each place she went either to help or to supervise: she worked with energy and the skill she had acquired, but no one approached her.

The word had got out. This lady was now past-tense. No use in bringing complaints to her; she would not be here to deal with them. Or was it just barely possible that the system at last worked like a ticking clock? Wind it up each morning and off it goes. Were she to come back after Easter, would it be all clockwork?

She stood for a moment at a window overlooking the tumbling waves on the seashore, and she made a solemn vow: Never, never, never will I work in this place again.

The morning came to an end and the women were all back in the cloakroom, with the exception of Mrs Duffy, who had discovered for herself a back entrance through which she could slip away.

"Lady Jane done a bunk," said Jinny. "She won't know what hit her next week when she has to fill out the chart, sure she won't, Miss?"

"Don't worry, Jinny," said Cassa. "I don't think she'll be a problem."

"Jaysus, dealin' with that wan would put years on the rest of us. She drives me spare!" This was from one of the two new cleaners who had teamed up with Mrs Loney.

"You are doing fine," Cassa told her. "You are simply a topper at the work – almost as good as Annette."

In an aside, she said to Annette, "I hear great things about your future. I hope you will go ahead. Study is not easy but you can do it, Annette, and the best of luck!"

"Gather round, girls," yelled Rose above the voices, "we are going to tell Miss Blake how much we will miss her."

The women came together in a knot around Cassa. She was overwhelmed. A flood of tears was long overdue and she had trouble holding back. Any show from the women was the last thing she would have expected.

"Go on, Rosy, you make the speech," they shouted at her.

Cassa looked at their faces, all smiling for her, and thought they were beautiful.

Rose, gabbling her speech and waving her arms like a magician, produced an arrangement of spring flowers on a little raffia hat, yellow daffodils and blue lobelia trimmed with greenery.

Cassa took it in her hands. "It is just lovely," she said. "I don't deserve such a lovely gift. Thank you, all of you, I cannot thank you enough. Please believe me, I could not have faced the day only for knowing you would be here. I shall miss you all."

She was thinking she did not deserve the sacrifice of their hard-earned cash. A tear slid down Cassa's cheek, and another tear.

Then the women were all babbling together: "Ah, don't cry, Miss. You'll get another job! We'll make it hot for Jane Duffy, never fear! Don't cry, we'll get our own back on flamin' Callous Anxious, the oul git! She was the fuckin' cause of all the trouble! Cheer up, Miss! Three cheers for Miss Cassa Blake! Hip, hip, hooray!"

When the women were gone, Cassa took time to tidy the cloakroom. She would give the key back today. She looked in her compact mirror and wiped away the tear stains.

As she was handing the key to the hall porter, he took an envelope from the cubbyholes behind his counter. "This is for you, Miss," he said.

She recognised the script of Robert Gray. "Thank you," she said to the porter, "there is no answer."

In the car-park she looked again at the unique penmanship of her name: Miss Cassa Blake. Then she tore the envelope, and whatever was in it, right across and into small pieces which she dropped into the litter bin.

Cassa placed the little raffia hat on the hall table beside

the telephone. The yellow and blue colours glowed in the dim hall. Jinny was surely the one who had prompted the thought of a gift, and Annette the one sent out to purchase it.

Maybe Cassa would never see that family again, but she felt sure she would never forget them and the litany of the husbands and wives in the flats: Joe and Eileen, Jinny and Mick, Danny and Gertie, Violet and Anthony, Rory and Dodo. Cassa smiled, remembering the pride in Jinny Corcoran's voice.

Last year, she had gone to the stations of the cross in the local church with Papa. A year had gone. This year she went alone. When the congregation had dispersed after the last prayers, Cassa remained kneeling.

She could no longer be sure of the old routines of her life. She had been through a year of doubt and difficulty. She could not pray for a return to the loving stability of that family world in which her father had ruled, any hurt inflicted on her magically forgotten in a word from his caring voice. That life was over, taken away for ever. All the props of that familiar old world were heaped up like broken stones at a crossroads.

Pray anyway, she told herself. Just pray, offer praise, don't ask for favours.

The service station was opposite the church. Cassa told the man to fill the tank and put a can of petrol in the boot. And would he kindly check the oil and water.

She was worried about additional expense, such as a new tyre, so she had drawn on her meagre savings.

"How do the tyres look to you?" she asked him.

"They're not baldy anyway," he said. "I'll give them air if they need it. The spare is game-ball. Takin' a trip, Miss Blake?"

"Well, it's Easter, Pat. Have a nice break yourself."

He grumbled about being on duty all the weekend, but he brightened up when he saw the tip.

Cassa smiled at herself. Papa had always honoured the

custom of tipping: the gentry of the Big House. Sadly indeed were the Blakes reduced when they had to consider the size of a tip. I should have given him much more, she thought.

After all, it's Easter.

CHAPTER SIXTY-TWO

A T THE HOUSE, she drove the car around to the side and stacked the two suitcases into the boot. Then she went upstairs to close all the heavy shutters in every room. She locked all the rooms, except her own bedroom and the door at the head of the stairs. They would be last minute. The bolts were drawn shut on the front door. The downstairs shutters would be closed at the moment of departure.

Cassa had formulated no final plan, her anxious mind refusing to construct a timetable.

Father Frank would be expecting her arrival in Carrick-on-Shannon tomorrow evening. Her sister expected her here on the doorstep of Firenze at six-thirty tomorrow morning. Fear of Nicole was a lifelong paralysing fear. Cassa had boasted of breaking loose, but now where would she find the courage?

She had no doubt but that Nicole had reasons for the hideous, cruel deed she intended, maybe good reasons of which Cassa could know nothing.

Her sister, who had never asked before, never asked nor included Cassa, had asked her for help. To refuse would be to break with Nicky, maybe for ever. Nicky has her husband, her pretty daughters, her friends, all the Gilbey aunts and cousins.

Who do I have of my own? If I lose my sister, I have no one.

There was the one single thing which was certain: she wanted nothing to do with this abortion. Nothing. Nothing. Nothing.

She felt sure that Nicky would come to Firenze tonight, to check on her. Nicky always checked.

She wandered into the front drawing-room and switched on all the lights. Courage, she thought, it's a lovely word. I must make one enormous attempt to change my sister's mind, to tell her, and to plead with her, that when this deed is done, it can never be undone – a deed she will regret all her life.

I'll make her listen; I will have the courage; I will.

She touched the keys of the piano, drew a little music out of them, then closed the lid.

At the French window, she paused. There was a stretch in the evening, a faint after-glow in the sky giving a dusky tinge of greenery to the trees. Even as she looked, a light illumined the trees, the headlights of a car coming up the drive.

Cassa thought instantly of John, somehow conscious of the need to rescue her. In the same moment she saw that the car was not the Bentley but the Tysons' Merc. This would be Nicole, advancing the time to make sure of Cassa's obedience. The moment for screwing up courage must be now, or it would be lost for ever.

Then she realised that only Dermot Tyson had stepped out of the car, and he was alone. He saw her standing in the lighted window and he walked across the grass. She opened the glass doors, suddenly remembering how kind he had been to her on the night of her father's death. It did not seem courteous to show surprise.

"Do come in," she said. "Nicole not with you?"

"As you see," he smiled. "She is, I gather, saying au revoir to her friends because she cried off spending Easter with them. Marjorie and Co. had Ashford Castle in mind for a bridge weekend."

"That's nice." Cassa played for time. "Perhaps you should sit down. Shall I make coffee?"

He sat on Sadora's couch. "Well, no thank you, I don't need coffee just now. Are you pleased Nicole is taking you for a little holiday? She got a yen for both of you to see London again. She's been there recently, but apparently you have not."

He's questioning me, Cassa thought. Nicky has admitted London, but not why. So he is in the dark after all.

"Was this holiday a surprise to you, Dermot?"

"Well, yes, rather a surprise. You are two such different

298

people. Are you happy to go?" His doubt was obvious.

Determined not to be caught in her sister's lies, Cassa said slowly, "London is always London. I guess Nicky told you that I am finished with San Salvatore."

"But that was my idea, Cassa. I never wanted you to take that wretched job. You are simply not the type. Nicole persuaded me against my better judgment." He added hastily, "She meant it for the best, of course."

"Well, it's over now," Cassa said.

"When you come back from London, what are your plans?"

She looked at his kind, interested face. "I don't have any plans. How could I have plans?"

"I have plans for you, Cassa. I should like to discuss them with you."

Cassa continued her examination of his face. His eyes deepened in colour, emphasising his friendly interest. Was he another Robert Gray come to rescue her and elevate her into the status of housekeeper, Queen of his teapot in his palatial Stillorgan house?

Best to be on the defensive before he mentioned his Lares and Penates. "I don't really like housework, Dermot."

"I want you to go back to the study of your music," he said, and he held out his hand to invite her down beside him. So astonished was she that she took his hand and they were seated side by side among Sadora's cushions.

"I could never afford to do that," she told him. "How could I?"

"My plan is that I can afford it for you, Cassa. In Paris. I have been making enquiries. I mentioned the possibility to Nicole. She said that your French was very good. You could have a little apartment convenient to the Conservatoire. How does that grab you?"

His voice was genially warm, although his reference to his wife was rather inaccurate.

In amazement, Cassa drew back. "It sounds just wonderful. A dream come true. But I'm not that good, you know. And terribly rusty."

He took her two hands in his. "No more scrubbing and polishing for these hands. They are beautiful hands. They will be used only for your piano."

Her great brown eyes were gazing out from under the dark up-turned lashes in absolute wonderment. The question was "Why?" It seemed ungrateful to ask him, but why would he do this? Why this change? Things he was reported to have said came back to her: "Dermot is livid" and worse.

"I should like to ask you, Dermot, how have I suddenly found favour in your eyes?"

"You were never out of favour, my dear Cassa, never." He was still holding her hands and willing her to recall the night of her father's death. All night long, they had sat together on this couch, his arms encircling her, his intimate touch giving comfort in her distress.

The spell of her nearness threatened his control. He was dreaming now of coming to her in their Paris apartment, coming to her with *droit de seigneur*, a role for which he was prepared, and for which he would prepare her in the long weeks of enchantingly leisured seduction, a pleasure he had never had. He was a man who had been bought and paid for. That had long been a bitter regret. The pleasuring of Cassa, the initiation of Cassa, would be his glorious release.

"Do you remember the very first time we met?" he asked. "I rescued you and your bicycle out of the traffic at Donnybrook church. You were a little girl of twelve."

"Oh, I do remember that day. I hope I thanked you."

What she remembered was the horrible old man in the ragged coat who had knocked her against the wall and tried to steal her bike, and even more clearly she remembered the punishments Nicole had heaped on her for weeks after-wards, calling her a sneak and a spy.

"You never said a word to me," his eyes twinkled in amuse-ment, "but I'll accept your thanks now. A grateful little kiss is years overdue."

Cassa turned her face to his handsome face. "Do I kiss you or do you kiss me?"

He took her into his arms and he was very careful. His kiss was gentle, almost humble.

"I am out of the way of kissing," she said, and she touched her fingers to his lips. "Kissing takes practice."

With a voice as light as air, he asked, "But didn't I see you racing down the hill with a handsome man the other day?"

For a moment she forgot, and then she laughed, "Oh that was John! John Gowan."

"A lover?" he queried, his tone even lighter, lacking all curiosity.

Now Cassa drew well away on the couch. "A lover? What ever gave you an idea like that?"

Her surprise pleased him, and he drew her back to him very gently. "Because you are so attractive. A man might like to kiss you. Why not?"

"Why not indeed!" she retorted. "But a kiss and a lover seem to me two quite different concepts."

A year ago, Cassa's senses might not have sprung alert, but the months in San Salvatore had been very enlightening months. This man was married to her sister, a sister more full of vengeance than of family loyalty.

"You know," she said, "I have just remembered that tomorrow morning is a very early start."

"But we will talk again in a week or two," Dermot said with a wealth of affectionate sincerity. "We can go ahead then. I am so glad you like my plans."

"Oh yes. Wonderful plans!" She could not but see the triumph in his very handsome face.

"Shall I walk you across to the car?" Cassa had become apprehensive of so much charm displayed for her who had no right to it.

"I prefer to say goodnight here. I like this room. A goodnight kiss, Cassa?"

His kisses evoked a rush of some feeling hitherto unknown and yet familiar, acceptable, needed. Her response was evident, her slender body was straining into the man's vibrant embrace.

Dermot Tyson was murmuring strange assurances. He would teach her, cherish her. Make up for all the years when desire was hidden. Her love was known and his love was known, but no need to tell the town. He had prepared a secret world for Cassa in another town far away. Everything would be for her, everything she had ever wanted, and it would all be perfect.

It was a bewildering and beguiling sensation to experience her body in so crushingly close an alignment with the hard male body of some other woman's husband. That he belonged so absolutely to that exact other someone made the magic of the feeling at once more exciting and more dangerous.

It was a love scene in a drama. Cassa felt she had a taste for this way of being desired, and of desiring in return.

At last, he let her go. "Soon, Cassa, soon."

Their arms entwined, they walked across the grass to his car.

As if touched by his sorcery, Cassa stood perfectly still until the car lights had dimmed into the distance.

Abruptly, the spell was broken, Cassa dashed off all the lights in the drawing-room as if she could not be rid of them fast enough. She ran up the stairs and took refuge in her bedroom. She sat hunched up in the dark.

She had let Nicole's husband into the secret of her urgent emotional needs. Another moment and she would have surrendered willingly and utterly. Nicole was right: I am a fool.

CHAPTER SIXTY-THREE

NICOLE'S CAR WAS not at the front of the house when Tyson drove up a little after ten. He walked around to the double garage but she was not yet home.

Upstairs, he stood looking quietly into the girls' room for a few moments, but they were fast asleep in their beds.

He was confident he had the audacity and the skill to forge the division in his heart into a steel band of boundary: love on both sides, tenderness to spare. He closed their bedroom door softly. His life was a wide and comfortable place. Orla and little Sandra would not be hurt.

He sat in the living-room to wait for his wife's return, thinking not of her, but of the woman who had come into his arms under the portrait of Elvira in the drawing-room of Firenze. From his first night in that room, the portrait had been a potent force. He would suggest to Cassa that it should come with them to Paris, to complement the pieces he had chosen for their *appartement*.

Exactement, he thought with a smile. Paris would be the youth he never had, and with this lovely woman who would depend on him for every breath she drew. He thrilled again to the intimate feel of her slender body against his. He had wanted to lift her up and fly through the air, across the trees, across the sea, his lips on her softly parted lips.

Never before had he known pure passion to course through his body. In the long drawn-out moments of the kiss, he had known for certain that she was newly awakened. She would come to him untainted, uninitiated.

Suddenly he was awake to find his wife close to him.

"Poor old darling, were you waiting up for me?" She was snuggled into the space between his out-stretched legs. "What's this, my hero? Were we having a naughty dream, then?"

Distaste for her rose up in his throat. He struggled to his feet.

"Look at that clock," he said. "It's long after twelve."

She kicked off her shoes, laughing up into his face. "Were we getting impatient?" she teased. "Cinderella is home from the ball! Let's into our bed immediately!"

"Nicole, why are you going to London tomorrow?"

"Taking my little sister for a holiday. Going to buy her some decent clothes. She has let herself go: not a fashionable rag in her wardrobe. She needs a little holiday. She's not a bad old thing really!"

"Does she want to go?" he asked.

"She can't wait for tomorrow. She's all agog! Silly old Cass!" Now she turned around to him. "Pet lamb, aren't you coming to bed? We are going to have a short night!"

She gave him all her usual gestures of invitation, her hands ruffling the back of his head, her lovely mouth in its most sensual pout.

He disengaged himself. "Truth to tell," he said, "I have a couple of urgent letters to write. You go on up."

So blatant a lie surprised her. His secretary attended to all his letters. For a second, she hesitated, but she needed her sleep. Tomorrow morning's flight to London was very urgent, no time to be lost.

She was determined on the abortion, but also frightened. She could not face this thing on her own. Cassa was the only woman she could absolutely trust. Marjorie would blab the delightful news of Nicole Tyson's abortion all over Dublin. Already, Marjorie knew too much.

"Darling," she said sweetly to her husband, "you will probably be still asleep when I am going in the morning, so give me a big love now, Dermy, please."

He kissed her lightly, steering her ever so gently towards the door. "Go ahead, my dear. You need your couple of hours."

When the footfalls and closing of doors had settled into quietness, Tyson showered in the den's shower. He changed into pants and sweater suitable for golf. In the kitchen he made tea and took it into the living-room.

Having set the alarm on his wrist-watch for six a.m., just in case, he again sat down to wait.

CHAPTER SIXTY-FOUR

CASSA REALISED SHE was acting in the very same way she had always acted when she had fallen foul of Nicky: sitting on her bed in the dark with her arms clasped around her knees, lonely and guilty and forsaken.

She wished with all her heart that the last two hours had never happened. Her sister would find out and, no matter what she could do to placate Nicky this time, she would never be forgiven.

When she had drawn back and he had pressed forward, did she imagine it or had he whispered, "Soon, my darling, soon."

That he might have said those words, surely a mocking promise, filled her with a piercing fear. Earlier tonight, she had wavered about disappointing her sister; she had almost veered towards sympathy for Nicole.

Now, escape was more important.

Now, urgently. Stir yourself, Cassa Blake, before he gets home to tell his wife. Get away from here before Nicole arrives.

She huddled into her coat and clutched her handbag. Careful not to touch a light switch, she locked her bedroom and the door at the top of the stairs. She fastened all the downstairs shutters, let herself out by the back door and tried the lock to make sure she had turned the key.

The night was very still and dark as she stood at the door, unable to move lest someone jump on her. She could not shake off the fear that Tyson might come back. Perhaps she should leave a note for Nicky, a note on the front door to say sorry.

Pity squeezed her heart for her sister's trouble. Nicole could not truly want this awful deed, but she would have to go through it without Cassa. That was the one certain thing in all the uncertainty.

She crept into the car, drawing shut the door with the merest click. The old car started silently as if it too wanted to steal away. Until she was well out of the avenue and on to the Merrion Road, her heart thumped painfully.

She crossed the city slowly, trying not to feel like a fugitive from her own home. She passed a taxi here and there until she was at the country end of the Navan Road, after which there was nothing. Too terrified to think about Dermot and Nicole, she kept her mind focused on the road. She was travelling north-west and at the end of this journey she hoped to find the one person who could keep her safe from harm.

CHAPTER SIXTY-FIVE

"YOU NEVER CAME to bed at all?" Nicole put the question lightly. Never intuitive, she was merely puzzled. "Playing golf so early, Dermy?"

"Later on perhaps. I thought I should run you and Cassa to the airport."

She took this to be his accustomed courtesy, to be as easily deflected. "Oh, I'll take my car. I can leave it in the long-term park. No need for you to bother."

"No bother at all. I feel like an early spin – before the city wakes up. Have you a suitcase?"

"In the hall."

It's all their fault, she thought inconsequentially. If men weren't so madly, sensually beautiful. Even Dermot, standing there with that withdrawn face: I could jump on him this minute.

Dermot was commenting on her new suit. "You look awfully soignée this morning," he said. "Have I seen that suit before?"

"This old thing? Of course you have!"

He detected the easy lie. A lie for no reason.

"So, will we get started, then?" He took up the case.

"I didn't say goodbye to the girls; they were sleeping like angels. Will you tell them for me?"

"Of course. And that you'll bring back something very special from London."

Nicole hadn't thought of that. Shopping? The clinic wasn't in the city. But of course she could send Cassa to buy presents on the day they'd be coming home. That would give her something to do, make it look like a holiday.

An awkward attempt was made at conversation as they drove through Stillorgan and on to the Merrion Road: lovely weather, nice if it keeps up for Easter.

Tyson was alert to these stumbling remarks because Nicole usually had no problem with endless gossipy chatter. As they turned into the avenue of Firenze, she went silent, not even a disparaging comment on the overgrown grass verges.

"No sign of your sister," he said cheerily. "Surely she should be out on the steps, all agog, as you said?"

He expected his wife to pass some derogatory remark about Cassa's laziness, her untrustworthiness.

She was banging on the big knocker on the hall door and shouting through the letter box. The knocker echoed loudly into the early sunshine.

Tyson took the car keys out of the ignition. He walked around the house to the kitchen door. It was locked and he could see that the inside shutters were closed. He inspected the other downstairs windows and the French doors. All shuttered.

Not only had Cassa fled from this holiday in London, but he had a feeling there was a message for him in this sudden shuttering. His so-attractive wife in her new and no doubt costly rig-out was standing on the steps in an attitude of helplessness. His keen eye caught the picture. He would never underestimate her ability to get herself out of an unpleasant situation.

Obviously suppressing rage, she asked, "You will still drive me to the airport, Der, won't you? I suppose I will have to go all on my own."

This was so plainly ludicrous that he did not answer, nor when she added, "It is just possible that Cassa has gone ahead to the airport."

They stood in silence for a moment, each with a guilty secret and each waiting for the other to uncover the mystery of Cassa's disappearance.

"Darling," she said to him, "either you drive me to the airport, or we may as well go home."

"If you tell me why you are so anxious to go to London, then I will drive you to the airport."

"Is that a solemn promise?" she asked. "People never keep solemn promises."

Dermot Tyson had not forgotten Cassa's agonised plea not to let this terrible thing happen.

"Yes, Nicole. There are solemn promises given in error, to be solemnly broken again and again. Now tell me, what is in London that you must have?"

"I hate being cross-questioned, I can't bear it." Her eyes were resentfully angry. "Let's go home."

"Very well," he replied.

With the utmost courtesy he held open the car door. They returned back along the Merrion Road in silence.

When she had stood on the steps of her father's house, outlined against the bright morning light, he had observed the gentle outward curve of her stomach. To Nicole curves and weight were anathema.

Was it possible that he would owe this future child in his wife's womb to Cassa, who had fled rather than destroy a tiny life?

Suppose his wife would give him a son. His heart leaped joyfully and his sympathetic understanding flowed to the silent woman beside him. She had intended an abortion, in itself an appalling act, but perhaps there could be reasons.

He glanced at her tense face. Pregnancy and giving birth had not been easy for Nicole. There had been dreadful pain, she had come close to death and her recoveries had been very slow. There was recurring relief when no more than two children came to them. And they were wonderful children.

But the possibility of a son of his own. The pride of it.

He drew up at their own door and, turning to her he said, "My dear, perhaps we could spend this day together?"

She was not smiling. "You have left it too late."

On the silent drive from Firenze, Nicole remembered Sadora's Rules and Regulations. Life, according to Sadora, had cruel priorities from which there was no easy escape.

She wondered, but very briefly, where Cassa had gone. Wherever it was, she would find her and punish her. She felt like beating her nearly to death.

But first, the abortion.

She was going upstairs and her husband watched her. He

310

caught her hand on the banister. "Nicole, should we not think of family love? We..."

Snatching her hand away, she rounded on him scornfully. "You don't know the meaning of love, any more than I do. There is only one difference between us. I am the one who would have to go through with it. I want rid of it. There is no way you can stop me." Her face glowered with contempt. "I hope you are not brute enough to use force."

Hearing her mistress's voice, Mrs Kelly walked out of her radio-filled kitchen. "Yes'm?"

"Mrs Kelly, there is a suitcase in Mr Tyson's car. Would you please put it into my car. I shall be leaving immediately."

CHAPTER SIXTY-SIX

CASSA THOUGHT SHE had memorised the map, in fact she thought she knew the road from of old, but as she grew sleepier she had to pause at crossroads and shine the beam on the signposts. Several times she felt she should pull in and sleep for a while, but there was the dread of being followed. She knew it was absurd, childish and stupid, but fear had governed her life.

Country roads are very eerie in the night as old wayside trees take on strange humpy shapes. Keeping well into the left she pressed on until she came close to Mullingar. With the torch she studied the road map. Should she cross the Shannon at Athlone and head north on the west side, or should she stay on this side of the Shannon and make for Longford? She realised she should not have gone through Kells, but out through Maynooth. She was tired and sleepy and the sun wasn't coming up quickly enough.

She decided on Longford. By the time she reached it, it should be long after seven o'clock.

She counted off the villages: Ballinalack, Rathowen, Edgeworthstown. With immense relief she saw the signpost for Carrick-on-Shannon, but she could not face the last thirty miles. It was a tremendous effort to keep her eyes open, and her steering was wandering over to the right.

On the first bungalow outside Longford there was a nicely painted board reading "Bed and Breakfast". She wondered hazily would they consent to "Breakfast and Bed".

She pulled the car into the driveway at the same moment as a woman opened the door to brush the entrance porch. The woman advanced smiling. "Driven up for the festival, have you?"

Cassa nodded, mumbling about a vacancy.

"I have, of course. A nice room. You could do with a cup of tea too."

It was like being invited to step into heaven.

Cassa followed the woman into the bright hall. There were already some people settling into their breakfasts in the dining-room and the radio was telling the eight o'clock news.

"Here we are," said the smiling woman, "and there's the bathroom: it's free now, if you would like to freshen up. Everyone is up and off early on account of the festival."

"Here are the car keys," Cassa handed over the keys. "Maybe someone could bring the small case."

"Jacky will get it for you, and he'll lock the car. Will I bring you a bit of breakfast? You'll want a lie down."

"I am very grateful to you. Please tell me your name."

"I'm Emily, Emily Frame. It's my sister runs the guest-house; she's May Johnson."

"I am Cassa, Cassa Blake. I have driven from Dublin."

Emily led the way into a bedroom, and Cassa sought the nearest chair.

"Emily, do you think you could make a phone call for me in a couple of hours to a family by the name of Gowan, in Carrick-on-Shannon. I will pay for bed and breakfast, but really all I want is a break in the journey. Would that be all right, Emily?"

Cassa yawned a long tired yawn. "Please excuse me," she said. "This is the phone number; my family will be expecting me. Just tell them I got so far, and I am resting."

When Cassa came out of the bathroom there was a neat tray beside the bed. The tea tasted great, but she was too tired to eat. She placed the tray outside the door and climbed into the bed. Within five minutes she was fast asleep.

Emily made the phone call as instructed, and John Gowan took the call. Father Frank, Deirdre and James all wanted to pile into the car, but John was adamant.

"There is some reason Cassa has arrived in Longford so early. Only one of us should go. Cassa may be upset. How about you, Frank?"

"You go, John. I was going up to the church for eleven o'clock, so I'll be expected up there. You don't mind?"

Deirdre could see that he wanted to go on his own. "I'll come and say a few prayers with you, Frank!" she said.

"I'll stop over at Mrs Hanley's," said James.

When Cassa woke up at midday, John Gowan was sitting by her bed waiting for her eyes to open. Emily had ushered him into the bedroom, assuming he was one of the family.

"Am I dreaming?" Cassa murmured as she struggled out of sleep to sit up and look respectable. "I must be dreaming."

John smiled at her. She was as young as a girl, her hair curling closely, her cheeks pink from sleep.

"You are not dreaming. You are in a guesthouse in Longford and I have come to take you to Carrick."

Suddenly all the thoughts which she had kept rigidly at bay during the long drive flooded back into her mind, and the tears she had not shed came coursing down her cheeks. Suddenly she was babbling out her fears of being watched and followed.

"You see, my sister asked me to help her in a very special way and I have let her down. I ran away like a kid out of school. I do love my sister, but I never seem able to please her, and now I really have let her down. Her husband came to Firenze and I think he was testing me in some way and I made a fool of myself and when Nicky finds out, she will... oh, I'm sorry, I'm sorry, John. I didn't mean to upset you. I thought I was lost on the roads. I thought the journey would never end. I seemed to have travelled the length of Ireland. I was sure Dermot Tyson would catch up on me. I was sure he would, he would... oh please, forgive me!"

She hid her face in the quilt.

"I am so ashamed to make a scene. It was just I got so tired. I seemed to have been tired for weeks. John, I'll be all right in a few minutes. I was afraid of falling asleep at the wheel. At times I was way over the other side of the road. I left home at two. The eight o'clock news was on the radio when I got here. Please forgive me. I'll be all right when I wash my face."

John had the strange sensation of a man who has come home from far away to find that which was lost. He held Cassa very tenderly, wiping her tears with his finger tips, kissing her forehead, comforting her with words deep in his throat. She protested how contrite she was at dragging him into her involvement with Tyson.

"I am glad to be here," John said. "Of course I am. Cassa, it's over, all over. Trust us to see you through."

"But I am afraid, really afraid of Dermot Tyson. He will keep on until he finds me; he knows people everywhere. Garda Commissioners, politicians. I am terrified of him. You could never imagine... oh, John!"

John held her closely for another moment, and then he let her go. She had pushed back the covers and she was standing out on the floor looking around for a towel to wipe her face.

She was wearing pyjamas of the sort his sister Deirdre used to wear the year she was in boarding school where the nuns insisted on warm pyjamas. She looked sweet and dear.

"I will wait for you downstairs, Cassa. Take your time. And cheer up! I know the very place for lunch."

He gave her a little kiss, feeling that he and Cassa Blake had linked up an enchanted circle. He turned at the door to smile back at her. "I'll wait for you. Take your time."

Walking out to his car he repeated the words again. He would wait for her. She could take her time. The circle would hold fast for the two of them. There was a certainty in his mind.

When Cassa came down to pay her bill, John had arranged with Mrs Johnson to leave the car in the drive until he could have it collected.

"I got your keys from their son, Jacky, and you were right out of petrol! I have put the other suitcase in my car."

It was a delicious feeling to be taken care of.

Cassa thanked Emily and Mrs Johnson. They still assumed that Cassa was bound for the festival. Emily urged them to hurry, the crowds would be enormous.

"The Bishop of Elphin is coming up specially," she told them as they were getting into the Bentley.

As they were driving away, Cassa asked John about the festival. "Is it in Carrick-on-Shannon?"

"No, Cassa, we have our festival in July, the boat rally on the Shannon."

He smiled at her, and she smiled back at him. Cassa felt a glow of pure contentment unknown to her for a long time.

"You mentioned lunch," she said happily, "I am very hungry. It just occurs to me I should have brought a flask, but I would never have opened it. I never stopped."

"Because you were afraid, Cassa?"

She nodded, still a little bit apprehensive.

"You can trust us Gowans to look out for you."

"It is not fair to impose on you, John. Who am I, after all?"

"I know who you are, Cassa," he said.

You are my angel of grace and I will never let you go. John always thought in his heart far more lovely compliments that he had words to say.

Cassa began to understand this in him from that first hour. She was often to read entire sentences in his dark blue eyes. There would never be a need to press for spoken words.

"We are on our way to lunch – a little hotel on the river-bank. I'll phone home from there. Of course Frank and Deirdre and James will be waiting eagerly to greet you."

Cassa found herself thinking of Father Frank, her cher-ished friend. There was something untouchable about him towards which she yearned in a way she had never experi-enced before.

He was a man to whom she could reveal herself, hidden and unknown, and open to him as a flower would open. To be again within his ambience would be to know the radiance of loving another person with nothing between them but that very radiance.

"Are you still tired, Cassa, from your long night?" John asked.

Cassa pulled herself together. "It is this fabulous car, John. It sends me off into a dreamy coma. The luxury of it! The silent engine!"

"Umm, you know the exact thing to say to flatter me. Look Cassa, here is the little place I told you about."

In off the road, and winding through a tunnel of trees, they came to the Rooskey. It was a small but rather splendid hotel, set back behind a white balustrade and overlooking the leafy verges of the mighty river.

Evidently John Gowan was a regular client: a great fuss was made of his arrival. Cassa was introduced to the manager and his pretty wife, and a special table was selected for them in an embrasure of ferny plants.

"Let us make this a celebration," John suggested.

Cassa smiled at him. "It is all like a fairy story," she said. "I am the forlorn princess and you are Sir Galahad, only instead of a white steed, you have a trusty Bentley!"

CHAPTER SIXTY-SEVEN

CASSA FELL COMPLETELY in love with Carrick-on-Shannon from the first glance. There was an open-up-wide atmosphere of waterways and rope bridges and painted boats. There were flags and music and the wafted aroma of cooking. There were treasures of space in the sky. It seemed as if the vista went on into the distance in all directions, giving a sense of unlimited freedom to lift the dullest day.

On Easter Sunday in that year of 1980 the sun shone out of an azure sky, and it went on shining for the long summer ahead. It was the summer weather which comes to Ireland one year out of every five.

With all the family of two brothers and their married sister together in John's house, Father Frank drew Cassa into his arms, fully and joyously.

He held her at arm's length after the first embrace. "We will have to build you up, Cassa! You certainly have lost weight."

And your eyes are tired and you have been crying and I wish I could show you all the tender love I hold in my heart.

Deirdre was very like Frank: the same wavy hair, the same sapphire blue eyes and the same friendly manner. James was a big Donegal man with a gift of immediate friendship.

John, who still held her hand introducing her, was very much in charge.

"Cassa and Deirdre are going to move on to the cruiser," he said, "and James, of course, he'll bring the old rod and won't be a trouble to anyone. Frank, maybe you could get Cassa's cases into your car. I have the launch down at the bridge jetty. We'll take Cassa over to her new holiday home, and we'll come back for the rest of you later." John was in jubilant form.

Deirdre hugged Cassa. "You'll never want to go back to Dublin. John brought me over earlier with supplies to *La Vie En Rose* – he was always an old romantic. Frank says old bachelors are all romantics. John loaded the fridge and the freezer; some of my concoctions went in also. Loads of wine, although come to think of it, I don't know if either of them drinks wine. Except altar wine, of course! Of course, all the men have a fondness for the Guinness! They are going to have a big party to celebrate your arrival – they never stop talking about you and worrying if you would survive that awful hospital."

Cassa was blushing with pleasure. "I am so lucky to find such wonderful friends, and to be invited to meet the family. I really am so grateful."

Deirdre hugged her again. "I am glad to have a friend, too. I live my life surrounded by men: two brothers, a husband and four galumping big sons. I hope you will tell me all about yourself, and about Dublin. I've never been there."

"And I've never been in Donegal," Cassa told her.

"We'll be exchanging visits!" Deirdre laughed. "It's lovely having another woman to talk to. I'm not a great reader and James spends hours hanging over the water. He should have married a mermaid!"

John was immensely proud of *La Vie En Rose*. He led Cassa around to show her every gadget and facility. He had a tape-bank of classical music. He showed her how to put on the lights, and run the showers. He invited her inspection of the fridge, full as it could be.

"Everything is so beautifully wedged-in," Cassa said in wonder, "and everything is spanking clean!"

"Spanking new!" teased Father Frank. "He has been renewing everything since the day you said you would come for Easter."

Cassa looked up at John. In his eyes she read a message that sent colour into her cheeks.

"Can I ever thank you enough?" she said, and she put her hand back into his hand, thinking of Chopin's music echoing on the water.

"Pay no attention to Frank! This gets done every year. The wear and tear on cabin cruisers takes the gilt edge off the profits. Did we tell you that Deirdre and James are – for the very first time – staying for the whole of Easter week? James has expeditions mapped out for every day. We'll give them the prow quarters and yourself will occupy the stern."

"And the dog at your house," enquired Cassa, "does she come aboard too?" Cassa had never stopped missing her father's dogs.

"Poor old Flacthna is tired of the water. I leave her with Mrs Tracey, a kind of a watchdog, though I doubt if she'd scare a burglar!"

"I never heard that name, Flacthna," Cassa said. "Where did you get a name like that?"

"Flacthna is the moon goddess of the ancient druids," John replied. "I hope I have it right – I like it. The moon goddess is worth watching some nights on the Shannon!"

"Oh, I like Flachtna," Cassa said warmly. "It is a lovely name. But you did not tell me if I am putting you out of house and home? Where will you and Father Frank be when we are here?"

"I seldom sleep aboard," Frank said. "Being rocked by the incessant movement keeps me awake!"

"And you, John?" smiled Cassa, amused at Father Frank's mimicking face.

"During the season I go home at night for security. The place is fairly overrun by tourists, and the house in the town is handy if there's a commotion – but that doesn't happen often. I'll show you over Carrick tomorrow, Cassa. Mrs Tracey looks after me very well, has done for years. She's in her seventies, but she is as nimble as a goat – I think I told you that before?"

Father Frank laughed gently: "Melia Tracey would relish that compliment! Goat indeed! A very well kept old lady she is – too good for you!"

Cassa made a determined effort to put Firenze and Nicole and Nicole's husband well out of her mind, and to enjoy the week ahead. Every time she caught Father Frank's eyes on her, or hers on him, she knew this holiday would be a once in a lifetime occasion. Her heart felt as light as a small bird. Her whole being was ready to soar and fly away past time. A week could last for ever taken in single seconds.

Their days began at nine o'clock when Father Frank came across from Carrick in the motorboat. Deirdre had his favourite Irish breakfast ready for him: bacon, egg and sausage with lots of buttered toast.

He had said his early mass in the nuns' convent, visited the sick in the old folks' home and had a cup of tea with Melia Tracey.

Cassa noticed breakfast was the main meal of his day. All Deirdre's wonderful recipes were, she said, "lost on him!" when it came to lunch, and later dinner when John came across to *La Vie En Rose*. It gave Cassa great pleasure to see Father Frank enjoying the breakfast and to share it with him.

"If the sun shines at Easter," he told them, "or so I have it on the authority of Melia Tracey who has been a weather watcher for fifty years and is a recognised local authority (so she says) and knows all the signs – never heard of on radio or television (they know nothing, she says)..."

"Frank, would you ever come to the point!" laughed Deirdre. "If the sun shines at Easter, so what?"

"Well," he said, "I have it on the solemn prediction of Melia Tracey..."

James threw a tea cloth at him, "You'll be telling us next about Saint Swithin's Day!"

"Oh, she has that one too," said Frank, "and it rhymes: If..."

"Fraaank! What about Easter?"

"I never knew such a load of interrupters as this family! Look how good Miss Cassa Blake is! Proper manners!"

Cassa was helpless with laughter. She had never experienced this kind of family camaraderie.

"Listen carefully, my children," intoned Frank. "If the sun shines on Easter Sunday – now all take a deep breath, there will be a wonderful summer. If rain is required by such miserable people as farmers, I have it from the wise lips of Melia

Tracey – now wait for it – rain will fall in a small sufficiency."
They all cheered. Hip Hip Hooray!

Cassa had never felt so happy, even in the great days with Papa.

John could not always come with them on their adventures. "Big Boss Man" Deirdre called him. He seemed to be needed in a hundred places.

Usually it was the inseparable four, as Frank said: "The two talking heads and the two wiseacres." Deirdre and Cassa found a million things to tell each other, James took out the fishing rod, and occasionally Father Frank said his office sitting parapet-wise with his feet in the flowing water.

As they drifted downstream from Carrick, Frank saw Cassa blossoming in health and looks and friendship. They explored a water wonderland of winding rivers which gradually widened as the Shannon began to gather size on its slow path southward. James, with his map, became an expert, steering them into the mysterious reed beds and winding channels of Carnadoe, Kilglass and lovely Lough Boderg.

On the Wednesday, John came with them and they pulled in at the pier of Rooskey. Cassa thought the food in the small but top-class hotel there was the best on the Shannon. They usually cruised home to Carrick by evening time. Cassa was always a lover of sunsets and, on the Shannon, they were gloriously spectacular.

On their last day before the week ended, the inseparable four cruised as far as Portumna to moor at Terryglass. John could not get away from base.

Here they went ashore and hired bicycles to explore the countryside. They didn't cycle all that far, but they found a very inviting farmhouse in which to eat. Afterwards as they sat in the garden, Deirdre got Frank to talk about Peru. It was a remark about his pullover which started him off. She had said, "You must have paid a heck of a lot of money for your jersey, Frank."

"Am I a millionaire?" Frank laughed at her. "This one is llama wool, made in a craft shop in our village. Ana, the woman who runs it, has a good eye for colour."

Deirdre ran her hand along Frank's shoulder. "She could make a fortune in Donegal with designs like that, all the blending of the colours. Tourists go mad for unusual jerseys. Who buys from the woman in your village? Isn't Sonaquera hundreds of miles from anywhere?"

"Buyers come," Frank said, "several times a year from the USA, and from Canada, and they take the stuff away. Loads of it. They don't give Ana much. It is a long way to come, and they are only the middle men."

Cassa asked him, "How do the craft women get the wool?"

"A tamed llama is a gentle animal, and they can be combed. Mostly the combings are made into cloth."

"How's the fishing out there?" enquired James, the perennial fisherman.

"The sea-birds themselves do a lot of the fishing, cormorants and even pelicans. There were hoards of anchovies some years ago but but there are strange currents. The Humboldt current cools the coast even within the tropics."

Frank looked around at the interested faces. His gaze stayed a little longer on Cassa's features, from which all the strain of anxiety had gone. She had the untouched beauty of a girl. Her close-cut curly hair was like a halo, full of sunlight.

"I'll bore you all to death if I go on about all the fish in the South Pacific," he said.

"I remember, once in a letter, you wrote about some islands? You wrote that they were fascinating." Deirdre had kept all of Frank's letters.

"Ah yes," Frank replied, "those were the Ballestras in the Bay of Paracas. These tiny islands have wonderful arches and natural caves with windowed turrets and amazing staircases leading to hidden balconies, hidden behind balusters formed by the lashing seas.

"A few times, I was taken out in sight-seeing boats. When the boats come into the vicinity, the sea-lions wade out into the caves and they call out in almost human voices: I always think they are asking us to go away."

Frank suddenly became conscious that his voice had gone on too long. "James, what are we thinking of! We have to get back these bikes and start for home."

It was too late to think of returning; they had delayed so long that twilight had come. It was decided they would sleep aboard.

James found a phone box at the landing bay in Killaloe, at the foot of Lough Derg. He was able to assure John that they had not upended his cruiser and that they would head back in the morning.

Late that night when Deirdre and James had gone off to their bunks, Frank and Cassa sat on the half-deck under the stars.

Each knew that the simple state of being alone together in the warm night was idyllic happiness. Only their shoulders touched, but each yearned for the other to move closer.

In an art gallery in Lima, John had seen a painting by Salvador Dali: two lovers who ached for each other, a man and a woman roped securely to trees opposite to each other but well apart. Dali's portrayal of agony. Frank's body rebelled against this apartness. In the absolute immobility of Cassa's nearness, he guessed the communion of her senses with his. There was elation and there was rhapsody. In a heaven of restriction, Frank knew this communion was their very apotheosis of sensuality.

When time passed and the stars were fading, they were mutually ready to go their separate ways to sleep.

"A goodnight kiss, Frank?" She dared to whisper the question, she who had so recently acquired a taste for being kissed.

"Why not, *querida Mía*?" He held her very closely and he kissed her hair, her eyes, her throat and her mouth with joyful desire as if he were well-versed in kissing beloved women every night in the week. He took his time.

Then he held her, as he did sometimes, at arm's length. "Now, off to bed with you, Cassa, and sleep well." That should take the harm out of it, he thought ruefully.

Cassa lay on her bunk with a feeling of easeful bliss, her

nerves savouring the recollection of his breath on her mouth. He had kissed her and let her go. I love him, she whispered the words into the darkness. I love him so much. Please, God, if that is wrong, could you forgive me?

CHAPTER SIXTY-EIGHT

FOR THE TUESDAY after Easter week it was proposed by John that he and Cassa and Frank would drive in convoy with Deirdre and James as far as Enniskillen. He knew the very place for a good lunch.

"You haven't been over the border in recent years, have you, Cassa? Well, don't be shocked. The British have built big iron Check-point Charlies at all the main exits. The Gardaí are there too, they have to be: double security. The Gardaí have wooden huts, but they're armed."

"I remember when we were kids," Frank put in, "we went back and forth with Uncle Tim and his tractor. I don't remember ever being stopped in those days. Now I'm told you can be searched, you and your vehicle."

Cassa suggested timidly, "Isn't it because of the IRA?"

"Sure they were always there," said James. "Away back a hundred years they were rapparees, and after that they were Fenians, and before that there were Dissenters, and United Irishmen." James stood up ready to make a speech. Deirdre gave him a push to sit down. "Yerra Jamsie, we've heard it all before. The people this side of the border have switched off."

"I wouldn't be so sure of that," James muttered. "Don't forget Donegal has a border too."

John said, "If you're nervous, Cassa, we'll stop this side of the divide – maybe go as far as Rossinver."

"That's a very good idea," James said. "I could drop a line in Lough Melvin." He saw his wife's face. "I mean to say Lough Melvin will put up a great fish lunch. I'll give them a call, Easter being over and the mayfly season a while off yet."

Deirdre put a protective arm around Cassa's shoulder. "We'll leave the old border for another time; it's frightening if you're not used to it. You'll see plenty of lovely scenery if we take the Lough Allen, Lough Gill roads."

James hooted at this. "Why don't we go home to Killybegs

through Cork and Kerry while we're at it! Talk about the long way home!"

Frank looked at him. "So it's short-cuts you want?"

"Lough Melvin for lunch," John declared. "Make the booking, Jamsie boy."

As it happened, on the Monday night Father Frank got a phone call from the Father Provincial of his order asking him to come to Dublin for a day. Cassa knew she would miss him every moment. John, however, was in his jubilant mood. "Sure and isn't it time I have her all to myself for a day? Isn't that right, Cassa? And won't a day in the Bentley be a change from *La Vie En Rose*? Admit it, Cassa, doesn't the water get very monotonous?"

"Never," she smiled at him. "I love every minute on the cruiser."

This was what he wanted to hear. He smiled at all of them, beaming, his dark blue eyes sparkling.

But after the parting with Deirdre at Lough Melvin, Cassa had grown silent. The holiday was over and she was thinking that love was over too. While they were together in the same place, they could share their days, they could almost be intimate, and no one passed a comment. Apart from the fact that loving him was inadmissible, inviting him to stay in Firenze was out of the question; an odd, rare visit was all she could hope for, and when his holiday ended, would there even be a letter? Peru was the other side of the world.

"I am glad we have a couple of hours on our own," John interrupted her thoughts. "I never get a chance to really talk to you."

"Talk away, John. In this wonderful car, flying along scarcely touching the ground, am I not the perfect captive audience?"

"Right," he said, "so don't jump out the door when I tell you I want you to stay for the summer. Think for a moment. Why shouldn't you have a prolonged holiday?"

She thought and she said sadly, "There are several reasons, John. One is that I don't have much money. Another is that I would worry about the house, standing there all alone with no one to look after it."

"There are some question very hard to answer, but would you tell me: do you miss your house very much?"

"I can answer that easily. No, I don't. Not at all. I wish my father had never left it to me. It is a burden, a great big place to worry about. It has come between me and my sister – it is like a nightmare."

He was surprised. "But it is a lovely old house and so well situated."

Cassa shrugged, "A hundred years ago, it was a possible house. Even in my mother's young days, there were servants and money. Before I was twenty-one that was over. No, John, I don't miss Firenze."

He knows I do, she thought, but he is so kind, so generous, how can I say? John pressed her hand. He knew, of course he knew. "And yet you say you would worry if you stay here for the summer?"

"Conscience, I suppose. The insurance is due in July. It is a lot because the house is full of antique furniture said to be valuable. Just think what Nicole would do to me if Firenze were burgled and vandalised and she found out that the insurance were not up to date. Besides, my father must have trusted me. I'll have to get a job somehow. A prolonged holiday? Oh John, you know I can't."

He slowed down the big car and drew over into a lay-by. "You could, if you allow me to look after the insurance, and to put the house under security." It took Cassa a few minutes to take in the meaning of his words.

"Why would you do all that for me? I am only a stranger."

Even if he were useful with words, it was too soon to tell her his reasons. He was able to wait. At this time, her spirit was in the hands of his brother. His brother deserved the chance of a choice, or the opportunity for a sacrifice.

It was a risk perhaps, but it was a risk he must take.

He turned around to Cassa, "I am, as you may have noticed, a very commercial sort of a bloke. If you stay for the summer, it will free me of the daily necessity of looking after our visitor, of entertaining him. Frank won't be home again

328

for seven years. As it turns out, I have my busiest ever summer schedule ahead. You would be obliging me."

"Are you sure, John? Really sure about this?" The deep-down fiery glow in her brown eyes told its own story.

"Never surer," and John was back in his jubilant mood, "and I'll look after the house."

"Will I ever be able to pay you back?" she said dolefully. "That will be my big worry."

Having her here beside him, knowing he would see her every day in the summer, treasuring within himself the hope of a future caring for her, what was there to say about paying back.

"Let's not be worrying right now. Tomorrow you will give me a few details and I'll look after everything."

He smiled at her. "Insurance is second nature to me by now and the girl in the office (you know Joan) deals with all that very well."

"I'll never be able to thank you enough."

"There's still a few hours of daylight left, and this is the first whole day I have had off for weeks. If we were in Dublin now, I could suggest a film or a concert. You must be missing Dublin, whatever about the house?"

"I miss nothing, John. There is peace and happiness for the only time since my father died." She caught her breath, afraid of tears. "You will never know the depth of gratitude I feel towards all of you."

John started the car with the satisfaction of a man who has jumped a first hurdle and landed on his feet.

"We'll go on so, and find a nice old pub. I notice it takes yourself an hour to down a small sherry."

"And I notice," she rejoined happily, "that yourself can be very handy with a pint."

CHAPTER SIXTY-NINE

WITH SO MANY cabin cruisers on all the rivers and lakes and canals, John Gowan decided to lay up *La Vie En Rose* until the autumn. Cassa was comfortably accommodated with Mrs Hanley, and Father Frank stayed, as always, with Melia Tracey in John's house in Upper Street.

A little two-person cruiser, *Morning Star*, was for Cassa's use, and for any friend she cared to bring aboard.

John knew that his brother would be the friend. No one of Cassa's family had contacted her, and the two brothers assumed she had not contacted any of them.

John was giving them the freedom of the summer and of the waterways. Frank was well aware of his brother's benefaction. Cassa was simply grateful for being allowed to enjoy long summer days with a man she loved more with each passing hour.

Never for a moment did she forget that he was a priest. The word "sacrosanct" stood upright in her mind like a mark of interrogation, questioning her gentle touch on his arm and ironically absolving the passion of their goodnight kiss.

The passion was a matter of minutes: over, done with and filed away until the next night. There were nights if John or others were of their company when their ceremonial kiss was postponed for twenty-four hours.

Occasionally they took John's second car and Frank drove across into Monaghan to show her places familiar to him since boyhood. He never revisited the farm in which he had grown up, although he mentioned it many times. Cassa had questions, but she never asked them. Her sympathy was in her eyes and her hand on his sleeve.

They liked best to take the *Morning Star* into the small secluded channels and anchor her under the verge trees where the hot sun filtered down through the leaves.

They listened to John's tapes over and over again, sharing an identical love of music. Frank talked for hours about the

Peruvian peoples, their problems, their poverty, and their achievements in writing and in art. Often he described the children dancing the *marinera*: no shoes, only their bare feet but their gaily colourful Spanish dresses which had been handed down for over a hundred years.

"You do not tell me enough about yourself, Cassa my girl. Your childhood. Your early years."

She evaded queries like that. What had she ever done? Attended on her mother for ten torturing years. That happy time alone with Papa, towards the end, such a little time. To recall Papa now would bring tears.

Work in the horrible hospital, unmentionable and best unmentioned. Jinny Corcoran and Lotty Slattery were people on another planet.

There were names in her memory which she tried to forget: Dermot Tyson, Robert Gray.

The thought of Louise's suicide was still too terrifying to speak of to anyone. A hundred times, the vision of a demented but beautiful Louise came out of the dark to haunt her friend who dared to be alive and happy on a sunlit cruiser. The thought of Louise was too poignant for Cassa to endure.

"What have I ever done, Frank? What kind of a story would I tell? I am only now awake and alive. I much prefer listening to you." And indeed she loved the sound of his voice, and the pause when he glanced up at her. In a side tooth, there was gold filling.

"It's how they fill teeth in Peru," he laughed at her asking. "Gold must be cheaper there than Polyfilla is here."

Gradually she absorbed his way of looking at things. Gradually, all unaware of doing so, she revealed the yielding womanly quality which was the essence of her personality.

They found they both loved history, especially very ancient history, folk history and legend. Frank brought some biographies he had told her about and she listened while he read pieces here and there. He was surprised to find her so far-flung in her knowledge, realising how very little he knew about women who did not live in the Andean mountains depending for wisdom on poor missionaries.

When he said this, Cassa replied, "During ten years of sitting by an invalid's bed, never leaving her alone, I made full use of my father's library."

They made plans for an expedition into the north to see the Grianán of Aileach. They would drive and stay in the north for a few days. John vetoed this trip. His farm-machinery trade, inherited from their Uncle Tim, brought him frequently over the border into Fermanagh and Tyrone.

"No," John advised them, "not at the present time. Think of somewhere else for your expedition. There is a restlessness up there like something in a cauldron. If it boils over, we could be in for a long bloody fight. Don't go north right now. The next time you come home, maybe."

"As far off as that?" asked Frank incredulously.

"Aye, and maybe further," answered John heavily.

There were fewer tourists in late August and *Morning Star* spent endless days drifting across Lough Key, mooring at Boyle and inspecting the town as if they were foreign visitors with not much English. This amused them greatly. Away over on the other side of Lough Key, they tied up to go over the relics of the fabulous Rockingham Estate.

Many evenings they cooked in the galley and drank wine from John's store of bottles. Afterwards they would sit on the half-deck, shoulder to shoulder, watching the sun go down in the west, away across the mighty river. This was a very precious part of their wonderful day, the going down of the sun.

"Have you ever known so marvellous a summer, Frank?"

"Never! And I hope we are not talking about the weather but rather about how rapidly the summer is going. Time is like Pegasus, streaking away through the evening sky on glittering wings. No one ever found the reins of Pegasus or the reins of time."

She knew she would remember for ever the tilt of his head, his turn of phrase, his accent polished by years of using another language.

"If only this one summer could go on and on," she murmured.

"Cassa, it is a tenet of philosophy that when we are certain, absolutely certain that nothing lasts for ever, we wish it would."

He was smiling and she smiled back at him, "I should have to think that one out, Frank!"

"The certainty is all, my very dear Cassa." He bent his head to look deeply into her brown eyes.

CHAPTER SEVENTY

QUIETLY, JOHN OBSERVED his brother and Cassa each evening when they came ashore. Their love for each other was in the air all around them: a perfume distilled from their nearness, or maybe from the golden tan of their skin, or maybe from the evening sun-rays caught in their hair. They never touched each other, never gazed. They remained always two separate beings, laughing and speaking and looking.

Nevertheless, John knew there was a fusing of their spiritual essence. Looking at them, their love affair was a frame enclosing fragrant roses in an alabaster vase, a perfect picture of untouchable beauty.

Another man would not notice anything in this couple stepping off the *Morning Star* at the Bridge Cove, but John was a man in his mature years experiencing the throes of first love for a woman as equally he was renewing his lifelong reverential love for his brother.

If Frank's spirit had newly fused with Cassa's spirit, the more had John's nature been forged in the smithy of his brother's nature. There were days when John's heart was drenched with pity for his brother, and there were days when the hopeless pity vied with helpless envy. Cassa was so very beautiful and she was so beautifully in love with a man entangled in a stifling web. There were yet other days when John grieved with the pain which could give no warning.

John sensed that Cassa would never plead. In her world, decisions were a male prerogative. John saw down into his brother's soul. It would go hard on Cassa when the day for decision came.

In September Father Frank's leave of absence was coming to an end. Before flying out from Dublin, he would be called in to the general house for a spiritual retreat.

John perceived the days when actual physical retreat began and his heart ached for Cassa.

La Vie En Rose was again moored in at the Bridge Cove. The cruiser office was not so busy now, and Cassa liked to cook an evening meal in the galley for the three of them. Frank was absent as often as he was present.

"I cooked for all of us today, and no sign of him. Is Father Frank packing every day?" she asked John.

"I think the packing is done. I think he is writing letters."

"That was on Sunday he said he had letters to get off. I hoped he would come this evening."

It was kinder to give her a clue. "Melia Tracey thinks he is 'putting on his considering cap'."

"Did she say anything else?" Cassa was puzzled.

Reluctantly, John said, "Melia Tracey thinks he is fasting and praying. He is not eating much of what she cooks for him."

"When he comes to the launch, he eats well," Cassa said. "I hope he is not going down with something. He has told me about tropical infections which may strike even when no longer in the tropics. Things like malaria."

"Will you miss him when he goes away?" John asked watching her eyes.

A cloud passed slowly across her bright face. "Oh yes, oh yes! He is my best and dearest friend. I have so much affection for him. I wish he did not have to go so far away – and for so long a time."

And that was not all she was wishing. After all the summer sunshine it seemed to Cassa that snow was falling on her heart.

Suddenly, without warning, the last few days were gone.

On the day of departure, Father Frank walked down to *La Vie En Rose* at the quayside. His brother would follow with the car.

Cassa was ready, standing on the half-deck watching out for him. She had a warm jacket about her shoulders and a pretty scarf tucked into a silky shirt. He noted these things and he would remember them.

She greeted him with a tender smile. "Oh how I wish you

were not going! I was hoping for that last trip, all on our own, to the Grianán."

Frank turned over the words. "All on our own" could well have proven fatal.

"Cassa, please don't come to the airport. Let me remember you here. *La Vie En Rose* is painted on the rail beneath your hands. The sun is shining on the glistening water. You are more beautiful today than I have ever seen you, and I will take this last picture of you with me. It will be with me always." He could scarcely conquer the emotional break in his throat, but he tried hard for a smile. "Now I have come... to say... this has to be... this is goodbye, my... darling Cassa." His sapphire blue eyes were glistening in the sunlight.

She waited for him to step aboard to enfold her in his strong arms. Then their farewell kiss, his ceremonial kiss on hair and eyes and his breath sweet on her mouth.

Instead, he stepped back a few paces. Cassa held out her hands to detain him, and somehow the words tumbled out: "Frank, I love you. I will love you always and always."

He came back to the rail. Gently, he placed his fingers on her lips and he spoke in a voice so husky it was almost gone.

"Dearest girl, for us there can only be a silence of the heart."

The Bentley zoomed over the bridge, and John called out to them.

"All set? Come on, Cassa! Come on, Frank! "

The pulsing car was tuned, ready for the long drive to Dublin Airport. When only Frank turned to the car, John quickly sized up the situation. The big car was gone with a last wave of a hand.

The sweetest part of Cassa Blake's life was over.

CHAPTER SEVENTY-ONE

CASSA HAD PACKED her two suitcases. The summer had faded and the days were drawing in now. It was time to leave *La Vie en Rose*, return to her own house, and see about learning again to live alone. A job! That too, she supposed.

She had prepared a little banquet for John, a farewell dinner. She listened for his car coming over the bridge and pulling up. He always tooted the horn a soft bip-bip so she would not be startled. In the last week the town had almost emptied out.

"Smells good!" John said. "Something special. I see the table looks like a party! Candles! And wine!"

Cassa gave him her usual affectionate peck on the cheek. "Sit there like a good man, and let me dance attendance on you for a change."

"Have I been a good man, then?" he smiled.

She handed him a starter she had found in Deirdre's cookery book. "You are the best in the world and I could never begin to tell you how thankful I am to you. Tonight has to be a last-supper kind of a dinner. I hope it is going to taste good. This is a Deirdre recipe, but the main course is all my own invention. Eat up!"

John was suspicious of this long speech. Head her off, he thought.

"Yes, you are right, Cassa. Your cruising days are over for the present, except for the odd good days when we might cruise south over a weekend."

She busied herself at the stove.

"John, you must tell me if this tastes really gourmet? Help yourself to the vegetables, please."

"It is delicious, girl, but it will probably choke me if I have to swallow the 'last supper' along with it."

"Then we won't talk until afterwards. Please don't choke; I spent hours preparing it." Cassa was trying to make him laugh as he usually did.

"It really is delicious, but I can speak and listen, while I eat. We are talking about your coming ashore. There is my house and there are also apartments now empty after the season."

"Well no, John, we are talking about my going back down to Dublin. My house is there, locked up, but still standing I am sure, because of your good care. Thank you again, John. You have been so good to me. This is a special dinner of profound appreciation."

He stood up and bowed with a flourish, so then she had to laugh as she busied herself with the dishes.

At the airport, when the flight was called, John and Frank had clasped each other in an unusually affectionate goodbye. At the very last minute, Frank said, "Now or never, John. Don't let the grass grow under your feet." They had smiled a mutual recognition of the clichés, but John had understood. That was nearly three weeks ago.

He had received a benediction, but had he given Cassa enough time to ease the heartache of a love that could never be?

All during the balmy days of the summer John had watched Frank and Cassa. He had depended on Frank not to cut the links of John's magic circle, a circle of which Cassa was not yet aware.

John Gowan had the same certainty as he had when he watched Cassa asleep on that first day: two brothers had become enthralled with the sleeping beauty. When she awoke at last, would she be given the chance of choice? John knew his brother.

"I had thought, quite honestly, Cassa, I had thought that Carrick-on-Shannon had cast its spell over you. That you would be reluctant to leave."

"Oh I am, I am. I have been more contented here than I have ever been. Ever. Ever. Ever. I love Carrick. But you know yourself, John, the house and the land are down there in Dublin. Houses go to pot if they are neglected, the garden too. The house will get damp. The heating had begun to be a problem for me lately."

Cassa and Father Frank had not crossed the barriers which barred them from each other, but perhaps that made their love all the more sacred and precious? The thoughts fell down through his mind like so many rattling stones.

Now or never, Frank had said.

John put down his knife and fork.

"Come on deck for a moment, girl. The tip of the moon is showing over that far breakwater."

Cassa loved to watch the moon rising at the edges of the waterways. The moon on the lapping waves had a silvery sheen. They stood together in the glinting stillness.

"Soon it will be winter in Carrick," Cassa murmured.

"Cassa Blake, before winter comes, please do me the honour of becoming my wife."

He held his breath as he saw the questioning wonder in the dark eyes she turned up to him. He wanted to plunge in with a hundred words: Don't answer now. Take your time. Think about it. I will wait. Please, Cassa, give it some thought. There's no hurry. I can wait.

None of this came out. Instead: "I love you, Cassa. I loved you from the first moment. I loved you before I saw you and then I loved you more."

It took a long, long pause to get the courage to answer and not to hurt.

"John, perhaps it is that ice-cold slip of a moon, your moon goddess Flacthna working her spell. You are a man fit to be king. I am an old maid, a tried-and-true ordinary old maid. Marriage for you is with a girl, a young and lovely girl."

"Cassa, I am the one who is ordinary. Would that I were the man my brother Frank is."

Cassa drew a long sigh. "Ah, Frank," she murmured. And then she added, "But you are equally, both of you, lovely men, and I love both of you. You must know I do. But John, marriage is different. If I were ever to marry, it would be to some old guy about to retire and needing a housekeeper!"

"Would I not be old enough for you?" he asked, hoping she would smile at him, and she did.

"You are a dear sweet man and I thank you with all my heart for the compliment I will remember for the rest of my life."

"Does love not count for anything?" John asked. "Love on both sides? You said just now that I am a lovely man and you love me, didn't you?"

She was not taking his proposal seriously, but treating it as a pretty compliment.

"Are you actually against marriage, Cassa? Marriage as a way of life? Or is this the conversation we had before about something called the biological clock?"

"I suppose that counts more than love," Cassa said slowly. "A woman's fitness, as it were."

"It doesn't count with me," John said very firmly. "I love you. I don't want to lose you."

He put his arms around her. "I held you like this in that little place in Longford. Don't move away now." John could feel her trembling against him. He held her more closely. "What are you afraid of, girl?"

Cassa whispered, "Of men, I think."

"I would never hurt you," he said. "Trust me, Cassa. Tell me you are ready for this man's love. Tell me."

Her whisper was even softer than before: "But I would not know how to respond, and you would have to endure my ignorance," and softer yet she added, "and you would be disappointed. And, after a while, you would be tired of me."

"Charity cuts both ways." Now John's voice was stern. "You could be in love with me, and yet tire of me. I am talking of marriage, girl, the taking of solemn vows. It is a sacrament. It would give us the grace, the strength. We would look out for each other. And I could take care of you, Cassa."

John bent his head to find her mouth. Her lips were soft and yielding. He kissed her very gently, keeping control of the sudden surge of passion rising within him from the very submissiveness with which she was trying to respond.

To win Cassa would take patience. Her body moved more closely against his.

"I love you, girl. Give me a little hope." Her lips sought the security of his lips again, her arms crept up around his neck. The thought came to him that Cassa was a natural. She would enjoy and invite his lovemaking when he was able to find a way past her inhibiting fears. It would take time, however, for her to be sure that his proposal was not a spell cast by the moon goddess, but a proposal for their future married life.

He was a man of certainty. He had given them the summer, and he had waited, and now he would reap his reward. They would be married at the end of Advent. Perhaps on Christmas Day? He began a countdown, and each day he drew her to him, establishing himself slowly.

Some of Cassa's fears redounded to John's benefit. At the end of September, she consented to his accompanying her to Dublin, and to staying in Firenze.

"I think you are my guardian angel, John," she told him. "Please don't be shocked by my fear of my sister. I try not to be, but it seems ingrained in me. I have made up my mind to sell Firenze, and she will try to stop me. She will find out I am here. If I could get enough to buy a little place on the bus route and then get a job… Could you stay with me until I get settled? And, John, you know all about the business end of these things, would you please deal with auctioneers and furniture people?"

She told John how her father always referred to Tyson as the godalmighty Tyson. And how Tyson had wanted this house and the land adjoining for himself and Nicole, rather than a dowry and their house.

"Nicole told me that about Tyson, fifty times at least, but the solicitor could not undo Papa's will, which had been drawn-up years before."

"It could be, then, that Tyson will bid at the auction," John said. "We will make it a condition of sale that we know the names of the rival bidders. There will be a great deal of interest in this sale. If Tyson is a bidder, I will outbid him."

"Would the auctioneer allow that?" Cassa wondered, and John chuckled. "Of course," he said. "The higher the bid, the higher the auctioneer's commission."

John Gowan chose the top man in Dublin, and within a fortnight they had set the date for the auction. Advertisements and pictures appeared in all the daily papers in Dublin and in London. The auctioneer appeared gratified to work for them.

"May I suggest we have three days of viewing, and that we show the house fully furnished as it is. In these cases, we usually add some valuable pieces, maybe articles and pictures we have in stock for sale. In this case, there is no need. The way this house is laid out is considered traditionally classic. Nothing much changed since Victoria reigned in her Empire. It is essential that we have an inventory."

Cassa was surprised when John took an inventory from his brief case. "You will find everything accounted for in this document. This was made shortly after last Easter. We had the house under security, as it was unoccupied."

"And your solicitors are Boyce and Boyce. I presume they have a copy of the inventory?"

"And we are keeping copies ourselves," John said.

Out in the street, Cassa looked up at him in admiration. "Where would I have been without you? I am so grateful to you, John."

Her gratitude was not unwelcome, but it was not the thing he wanted most. Cassa was still talking about a little house on a bus route and getting a job. Their daily nearness was not enough. He was looking for a sign and forcing his patience to stay firm.

"I love walking through the streets with you," she said. "I love when you take my hand to cross the traffic."

She would have liked to add that she liked his outdoor handsome looks and the country-gentleman style of clothes he wore; that it gave her pride to walk with him. But she felt that such talk would be like drawing attention to herself, as if he should be returning the compliments.

His brother Frank had been so easy with the little compliments. They had been so open with each other. She missed him every moment of the day, and far into the night. She found herself praying, almost frenziedly, that she might forget. Other nights, she implored the saints in heaven and all the holy angels that she might dream of him, that he might come to her in a dream, that once more, even once and never again, O Lord, allow me to be kissed in that way he had.

Cassa was in love and she was slow in coming to the forlorn realisation of his words: "For us there can only be a silence of the heart."

That was all. He had not left her any guiding rules to carry her forward. Only silence.

CHAPTER SEVENTY-TWO

DERMOT TYSON HAD his own ways of watching out for Cassa's return. He was aware that the house was secured and occasionally opened up, apparently for attention. For May, June, July, August and September the procedure of attentive care continued. Sometimes he took Orla and Sandra for a drive up the hill past the locked gates. From the top he viewed the gardens flourishing, the green lawns, the hedges trimmed.

"When will Auntie Cassa be coming back from her holidays?" Sandra always asked.

In the first week of October he saw the advertisements for the sale of Firenze and thirty acres, very costly ads and large pictures of the house showing the conservatory in colour as it may have been twenty years ago.

Dermot rang the auctioneer, whom he knew. "Of course you know, Tom, that was my wife's family home. I suppose her sister is selling it at last – much too big for one person."

"Are you interested, Dermot? We think it may go over the top. Although it is the worst time of the year to be selling. Wait for the spring, I told them. Let me know if you're interested."

"It's a fine place, plenty of land. I could be interested."

He was not interested in bidding but he wanted to hold the auctioneer's ear for a moment. "I expect you will have met my wife's sister, Cassa Blake?" Tyson enquired.

"Well no, as a matter of fact, I have not actually had the pleasure. Dick Boyce tells me she is the sole owner, but she appears to have a man-of-business to deal for her. She may be the lady who came in with him on one occasion, but mostly he comes in on his own. A big country fellow, northern accent, name of Gowan."

Tyson's memory clicked. John Gowan was the fellow running down the hill with Cassa. Not a lover, she had said. But, maybe a fortune hunter. Driving a Bentley?

"The lady who came with this Gowan, were you not introduced to her, Tom?"

"Not that I remember. He did all the talking. Pretty well
versed. You think it's your sister-in-law? I'd say a smasher: big
brown eyes and close-cut curly hair, tanned like the South of
France. Is that the one?"

"It may very well be. I'll see you on the viewing day, Tom."

"Three viewing days," Tom reminded him.

Dermot Tyson whistled softly as he put down the phone.
He left his office and walked jauntily down Harcourt Street
and into Stephen's Green. He found a bench in the sun
where he admired the happy little ducks pottering away in
their pond.

The weight was off his mind. He was back in command.
Cassa was not lost to him. He was supremely confident of his
powers of persuasion, recalling yet again the effect he had
had on Cassa in the front drawing-room of Firenze; it was a
few months ago but the warmth of her slim body against his
mounting desire was still fresh and very much to his taste.

His plans for Paris were still in readiness, and all the easier
when Firenze was disposed of. She could save whatever
money it fetched. He would keep Cassa in silken luxury.

He fancied Tom Dwyer's picture of her: big brown eyes and
a tan like the South of France. He closed his eyes and smiled
in the sunshine. He would cherish Cassa. Wherever she had
hidden herself for the summer, no doubt from fear of
Nicole, his deepest instinct told him she was still untouched.

Later in the evening, he phoned his mother. She had
always admired Firenze, but she had been in the house only
once, the day of his wedding. He knew she would like to walk
all over it and peep into the bedrooms and up into the attics
where the servants used to sleep.

"Will they be auctioning the furniture?" she asked. His
mother dearly loved a furniture auction. He supposed they
would. What would Cassa do with all that stuff when the
house was gone?

He remembered the portrait of Elvira. He would remind

345

her how well it would look in their Paris *appartement*. Had he told her of that plan ? Perhaps on that night she hadn't really taken in the golden change he was about to introduce into their dual life.

He had thought so much about Cassa and that night of revelation, endless dreams in the last few months. But then Cassa had always belonged to him since she was twelve years of age. That night he had recognised their identical urgent sexual arousal... the mutual thrust... he would give and she would take and he would give again. Her lovely little tear-stained face was his treasured medallion. It was to him that fate had sent Cassa. To him, Dermot Tyson, in the midst of a Saturday morning's traffic outside Donnybrook church. How young he was then, how green and gauche.

It would be good strategy to have the company of his mother walking around with him at the viewing. He was very fond of his mother. She took a pride in being the least pass-remarkable of women. Nor was she ever critical. Nor did she ever offer advice. She had a host of friends and the family were devoted to her. Cassa's face would light up when he would introduce his mother. There would be an element of safety. It would give him a head start.

CHAPTER SEVENTY-THREE

ONE DAY THEY were walking around the house and Cassa was trying to decide which pieces of the furniture she could bear to part with: and if she kept anything, where would she store it?

Cassa had begun to find John an indispensable part of her days, but his marriage proposal had been stacked far back in her mind. Her thirty-four years of age seemed an impediment to her.

"You know," John said, "I cannot help thinking that there was a conspiracy against you last year. If Tyson had advised you to sell after your father's death, you could have lived quite comfortably and never taken up that wretched job. Tell me something: if Nicole had not (you know), and if you had got to the point of desperation (Frank told me a lot about San Salvatore), and if Tyson had offered a price for this place (his price, of course), would you have sold to him?"

"I was at the limit of enduring. I didn't realise how scared and beaten down I was until Tyson came to the house and, and, and he was... was..."

The recollection stung her eyes and she moved over into John's arms. "Yes, that night I would have agreed to anything about selling, just to get out of telling him about Nicole and... instead I ran away, stupidly to get, to get free of him. But because I was afraid as well and, and I..."

"Frank told me," he said as he held her and pressed his lips to her hair.

Cassa was tempted to cling to him, but she had not told Frank about that night. Not all. Not everything. A dim feeling of guilt moved her away from John.

"We have so many decisions to make," she said.

John said, "May I make a suggestion about the furniture? Once the property auction is over, why do we not have a pantechnicon van come with four stout men to carefully remove the lot? I recognise that much of it is antique. To have a few hundred people tramping through the house for a public auction is going to be a sacrilege. Maybe idiots testing out that lovely piano."

"And what would I do with the pantechnicon?" Cassa enquired. "Where would I store the furniture?"

"It is only a suggestion," he said, "but I have loads of storage space – that is, until you decide."

His practical business sense told him that to auction-off antiques in a private house was offering colluding dealers the chance of bargains.

Cassa was smiling broadly. "You are a good one to talk about conspiracies! If I don't jump into the Bentley and go back to Carrick, at least my piano and my bed and my books will travel off in this wonderful pantechnicon: one half of me will be stored in your vicinity!"

"Well," John grinned, "Melia Tracey would enjoy polishing the piano."

He was quite sure he had made another little advance when Cassa said, "I'll agree to that, John." Slow but sure and getting there, John thought.

John had made up his mind that if the interest in the sale was not keen, he would buy-in himself and hold it for Cassa until the spring. The auctioneer had told them that sales were better in spring. The furniture would furnish Firenze as it had done for a hundred years for the three days of viewing, and after that the pantechnicon.

CHAPTER SEVENTY-FOUR

ALTHOUGH IT WAS late into October, the viewing days were autumn at its best, with the leaves on the chestnut trees turning golden brown in the warm sunshine. From early the first morning the avenue was lined with cars and an extra car-park was made available in the first field.

John Gowan had brought down some of his own men from Carrick, to add to the patrol of the auctioneer's men watching out for light-fingered viewers. Cassa teased John that he was like the keeper of the Tower of London guarding the crown jewels! She named him "my halberdier", to which he replied that he was happy to be her dear anything.

Their relationship in their daily intercourse, chaste as it was, had deepened. Cassa was the sort of woman who depended on a man, and she had grown to depend on him completely. And he quite simply adored her.

On the first morning of the auction-viewing, Cassa was interested in walking around the house, seeing it through the viewers' eyes and listening to these strangers' comments. Thankfully there was no sign of Nicole.

After lunch, she decided to stay out in the garden. She chose a couple of garden chairs which John carried far up over the lawn to the sunny side of a beech hedge, saying he would join her in a while.

In the sheltered warmth, it was dreamy to think of the summer, when Frank steered *Morning Star* into the willow reeds to the music of a Mozart sonata and their eyes had held in a long look of sheer delight in each other.

A shadow passed across the sun, and she looked up smiling, expecting to see John Gowan. It was Dermot Tyson, his handsome face alight with admiration as he stood looking down at her.

"Cassa, my dear, you are looking splendid! How good to see you again. I have missed you. Your holiday has done you a world of good. You needed that break."

He stood back the better to admire her.

She clasped her hands on her breast to still the urgent beating of her heart. He was a very handsome man, and so effusive he would make a woman's heart flutter, but not with the desperate fear which clutched Cassa's. Surely, at any moment, Nicole would step from behind the hedge, and between them they would beat her to death with vile accusations.

Tyson asked very nicely, "May I sit down beside you? I brought my mother with me to view your house."

He chuckled charmingly, turning his face fully towards Cassa. "My mother is so curious about old houses. She would really like to meet you again. She tells me you talked to her on our wedding day when you were making the guests feel at home. We danced together, you and I, do you remember? You were a slip of a girl of eighteen, and do you know what it is, Cassa, you have not changed a day. Do you find me changed since that day?"

Beyond all knowing, she wanted to say, but she made an effort to match his flirtatious manner. "You have become even more handsome," she said softly.

His smile was devastating. "May I tell Orla and Sandra that you said so?" There seemed to be no end to his winsome ways. And still there was no mention of his wife.

He leaned towards Cassa. "You aren't forgetting about our plans for Paris? Later we can talk. May I take you to dinner this evening? The Glen of the Downs: just like our very first lunch?"

Cassa felt the old familiar fear, and yet an unwanted fascination. She looked around warily. Tyson reduced her to being a child again, a small sister waiting to be caught by a lurking Nicky.

"Will you come over to the house, Cassa, so I can introduce you to my mother, or shall I ask her over here? I am sure she would like to walk through the gardens."

He was aware of being irresistible, and Cassa knew she found him so. He held out her hand to her, and they both stood up.

She had to force out the words as she turned to accompany him: "Is Nicole viewing the house with your mother?"

He caught her hand back in his. "You did not know then? Nicole has gone away. Did she not write to you?"

This was not credible. Cassa felt weak and she sat down, looking around again, uneasily, fearfully. "Where is Nicole?"

The hazel glints were gone from his eyes and his voice had lost its persuasive warmth. "She is in America. She has presumed to take what she calls a sabbatical for a month or two. She is studying the contract cleaning business in the States, or so she writes in a letter to my daughters. A sabbatical is a useful word to make light of a mother's absence. Let us not talk of your sister."

"But she is my sister, Dermot, and I must know. Did you send her away... Did she go because... Did she go through with...?" Cassa's voice broke.

"You are asking me about the abortion? I have never forgotten my blind stupidity on that night. You tried to tell me..." Now his voice failed completely and he turned away to conceal his anger and his pain.

"That was the unforgivable act of a vile creature, and I cannot forgive her. She may have murdered my unborn son. Did she think of me in that terrible act?"

It was a moment before he could control his emotion, and then he turned to Cassa as if asking for her sympathetic understanding. "After that weekend, your sister thought she would resume our family life exactly as it was before. Her pursuit of her former pleasures verged on the shameless. It took strength of purpose to disengage her from her rights as my wife. My daughters were my first consideration, their serenity and security. Eventually your sister realised she no longer reigned supreme. You may never have known it, Cassa, but your sister is overwhelmingly possessive."

Cassa had never quite forgotten the sight of her sister and Clive Kemp acting like a couple romantically in love. Cassa pushed the thought away. "I feel infinitely sad for you, Dermot," she said.

Now Dermot Tyson turned on the charm, his eyes appraising and reassuring. "I know you do, my dear. Thank you, and I trust you will give me the opportunity to rid you of all sadness? You did not know, then, that your sister searched for you, Cassa? When she didn't find you, I knew you didn't want to be found. Finding you now, my dear, I begin to live again."

Cassa thought he seemed in no danger of dying.

"So, Dermot, you sent her away?"

"No," he answered at last, unwilling to be put in a bad light. "I had my daughters to consider. I simply made it plain that we did not belong to each other, then she left."

He moved a pace, and looked away over the hedges towards the people milling around the big house. A silence fell across the grass.

Then he said decisively, "She is gone out of my life."

But Cassa knew her sister better than that. Nicole would never relinquish her hold on him, nor on her beautiful daughters, nor on any of her possessions. Nicole would let him cool his temper, knowing that he could not be shut of her easily.

He was too proud a man to face the odious publicity of a small city like Dublin, even if there were a law for divorce, which there was not. Nicole would recapture him when she judged the moment fit for the retaking.

"And what are you going to do without her?" she asked sympathetically, in her voice the freedom of relief from fear.

The fulsome light came back into his hazel eyes. He was buoyant again. "Cassa dear, you know what I am going to do. I am going to see to it that you get your chance: the music lessons, the gay Parisian life, the being young again! Your place in the sun, my darling Cassa, and I will give you that place."

His handsome smile was a smile to light the world. The ugly picture of the trailing-haired woman with the lusting Robert Gray lit up her imagination for a second.

"Dermot, let's go over now to the house and meet your mother. Perhaps she would like a nice cup of tea in the kitchen."

He was all beams and smiles and extravagant compliments as they walked across the grass.

At that moment John Gowan was standing out on the steps directing a queue of viewers. He saw them and walked towards them.

"John, I would like you to meet Dermot Tyson, my sister's husband and my ex-employer."

Cassa's voice was as sweet as any voice either man had ever heard. Her hand on John's arm was a signal. "Dermot, I have much pleasure in introducing John Gowan, my fiancé."

"Oh yes!" John boomed in a north countryman's hearty voice. "Sure it's great to meet you. Cassa speaks very highly of you!"

"Shall we find your mother now, Dermot?" Cassa asked as sweetly as before.

"Thank you, no. I will attend to my mother." Abruptly, he turned on his heel.

Cassa and John stood until they saw Tyson escorting an older woman to his car. She looked a very pleasant lady.

Cassa looked up into John's friendly face. She linked her arm through his arm.

"My halberdier and my guardian angel," she murmured.

John gave her a little hug. "Just for a moment there, I was getting my hopes up."

CHAPTER SEVENTY-FIVE

I N THE DAYS before difficult planning permissions, the lands around Firenze were completely open for redevelopment. Close enough to the new arterial highway out of Dublin city and through Wicklow all the way to Wexford, the rising value of the land was now apparent. Speculators thronged the auctioneer's office. John Gowan had no need to safeguard the estate by putting in a bid; all bids were topped at a dizzy rate by high-speed entrepreneurs.

Cassa stayed at home on the day of the auction, which took place in the auctioneer's office in Dublin. She had not been all alone in Firenze since the night she had run away. Now she found the hours long and very lonely. She had grown away from the old house which once held all she ever knew about the nature of loving. She found herself going out on the steps to wait for John's car.

It was his pleasure to tell her the final, dazzling result of the sale.

"There were none of the usual cock-ups," he said gleefully. "Your solicitor had done his homework. Less his fees and the auctioneer's commission (hefty, I should think), the cheque will be ready on Friday at midday."

"What happens then?" Cassa asked, pleased that he was pleased. He had taken it all so seriously.

"You will lodge the cheque to your account in your bank. Sure, what else would you do, girl?"

"I don't have an account," she said. "I still sign my name twice a year when I draw the dividends left to me by my grandfather. That just about pays the electricity and phone, and taxes the poor old car which is insured to the end of this year."

"I guess your financial worries are over now, Cassa," he said.

John was slightly miffed that she was not jumping for joy. The actual sum of money did not seem of much account to her.

"John Gowan, look at me! I need you to be happy. I depend on it. Just tell me, is it a lot of money? I have never had any, you know?"

"It is a lot of money, Cassa. You will open an account in your own name, and the bank manager will perform a highland fling on the counter."

Her laughter was very precious to him, the laughter which always held a tiny echo.

"And you will come with me to see him dance? What will I do to you, if he doesn't know how to dance?"

On Thursday evening, John and Cassa watched the sunset over the trees. They listened to the birds settling for the night.

"This is my last night to sleep in Firenze," she said in a soft, regretful voice.

"'Fraid so," John told her, "because tomorrow evening, about this time, the auctioneer's man will be coming for the keys. I told the removers to be here at nine a.m. and they are reliable; I know them."

She reached up to give him a little kiss of thanks. "You are a trusty halberdier; you think of everything. There is just one last thing I want you to share with me."

She took his hand and they walked up along the curving paths still faintly perfumed by lavender until they came to the high stone wall. John read aloud the names and dates on the gravestones of the dogs' little cemetery. His arms were around her, her head against his coat. He felt her shudder of grief, a grief he shared with Cassa because he also was a dog man. Almost in prayer, they stood for a long time as the evening grew cold.

"We have made a requiem," Cassa whispered to him, "not only for the doggies, but for all the Blakes who live here no more."

He wanted to ask her if she would regret selling, regret leaving this pleasant place, the lovely house on its hillside, but he did not. He was a man of certainty, and he must be certain of her reply before he could finally believe her.

Next morning, they collected the cheque from a very genial Tom Dwyer and they went together into the Bank of Ireland in College Green. Her face was pale and her hands unsteady when she accepted a cheque book from the bank manager. He turned out to be a suave, quiet man who had probably never flung up his dance legs in his life. There was talk of charge cards and checking accounts, but Cassa showed no further interest.

"Just the cheque book for the moment," John said, taking her arm to steer her out into the street.

They stood on the broad steps of the building which had long ago been the Parliament of Ireland.

"Is it a lot of money?" she asked him again.

"Put it this way," John grinned down at her, his blue eyes glinting with laughter, "you won't have to look for a job and you will never know a poor day."

"There are so many poor people I got to know in the past year," Cassa told him sadly, "so many women who have to scrimp and save for a miserable few shillings."

She looked up into John's face inviting him to share her wish. "I should like to go out to Seacoast, into the car-park of San Salvatore, and scatter twenty pound notes all around, and call out to the women to come out and dance!"

"I am glad I am here with you, Cassa," John said very seriously. "You will please leave the money in the bank, withdrawing only whatever is your normal need. I have learned one very big lesson in life: nothing loses its value as fast as money."

She linked his arm as they crossed the road, smiling up at him. "Let's walk through Trinity College. Perhaps it is not too late for me to take a degree in musicology?"

He pressed her arm and joined in the teasing: "As I am already a bachelor – and for far too long – maybe I could become a bachelor of law in this college."

"We would have to become students and live in Dublin," she was laughing. "Could we descend to a house in Dublin after *La Vie En Rose* on Lough Key?"

As they paused beside the campanile, in the middle of Front Square, John turned to her: "Cassa? Cassa?"

"I am thinking about it!" she answered, and she actually winked up at him.

It is a wonderful thing, thought John, what a few pounds in the bank will do for a mature spinster! No doubt, she was thinking much the same thing.

John was anxious to get back to Firenze to see the pantechnicon off on its way.

Until five in the evening, the men removed and wrapped and packed. Cassa made tea and loads of sandwiches.

There were many items of ware, pots and pans, and tins stored against emergency, jams and marmalades, dried fruit for cakes: stuff Cassa had put aside when she toyed with the idea of taking in students. That whole crazy idea seemed ages and ages ago, but it was only last year. She asked the men to take the lot, for their own use. John packed all the bottles from the drinks cupboard into the Bentley.

At last, the huge van off took on the first leg of its journey.

At six o'clock, Tom Dwyer arrived for the keys.

"Fantastic place," he said. "It would break my heart to leave it. They tell me the buyer will be pulling it down! Shame! There should be a preservation order put on these places!"

He drove off with a cheery wave. Not a bad day's work.

"He said it would break his heart," John observed. "What about your heart, Cassa?"

"Still in one piece," she smiled at him, "and I wouldn't share it with a house, anyway. But don't let's hurry away too quickly. One last look at poor old Firenze."

With his arm about her shoulder, they turned into the hall and gazed up the elegant staircase. They walked down the avenue and stood for a long time staring back up at the house. John did not hurry her, nor did he ask her what she was thinking. When she glanced at her wristwatch, he broke the silence.

"It's going on for seven o'clock," he said. "What do you

propose we do when we shut the back door, and we must bang it strongly to make sure it is truly closed."

"Would it be too late to head for home?" Cassa asked. John beamed.

Just then the phone rang. John's eyebrows shot up, and Cassa nodded for him to take the call.

"John Gowan here. Yes, Miss Blake is right here."

John listened, and then he said, "Hold on a moment. It's the auctioneer, Dwyer. He's had a call from a client enquiring about a picture."

"Which picture?" Cassa asked, and John listened again.

"He says, a portrait of a lady named Elvira, which hangs in the front drawing-room."

"Yes," Cassa said, "I know that picture. We are leaving it with the others for Dwyer's art auction at Christmas."

John explained this on the phone. "Dwyer's client wants to make an offer now. He is going to hang it in his office, and please name your price. What'll I tell him?"

"I have no idea," she replied.

He handed the phone to Cassa.

"Mr Dwyer, did you say where the office is?"

John could hear Dwyer's loud voice: "I believe it is in Harcourt Street."

Cassa said, "I should like to make the man a present of the picture. Goodnight, Mr Dwyer."

John did not mention his surprise.

"Dwyer's men are clearing the rest of the house tomorrow," he said, "and from six p.m. tomorrow the phone and the electricity will be cut off. But I would like to go in and see this picture."

They went into the front drawing-room and Cassa switched on the light beneath the picture.

"I suppose it is like you, Cassa, but she is the saddest lady I ever saw – but colourful all the same. Who is she?"

"She is Elvira, our great-great-grandmother on the Blake side. When I was a little girl, I asked my Papa who was this lady who was always looking out at us. She was very beautiful but she seemed to stare a lot, sort of curiously. I remember how he laughed when I asked him about her. His grandfather told him, he said, that Elvira was famed for her beauty, but she was the very devil for the men, a bold bad piece and slippery as a serpent. So I was always afraid of her." Cassa snapped off the light under the picture.

"Time to go, my halberdier, and I am glad. Now it is over."

As the slam of the heavy door echoed away into the trees, Cass took John's hand, leading him out to his trusty Bentley.

Navigating his way across the city of Dublin, John Gowan fell silent. Cassa was lost in her thoughts and he let her be.

All her life Cassa had felt off-centre, out on the edge. The events which go to make up a woman's life had missed her out: the sensual joys Louise had practised with Robert Gray; the warm family love that Deirdre enjoyed; Nicole's prize, she who owned Dermot Tyson.

And Frank? She burrowed down into her car seat, suddenly cold as if whipped by a chilling wind. With Frank, she was further than ever out on the edge, her passionate yearning for him choked off, his love for her forever inaccessible. A silence of the heart.

Now another man was offering her the chance to enter a grown-up woman's world where she would be the centre, the hub, the core. Where she would never know fear again. And John Gowan was safely all hers. Safe. Always, and in all ways safe. For Cassa, that was the jewel in the casket.

CHAPTER SEVENTY-SIX

JOHN GOWAN KNEW that setting the Marriage Date (always spoken in capitals) for Christmas would give them the whole month of January to be together. Spring would begin in February with cruiser bookings for the following summer. A honeymoon pair: he liked the sound of that.

Meanwhile, October and November would be given up to the business of courting. This he took very seriously in the time-honoured way, constantly surprising Cassa with flowers and jewels and music and books and every dazzling wonder he could think of.

He was a man of certainty and when Christmas came he was certain that his beloved was as much in love with him as she was ever going to be. And that that love was deep, and very tender. Passion would come. He was prepared to wait.

That his brother Frank had a special place in Cassa's heart did not worry John, because in John's heart Frank always came first. The married couple had very quickly achieved a perfect understanding of each other.

When snow came in late January, Melia brought up their tea and toast at nine o'clock.

"Ye may as well stay in the bed until I have the house warmed up. If there's any post, I'll land it up to ye."

"She has us spoiled," Cassa said as they finished the tea. They turned again to be close to each other. "We're not in any hurry, are we?"

"You say that every morning, and in another hour you'll want to be up."

"That's because I don't want Melia to think I'm lazy." Cassa kissed him. "Or at least, not as lazy as you!"

"You get along very well with Melia Tracey, Cassa," John said, taking time to return the kiss. "I was afraid in the beginning that she would resent a mistress after ordering me around for years."

"I had a fear of that, too," Cassa confessed, "but I gave it time because I was tired of having fears. You know, there should be a world of difference between my mother, Sadora Gilbey Blake, and Melia Tracey, but I discovered they are identical while having different ideologies."

"Melia Tracey has an ideology? Fill me in on that, girl."

Cassa loved talking in bed, held warmly in his arms, enjoying his attention to every word.

"My mother had a Rule Book, and she queened it over everybody. The Rules built up your character, she told us. Melia has a Rule Book which works very well for the comfort of the household... but it is a Rule Book none the less. As she tells us daily: she is set in her ways. And another similarity: I cannot remember an original remark from my mother. She always used accepted proverbs and phrases and clichés to cover all eventualities."

"And isn't that the very thing that Melia does! Now that you mention it, and I never took much heed to it before, but you're right."

"And don't go paying any attention to it now, my darling husband. Just accept that the predictable is comfortable. Hear that? I'm getting the hang of it!"

They loved each other's company so much they went everywhere together; especially when Cassa was carrying their baby.

As Melia remarked daily to her niece Aggie who came to help, "It is a marriage made in heaven."

The baby, of course, was "a nine months wonder to the tick of the clock", as he was due to arrive on 26 September. The proof positive of the exact union, Melia announced, as the lovely couple had been wedded and bedded on 26 December. "That is how you calculate these things," Melia explained to sixteen-year-old Aggie, who knew perfectly well.

Cassa felt no reason to dwell regretfully on the past but, all the same, there were times when Firenze came to mind. Cassa's domestic background was not of the order that Sadora Gilbey Blake would have envisaged. Not even when the staff was augmented by another girl (another niece of Melia's naturally) and a gardener for the big back garden which stretched down to a stone-built jetty on the river. Not even when John had a glass summerhouse constructed for their pleasure; not even when the summerhouse was full of colourful blooms.

Cassa would love to have known her mother's approval, her sister's approval, even Dermot Tyson's approval. The engraved invitations had been sent for the wedding, but there had been no reply from the Tysons. No word ever.

Some day in the future, Frank would come home for his leave of absence from Peru. He would see they had made a success of their life, that they were doing all the things they talked about in their letters to him. His approval would be enough.

His letters, rare enough, were the real treasures.

Melia and the nieces were contented to spend their kitchen evenings knitting and praying and planning, all for the coming baby.

"We'll make sure he'll get his vitamins," Melia said. "I've been reading about it, there's vitamins in the sunshine. They're fairly new things, those vitamins... said to be very nutritious."

Cassa was able to tell John they were going to have a son. No doubt about it: Melia Tracey was using the masculine gender!

I'm coming along nicely, Cassa thought, laughing to herself: another Melia phrase.

So there was love. There was comfort and security. In the air around the house by the water there was a breath of happiness.

Sometimes Cassa stood at the window watching a cabin cruiser cutting along up-river. This year I have John and my baby is on the way, but last year Frank and I were on that cruiser. Last year was so long ago. A line from a poem she had read somewhere always came to her, and she whispered it out through the window to catch the wake of the cruiser: "For you abide, a singing rib within my dreaming side."

Lotty Slattery had once remarked to Cassa, "Life is a bugger, Missus, you have to watch out." You have to watch out, you cannot ever be prepared for the next blow, but neither can you ever be sure there will not be one.

In the last week of May, John and Cassa were lazily watching late night golf on the television.

A newsflash suddenly announced an earthquake in Peru. At first, they could not accept its meaning to their life. Peru is a huge country. The Andes are hundreds of miles across. Why should this earthquake be in the one place and not in some other place?

John stayed on the house phone, and he arranged for the office phones to be manned through the night. Embassies were phoned. If Father Frank were safe, perhaps in the city of Lima, he would get a message through. No call came. No message.

Melia and her nieces prayed all night in the kitchen, and again all the next day. Father Frank was Melia's favourite in the whole world, a saint he was, a saint who gave up his life for pagans.

Cassa and John were shattered. They could not accept each other's grief. They were no solace to each other. There was in each of them a passionate love which would never die, but it was not the same love, and not the same passion. For a week, the longest week in life, they fought against accepting the facts. They refused to believe that the mission of Sonaquera and its faithful pastor and thousands of his people had been swallowed up in the peaks of the Andes and would never be seen on this earth again.

John wanted, as he had never wanted anything before, to fly on the next plane out to Lima, to journey to that awful place, to scrabble with his bare hands in the blackened soil until he found his brother. But the News told him that an area of hundreds of miles was cordoned off, and all transport was forbidden.

And he was not free. Cassa must be his first concern. She was nearly six months pregnant. He held her as she cried in the anguish of her grief. His own grief for his own beloved brother had to be held in check.

*   *   *

"Dearest girl, why are you standing at the window again? You are cold, and you must eat."

"John, don't send me to the hospital for the baby. I want to stay here in our own room, near the window, near the river, and..."

"Wouldn't the clinic be safer, dearest?"

Her dark eyes seemed to reproach him. "Safer? Other women in Carrick stay home to have their babies. Is it dangerous because I am too old to have a baby? I told you that in the beginning."

John, close to tears, took her into his arms. "You will never be old, Cassa, and thirty-four is not old." He tried to smile cheerfully, "You said, only the other day, that the clinic is so up-to-date, so bright and welcoming. Real 'into-the-eighties style', you said!"

He realised that was something she had said a few days before the earthquake. She was murmuring to herself very softly and her eyes closed against John. He tucked her into bed and tiptoed out when she was sleeping.

"I'll eat in the kitchen," he told Melia.

"You'll eat a proper dinner, same as usual," Melia said. "What'll the mistress have, John?"

He shook his head helplessly.

"I'll take an egg-flip up to her later. I'll put in a small drop of brandy. She needs to sleep, the dote."

"Melia, this new maternity clinic in the hospital, wouldn't every woman approve of that?"

"Sure, hardly anyone stays at home these days, and the paying part of that clinic is sheer luxury they say!"

"Doesn't she realise her time is due, Melia?" he asked.

"She does, but the interest is flaggin' – the poor mind is elsewhere. She's in a state of shock. A woman with her first

364

baby, and in a state of shock, mightn't want to be moved; a first baby is often slow and frightenin'. She'll not be travellin' for the baby. She'll stay home."

"That is out of the question. This is not a hospital, Melia."

"She'll stay, all the same," Melia said, "or she'll slip away on you."

"Absolutely out of the question."

He was surprised with this turn of things. He did not want to deal with a new emergency. He was trying to compose his thoughts until he could let loose the weight of grief that was turning like a treadmill in his chest. What was Melia going on about?

"Dr Magner was here this morning when you were at your office, John. He agrees with me. And she will need you to stay with her for the birth."

He looked at her. Bewildered.

"There's only half of you here half the time," she said. "Pull yourself together, John. The mistress needs all you can give her. I'll make the arrangements."

"Did Eoin Magner say it's today?"

"No, probably not," she said, "but in a day or two surely. If you go out, be home by nightfall."

Melia knew him well. He had to get away .

He took out the old car which Frank used in that un-forgettable summer and drove, Melia would say, like the hammers of hell, all the way back to boyhood, to the house in Monaghan which was the only home his brother Frank had ever known.

When he himself was sixteen years of age, their mother had waved Frank goodbye and sent him over the fields to catch the bus for the town where the local priest would put him on the train for the seminary. Frank walked away with one miserable little suitcase in his hand. He walked proudly and only Johnny knew that Frank's heart was breaking.

He never wanted to become a priest and he knew Johnny was scarcely able to manage without him. After the years of slavery, the ceaseless work he and John and Deirdre had known since they were six, and five, and four, they were very close and depended on each other.

John could still see their mother at the door, a triumphant smile on her face, her rosary beads held aloft in her hands. Twenty-five years ago. No one disobeyed in those days.

At the house, he spoke briefly to his tenants. They had heard the tragic news. He walked away across the back fields and climbed the rising ground where only the stones were harvested, to the dolmen. It seemed like a hundred years ago when twelve-year-old Frank had told him that the dolmen on the ridge had been there before history was written.

"Before Rome was built, before America was discovered, before Christ was crucified, that stone dolmen was standing there in our fields. Johnny, don't be afraid: touch it with your hands. Deirdre, feel the coldness. It may be half a million years old. It will still be there when our history is forgotten."

In the late summer evenings when the farm work was finished, the three children came up to their dolmen. It marked their seasons; it stood as their guardian when the light faded from the fields; it was safer and more secure under the dolmen sacrifice stone than in the erratic woman's kitchen.

John buried his head in his hands on the dolmen. The pent-up tears could fall now on this ancient altar, in this place where the tears of unhappy childhood had fallen many times.

"You were my history, Frank. Without you, I have no beginning. You were my father and my mother and you were all my childhood. Boyhood ended the day she sent you away. I came up to the ridge that night, and I cried for you to come back, Frank. And our sister Deirdre cried too like her little heart would break.

"I never got the chance to thank you, Frank. Words are always difficult for me, but you know now. You hear me, my brother? You gave me everything you could give, and then you gave me Cassa. Each time she offers herself to me in love, it is your gift to me.

"I knew you had forged a vocation out of nothing. I knew you had taken solemn vows, and I knew you would honour your priesthood, but I knew you could take her if you called her, but you gave her to me because you loved me more.

"Frank, Frank, Frank, I cannot help but think that if you had reneged, if you had broken your vows, if you had turned your back on Peru and its terrible earthquake, if you had chosen Cassa, you would still be alive. But, my brother, reneging was not a part of your nature."

Remembering the way Frank's hands used to touch the sacrifice altar with reverence, John placed his hands on the same place. "I depend on you, Frank, same as always." The stone was wet with tears and icy cold as it had been since he remembered.

CHAPTER SEVENTY-SEVEN

WITHIN THE WEEK a solemn requiem mass was arranged for the repose of Father Frank's immortal soul, and in remembrance of all his mission people who had perished with him in the disastrous earthquake. The bishop and the priests from five parishes as well as the priests of his own order concelebrated. There was no coffin and no grave, but many folk brought flowers and cards, making a concourse of colour in the chapel yard. There were hundreds of old friends who had known Frank all his life, and all were grief-stricken. People called all day to the house and to the Gowan offices in the town.

Melia Tracey was worried when her mistress was preparing for the mass. She could not restrain her own tears, and to pray with all the congregation in the chapel would be a sorely-needed comfort. Nevertheless, she was ready to stay and pray at home with Cassa safely at rest in bed. Something in Cassa's stricken face frightened the tender-hearted old servant and something in the slow stooped way Cassa was moving.

"Let me help you, Mrs G. Is it something you've lost? Sit down, let you, ma'am, and tell me what's the matter." Cassa only shook her head and went on searching in the tallboys that had come from Firenze. At last she took out a black mantilla which she placed on her head, giving herself the look of a widow. She was ready now to go to the requiem mass for Father Frank. When John came into the bedroom she took his arm, silently indicating her readiness.

During the long ceremonies, Cassa kept her hand in John's hand and her eyes fixed on the altar. He wondered if the prayers made her feel as close to his brother as they did him, but when he pressed her hand within his hand, there was no reassurance in her fingers. John held her close to him as they made their way out of the chapel yard and through all the sympathising mourners crowding around them.

At home Cassa continued out of the hall, slowly climbing the stairs, into the bedroom where she collapsed on the bed. Always a very private person in undressing, now she allowed John to take off her clothes and slip the roomy nightdress over her head. Unaware of his presence, she lay all night in his arms as if she had become a mere ghost, scarcely breathing. John counted the hours as each hour rang out from the Town Hall clock. He was counting six when Cassa turned towards him, moaning a little and searching with her fingers for his face.

They murmured words of love, as Cassa's fingers moved tenderly, caressingly.

John switched on the bedside lights. "Is there anything you would like to do today, Cassa? Any place you would like to go?"

"I don't think so, darling. When Dr Eoin was here yesterday he advised a few days in bed. Something about my blood-pressure being slightly up. He said he would look in this morning to check on it."

"And how do you feel, girl?"

Cassa smiled at him. "A little bit afraid, John. I wish I were that girl of twenty! But a little bit excited that it will soon be the time. Will you be glad too? Will this make up even a tiny bit for... will we be able...?"

He knew she was thinking again of Frank. He tried to tell her that if there were never to be a baby, she herself was a sufficient miracle to make up for all their loss. And since they were to have their baby, he would lessen their loss with each year he grew into manhood. Of course the baby would be a boy and of course they would name him Richard Francis and they would call him Frank. His emotion threatened tears, his words were like a breeze rustling against her hair, invented words that came and went in all their amorous intercourse. He held her protectively.

Dr Magner came promptly at ten o'clock. John sensed immediately that Eoin was worried. His usual genial greeting was subdued, and when he took Cassa's blood-pressure his face was grave.

"Any dizziness, Cassa?" The doctor held her two hands in his. "Have you been overdoing things lately? Sailing? Gardening?"

Cassa's smile appeared radiant, but John recognised the smile as a smile of alert apprehension. That she was too old to be having a baby was the thought bravely concealed by the bright-eyed smile. In this year of 1981, Cassa would have her thirty-fifth birthday.

"No sailing, no gardening, Eoin – not even in our gorgeous new conservatory. Why should I be feeling dizzy?"

"Your blood-pressure could cause concern, Cassa. Your baby could become a little distressed. Perhaps it is too early to be alarmed. Promise me you will rest, right there in your comfortable bed, until I come back later on."

"Later on?" Cassa whispered, her brown eyes now betraying her very real fear.

Going down the stairs to the hall, John asked, "What is it, Eoin? Tell me what exactly is happening, please."

"Look, John, I know we agreed on a home birth and I have several nurses on call, but if the blood pressure flares up, Cassa would be in better care in the maternity wing of the hospital. I know all her fears and I know she is banking on the idea of staying here with you close at hand. Yes, I know she will be disappointed, but high blood-pressure takes a tough toll of both. An early induction, or a caesarean, may be necessary. Neither is fatal, John, taken in time, so keep you heart up. Say very little to Cassa, don't alarm her, and look a bit more cheerful. Stay with her; I will be back very soon."

John knew he could trust Eoin Magner, a Monaghan man like himself.

When he went back to the bedroom, Cassa was curled up on the eiderdown fast asleep. He covered her gently, careful not to waken her. John stood tall at the window with his shoulders drawn back, like a man on guard. It was not in his nature to be less than certain of the next move, but now his anxiety about Cassa and the baby and the future he had hoped for the three of them produced a flood of thoughts he could barely hold at bay.

When the doctor returned within an hour, John had no option but to act on the doctor's instructions and to persuade Cassa that he must get her to the hospital.

"It is safest, dearest."

Her dark eyes filled with reproach and sad tears glinted on her ink-black lashes. Her voice was barely audible: "John, you promised. It is safer here with you. Don't let them keep me in the hospital. John, I dread hospitals, you know I do... you promised... you promised..."

With Melia's help, loving and fussing, John carried Cassa down the two flights of stairs and seated her into the Bentley. In twenty minutes they were at the hospital and soon Cassa was lying in a cool high bed in a cool high room.

Gripping his cuff she struggled valiantly with the tears. "Don't go, don't go," she whispered. "What are they going to do to me? Don't go, John, don't go!"

Then Dr Magner, very brisk and professional, came into the room. Again her blood-pressure was taken and again the doctor's face was compressed and grim. "No more tears now, Cassa. You are in the right place. Don't worry. Relax, Cassa, and stay calm."

Now a nurse sailed serenely into the room and Eoin Magner motioned John out into the corridor.

"It would be for the best if you make your goodbyes now – John, try and look a bit more cheerful – I have called in a second opinion and if we decide on operating, there is preparation to be done."

"The blood pressure?" John asked fearfully.

"Sky high," Eoin answered, "but we can work on that. I would prefer you to go home and stay by the phone. I'll keep in touch, but it may be slow. Say goodbye now."

Cassa was trying to be brave, but her grip on his hand told him how terrified she was. "I don't feel sick," she whispered. "I'm not in pain. Couldn't all this wait until another two weeks? I didn't know this was how it was going to be... please, John, take me home... please..."

The head-sister, a nun, now appeared. Patently she had no time for gushing tears, nor endless farewells, nor passionate kisses. Her energetic movements around the bed made it impossible to linger.

Cassa drew John's head close to her, "I love you, darling," she managed to whisper, "but I was never lucky with nuns."

This was so typical of Cassa's quiet sense of fun, he thought as he left the room, a little piece of Cassa he would treasure for ever.

On his return to the house Melia and the two nieces were standing in the hall. They knew by his face not to ask. Melia followed him up the stairs carrying a tray with a bottle of Jameson. She had tidied the room and she left him there. It was a very rare occasion when Melia Tracey did not burst into speech. He appreciated that. To be alone in Cassa's room with Cassa's spirit was the most he could hope for.

John filled the whiskey glass and took it over to the window, Cassa's window, Cassa's look-out on the river, on the season's sailing craft and on her fondest memories. John guessed at Cassa's every thought and there was never any resentment, rather was there comfort now in knowing that Frank had had his one and only summer with Cassa; every hour of that idyllic summer was as precious to John as it had been to Frank and Cassa. He had shared with his brother and his brother had shared with him.

Tired now, he sat down in Cassa's armchair beside the fireplace where someone had placed an urn of silk flowers. Distantly he heard the Town Hall clock strike an hour. He did not count the strokes, but with each toll of the bell his certainty diminished. The sound came again and again as time inched on in an ever-widening circle of futile fear until at last the changing light drew him back to the window. The sunset was sending thousands of slanting sunbeams into the river. Cassa loved this time of day. Often she had commented, as the yellow sunlight departed into the west, that soon her moon goddess, Flachtna, would come up from the east to spread her silver mist over the Shannon.

John watched the glowing circle of the sun sinking slowly beneath the far rim of the river. Suddenly he remembered standing, long long ago, with his brother and sister by their dolmen as they watched this same glittering spectacle. Frank told them, "You see this huge golden orb? That could be the eye of Almighty God and all that wonderful gleaming brightness could be heaven. You know, Deirdre, heaven is the next world where we go when we die."

Frank, Frank, please don't do this to me. You could have claimed her then, not now, please not now. If you are out there in all that dazzling light, please plead for me, beg God for me. You gave her to me, remember. Frank, beg God for me. Please, please, my brother, plead for me …

*　　*　　*

The last curve of the setting sun had disappeared and the river was settling into twilight gray. Deep inside the house, the telephone was ringing, ringing. John's feet refused to rush down the stairs. This was the moment he would wish to postpone for ever. Someone had picked up the phone; there was a faltering footstep outside the door, and a timid knock. His reluctant throat held him silent for one long protracted moment, then he said, "The door is open. Come in."

Framed by the landing light, Melia's niece had brought a nervous message. She had been crying, her eyes were red-rimmed. "It's the phone, sir. They're wanting you on the phone, sir."

He listened to her retreating footsteps, and then he turned to draw in the casement window. His words went out into the night, strong and clear: "Depending on you, Frank, same as always." Suddenly he was racing eagerly down the stairs, catching up again on his old familiar certainty.